M. LEIGHTON IS

"INSANELY
—The Bo

"FREAKI
—Nette's Bookshelf

AND "SERIOUSLY SCANDALICIOUS."
—Scandalicious Book Reviews

PRAISE FOR *THE WILD ONES*

"This book is worth every second I spent reading it. Ms. Leighton is a phenomenal writer, and I cannot give her enough praise."　—*Bookish Temptations*

"Hands down one of the hottest books I've read all summer . . . Complete with love, secrets, dreams, and hidden pasts! *The Wild Ones* is romantic, sexy, and absolutely perfect! Drop everything and read this RIGHT NOW!"　—*The Bookish Brunette*

"I can honestly tell you that this is one of my top books of the year and easily one of my new all-time favorites. I couldn't put the book down."
　—*The Autumn Review*

"You will laugh, swoon, and even shed a few tears. M. Leighton knows how to write an amazing story. Get your copy of *The Wild Ones* today. You will not regret it."　—*Between the Page Reviews*

"This book was one of the best books I've read this year. It may sound like just a love triangle on the surface, but inside there's so much more going on."　—*The Book Vixen*

"One of the best books I've read this year so far."　—*Sim Sational Books*

continued . . .

Some
Like It Wild

M. LEIGHTON

BERKLEY BOOKS, NEW YORK

THE BERKLEY PUBLISHING GROUP
Published by the Penguin Group
Penguin Group (USA)
375 Hudson Street, New York, New York 10014

USA • Canada • UK • Ireland • Australia • New Zealand • India • South Africa • China

penguin.com

A Penguin Random House Company

This book is an original publication of The Berkley Publishing Group.

Library of Congress Cataloging-in-Publication Data

Leighton, M.
Some like it wild / M. Leighton.—Berkley trade paperback edition.
pages cm.—(A wild ones novel ; 2)
ISBN 978-0-425-26781-3 (pbk.)
1. Horses—Breeding—Fiction. 2. Ranch life—Fiction. 3. Daredevils—Fiction. I. Title.
PS3612.E3588S66 2014
813'.6—dc23 2013044564

PUBLISHING HISTORY
Berkley trade paperback edition / March 2014

PRINTED IN THE UNITED STATES OF AMERICA

10 9 8 7 6 5 4 3 2 1

Cover art by ImageBrief.com/Greg Daniels
Cover design by Lesley Worrell

I thank God for Southern guys like my husband,
Southern girls like the ones I used to know,
and the Southern series that started it all for me.

ONE: *Laney*

Four years ago, summer

"Come on, Laney. You gotta live a little. You'll be eighteen in a few weeks and then you'll be leaving for college. This is the last fair you'll ever attend as an adolescent. Don't you want this summer to be memorable?"

"Yes, but that does *not* include getting busted for drinking under age." My best friend, Tori, gives me that look that says I'm hopeless. "What?" I ask defensively. "Daddy would kill me."

"I thought preachers' kids were supposed to be wild as hell?"

"I can be wild," I tell her, avoiding her disbelieving blue eyes. "I just don't want to be wild *right now*."

"Then when? When are you gonna do something? *Anything?* You won't make it a single semester away at college if you don't learn some of this worldly stuff now, Laney."

I chew the inside of my lip. I *do* feel ill-prepared for college. But the thing is, I don't *want* to do wild things. All I've ever really wanted out of life is to find the perfect man to sweep me off my feet, get married, have a family, and live happily ever after. And I don't have to get wild to achieve any of those things.

Looking at Tori's expression, however, makes me feel like some kind of freak for not wanting to break the rules. At least a little. But she doesn't understand my dreams. No one does, really. Except my mother. She was the same way when she was my age, and she found everything she wanted in life when she met my father.

"Come on, Laney. Just this once."

"Why? What is the big deal about getting it here? Getting it now?"

"Because I want to get it *from him*."

"Why?" I ask again. "What's the big deal?"

"I've had a crush on him for years, that's what the big deal is. He went off to college and I haven't seen him since. But now he's here. And I need a wing woman." When I don't immediately relent, she presses. "Pleeease. For meee."

I sigh. I have to give Tori credit for being one seriously gifted manipulator. It's a wonder I'm *not* wild as a buck. She talks me into doing things I don't want to do *all the time*. It's just that, so far, they've been fairly innocent. Being the preacher's daughter and living with such strict parents makes it hard for me to get into *too* much trouble. Tori ought to be happy about that. If it weren't for the restrictions being my friend has placed indirectly on her, she'd probably be a pregnant, drug-addicted criminal by now.

But she's not. Partly because of me and my "taming" influence. And it's those stark differences in our personalities that make us such good friends. We balance each other perfectly. She keeps me on my toes. I keep her out of Juvie.

"Fine," I growl. "Come on. But so help me, if he tells on us, I'm blaming you."

Tori squeals and bounces up and down, her ample boobs threatening to overcome the extremely low neckline of her shirt.

"Why don't you just go over and do that in front of him a couple of times? I'm sure he'd give you anything you want."

"That'll come later," Tori says, ruffling her blond bangs and waggling her eyebrows.

I roll my eyes as we start off across the fairgrounds. As we near the farm truck where the shirtless guy is unloading crates, I ask Tori again, "Now who did you say he is?"

"Jake Theopolis."

"Theopolis? As in the peach orchard Theopolises?"

"Yep, that's his family."

"Why don't I remember him?"

"Because your hormones slept through your freshman year. He was a senior. Jenna Theopolis's older brother. Played baseball. Dated pretty much all the hot girls. "

"Except for you," I add before she can.

She grins and elbows me in the ribs. "Except for me."

"And you're sure he won't try to get us into trouble?"

"I'm positive. He was a bad boy. I'm sure there's nothing we could think of that he hasn't done ten times over." We stop a few feet behind him, and I hear Tori whisper, "Good God, look at him."

So I do.

I can see why Tori would find him appealing. His tanned skin is glistening in the hot Carolina sun. The well-defined muscles in his chest and shoulders ripple as he picks up a crate from the back of the truck, and his washboard abs contract as he swivels to set it on the ground. His worn blue jeans hang low on his narrow hips, giving us an almost-indecent look at the way the thin trail of hair that leads away from his navel disappears into the waistband.

But then Tori's words come back to me and I'm immediately turned off. She said he's a bad boy. And I'm not interested in bad boys. They don't figure into my plans. At all. In any way. That's why I don't have to worry about being attracted to him.

Even though he's hot as blazes.

Tori clears her throat as we move closer. "Hi, Jake."

Jake's dark head turns toward us as he pauses in his work to wipe his brow. He looks first at Tori. "Hi," he replies around the toothpick stuck in one corner of his mouth. His voice is low and hoarse. His smile is polite and I think to myself that he's handsome enough, but nothing to warrant Tori's insistence on talking to him.

But then he looks over *at me*.

Even with him squinting in the bright sun, his eyes steal my breath. Set in his tan face and framed by his black hair and black lashes, they're striking. The amber color is like honey, honey I feel all the way down in my stomach—warm and gooey.

"Hi," he says again, one side of his mouth curling up into a cocky grin.

For some reason, I can't think of one single thing to say. Not even a casual greeting, one that I would give a perfect stranger. I stare at him for several long seconds until, finally, he chuckles and turns back to Tori.

"What's wrong with her?"

"Uh, she's just shy."

"Shy?" he asks, turning his attention back to me. I almost wish he hadn't. My belly is still full of hot liquid and I'm starting to feel breathless. "Hmmm, I don't meet shy girls very often."

From the corner of my eye, I see Tori wave her hand dismissively. "Eh, she'll loosen up in a minute. In fact, that's sort of why we're here."

Jake glances back to Tori, releasing me from the prison of his strange eyes. I take a slow, deep breath to settle my swimming head.

"Oh, I've gotta hear this," he says, leaning back against the tail-gate and crossing his arms over his chest. I can't help but notice how his biceps bulge with the action.

Tori steps closer to him and whispers, "We were sort of hoping you'd sell us a bottle of that peach wine. You know, on the down low."

He looks from Tori to me and back again before he bends to pick up one bottle. "One of these? To loosen her up?"

"Yep. It's sure to do the trick."

His golden eyes return to me as he slowly straightens to his full height. "I don't believe you. I don't think she'll drink it." His gaze drops to my mouth and then on down my neck and chest, to my stomach and my bare legs. I wonder what he's seeing—just the light green strapless sundress that sets off my tan? Or is he imagining what's underneath? What's underneath my clothes? Underneath my skin? "I think she looks like a good girl. And good girls don't drink."

The fact that he so accurately pegged me stirs up my temper for some reason. Immediately defensive, I pull in my stomach, puff out my chest, and jack up my chin. "What? I'm just some simple, one-dimensional country girl? Is that it?"

He shrugs, his eyes never leaving mine. "Am I wrong?"

"Yes," I declare defiantly, even though it's an outright lie. "You couldn't be more wrong."

One raven brow shoots up in challenge. "Oh yeah? Prove it."

Too proud to back down, I reach out and snatch the bottle from his fingers, unscrew the lid and tip it back, taking one long gulp.

It's just local, homemade wine from his daddy's peach orchard, but that doesn't mean the alcohol doesn't sting the throat of someone who's not used to drinking.

As I lower the bottle and swallow what's left in my mouth, my eyes water with the effort not to sputter. Jake watches me until my cheeks are no longer full of the wine.

"Satisfied?" I ask, shoving the bottle into the center of his broad chest.

"I'll be damned," he says softly.

Ignoring the way his voice makes my stomach clench, I reach for Tori's hand. "Come on. We have to get back for our shift in the booth."

Tossing my hair, I turn and stomp off with as much dignity as I can muster. Tori is reluctant, but when I tug, she follows along.

"What the hell are you doing? You just totally screwed that up for me. Not to mention that you left the wine."

"We don't need that jerk's wine."

"Uh, yeah, we do. And what's this about the shift at the booth? We aren't supposed to be there for another forty minutes."

"Then we'll go early. It's just a kissing booth, for Pete's sake. It won't kill you to work another forty minutes. In fact, you'll probably like it."

"What's that supposed to mean?" she asks indignantly.

I pause in my mad trudging to look at her. I shake my head to clear it. I don't know how that Jake guy managed to get under my skin so quickly, but he did.

"Sorry, Tori. I didn't mean anything by it. I'm just aggravated."

"I can see that. But why? What did he ever do to you?"

"I don't know. Nothing, I suppose. I just hate it when people assume the worst about me."

"Assuming you're a good girl is not a bad thing."

"He sure made it seem like it was." I start walking again and look back at Tori until she catches up. "Besides, weren't you just fussing at me for not living a little?"

"Yes, but this is not really what I had in mind."

I smile and loop my arm through hers, hoping for a quick reconciliation so we can leave the topic of Jake behind. "Be careful what you ask for then, right?"

She sighs. "I guess."

"Now then, let's go."

Twenty minutes later, I'm regretting my rash decision. I've kissed the cheek of every pimple-faced boy in town. Tori has jumped in front of me to take all the cute guys that have come. Not that I have a problem with that. I guess I owe her since I messed up her plans for Jake. Besides, I'm not interested in any of the boys from Greenfield. The only reason I'm working the booth at all is to raise funds for the church.

I smile politely as I take two dollars from the next boy in line. He looks like he can't be a day over twelve. I bend forward to give his cheek a peck. I press my lips to it and then offer mine. He kisses it sweetly then looks shyly away. "Thank you for the kiss," I say for the hundredth time. I look down as I put the money in my till. When I glance up, prepared to ask for the next person in line, my heart stops and the words die on my tongue.

Standing in front of me, smiling like he knows I can't breathe, is Jake Theopolis. He's wearing a T-shirt now, a blue one that fits snugly over his wide shoulders. His pecs shift beneath the material as he digs in the front pocket of his jeans. I see him toss a ten dollar bill onto the counter in front of me. Confused, my eyes flicker back up to his. The bright, liquid orbs are intent on mine.

"I came for the peaches," he says quietly. He reaches up to take the toothpick from between his lips. I watch, spellbound, as his face gets closer and closer. "I need a taste before I go," he whispers, his sweet cinnamon breath fanning my lips.

And then his mouth is brushing mine. I don't even think to resist. In fact, I don't think at all. I only feel.

His lips are soft against mine and he smells like soap and clean sweat. His touch is featherlight until he tilts his head to the side and deepens the kiss. I feel his tongue trace the crease of my lips until I part them to let him in. In long, leisurely strokes, his tongue licks at mine, like he's savoring the flavor of it. I savor him right back, drinking in the hint of cinnamon in his mouth. I lean toward him, bracing myself on the counter, afraid my legs won't hold me up much longer.

Finally, he leans back and looks down into my stunned face. "Mmm, that's the sweetest peach I've had in a long time," he purrs. When he winks at me, I feel a gush of heat pour into my stomach like hot lava.

Without another word, he turns and walks away.

TWO: *Jake*

Present day

The screen door bangs shut behind me. After having been out in the fresh air of the orchards, the sweet, fruity smell of the house is even more pronounced. My family's farmhouse has seen too many harvest seasons *not* to smell like peaches.

It smells exactly the same as it has my whole life. In fact, very little about the house has changed at all over the years. Except for the dwindling of its occupants, of course.

First Mom, now Dad. It took a few years for it to feel like home after Mom died, but it finally did. With Dad, it'll be different. I can already tell. Although his death was sudden and accidental (he fell off a ladder out in the orchard and hit his head on a rock), I don't mourn him like I did Mom. Or like Jenna mourns him. She can barely come into the driveway, much less spend time indoors. Then again, she was always his favorite. But that's understandable, all things considered.

Feeling the sting of old wounds, I walk to the fridge for a beer. I jerk the door open with much more force than what's necessary. It feels good to get a little of my aggression out, though. It'll do until I can get back to work, making a living at staring death in the eye. Adrenaline—it's my drug of choice to numb the pain of the past. And of the present, if it decides to act up and give me shit.

But right now, I have to shower before the bloodsucking douche paralegal from the estate attorney's office arrives to start cataloging all our family holdings.

I pop the top on the bottle and down half of it before I even reach the stairs. I try not to think of the good ol' days, just a few short weeks ago, when I was living the life I chose rather than the life my father left behind when he died.

What the hell was I thinking, coming back here?

Less than half an hour later, I'm freshly washed, cleanly shaved, and dressed in jeans and a T-shirt that reads: SKYDIVING: THE GROUND IS THE LIMIT. I grab another beer from the fridge and sit in the den, waiting for the tight-ass from the attorney's office. The only sounds are the dog, Einstein, barking at something out back, the tick of the grandfather clock in the dining room, and the wind whistling through the crack in the screen door. It takes exactly seven minutes for this quiet combination to drive me nuts. Finishing my beer, I decide to get some stuff from the garage and wash my Jeep while I wait.

And if this straightlaced asshole doesn't like it, he can kiss my puckered ass.

Twenty minutes later, I'm rinsing soap off the Rubicon when I see the flash of sun on a windshield, drawing my eye to the far end of the driveway. A little dusty blue car is making its way slowly along the path, moving in and out of the dappled patches of shade thrown onto the pavement by the trees stretching overhead. Every now and then, the sun will shine through the glass and hit the platinum blond hair of the driver. The *long* platinum blond hair of the driver. This immediately piques my interest. I never considered they might send a female.

I continue spraying, keeping an eye on the car as it comes closer. I watch as it rolls to a stop a few feet from where I am, parking in front of the house with its rear facing in my direction. The engine shuts off, and I see the driver reach onto the seat beside her. She fiddles with something before opening the door.

The first thing that comes out is legs. Two mile-long, perfectly toned ones capped in a pair of high, high heels. I wait anxiously to see the rest. She pauses for a second before scooting out of the car.

I see her first in profile as she reaches down to tug on the rising hem of her slim black skirt and then tucks her hair behind one ear.

When she finally turns toward me, her head is down as she looks at something in her hands. That's fine by me. It just gives me time to ogle the shit out of her without getting a nasty glare for it.

The long legs were only the beginning of the package. Narrow hips curve into a tiny waist and lead up to what looks like a nice-sized rack. Not too big, not too small, although it's hard to be sure through her loose-fitting blouse.

She walks gracefully toward me and, when she's a couple of feet away, she looks up.

Just as my jaw drops in surprised recognition, the spray of the water hose hits the front bumper of the Jeep and shoots water all over my chest and stomach.

"Shit!" I yelp, jumping back when the cold water makes contact.

I redirect the hose and glance at the girl standing just outside spray reach. She's smiling down at my wet shirt.

My mouth waters when I look at the lush pink lips spread over her perfect teeth. I remember the way they taste—sweet and innocent.

Like peaches.

And like a challenge.

THREE: *Laney*

I knew going into this whose estate I'd be recording. I saw the names on the paperwork and recognized one immediately.

Jake Theopolis.

It's been a long time since that kiss at the fair, so I didn't think twice about taking the assignment. It gets me home for a while and that's what I wanted most.

Space.

Distance.

Escape.

Although I'd forgotten how incredibly handsome he is, I feel perfectly in control of myself as I look at him in his soaked T-shirt.

That is, until he lays the hose to the side and peels the dripping material from his body.

My breath is suddenly stuck in my chest, my pulse is racing, and my skin feels warm and damp.

Inches and inches of glistening golden skin cover wide shoulders, a powerful chest, and rippling abs. His jeans sit low on his hips, as though they were made to fit his lean body. If all that weren't enough to get me flustered, the cocky grin on his face would be.

He knows exactly what he's doing to me. Might've even done it on purpose. I guess that's what I get for smiling at his mishap.

Who's laughing now?

"Something wrong?" Jake asks, his deep voice dripping with knowing amusement.

My eyes fly up to his, hoping for a break from the onslaught of his hotness. But I don't get one. I fall headlong into those honey yellow eyes of his. I'd forgotten how disconcerting they are.

I've never seen honey like that before!

The movement of his hand draws my gaze downward again. Jake is wiping his wet palm on the leg of his jeans. The action causes the muscles in his chest to flex, making me feel even warmer.

I squeeze my eyes shut and pray for some composure.

Oh God! Oh God! Oh God!

"Jake Theopolis," I hear him say. I open my lids a crack and see his hand extended toward me. Slowly, I reach out and slip my fingers into his. They curl warmly around mine. "Welcome to my lair."

Again, I see amusement when my gaze flickers back up to his. He's really enjoying me making a complete fool of myself.

Pulling my hand from his grasp, I clear my throat and look over at the house. "So, this is the main home on the estate?"

When Jake says nothing, I'm forced to glance back at him. He's smiling at me, a devilishly wicked grin, as he wrings out his shirt. He's chewing a toothpick again, reminding me of the way his mouth tasted all those years ago. "Yes, this is it. Would you like me to show you around?"

"That would be helpful, thank you," I say stiffly, feeling mortified by my reaction to him.

He tips his head toward the house, his lips still curved in a cocky half smile. "Then come with me."

As I follow along behind him, I wonder at his ability to make every look, every word, and every gesture seem so . . . so . . . suggestive. I have no doubt it's intentional. He obviously knows I'm flustered and is exploiting that, which makes me mad. Unfortunately, that anger isn't nearly enough to help me keep my head on straight, as evidenced by the fact that I watch his butt all the way on the walk to the house.

After mounting the steps, he turns at the front door to allow me to precede him. I jerk my eyes up, looking guiltily away from his backside, hoping he didn't see what I was doing.

When he winks at me as I pass, I realize that he did. I feel my face go up in flames.

Oh my God! Just kill me now!

The house is quiet and dark, and the interior smells slightly sweet and homey. At first glance, it's hard for me to fathom a guy like Jake Theopolis being raised here. He's the type that I imagine landing on the scene with a loud bang, like life just spit him out, fully grown and wild as a buck. Never a sweet, innocent child.

Jake tips his head toward a sage green couch in the den. "Have a seat and I'll get us a beer."

"No, no thank you," I rush to say as I make my way to the sofa. As I perch demurely on the edge of one cushion, I glance over at Jake. He's eyeing me from the doorway leading into what I presume is the kitchen.

He shrugs. "Suit yourself."

A few seconds later, he returns carrying a beer and a glass of some other kind of golden liquid. I look up at him, frowning as I take the proffered wineglass. "What's this?"

"Peach wine," he says, watching me intently. "Did you think I'd forgotten?"

My cheeks flame and I take a nervous sip of the sweet drink, any excuse to get my eyes off of his. "Thank you," I mutter, avoiding his question.

After a tense moment, Jake plops down in an armchair across from me, crossing his legs to rest one ankle on his knee. He still hasn't put on a shirt and, when I look up, all I can see is an ocean of flawless skin.

"Would you mind getting dressed so we can discuss what's ahead for your family?"

With his golden eyes trained on mine, Jake rubs his hand across his bare chest. "Why? Does this bother you?"

I know he's teasing me, but I'm trying to keep things professional. And I can't do that with a gorgeous, half-naked man sitting a coffee table away.

"Not at all, but it's hardly appropriate."

One black brow shoots up. "Not at all, huh?"

I hold his gaze, hoping he doesn't see the lie of my words. "Not. At. All."

"Well, then I'll just have to see what *does* bother a prim and proper woman such as yourself."

The warning is not lost on me. However, my only option is to ignore it. I can't very well do my job if I let Jake Theopolis strike me stupid and speechless every time he's in the room.

Jake gets up to leave. With one foot on the bottom step, he turns toward me. "Are you ever gonna tell me your name? Or should I just call you 'peaches'?"

"Laney," I offer, adding another brick to the huge pile of my embarrassment. "Laney Holt."

He nods slowly. "You from around here, Laney Holt? Or were you just working the kissing booth for pleasure that day?"

"Originally I'm from around here, yes."

Jake starts to turn away again, but stops himself, his brow furrowing. "Holt. You're not related to Graham Holt, are you?"

"Yes, I am. He's my father. Why?"

Jake throws back his head and laughs heartily. "Oh, God! That's perfect! The preacher's daughter!"

It seems like he's making fun of me, and I bristle. "And why is that *perfect*?" I ask sharply.

Jake lowers his head and looks me square in the eye. "Because I've got a thing for forbidden fruit, Laney Holt. Consider yourself warned."

With another cocky grin tossed my way, Jake turns to mount the steps, leaving me feeling nothing short of breathless.

FOUR: *Jake*

The following afternoon, I'm driving home, thinking to myself that this unforeseen, undesirable incarceration in Greenfield on my family's peach farm is looking decidedly more promising. Between the part-time job I just got and the tasty little piece that'll be wandering around my house for the next couple of weeks, I'm feeling pretty optimistic about the time I'll be spending here. Boredom and I don't mix, but it's looking like I won't have to worry about that any time in the near future.

When I turn into the driveway, I see a speck of blue through the trees. That's bound to be Laney. She said she'd see me today, but she didn't say when. I just assumed she'd call. Luckily, hers is the kind of unexpected visit I could get used to.

As the lane widens just in front of the house, I see Laney marching angrily toward her car. I steer the Jeep toward the garage and cut the engine, hopping out before she can leave.

"Where you off to?" I ask as I approach.

She doesn't answer, just yanks on the car door handle. It doesn't open on the first try, which seems to make her that much madder.

"Hey," I say, reaching out to touch her arm and turn her toward me. She whirls to face me, her eyes flashing furiously. "Don't touch me!"

I hold up both hands in surrender and take a step back. "What the hell is the matter with you?"

I'm not irritated, just curious. It's a simple question, but she gets all huffy. Which totally turns me on.

Laney takes a deep breath and pokes me in the chest with one finger. "Listen here, *Mr. Theopolis*, I didn't come here to be trifled with. I'm here to do a job, but if you refuse to show me the most basic respect and common decency, I'll be more than happy to turn your case over to another paralegal."

I feel my lips twitch. "Trifled with?"

First her mouth drops open, like she can't believe I just said that. Then she makes a growling sound and turns around so fast, her hair nearly whips me in the face.

Quicker than she is, I reach out and grab her arm again, spinning her back toward me. I pull her in close and look down into her beautiful sapphire blue eyes. They're sparkling with irritation and indignation, and I've never before wanted a woman so badly.

"Hold on just a second. What have I done to show you anything less than respect and common decency?" My voice is low and reasonable, and my hold on her is light. Just enough to keep her from leaving.

"I told you I'd be back today and you didn't even have the decency to be here."

"If I'd known when you were coming, I'd have been here. You said you'd see me today, but you didn't say when."

I see the doubt flicker through her eyes. They lose a little of their heat as she relaxes in my arms.

"I told you . . . I mean, I thought I told you . . ."

I shake my head. "No, you didn't. You didn't give me a specific time. I figured you'd call first."

Doubt turns to reluctant contrition right before my eyes. "Then I must apologize for getting angry. I just thought . . ."

"You thought the worst," I finish for her. "Lucky for you, I'm used to it."

"Mr. Theopolis, I—"

I reach up to lay one finger across her lips. "First of all, call me Jake. Secondly, don't go apologizing too soon."

"But I owe you an apo—"

"Not after this," I reply as I lower my mouth to cover hers.

Her lips are just as soft as I remember and, when I slip my tongue between them, she tastes just as sweet, only without the hint of peach this time.

I caught her off guard and, for a few seconds, she responds to me, tilting her head and dragging her tongue along mine. But then, as if someone dumped a cold bucket of water on her head, she snaps out of it and pulls away.

She glares at me, all the fury back like it never left. She raises her hand to slap me, but I catch it, winding my fingers around her wrist and pulling her arm behind me. Her chest crashes into mine, and I whisper in her ear, "Now *that* was disrespectful. And I won't do it again until you ask me to."

With a featherlight kiss to her jaw, I lean back and let her go. For a few seconds, she stands staring at me with her mouth hanging open before she huffs once, pivots on her high heel, and flings open her car door to climb inside. I watch as she starts the engine, backs up, and speeds down the driveway without a backward glance.

Damn, this is gonna be fun!

FIVE: *Laney*

Jake Theopolis is bothering me. I feel like my insides are in turmoil, yet I can't stop thinking about him long enough for them to settle down. That both frustrates and angers me.

My lack of sleep isn't helping matters. Neither is the memory of our phone conversation.

I had to call Jake last night to tell him I'd be by around nine this morning. The call was short and he was agreeable, but there was something about his tone—something smug and satisfied and . . . teasing—that has left me feeling off-kilter. And I don't like it.

"Why are you up so early?" my mother asks as she makes her way into the kitchen. She's wearing the same robe she's worn since I was a little girl—dark blue with tiny pink flowers embroidered across the chest. Her short, sandy hair is perfectly coiffed, like she didn't just sleep eight hours on it, and her brown eyes are soft and sleepy, and as angelic as always.

I shrug, bringing the coffee mug to my lips and taking another sip. "A lot on my mind, I guess."

"Is it all this mess with Shane? I don't know why you can't just forgive him and move on. It's the Christian thing to do, no matter what he did."

I bite back my waspish response. She has no idea. But that's not her fault. I haven't told my parents the details of my breakup with my fiancé, Shane Call. They just think I'm being impulsive and petulant. "Mom, I've told you, Shane and I are *not* getting back together."

She shakes her head, a sad expression on her face. "I hate to see you let anything get in the way of your happiness, sweet pea."

"Sometimes it's not up to us, Momma."

"It's always up to us."

I feel my frustration rise and realize it's high time for a change of subject. "Do you remember Cris Theopolis?"

"Of course," she answers, moving right along with my new direction. "He was a wonderful man. Such a tragedy, especially after what happened with Elizabeth."

"Who's Elizabeth?"

"Cris's wife. She died many years ago. She was very sick. It just broke Cris's heart. I don't think he ever really recovered. But he always made sure to do right by those kids of his. At least he tried."

"What's that supposed to mean, 'he tried'?"

"Well, it's not an easy thing, to be a single parent and tend an orchard as large as his was. It's no wonder—"

"Who's a single parent?" my father asks as he strolls into the kitchen. He's already dressed in slacks and a white button-up shirt, his dark hair still damp from the shower. His commanding presence fills any room the instant he walks into it. This one is no different.

"*Was*, honey. Cris Theopolis. It's his estate Laney's going to be working on."

Dad pauses in his bend to kiss Mom, his brow furrowing. "Does Shane know?"

"Know what?"

"What you're down here doing?"

"I'm not down here *doing* anything but working."

"I mean, does he know *what* you're working on?"

"No, it's none of his business."

"I'm sure he wouldn't be happy about it," Dad says, ignoring my comment.

"Lucky for me I don't care. I don't have to worry about what Shane does or doesn't like anymore. Besides, I'm not doing anything wrong."

"No, but associating with people like the Theopolises . . ."

"Mom was just talking about what good people they are."

"I said *Cris* was a good man," she clarifies.

"And his kids aren't?"

"You're smart enough to know the answer to that, Laney," my dad says. "You went to school with the youngest, Jenna."

"Yes, but I didn't really *know* her."

Dad gives me "the look." "No, but you know enough, young lady."

I slide my bar stool back. "So much for not being judgmental," I snap, walking to the sink to rinse out my half-full mug.

"Avoiding a bad element is not being judgmental. It's being prudent."

I turn to face my father. I hold my head high, tired of a lifetime of cowering under his disapproval. "And how, exactly, do you determine who the 'bad element' is then, Daddy?"

I walk out of the kitchen before he can respond. I'm sure he'll have some valuable bit of wisdom for me. No doubt it'll be true, too. But right now, at this point in my life, I'm not looking for wisdom. I'm not looking for prudent or safe or reasonable, any of the things I once attributed to Shane.

In fact, I think to myself as I head up the stairs, *I might just be looking for the exact opposite.*

Having cut short my morning at the house in order to avoid my parents, I arrive at the turn to the Theopolis orchard twenty minutes early. I figure I'll just sit in the car and start on my paperwork before knocking, just in case Jake is still asleep.

He seems like one of those up-all-night-partying-sleep-all-day-afterward types.

The thought has barely had a chance to make it through my head when I see a lean, tan, shirtless jogger just up ahead. Even if the guy wasn't running on the long, winding Theopolis driveway I'd have no trouble identifying him—Jake. His physique and dark good looks are unmistakable, even from behind.

And my stomach reacts accordingly.

I ease my foot onto the brake, debating what to do. Go forward, turn around, stop and wait? What's the right thing here?

Jake takes the decision out of my hands, however, when he slows to a stop and turns to look down the road at me. His eyes meet mine, and he smiles. Even from a distance, he makes me feel breathless.

For one second, I get the feeling I should turn and run. But it's gone almost as quickly as it came when Jake starts to jog in my direction.

My foot presses harder on the brake as I watch him approach. His skin is slick with sweat and his muscles move and shift beneath it. He stops at my window and bends, laying his forearms along the opening, his face but a few inches from mine. He's winded and his breath tickles my cheek.

"You're early."

"I know. I was going to do some paperwork before I woke you."

"Woke me? I've been up for hours. But if you'd prefer to wake me, I'm sure I can arrange to still be in bed when you get here." His wink tells me that he means exactly what I think he means. I want to curse my light complexion when I feel my cheeks heat up at his insinuation.

"I hardly think that will be necessary," I reply, trying to sound unflustered, but likely doing a poor job of it. "Continue your run. I'll just meet you at the house when you're done. If you don't mind me waiting there, that is."

"I can't think of anyone I'd rather stumble upon when I'm hot and sweaty and headed for the shower."

Giving me his trademark cocky grin, Jake straightens and jogs off before I can respond. And it's a good thing. I don't even know what to say to that. For a few seconds, I watch the way his shorts cling to his tight butt as he moves. But he shakes me out of my dumbstruck state when he turns and jogs backward for a few seconds, openly laughing at me.

Ohmigod, he knows I was looking at his butt!

And, of course, I'm mortified. I push on the accelerator and swerve far away from Jake when I pass him. I keep my eyes glued on the road ahead.

When I reach the house, I park and pull my briefcase from the backseat. I take out the folder labeled *Theopolis Estate* and flip it open in my lap, but that's as far as I get. My eyes keep straying to the rearview mirror, waiting for Jake to appear in it. It's like my brain is stuck and won't move forward until he does.

A flash of red catches my eye. Jake's shorts. Moving at a steady pace, he jogs into my frame of view, moving closer and closer. Again, I admire the way he glistens in the sunlight, like a champion thoroughbred in peak physical condition.

I force my eyes back to my folder when Jake gets near the rear of my car. From the corner of my eye, I glance at the sideview mirror as he passes. He doesn't even look down, just jogs right on by. He takes the steps two at a time and opens the unlocked front door.

I'm watching him, expecting him to disappear indoors, when he turns. He meets my eyes and tips his head toward the inside of the house before he crosses the threshold, leaving the door ajar for me.

"I guess that's my cue," I mumble to myself.

I gather my things, trying to keep my mind off the image of Jake stripping off those red shorts to get in the shower. Absently, I wonder if his skin is tan all over, or if he has a tan line.

Holy crap! Laney, you've got to stop this! I warn myself. I won't be able to concentrate at all if I don't get a grip.

I focus on the list of things I need to get done and in what order as I get out and walk up the steps. Once inside, I listen for Jake. I hear nothing but muffled sounds coming from upstairs. Thankful for the short respite in which I can attempt to reset my wayward brain, I make my way into the dining room and begin spreading out my things onto the table.

Firmly back in work mode, I'm making mental lists and dividing up areas to inventory together when I hear a throat clear behind me. I whirl to find Jake lounging in the doorway, smiling as he watches me.

"I didn't want to scare you. You looked deep in thought," he observes.

"Thank you. I was."

"So," he begins, straightening away from the doorjamb, "what do I need to do?"

I can't help but notice the way his pale yellow T-shirt clings to his still-damp skin, or the way his thick eyelashes look spiky and wet.

"Uh . . . well . . ." I stammer, struggling to get my mind back on the task at hand. I squeeze my eyes shut and then turn them to the documents spread out in front of me. "Actually, there's nothing I really need from you at this point. It's a matter of going through each room and inventorying what's here. If I have any questions, I'll make a note and ask you later."

Now that I've managed a coherent sentence, I look back at Jake.

"All right, I guess I'll just check back with you after a while then."

"No need," I assure him. "I'll be fine."

He grins, a wicked gleam lighting his amber eyes. "Regardless, I'll be back in a couple of hours."

There's no point in arguing. I feel like the more I protest, the more it will give away my discomfort with his close proximity. Instead, I nod and give him a tight smile. "Okay. See you then."

I pick up some random papers and study them as if they're important when, in reality, I don't even process what I'm looking at. It's not until, from the corner of my eye, I see Jake leave that it registers that I'm holding them upside down.

SIX: *Jake*

"I'm taking care of it, Jenna. Would you stop worrying?"

"It just kills me to think of those two losers living in our house, destroying everything Mom and Dad worked so hard for."

"I know, Jenna. That's why I told you to stop worrying about it. I'd never let that happen. I'd burn this place to the ground before I let her ruin it. Now stop aggravating me about it."

"I'm not aggravating you about it. I just feel helpless being up here in Atlanta, not able to do anything about it."

"You couldn't do anything about it even if you were here. I'm doing what needs to be done. Atlanta with Rusty is where you belong." I hear her sigh. She knows I'm right. "Control freak," I mutter teasingly.

"Asshole."

"But you love that about me."

"Not hardly."

"Liar."

I hear her light laugh. We play rough, as we always have. But if I was ever going to love someone in life, it would probably be Jenna.

Guys like me, though, we're better off without much love in our life. Keeps us focused, keeps the edge sharp. And that's the way I like it. That's the way it works best for me. Why change it? I get what I need without complications. End of story.

Or at least that's what I tell myself.

"Fine, have at it then, dick."

"I was going to anyway, wench."

"Call me next week."

"K."

"Love you," she says.

"You, too," I reply. It's all I ever say.

I stick my phone back in my pocket and turn toward the door of the barn. I stop in my tracks when I see Laney standing there. She's backlit by the sun, making it seem as though she's surrounded by a golden halo. She looks every bit the angel I'm sure she is. That only makes me want to corrupt her that much more.

"Please tell me you came looking for a little afternoon delight," I tease, walking slowly toward her.

Laney squares her shoulders, clears her throat, and ignores my comment, which makes me smile. "I'm sorry to interrupt. I was just coming to tell you I'm driving into town for lunch."

Her head is held high and her expression is as unaffected as she can make it, but still, she can't hide from me what she's feeling. She's attracted to me, and disconcerted by me, whether she'll admit it or not. I can see her nervousness in the way her fingers are fidgeting with the hem of her blouse.

"Are you sure you wouldn't rather stay here? I'm sure I could come up with something to . . . satisfy you."

Her cheeks turn bright red and her eyes round ever-so-slightly, making me want to pull her into my arms and kiss her senseless. But I won't. I promised I wouldn't until she asked me to. And I have no doubt she will. I'll just have to make sure it's sooner rather than later. She's giving me an itch that I don't want to wait to scratch.

"Thank you, but no. I've got some errands to run as well." I say nothing, just shake my head as I study her. Her eyes dart away and I know she's looking for some way to ease the tension. "So, I couldn't help but overhear part of your conversation. If neither you nor your sister wants to stay here in Greenfield with the orchard, why not just let your aunt have it?"

I feel like sighing. Every time I think of my aunt Ellie, I get angry. And right now, in Laney's presence, there are several other emotions I'd much rather be focusing on.

Another day . . .

"My parents wanted it with either me or Jenna. They'd roll over in their graves if we let Ellie take it."

Mom especially. She always dreamed of her grandchildren playing in the orchard. She's the reason I'm so determined to keep it with us, just like Dad is the reason Jenna wants to.

"Why? She's family."

"Not all family is the good kind."

"And you think your aunt falls into that category?"

"Yes. She's nothing like my mother. My mother was a kind and caring woman, and she loved this place. When my grandparents retired and moved to Florida, they left the house and the orchard to her as the oldest. We only found out after Dad died that Ellie was given a portion of the income. And now, true to the selfish person that she is, she wants it all."

"Why now?"

"Ellie never liked the orchard to begin with. She and her husband had big plans to get out of this place and make a shitload of money. I guess she always thought the orchard money would just be extra. But things didn't work out the way she had planned. She could never do anything about it while Dad was alive, though. But with him gone, and just me and Jenna left . . ."

"She's contesting that she should have the right of survivorship, rather than you two," Laney finishes.

I nod. "And that's why you're here, inventorying everything my family has ever owned."

It's Laney's turn to nod. She casts her eyes down, like she's afraid to meet mine. Finally she speaks. "I'm sorry, Jake. I can't imagine how hard it must be to go through something like this right after you buried your father."

She's sweet. And sincere. I can feel compassion rolling off her in waves.

And it makes me distinctly uncomfortable.

So, I do what I do best, and I deflect.

I step closer to Laney, close enough to smell her perfume. It's light and sweet. Sexy. Like sunshine and sin.

I take her chin between my fingers and wait until her eyes meet mine. "Don't feel sorry for me. Unless you plan to do something to make me feel better."

Her cheeks turn pink again. "You really are a bad boy, aren't you?" she whispers, almost like she's thinking aloud.

"I can be as good or as bad as you want me to be."

"I've always wanted the good guys," she muses. I'm not a bit surprised. I'd be willing to bet she's never broken a rule in her entire life.

"Maybe it's time for a change."

"Maybe it is," she says softly, her blue eyes flickering down to my mouth and back again.

"Tell me to kiss you," I say quietly as I lean slowly toward her.

Like I poked her with a cattle prod, I see her eyes widen and a startled look come over her face. She steps back, as though she's stepping away from danger. "I need to go. I'll be back after lunch."

And with that, she turns and walks quickly to where her car is parked, slides behind the wheel, and drives away. I step out of the barn to watch her go. And I see her watching me through her rearview mirror.

I grin at her and wink. Whether she can see it or not, it doesn't matter.

It's just a matter of time.

SEVEN: *Laney*

Sunday morning, and I've never been happier to hear the pianist start the first hymn. Here I thought I'd have to worry about sinful thoughts of Jake during church. Little did I know today's torture would be about Shane instead.

I'm already tired of all the good-natured, well-meaning questions about his absence. I can't remember the last time I came home and went to church and Shane *wasn't* with me. Evidently everyone else noticed that, too. One of the major downsides of small-town life is everyone knowing your business. It hasn't yet hit the gossip mill that we aren't together anymore, but it's sure to spread like wildfire now.

I exhale in relief when Mom slides into the pew beside me. The grilling is over. For the moment, anyway.

As the choir fills, the banging of the door at the back of the church turns nearly every head in the building. My blood boils when I see Tori, my *ex* best friend, duck and walk quickly down the aisle toward the front. Toward me.

Surely to God she doesn't have the audacity to come sit with me!

And yet, she does. My mother shifts her legs to the side to allow

Tori to pass. I do not. I keep my back straight, my feet planted, and my eyes trained straight ahead.

When she sits down beside me, I scoot a fraction of an inch toward my mother. I hear Tori's sigh, and I grit my teeth.

"Really? This is how you're going to act? In *church*?" Tori whispers.

As much as I'd like to say to her, as much as I'd like to blister her ears, I keep my mouth shut and ignore her.

"Nice. Real Christian of you, Laney."

I turn my blazing eyes on her. "*You* are telling *me* what's Christian?" My laugh, though soft, is discernibly bitter. "Oh, okay."

"What's that supposed to mean? You won't even give me a chance to explain. You're judging me without knowing all the facts."

I whip my head back around to look at her. "I don't need an explanation, Tori. I found you in bed with my fiancé. Unless you have a twin that I don't know about, I'm not interested in your explanation."

"It's not what you think, Laney," Tori says, her eyes pleading with me.

"I might be the preacher's daughter and I might be tame by *some people's* standards, but I'm not an idiot. I know what I walked in on."

"You *think* you know what you walked in on," Tori replies.

Suddenly, I'm tired. Tired of feeling hurt. Tired of feeling betrayed. Tired of trying to figure out the why of it all. Tired of feeling . . . less. Shane wanted a wild girl. He found one. End of story.

It just sucks that it was my very best friend in the whole world.

"It's done, Tori. I'm over it. Over Shane. Over you." I turn my attention back to the choir. I school my features to look politely interested, something I learned to do years ago so my father wouldn't fuss at me for misbehaving in church. But inside, there's a hole in my heart. I don't know if she can hear me, and I don't really care when I add, "It's time to fill my life with different people. People who don't lie."

Despite the fact that I'm still aching over what my best friend and my fiancé did to me, the first person to pop into my head is Jake Theopolis. He doesn't lie about who or what he is. What you see is what you get. Plain and simple. He's a bad boy, yes. But he's also a breath of fresh air. And my stagnant life feels very much in need of just that.

I'm glad I drove to church. This way, I can escape just after Daddy closes the service. I can get away before anyone else asks me about Shane, and before Tori can catch me.

I drive through town, not really thinking of where I'm going. I only know two things: I don't want to be at church and I don't want to go home. But what does that leave? As I drive aimlessly up and down the streets, through a town full of people I've known most of my life, I feel completely and utterly alone.

After half an hour of wasting gas, I hear the *ding* of the low-gas alarm, signaling that I have five miles left before I'm empty. I pull into the parking lot of Big A Grocery and turn around, heading back down route sixty, the way I'd come.

As I pass the fire station, a familiar Jeep catches my eye.

Jake.

My heart speeds up. How did I miss that before?

Several guys are standing just inside the huge, open bay door, gathered beside a bright red fire truck. I crane my neck to see if one of them is Jake, but I pass too fast to get a good look.

I glance in my rearview mirror, hoping to get a glimpse of him, but I don't, and within a few seconds, they're too far away for me to discern much, anyway.

Pressing on the accelerator, I try to put my curious desire to see Jake again out of my mind. But it's no use. Within a mile or so, I'm hanging a U-turn in front of the Stop-N-Shop convenience store and heading back toward the fire station to make one more pass.

This time when I go by, the guys are dispersing. I slow down a bit and watch two men back toward some cars parked in the right side of the front lot. My stomach does a little flip when I see Jake step around the corner at the mouth of the bay and yell something to one of the guys leaving. They all laugh, and the man nearest Jake jabs him in the ribs with his elbow.

I don't realize that I've slowed almost to a stop to stare at Jake's gorgeous, laughing face until he turns and his eyes meet mine through the open passenger window of my car. My cheeks go up in flames.

Busted!

Quickly, I turn to stare straight ahead as I punch the gas pedal. The car takes off, but then with a chug-chug-chug, it comes to a stop just a little way past the fire station.

Mortified, bedazzled, and totally confused, I pump the gas and turn the key in the ignition. I glance around helplessly, unable to think of anything else to do. My brain isn't working right and it only worsens matters when I hear the velvety voice rumble through the quiet interior of my car.

"Car problems?"

Leaning down at the passenger side window, looking inordinately pleased and ridiculously handsome, is Jake.

Of course it's Jake! He's ever-present when there's humiliation to be witnessed.

"Uhhh, car problems?" I repeat, still feeling scatterbrained after seeing Jake laughing with his friends like that. I've never been more physically attracted to someone. Ever. "I guess. I mean, I don't . . ."

Then it hits me. And my embarrassment triples.

I freakin' drove back to stare at freakin' Jake Theopolis and let my freakin' car run out of freakin' gas!

Dear God, just let me die!

I close my eyes and lean forward to rest my forehead on the steering wheel. For one fleeting moment in time, I think, *Maybe, just maybe, I'll be back in church when I open my eyes*, and that none of this is real. That I didn't just run my car out of gas to gawk at a guy. And then get discovered doing it.

But, alas, I'm not so fortunate. When I crack my lids and look straight ahead at my dash, I see the needle of accusation pointing to the E of humiliation on my gas gauge.

In the absence of any kind of intelligible speech on my part, Jake leans into the car and takes a look at the dials, too. He smells like soap and cinnamon, and I notice that he's chewing a toothpick again.

He turns his head toward me, catching me looking at him. His amber eyes flash and his lips spread into a grin as he wiggles the toothpick between them.

"I've never had a girl run out of gas just to get my attention before."

My face burns and my mouth works itself open and closed like that of a fish out of water as I try to deny it. But the words won't come, mainly because they're only half-truths. It wasn't purposeful, but still, I let myself run out of gas because of Jake Theopolis. There's just no getting around it. "That's ridiculous!" I finally manage.

"Is it now?" Up close, I can count every long, black lash that surrounds his warm eyes, and all coherent thought goes right out the window. "Either way, you're mine now, so let's get this car out of the road." Before I can argue, Jake backs away and puts his shoulder against the frame of the window. "Put it in neutral," he shouts. I do as he says, not really having much choice.

With a grunt, Jake pushes until the car starts to roll. "Steer it to the curb," he instructs, which I do. In no time, he has used his admittedly impressive strength to get the car out of the road. He walks around the front of the car and opens my door. "Set your emergency brake and roll up the windows." When I've done both, he reaches into the car and takes my hand. "Now, come with me."

I grab my purse and let Jake tow me back toward the fire station. "I didn't lock the doors," I tell him.

Jake grins down at me. "You're worried about that in *this* town? No one would dare vandalize the preacher's daughter's car. They'd be afraid of getting struck by lightning."

"What if they don't know it's my car?" I ask, ignoring his teasing.

He stops suddenly and turns toward me. "I guarantee you that everyone in this town knows. You make people notice you whether you intend to or not." His eyes rake me from head to toe. "You just can't help it. You have this touch-me-not quality about you that makes people want to touch. Even dressed like this. I've never found church clothes to be attractive until right this minute." He leans in to whisper in my ear, "I've never wanted to peel them off someone before, either."

Chills shoot down my arms and chest, making me glad I wore layers, even though they're light ones. I can feel my nipples pucker into pebbles and I'd hate for him to notice something like that.

"You really have no shame, do you?" I ask.

Jake's grin returns, more wicked than ever. "Not one bit."

He tugs me forward and on to his Jeep. "Where are we going?" I ask as I climb inside. It smells like him. Soap and man. Clean, yet dirty. Sexy.

He doesn't answer me. Instead, he yells to the men gathered at the door, watching the spectacle. "See you assholes tomorrow. I'm taking her to get some gas."

I wait until Jake is situated behind the wheel and the motor is running before I speak. "Assholes? Friends of yours, I presume?"

"Nah."

"They're not? Then what are you doing here?"

"I'm going to be working here."

"Working here? Doing what?"

"Fighting fires. I'm a fireman."

Oh precious God! He's a fireman.

Big, long hoses and sweaty skin flash through my mind.

With a wink that says he knows exactly what I'm thinking, Jake backs out of the parking lot. "So if you have any fires that need to be . . . put out, just let me know."

I resist the urge to fan my hot face as we turn onto the main road. I make no reply to his comment; I just focus on the road ahead.

I'm counting the seconds until we get to the gas station when Jake surprises me by stopping right in the middle of the road. I turn my puzzled gaze to him just as the car behind us honks. "What are you doing?" I ask.

Jake doesn't respond; he just watches me. His golden eyes are narrowed on me, turning my bones to warm liquid goo.

"Come to the Blue Hole with me. You look like you could use a little fun."

"I-I don't think—I mean, I don't think I should—"

"I'm not inviting you to an orgy, Laney," Jake interrupts. "It's just a few locals getting together for some hot dogs and beer, and some music. One of my high school buddies will be there. He plays with Saltwater Creek."

Saltwater Creek is a local band. I know this because my father has disapproved of them for the last decade.

"That doesn't sound like—"

Before I can finish, he butts in again.

"Rather than put so much energy into making excuses, why don't you just come with me? It'll do you good. I promise."

Years of my father's warnings and my mother's advice, coupled with a lifetime of knowing exactly who and what I want give me pause. But before I can turn him down, something else bubbles up. Some part of me that is inexplicably drawn to Jake, to the freedom he represents. He's nothing like what I've ever thought I wanted or needed in my life, yet, at the same time, he feels like everything I want and need in my life *right now*.

If I go back to my car, there is only the drive back to my parents' house awaiting me. That and possibly another run-in with Tori, which is not something I really want to tackle right now. But if I go with Jake . . .

Before I can think better of it, I find myself agreeing. "Okay. I'll go. But if I need to leave, you have to promise to bring me back to my car."

"Damn, it sounds like you think I'm going to kidnap you."

The thought of being held by Jake, of being restrained and at his mercy sends an unexpected thrill down my spine. Throwing caution to the wind and going out with someone like him only intensifies it.

Pushing all troubling thoughts aside in favor of letting go of it all for once, I smile and lean my head back against the headrest, closing my eyes. "Maybe today I want to be kidnapped."

Even over the revving of the engine as Jake takes off down the road, I can hear the smile in his voice when he says, "I'll see what I can do."

EIGHT: *Jake*

glance at Laney where she sits in the passenger seat. I'm sure this is her version of relaxed—hands folded demurely in her lap, spine ramrod straight, head tilted back, eyes closed. Something tells me that not only does she not kick back and *really* relax very often, but that today she needs it more than ever. She seems . . . troubled. A little more agreeable to leave care behind her. And I'm just the guy to drive her away from all her hang-ups. Whatever it is she's running from, I can take her mind off it. I'll give her something much more enjoyable to think about if she'll let me.

And she will.

She's already mine, whether she realizes it or not. We can be the perfect distraction for each other while we're in town. Then we'll go our separate ways. Her to the quiet, predictable life she's no doubt always dreamed of, and me to the next rush. It's the ideal arrangement—a short-term, no-strings romp with a girl that offers a little bit of a challenge. I'm all but licking my lips just thinking about it.

"So, you gonna tell me what it is that you're trying to escape?"

In my peripheral vision, I see Laney's eyes pop open, but she doesn't raise her head. "What makes you thinking I'm trying to escape something?"

"Oh, come on. A girl like you—gorgeous, great job, bright future—comes back to *this place* to take a random assignment and move back in with her parents. That's got 'running' written all over it."

I hear her sigh as she turns her head on the rest to stare out the window.

"Just trying to figure out what to do with my life. That's all."

"Seems to me like you've got everything going for you. What's there to figure out?"

"You'd be surprised," she says softly.

I get the feeling there's a lot she's not saying and doesn't want to talk about, which is fine. I'm not really the kind of guy that likes to get that involved, anyway. I'm more curious than anything. I've never met a woman quite like Laney. She intrigues me. But beyond that, I just want her. Plain and simple. Nothing more. Just her in my bed, warm and soft and moaning my name. Yep. That's it.

And I'd prefer it sooner rather than later.

"Well, lucky for you, you're in the company of the one man who can make you forget all your worries. Just leave it to me."

The Blue Hole is actually a deep spot in the river that happened to coincide with a brief widening, so it's like a private cove, surrounded by trees. There's a beach area between two big boulders, one of which is flat at the very top, making it the perfect platform for diving. There's also a tire swing that flings you right out into the deepest part of the hole. I mean what the hell kind of country hangout would it be without a tire swing? All in all, it's a damn cool place to chill out with friends.

Or work your charms on a goody-goody preacher's daughter.

It takes about an hour to get there. Neither of us has said much, and that's fine with me. I'm not one of those people who feels the need to fill every silence with small talk. Quite the opposite, in fact. I'd rather people keep their mouth shut unless they have something to say. Don't talk just for the sake of talking. That's one thing that ninety-nine percent of the women I've been involved with (however briefly) have done to irritate the shit out of me—talk too much.

But not this one. Laney seems content to stare out the window and keep her thoughts to herself. I must admit it makes me wonder what she's thinking about, though. Is it possible that she's daydreaming about me pulling off the road and shutting off the engine? About me dragging her out of the Jeep and walking her into the woods? About me raising up her chaste little skirt and feeling her wet panties? About me tearing them off and putting my fingers inside her? About sliding her hot, tight little body down over my cock until she loses her breath?

Damn, I hope that's what she's thinking about!

Just in time to save me from getting a raging hard-on, I see the line of cars that leads up to the turn off the main road. I bypass all of them in favor of exercising my fully equipped four-wheel drive and taking to the woods to park right up next to the edge of the cove. When I cut the engine, I can hear the music before I even open the door.

I glance over at Laney. "Ready to have some fun?"

She gives me a small, doubtful smile and nods once.

I walk around to open the passenger door and help Laney out. For one thing, my Jeep is pretty high and she's pretty tiny, but more than that, my mother taught me better. Even though I was young when she died, there are some things that stuck. This is one of them.

I take her hand in mine and lead her through the trees to the waterfront. There is a total of about thirty people in attendance, I'd guess. Some are in the water playing chicken, some are lined up to try out their acrobatic skills on the tire swing that hangs from a tree, and some are lounging on beach towels in the dappled sun.

I see lots of tan skin revealed by lots of skimpy bikinis, which is just the way I like it. Makes me wish Laney had something else to put on.

I glance at the three guys sitting on a fallen log at one end of the beach. Two are playing guitar and one is thumping his leg in time with the music as he sings backup to the lead guitarist. He's the drummer. Drum-less, of course.

Since they're in the middle of a song, I steer Laney toward the table set up at the edge of the trees.

"You hungry?" I ask as we approach.

She nods.

"Somebody always brings a shitload of food to these things so everyone can help themselves."

"Should we have brought something?"

"Nah. He who throws it feeds it," I tell her as I walk up behind the "chef" and tap him on the shoulder. "Can I get two hot dogs, man?"

When he turns around, I see a face that looks vaguely familiar, but like most of my life here in Greenfield, I've tried (and have mostly succeeded in) blocking it out.

"Sure thing, Jake," he answers. He starts to turn around, but does a double take when he sees who's at my side. "Holy shit! Laney Holt. I never thought I'd see the day . . ."

I watch the guy's eyes slide slowly over Laney from the top of her shiny head to the pink-painted toes peeking out of her shoes.

"See what day? When she'd take her chances on a guy like me?" I ask amicably.

The guy's eyes flicker back to me and widen for a second before his cheeks turn bright red and he starts fumbling through an apology. "No, that's not what I meant. I meant to say . . . um . . . what I really meant was . . ."

"It's all right, Marshall," Laney jumps in, sweetly rescuing the poor bastard before he makes things worse. "I knew what you meant. I guess we all grow up and start living our own lives after a while, right?"

Marshall, who I can almost remember but really don't want to, laughs uncomfortably. His eyes dart over to me a few times before he finally just gives up and turns around to stab us each a fat, blistered hot dog.

I grab a couple of plates and buns, and hand one to Laney. We walk along the table, putting condiments on our dogs and taking a handful of chips before we make our way back past Marshall whatever-the-hell-his-last-name-is.

"What's to drink, Emeril?"

"Beer on tap in the barrel over there and purple people eater in the cooler right beside it. Take your pick."

I nod my thanks, snag two cups, and lead Laney over to the drinks.

"What's your poison?" I ask as I set my plate down to fix our drinks.

"Uh, what's a purple people eater?"

"Pure grain, grape pop, and fruit."

"Mmm, that sounds good. I think I'll have that."

"Are you sure?"

"Of course, why?"

I shrug. "No reason." I think she has no idea what pure grain is.

I fill her glass and then pour myself a cup of beer from the tap. We head to a grassy spot in the shade, right at the edge of the sand and sit down to eat.

By the time Laney delicately picks her way through her hot dog and chips, I've already gone back for seconds and thirds. When she finally wipes her mouth with her napkin, I ask, "Done?"

"Yes."

"Good?"

She grins. "Yes."

"More?"

"No, thank you."

"More to drink?" I ask, eyeing her empty cup. She debates for a second before she agrees.

"Yeah, I think I'll have one more glass."

She comes to her feet and we take our plates to the trash bag and get refills on our drinks.

"Hell, if it ain't Jake Theopolis," I hear someone say loudly from behind us. I turn to see Jet Blevins making his way toward us. He's an old high school buddy, as well as the lead guitarist and singer of Saltwater Creek.

"Damn, you look scruffier every time I see you, man," I say to him when he stops in front of us. He looks like a typical band member with his pierced brow and various visible tattoos. God knows what we *can't* see.

He grins and playfully punches my shoulder.

"And you get sturdier. What the hell are you eatin', bro? Steroids? You know that shit'll turn your balls into raisins, right?"

"Are you kidding me? The only juice that goes into this body is right here," I say, indicating my beer. "Nectar of the gods."

"You got that right," he says, clasping my hand and pulling me in for a bear hug. "Good to see you, man. Where you been?"

"Oh, you know, dragging bodies out of burning buildings, saving lives, playing hero. Same ol', same ol'."

Jet turns to look at Laney. "I think your humble date here forgot leaping tall buildings in a single bound."

I laugh, but Laney doesn't. "Um, he's not my date. We actually work together."

"Hot damn, you're a fireman, too?"

That makes her smile. "No, I'm a paralegal. I'm working on Jake's family's estate. Laney Holt."

"Immune to superman's charms, huh?" he asks Laney as he reaches for her hand, his eyes taking her in like he didn't really see her before. And like he's hungry for what he missed.

With longish black hair and pale blue eyes, Jet isn't a bad-looking guy. I've never really paid much attention. He's got a decent personality. Again, nothing I've ever given much thought. Until now, when he decides to flirt with Laney. And for some reason, that irritates the shit out of me, making it harder to play nice.

"I haven't even begun to charm her yet, so back off, man," I say, lightheartedly cutting off his handshake. I temper my words with a smile, but there's still a bite to them. He'd be wise to take note of that.

"Wait, Holt. As in Graham Holt, the preacher?"

Laney all but sighs. "Yes."

Jet throws back his head and lets out a howl of laughter before he sobers and looks back to me. Appreciation is in his eyes. He holds up his fist. "Dude! Nice!" I bump my curled fingers against his and then he turns his attention back to Laney. "Well, the pleasure is all mine, Laney Holt, preacher's daughter. I'm Jet Blevins, singer, guitarist, damn fine man."

"I see I'm not the only 'humble' one," I mutter.

"Gotta let her know her options," he teases, giving Laney a wink. I make a point to keep my fingers relaxed, even though I want to ball them up into a fist and punch Jet right in his shit-talking mouth.

"Laney Holt! Ohmigod!"

The shrill voice saves Jet from getting himself into trouble. Or at least that's the way I see it.

We all turn to see a curvy redhead making her way toward us. She's wearing a string bikini that shows off her ample cleavage to perfection. Her face isn't bad, either.

"You probably don't remember me. We met at Shane's apartment last year. I was dating his cousin, Rod."

I watch expressions flit across Laney's face as she digs for the memory. "No, no, I *do* remember you. Hannah, right?"

"Yes. Ohmigod, you *do* remember!" The girl seems overly pleased. Good God, what's the big deal?

Women.

"So nice to see you again."

"You, too," Hannah says. "I didn't think I'd know anybody here.

Shane was supposed to be coming, but he couldn't make it. So now it's just me and my friend, Lisa. She's a freshman in college this year, but she grew up here in Greenfield. Shane knows her, but I doubt you would. I think she's a few years younger than you. "

"Of course Shane knows her," Laney mumbles.

"Pardon?" Hannah asks.

"You're probably right," Laney says, glossing over her comment. Hannah might not have heard her, but I sure did. "Greenfield is small, but I'm sure I don't know everyone."

"So, are you gonna swim? The water feels great. This is such a cool little spot." Hannah giggles. She's very enthusiastic. And bubbly. And she makes my head feel like it's about to explode. I'm about thirty seconds from excusing myself to go jump in said water and not come back out until she's gone.

"No, I didn't bring a suit. This was an . . . impromptu trip."

"No worries. I can loan you something. When I heard this was a swimming hole, I brought a suit and some shorts, too. Just in case. I mean, you never know. You're welcome to the shorts."

"No, thank you. I'll just—"

I perk up at her offer, even if Laney doesn't. "Oh, come on, Laney. Didn't you hear? The water's great. And everyone needs to ride the swing at least once," I add, glad that I didn't leave the girls to their conversation and miss this turn of events. Laney. In shorts. Wet. This is definitely heading in the right direction.

"I'd really better not."

"Today's about fun, remember? And I'm not in the habit of taking no for an answer."

She wants to argue. I can tell. But she's too polite. Southern girl all the way to the bone.

I turn to Hannah. "Go get them. I'll talk her into it."

Hannah grins, happy to be a part of the pile-on. "I've got an even better idea. Come with me, Laney. You can change in my car."

The smile Laney gives her is almost as tight as her ass. "Okay."

"Here," I say before she walks off, pushing her refilled cup into her hand. "Seems like you need it."

She gives me a frosty glare and stalks off with Hannah.

NINE: *Laney*

The only reason I'm letting Jake talk me into any of this is because I need it. As much as I hate to admit it, I know I do.

It's out of character for me to be going to parties and drinking purple people eaters and jumping off things, but that's what I want most right now—*not* to be the same old Laney. I don't want to be the boring, predictable, good girl anymore. That got me nothing but heartache. At least I know I don't have to worry about that with Jake. Trust isn't really an option. I know who and what he is. He makes no bones about it. And I have no more intention of getting deeply involved with him than he does with me. That's part of what makes this so perfect. It's fleeting. And dangerous. Two things I've never before craved or pursued in my life. And two things I know I could never settle for in the end.

But there's no reason I can't lose the old me in *this person* for a while. Just a little while. If only I could learn to embrace her . . .

Hannah's chattering stops, making me realize that I have been lost in thought and completely ignoring whatever it is she's been talking about. "Is that okay?" she asks.

I have no clue what she's referring to. "Sure."

She gives me a bright smile and hits the keyless entry for a bright purple two-door car. "Great."

She opens the door and disappears inside for a few seconds before reemerging with a couple of scraps of clothing. I look at her in question and she smiles again. "I'll keep an eye out."

With that, she turns her back to me, crosses her arms over her chest, and assumes the stance of a sentry, leaving me to climb into the passenger side of her car and change clothes.

After some creative maneuvering, I'm sitting in Hannah's front seat, staring down at my bare stomach and a whole lot of bare leg. When Hannah said "shorts," I made the very erroneous assumption that she meant real shorts, not these teeny tiny cut-off denim . . . things. And the T-shirt that goes with them? A scrap of cotton that might fit a doll.

Might.

I take a deep breath, reminding myself that I'm easy, breezy, and fun girl right now, not uptight Laney. I spy my glass of grape drink sitting in the cup holder. Impulsively, I drain the entire cup.

Liquid courage.

A burp bubbles up and surprises me. With a gasp, I clamp my hand over my mouth, hoping Hannah didn't hear. I look out the window at her, but she hasn't budged. I imagine that, if she'd heard, she'd be the type to mention it. So, figuring my embarrassing gastric mishap is still a secret, I grab my clothes, open the door, and exit.

Hannah turns around to size me up. Her eyes round. "Damn, look what you've been hiding under those clothes, Laney! You look hot!"

I feel my cheeks sting and resist the urge to cover myself with the skirt and blouse I'm holding.

"Thank you."

Hannah reaches for my hand, taking the empty cup from my fingers, crumpling it up and tossing it into the bed of a truck as we pass. "Come on. Let's drop your clothes off and then go show you off."

After telling her which vehicle I arrived in, Hannah puts my clothes in Jake's Jeep and then we make our way back to the party. We stop by the cooler for Hannah to refill her drink.

"You want another one?"

I know I should say no, but I'm feeling lighter by the minute. Happier. More carefree. Like my smile just might be permanent. And the drink really *is* good . . .

It takes me all of three seconds to consent.

"Sure."

After she hands me a cup as well, we head toward the beach.

The sun is glistening on the water and laughter can be heard from every direction, even over the music the guys from Saltwater Creek are playing. The smell of grilled hot dogs hangs in the air, and my head is as light and fluffy as the few clouds overhead.

Feeling bold and brazen for some reason, I stop and scan the crowd until I see Jake. He's talking to a couple of guys that look vaguely familiar. They're both laughing at something. That's the only attention I pay them before turning my gaze back to Jake. He's the one I'm most interested in. And getting more so by the second.

Jake changed his clothes, too. He's wearing black swim trunks. And nothing else. I scan him from head to toe. I notice two things. Number one, he makes my stomach quiver. Number two, his smooth chest and rippling abs seem to be begging for me to touch them. Then maybe kiss them.

As if sensing my eyes on him, Jake looks up from his place near the water and his gaze collides with mine. His mouth drops open a fraction as his eyes cruise every inch of my exposed skin. I tingle everywhere they touch—my throat, my stomach, my legs.

The song the band is playing brings a smile to my lips. It's an old Warrant song called "Cherry Pie." It makes me feel sexy and wanted and . . . daring as I step off the grass and into the sand to make my way to Jake.

The cool grains tickle my toes as I walk and a pleasant warmth suffuses my entire body. I'm not sure if it's from the drink or from Jake, but, at the moment, I couldn't care less.

He backs away from the other guys as I approach. I stop in front of him, pleased to see the heated glow in his eyes. "You're gonna make me regret your change of clothes, aren't you?"

"Why would you regret it?"

Jake takes a step forward, bringing his body to within an inch of mine. "Because I promised I wouldn't be kissing you again until you asked me to. And this," he says, reaching down to drag the backs of his fingers over the skin of my bare stomach, "isn't going to make it easy."

I'm trapped in the caramel pools of his eyes, in the low rumble of his voice, in the delicious web of this unfamiliar desire. The part of me that would normally resist him is curiously absent, leaving only the part of me that is fascinated by him and what he makes me feel.

I sway toward him. "Maybe I don't want it to be easy."

One inky black brow shoots up. "Are you teasing me, beautiful?"

"Maybe."

"Have you ever heard that expression about messing with the bull?"

"Are you threatening me with your . . . horns?" I ask, knowing full well that I'm playing with fire, yet not quite able to care. I just feel the heat. And I want it.

I want him.

"Baby, I don't make threats. I make promises."

For a second, I forget that we are in the middle of a crowd, that we aren't alone and that I shouldn't be tempting fate this way. For a second, I just want him to kiss me. And touch me. And make me forget everything in the world and in my life except him. And I know Jake is just the kind of guy that could do that.

An unwelcome voice interrupts the moment. It's Hannah. "There's no excuse for you to still be dry, Laney," she says. I don't even glance her way, hoping that if I ignore her, she'll go away. Only she doesn't. "Come on, you two. Let's go give that tire swing a whirl."

One corner of Jake's mouth curves up into a wry grin. "Didn't you say you were here with a friend? What was her name, Lisa? Where's she at?" he asks without taking his eyes off mine.

"Oh, she's off flirting with some guy she met."

While I am a bit irritated by the interruption, Hannah has been very nice to me, and I feel bad for her that her friend abandoned her so easily.

Swallowing my sigh, I turn to her and smile. "Lead the way."

"Yay!" she exclaims, clapping her hands as she bounces, setting her generous boobs ajiggle. She flips her red hair and turns toward the huge rock where several people are waiting for their turn on the swing.

Jake and I follow, stopping behind her in line. I feel his warm palm slide around the curve of my waist to settle at my hip. It's an intimate gesture, and I feel the heat of his hand all the way to my core, making me wish again that we were alone.

I don't turn to look back at him. I don't want him to see my smile.

I sip my drink until it's my turn to climb up on the rock, then I hand it to Jake. "Here. Hold this."

Jake takes it in one hand, glancing down at it before he winds the fingers of his other around my upper arm. He stops me from moving forward to take my turn. "Hey, are you sure you're okay to do this? I get the feeling you're not used to drinking, and this stuff isn't exactly a wine cooler."

His comment stirs up the resentment that I've been battling since things with Shane took a turn for the worse. I pull my arm free. "I'm fine. I'm not the goody-two-shoes you think I am."

He quirks one brow, but says nothing as I turn and climb onto the rock.

The first level isn't too bad, but the thing is, you have to climb up onto another, higher part of the rock to get to the tire and swing out over the water. When I reach the top and a guy pushes the rope tied to the tire into my hands, I look down. It seems that I'm at least a mile above the surface of the water.

"Uhhh . . ." The guy looks at me, raises his eyebrows and tips his head toward the water. "Umm, I'm not sure I want to do this," I tell him.

"Aw, come on. It's fun. You'll be fine."

I start to back away. "I don't think I should."

"Can you swim?" he asks.

"Of course I can swim." I feel like saying *Duh! Why would I be up here if I couldn't swim?* But I don't.

"Then you'll be fine. Just put your foot up here and I'll swing you out."

I pause, teetering between sucking it up and doing it to save face, or braving the humiliation of climbing back down.

A familiar voice interrupts my musing. "Want me to go down with you?" Jake rumbles at my ear.

I feel a sigh of relief swell in my chest before I ask, "Can we do that?"

Jake reaches around me to take the rope from my fingers. For just a second, nearly every surface of his front is pressed to my back. He pauses before he straightens, as if he's giving me time to enjoy the feeling of being enveloped by him, of being touched all over by him.

"We can do anything we want," he answers softly, his breath tickling my neck.

And just like that, we're talking of much more than just the swing.

I turn around to face him. He's so close I can count the dark stubble that dusts his cheeks.

"So how do we do this?"

Without taking his eyes off mine, Jake winds his arm around my waist, pulls me in tight against him, then lifts me off the ground. "Just hold on to me. I've got you."

I don't know if it's just in my head or if Jake *means* to make that sound like more than the obvious. Either way, my brain, spinning with drink and fear and anticipation, interprets his words differently. In some ways, I think Jake *does* have me. My attention, my attraction, my curiosity, my desire—but what comes next? Some part of me anxiously awaits the answer to that question. And maybe, just maybe, I'll be able to let go of the old Laney long enough to enjoy what I find.

My arms slip easily around his neck and my legs intertwine with his, leaving no space between us. We fit together perfectly, like our bodies were designed with the other in mind.

"Ready?" he asks as he watches me intently. Again, in my mind, it seems he's asking me about so much more.

"As ready as I'll ever be."

With a grin, he pulls back on the rope, steps up onto the bottom of the tire and pushes off. We swing way up into the air, enough for my stomach to drop, before Jake lets go.

Then we're flying.

And I'm falling.

Down, down, down we go, and I hear Jake's whoop just before cool water engulfs us. I can still feel the heat of his body and, even as our momentum slows and I begin to swim upward, Jake never loosens his hold.

We break the surface at the same time. Jake's laughing as he shakes his head, sending droplets of water in every direction. When his eyes meet mine, they're sparkling.

"Well?" he asks.

"That was awesome." My heart is still hammering, although I'm not sure if it's from the swing or from Jake's legs tangling with mine. "Thank you for doing it with me."

His smile turns wicked. "There are many, many things I'd like to do with you. I hope this was just the beginning."

"There are?"

"Oh, I think you *know* there are." I smile into his eyes as his arm tightens around my waist and he drags me slowly toward shallower water. He stops when his feet hit solid ground. Mine are still dangling freely. My head spins with purple drink. My stomach flutters with anticipation. My heart races with excitement. "Tell me to kiss you," he commands in his gravelly voice.

Uptight Laney would pause to consider. And then politely decline. But today . . . right now . . . she's not here.

I don't give it a second thought. I want him to do it; I want him to kiss me. "Kiss me," I whisper.

His lips twitch with satisfaction just before he lowers his head to mine.

The touch of Jake's lips is familiar, yes. His lips are firm yet yielding, and, even after eating, he still tastes vaguely of cinnamon. But in all other ways, this kiss is different. There's promise in it, the promise that this is where the ride starts, that this is where I have to take a deep breath and *really* jump into the unknown.

His mouth teases mine until it opens and he can slide his tongue inside. As it tangles with mine, stroking it, licking it, his hands skate down my back. He angles his head and deepens the kiss. I'm caught up in sensation as his palms cover my butt and then slide down the backs of my thighs to pull my legs around his waist.

With the intimate contact and no one to jerk on the reins, heat explodes between us. An urgency flourishes between us, making lips hungry and hands desperate. Suddenly, none of this feels too soon or too rushed or too dangerous. It feels just right.

Out of breath, Jake drags his mouth away from mine, trailing it to my ear, where he nips at the lobe. "I was thinking earlier about rubbing my hand over your wet panties, about what it would feel like to put my fingers inside you." He groans. Chills shoot down my back and my nipples tingle into tight points that beg for the brush of his chest against them. "You know I'm going to do that, right? Maybe not today. Maybe not tomorrow. But it *will* happen. You'll be mine, Laney. Before all is said and done, you *will* be mine."

With his words ringing in my head, he crushes his lips against mine again, threading the fingers of one hand into my wet hair as his other hand presses my hips against his.

It's not until I hear a delighted squeal that I remember we aren't alone.

Reluctantly, I pull my mouth away from his. My thoughts are foggy. I can't think right with him touching me, kissing me, talking to me this way.

Dazedly, I look around, prepared to be mortified. But no one is paying us any attention. Jake had enough sense to pull us to the bend at the edge of the cove, practically hidden from the view of the others.

"Don't worry. They can't see."

"I know, but still . . ."

I lean away. The spell is broken. This conversation, this *moment* deserves privacy. Of course, privacy could mean that we'd get carried away. And I'm not sure yet just how far it's safe for me to let Jake carry me. I'd thought there was no danger of me getting attached to him, but as I look at his handsome face and think of the great care and consideration he's shown me today, I worry that Mr. Wrong might start to feel like Mr. Right.

My shorts are finally dry. Well, Hannah's shorts are finally dry, I should say. After Jake and I got out of the water, we sat on a log in the sun to let our clothes dry. It took just long enough that my head finally began to clear.

And indecision set in.

Am I really capable of engaging in even the most casual of relationships and banter with a guy like Jake? Earlier, I definitely thought so, but now . . . It seems that no matter how badly I get hurt or how much fun there is to be had on the "other side," I'm still the same girl at heart. Some like it wild, but not me. At least not forever. I still want the same things. A man to love me more than anything. A man to put me and our family first. A man to build a life with. And I'm not crazy enough to think that Jake is that guy.

I might be crazy enough to wish he was, though.

I notice the low position of the sun and start to feel guilty about running off the way I did, without so much as a word to my parents. Yes, I'm an adult, but it was a really inconsiderate thing to do.

"I think I should probably head home," I say to Jake when the music dies down again. Saltwater Creek has played intermittently since we arrived, and they're actually quite good. I don't really want to leave yet. The thought of curling up next to Jake, after dark, in front of the fire I can see them building on the beach area, is extremely tempting. But . . .

Jake is agreeable about leaving. He doesn't seem to have any preference for staying or going.

He's quiet on the drive home, but I don't think that really says much. I get the feeling he's not one for small talk.

It's fully dark by the time we reach town. "You know, you could just drop me at my parents' house if you wouldn't mind. I can get one of them to take me to my car in the morning. It's getting late."

Jake shrugs. "Okay."

"It's not far from here."

"I know where you live."

"You do?"

"Everyone knows where the preacher lives."

He falls silent again. He guides the Jeep competently through the turns that lead to my street. I study him surreptitiously from beneath my lashes. The sharp angle of his cheekbones and the sculpted edge of his lips are highlighted by the soft glow of the dashboard light. He doesn't seem mad or upset, or inconvenienced. He just seems like . . . Jake.

Handsome, charming, sexy Jake.

Jake who sets my blood on fire. Jake who I can't get out of my head.

"Home sweet home," he says lightly as he parks at the curb in front of the house I grew up in.

I grab my rumpled clothes and purse from the floorboard and reach for the door handle. "Thanks, Jake. I had a good time."

"My pleasure," he replies.

He seems . . . off somehow, but I can't put my finger on it. I want to ask, but there are a thousand reasons why I shouldn't, why I shouldn't even care.

"Well, good night."

"Good night." I start to climb down, but Jake's voice stops me. "Oh, wait." My heart speeds up in anticipation. Jake cuts off the engine and pulls the keys from the ignition. He works one free and hands it to me. "Here. I won't be there for a few days. It's a round-the-clock shift at the fire station. Let yourself in, make yourself at home. Call my cell if you have any questions about anything."

I take the key from his fingers. "How will you get back in tonight?"

He waves me off. "I didn't lock the door. Besides, we have a spare key hidden in one of the barns."

I nod and give him a small smile, feeling bereft that the night is ending like this. So cool. So casual. So disappointing in the face of what happened earlier.

You've got no one to blame but yourself. Besides, you should be pleased. Jake Theopolis is a complication you don't need.

"Sweet dreams, Laney," Jake says as I'm shutting the door. I look back, but he's already pulling away.

But I could've sworn I saw him grinning, and that elevates my mood considerably. That seems a little more in character for him. Enough to bring a delighted smile to my face.

I'm still grinning in pleasure as I walk through the unlocked front door of my parents' house. When I shut it behind me and hear nothing but unnatural quiet and the tick of the mantle clock in the living room, my guard goes up immediately.

There's trouble brewing.

Quietly, I creep toward the steps. I feel like a teenager again, trying to avoid a confrontation that will end in a lecture and then me being grounded for all eternity.

Only I'm not a teenager. And I'm beginning to resent that I still feel that way when I come home.

"Laney, can you come here?"

My father. And I recognize that tone.

My stomach drops.

Curling my clothes into a tighter ball, I straighten my spine and walk to the living room. I smile casually when I stop just inside the doorway. "What's up?"

Both my parents look like I've just slapped them across the face. And they're both staring at my wad of clothes.

"Laney, what on earth?" Mom asks, holding a hand to her throat like I just announced I'm pregnant or joining a cult.

"Where have you been, young lady?" Daddy asks.

"Out."

I know such a short answer will only incur more questions and more wrath, but I'm still feeling a bit defiant from the taste of freedom I've enjoyed all day.

"Out where? And with whom? And whose clothes are those? Because I *know* they're not yours."

"And just how do you know that, Daddy?"

"Because *my daughter* would never dress like that!" he booms.

"And what's wrong with this? I'm not showing anything inappropriate. And, for what I was doing, this was actually quite concealing."

Mom gasps.

"And just what *were* you doing?"

"Swimming. Is that a problem?"

"Where?"

"A place called the Blue Hole."

My father's face turns red. "You know you're forbidden to go to places like that."

"Yes, Daddy. I know I *was* forbidden to go to places like that. But that was before I went to college, became an adult, and got a job out in the real world."

"Just because you're a few years older doesn't make places like that any more appropriate. Or the people that frequent them." I say nothing. There's no arguing with him when he's like this. "Who were you with? Who took you to that hellhole?"

I grit my teeth. This will just be icing on the cake. "Jake Theopolis."

"Laney, I've told you—"

I interrupt my father's blustering. "I know, I know. You don't think he's good company. You don't think he's the right kind of friend to have. You don't approve. Well, you know what, Daddy? I like him. He's kind and he helped me when I needed it today. And I think you've misjudged him."

"And just what would Shane think about you spending time with someone like that?"

He thinks that's what will cinch up his argument. A veiled threat to tattle on me to my fiancé.

Ha! He's my ex-*fiancé!*

"I don't care, Daddy. And it doesn't matter. How many times do I have to tell you that we broke up?"

"Well, until you give me a good reason, I'm not giving up on the two of you. Shane's a good man. The right kind of man. Good for you. You need to hang on to him. And cavorting about with a person like Jake Theopolis could ruin what you have with him. And I won't stand for that. Someone has to look out for you, do what's best for you."

"Maybe so, Daddy. But you're not it. From now on, *I'm* the only one that's looking out for me. And if I ever find someone I feel like handing the reins over to, I'll be sure to let you know. But until then, back off!"

With that, I whirl away from my stunned parents and storm up the stairs and to my room, slamming the door behind me.

If they want a teenager back in the house, I'll give them one!

Between that devilish drink I had at the Blue Hole, the drama with my parents, and the miniscule amount of sleep I was able to get after it, I'm tired and cranky by the time I drive back home from Jake's Monday.

As I pull up in front of the house, I wonder absently why Mom's car is parked on the street at the curb rather than in the garage. When nothing comes to mind right away, I shrug it off and grab my stuff from the passenger seat to head inside.

Something wonderful teases my nose when I open the door. I inhale deeply, feeling better already. "I'll be back down after I change clothes, Mom!" I call, aiming my voice toward the kitchen as I head for the stairs.

In my room, I dig through my still-packed suitcase and pull out some yoga pants and a T-shirt with a rip at the neck. I'm hoping my most comfortable clothes will bring me good luck. Maybe my parents can just leave last night where it belongs—in the past.

Maybe.

I hope.

I jog back down the steps and make the right that will take me through the dining room and into the kitchen. I see the table is set. Quite formally, actually. I think back for a second to any plans Mom might've told me about, but I come up with nothing.

Again.

I stop dead in my tracks after one step into the kitchen. My mouth drops open and all thought flies out of my head when I see what's waiting for me.

Or, rather, *who*.

Sitting at the island, still dressed in his work clothes, is Shane. My ex fiancé. The man I have no desire to see or speak to ever again.

At first, I'm just confused. I look to Mom then to Dad, asking, "What's he doing here?"

Shane stands and walks to me, reaching out to put his hands on my shoulders. I flinch at his touch, backing away from him. "Laney, we need to talk. And your father thought this might be a good time for us to do that."

His voice is well-modulated, purposely made to sound reasonable and confident. But all I hear is the voice of a liar. Of the man who broke my heart and betrayed me. With my best friend.

I'm flooded with disbelief. This can't be right. My parents would never, never be so manipulative and inconsiderate.

I lean to look around Shane's shoulder, expecting to see some sign of outrage at his lies. Or at the very least something to show me that he was gravely mistaken.

But that's not what I see at all.

I see the support of my parents. But not for me. For my ex fiancé.

It's an ambush.

"You did this?" I whisper, addressing my father. My throat is closed around a knot so large it feels like a fist. "Please tell me he's wrong. Please tell me this is just a misunderstanding."

My mother has the good grace to bow her head. This obviously wasn't her idea.

My eyes slide back to my father, standing tall and proud and unapologetic behind the island. Behind Shane.

"How could you?" I can barely squeeze out the words, but I know they are easily intelligible in the absolute quiet of the room.

"I can't let you make a mistake with that Theopolis boy that you'll regret for the rest of your life."

With an ache in my chest that feels like a raw and bleeding cavern, I turn away from my father. "The only two mistakes I've made, Daddy, are trusting Shane and coming back here."

Without a backward glance, I retrace my footsteps back up the steps, throw my few toiletries back into my suitcase, grab my purse, and go right back out to my car.

As I'm pulling away from the curb, away from the home and the people that seem barely recognizable to me right now, I have no idea where I'm going. I just know I can't stay here.

TEN: *Jake*

I'm tired. Not from overexertion like I might've been after a forty-eight-hour shift in Baton Rouge. No, this is from boredom. From being static for the better part of two days. It's no wonder there's only a dozen guys on the entire fire department force here. There just isn't enough activity to keep many people busy.

I worked an extra eighteen hours, bringing my total to sixty-six hours straight. I was hoping to at least get some kind of call where I could exercise my response skills, but no such luck. It was just . . . quiet.

Damn.

Since it's the middle of the night, I figure I'll get a few hours' sleep then get up and go for a run. At least working here at the orchard is a *little bit* stimulating. There's more to do than eat and play cards and watch television.

I stretch my neck as I pull into the long driveway that leads to the house. I'm missing Baton Rouge and all its excitement and activity, right up until I see the dusk-to-dawn light shining on a familiar blue car parked in front of the garage. The sight pushes Baton Rouge—

and every other desire, for the most part—to the very back of my mind.

"What the hell is Laney doing here at this hour?" I ask out loud as I recheck the dashboard clock to make sure I'm not missing something.

Nope. Sure enough, it's three o'clock in the morning.

I park beside her car and make my way quietly into the house. There are no lights on, no signs of life, which makes me wonder if maybe she had car trouble and had to have someone pick her up and drive her home.

That's possible. But, even though I can't imagine why, it's still also possible that she's asleep in my house right this minute.

Where I was tired before, now I'm wide awake. And feeling all kinds of stimulated.

Silently, I mount the stairs and stop at the top of the steps to look around and listen. There are no sounds, and nothing seems out of place.

Except for the fact that my bedroom door is closed. My dick twitches behind my zipper as all manner of lewd, hot scenarios involving me and Laney flit through my head. I bite back a groan and take a deep breath before moving on down the hall, in complete stealth, toward my door.

I twist the knob and ease the door open. There, lying in a shaft of moonlight with her platinum hair spread out over my maroon pillowcase, is Laney, fast asleep. The covers are pushed down to her hips, leaving her entire upper body exposed. She's wearing a form-fitting tank top that hugs her chest so tight I can see the outline of her nipples. They make my mouth water. And from what I can see, the only other thing she's wearing is a pair of light-colored panties.

I debate the best course of action from this point. The *right* thing to do would be to shut the door and leave her undisturbed while I go sleep on the couch. But that's not what I *want* to do.

As I stand in the doorway staring at Laney, I remember our kiss at the Blue Hole. We have unfinished business. And that business is what has me throwing the "right thing" right out the window, in favor of the thing I want.

Laney.

It only takes me a few seconds to strip down to my boxer briefs. She's lucky I've been bunking with a bunch of guys for the last few days, or else I wouldn't be wearing any.

As gently as I can, I peel back the covers and slide in beside her. I can feel her body heat radiating toward me under the sheet, warming my legs. My cock throbs with the desire to part her thighs and sink into her like I sank into the mattress—slow and easy.

I fold my hands behind my head, grit my teeth, and close my eyes, counting to twenty-five in an effort to get my body back under control. I hear Laney shift beside me right before I feel her hand sneak across my stomach. She drops one leg over mine and snuggles in. I wait a few seconds before I lower my arm and cup her shoulder with my hand. She sighs, and I relax against her.

But then I feel her stiffen.

I know the instant she comes awake. It's like her whole body goes on alert, even though she hasn't moved a muscle. Her hair tickles my chest as she raises her head to look up at me.

"What are you doing?" she asks softly, as though she's not quite sure she's awake.

"I'm going to bed. What are you doing?"

"Sleeping."

"I can see that."

Her brow furrows like she's still working all this out. Her blue eyes are heavy and I can see her struggle to push her way through the cobwebs. She's trying to find her way to wakefulness and reality.

"Are you really here?"

"Why wouldn't I be?"

"Because you should be at work and I could be dreaming."

"So you dream about me?"

"Yes," she replies candidly.

"Are they good dreams?"

"Mostly, yes."

"Mmm, would you like them to be real?"

"Sometimes."

"What about now?"

Her eyes search mine before they drop to my mouth. That tells me at least part of what she dreams about—kissing me. "Yes," she whispers.

"Were you dreaming of my lips?" I ask, keeping my voice low so as not to fully wake her. I know what her answer is; I just want to hear her admit it.

Gently, I roll until she's on her back and I'm hovering over her. I brush my lips over hers, using just enough pressure to tickle her, tease her.

"Yes," she sighs, her minty breath fanning my face as she relaxes back into the mattress.

"How about my tongue? Were you dreaming about it?" I trace the outline of her lips with the tip of my tongue, dipping inside only long enough to make her want more.

"Mmm-hmmm," she moans in answer, tilting her face up in open invitation.

"Do you dream about it here?" I ask, flicking her earlobe with my tongue. I descend to her collarbone, easing my fingers under the thin strap of her top. I feel her fingers push into my hair, and I know I'm getting warmer. "Or do you dream about them here?" I pull one side of her top down until her creamy breast and pink nipple are exposed. I draw the pebble into my mouth and feel her fingers clench into a fist, tugging on my hair. "Mmm, you like it there, huh?" As I tease and suck her nipple, I slip my knee between her legs, parting them a little farther. "What about here? Do you dream of my tongue here?" My hand glides down her flat stomach to the damp material between her thighs.

I knew they would be wet.

"Yes," she breathes heavily.

Moving the cotton to the side, I slide one finger between her slick folds. "I bet you dream of my tongue here, don't you?" I ask, caressing her wet skin.

Her answer is more of a moan, but it speaks just as clearly as any words. I move down to kiss her bare stomach. "And here," I whisper as I ease my finger into her. When her muscles squeeze, I can't hold back a groan. "Oh, shit, you're so tight!"

She moves her hips against my hand and I can feel her body sucking at my finger, begging me to fill it with something bigger, something harder. But as much as I want to do exactly that, I want her to be fully awake and fully consensual for it. I've never had sex with a woman who wasn't aware of what was happening. And although I can feel how willing her body is, I want her mind to be on board, too.

"Laney, you know this is real, right?" I ask, reluctantly stilling my hand and looking up past her luscious nipple to her passion-filled face. "You're here with me, in my bed, and I'm getting ready to make you come so hard, you'll scream my name. Tell me you want me to do that."

Her eyes are wide and very much awake, but now that I'm giving her an out, I can see the indecision rushing in. I can feel it in the way she's tensing beneath me.

Why the hell did I do that? Fu—

"I'm sorry," she whispers, interrupting my thought and confirming my suspicion. "I can't think straight around you, and certainly not when you're . . . touching me."

I hold back a sigh and give her a wry smile. "I kinda figured as much." Reluctantly removing my finger from inside her, I move back up her body to lean over her. I pull a strand of hair away from her face. "This *is* gonna happen. You know that, right?"

She says nothing. She doesn't agree, but she doesn't *disagree* either, which tells me she knows it, too.

"Just not tonight," I say, rolling off her and sitting up to run my fingers through my hair. With my back to her, it gives her time to straighten her clothes without me looking on. It gives *me* time to focus on not getting harder. And not trying to persuade her. Which I could do.

I know if I pressed her, I could get her to give in. But I won't. When we do this, I want her body *and* her mind begging for it. "Tonight, I'm very interested to know how I came home to find you in my bed."

"Are you complaining?"

I turn around to look at her, to see if she's kidding. Her expression is unreadable. "Hell no!"

She smiles and draws her knees up to her chest, resting her chin on them. Even though it's an innocent gesture, it's so prim it's somehow sexy. And it makes me want her all over again.

I stretch out on my side, crossways in front of her, resting my head on my palm. "So, tell me your tale, Goldilocks."

Laney focuses on her toes as she wiggles them. I don't say anything else to prompt her. She'll tell me in her own time. She has to. She's been sleeping in my bed, for God's sake.

Finally she speaks. Her voice is quiet. Wounded.

"It won't make any sense unless I start from the beginning."

"Okay, then start from the beginning."

She glances up at me then quickly away, almost like she's embarrassed. Now I'm more curious than ever to know her deal.

"My whole life, all I've ever wanted was to get married and have kids, and find in life what my parents have." I suppress a groan.

Damn! Why does she have to be that *kind of woman?*

"I met a guy my freshman year in college. He seemed like the perfect man. He was smart, responsible, ambitious, loving. He had pretty much the same goals as me. And I thought he was trustworthy. Turns out he wasn't. I found him in bed a couple of months ago. With my best friend."

"Oh shit! What an asshole!"

Laney nods, still staring at her toes. "I'm sure you know . . . I mean, I doubt it's any surprise to you that . . ."

When she doesn't finish, I prompt her. "What? Spit it out? What should I know?"

She struggles with how to phrase whatever she's getting at. I watch her small, white teeth chew nervously at her bottom lip. It's distracting as hell. Makes me wish she'd finish her story and then ask me to lick her from head to toe.

Although I doubt that's likely.

At least not tonight.

Maybe tomorrow night . . . If I can get her to stay . . .

When she still doesn't speak, I bark, "Damn, woman! Out with it."

"Look, I'm sure it comes as no surprise to you that people see you as a . . . a . . . kind of a wild guy."

"Seems like I've heard that a time or two, but what's that got to do with anything?"

She shrugs. "Well, my parents know that I'm working on your family's estate, and . . ."

"Ahhh, and they don't like you associating with the likes of me," I finish for her.

"It's not really that. I mean, I told them it was just work, but . . ."

"But what?"

"But they don't believe me, of course. At least not after Sunday."

"Why? What happened Sunday?"

"Well, you dropped me off at the curb and I had to walk in wearing a hoochie outfit, carrying my church clothes. It doesn't make a very convincing argument for professionalism."

I can't help but laugh. "Those were hoochie clothes?" I nod. "Good to know."

"To me they are. To my parents, they *definitely* are!"

"So the parents think I'm corrupting you?"

She shrugs. "I suppose so. They know I'm not *that* girl."

"The kind that wears hoochie clothes," I say, trying to hide my grin.

"Right. And goes to fun parties and indulges in meaningless flirtation."

"Maybe they don't know *what* kind of girl you are. 'Cause Sunday, you sure seemed like you were okay being 'that girl.'"

"That's exactly the problem. They know it's not like me. So . . ."

"They think it's me."

"Right."

"And the preacher disapproves."

"Very much so."

"And this is why you're in my bed? You're sticking it to the preacher by making it look like I'm sticking it to you?"

She gives me the stink eye, and I grin.

"No one is sticking anything to anybody."

"That's a damn shame, too."

She looks surprised when she giggles, like she wasn't expecting it. Couldn't control it.

When her smile dies, she asks, "Are you gonna let me finish?"

"Of course. You have my full attention," I say, narrowing my eyes on her. She gives me a dubious look then rolls her eyes and continues.

"*Anyway*, after my parents and I discussed where I was, who I was with, and why, we got into an argument. You see, they don't know why Shane and I broke up."

"Shane's Mr. Perfect?"

Another withering look.

"Anyway, long story short, they didn't like that we broke up, they didn't like that I was with you, and they took it upon themselves to fix it. So after I came here and worked on the estate all day Monday, I went home to find that they'd invited Shane for dinner. Without even asking me. They totally ambushed me. Wanted us to talk so they could all tell me how stupid I'm being and how wrong I am to throw what we had away. So I left. And I haven't been back since."

"They brought the guy in behind your back?" She nods solemnly. "Damn, that *was* a pretty shitty thing for them to do."

"I thought so, too. It's like they just can't understand. Or don't want to. They see what they want to see, no matter how wrong or biased," she says bitterly.

"Over the years I've learned that most people are judgmental as hell. They may *think* they're not. And some probably even try not to be. But most are. It's human nature."

"I try really hard not to be like that."

"And I think you do a good job. The fact that you're here right now shows that you're not as bad as most. Especially in this town."

She raises big, sorrowful, blue eyes to mine. "I'm sorry people have been so unfair to you and your sister."

It's my turn to shrug. "Nah, don't be. We've earned most of it. I've pissed off enough people in this town to get that 'trouble' label fair and square."

"Is that all you did? Piss people off?"

I reach out to glide my fingertips up one of her smooth calves. "There might've been a few corrupted daughters and compromised wives in the mix. I can't remember just now."

"Compromised wives?" she balks.

"Hey, I was young. And they were . . . needy."

"Oh my gosh! You really *are* a bad boy."

"Don't wilt on me now. You were so close."

"Close to what?"

"Coming to the dark side."

"No, I wasn't."

"Yes, you were. You can sense how much fun it is to stop worrying about what other people think, to just enjoy life as much as you can. We only have a handful of short, sometimes painful days on this earth. You've gotta take your pleasure where you can get it."

"Is that what you're offering me? Pleasure?"

I sit up and lean toward Laney. She doesn't back away, just watches me. I can hear as much as feel that she's holding her breath. "Isn't that enough?"

I edge in closer and lick over her bottom lip with my tongue.

"I don't know," she says softly.

"It can be. You just have to let it. You just have to realize that you're better off without love. It makes people weak. It makes people lose their common sense and they end up hurting each other. Listen to *you*! Love has brought you nothing but pain and suffering. But I can make all that go away. I can take your mind off the hurt. Make you feel better than you've ever felt before. You just have to let me."

"I don't know if I can just jump right in like this," she whispers.

"That's okay. Jumping can be fun, but so can . . . exploring. As long as we're on the same page, with the same expectations, we can't go wrong," I assure her, reaching forward to circle my fingers around her upper arm and tease the curve of her breast with my thumb.

"So where do we go from here?"

As much as I'd like to go straight to banging her head against my headboard, I know that's not the smart move right now. So, I bite back my frustrated sigh and opt for a long kiss instead. When she feels a little more relaxed, a little more pliant under my hands, I lean back.

"We go to bed," I declare, biting her chin and giving her thigh a teasing slap. She yelps playfully and I wink at her. "And we see what we can get into tomorrow."

"So just fun? No pressure, no promises?"

"Just fun. Lots and lots of fun." I scoot to my place in the bed and lift an arm, waiting for her to curl up against me, which she does. When she snuggles in and I hear her contented sigh, I smile.

And lots and lots of sex.

That's my last thought as I drift off to sleep.

ELEVEN: *Laney*

growl at the skillet and pull it off the heat. The other one is already in the sink, sitting in hot water.

Laney, what were you thinking?

What started out as an attempt at cooking breakfast has morphed into a nightmare. First, I should've checked to make sure I could find everything I needed before actually beginning to cook *anything*. The kitchen looks like a demilitarized zone, and I'm pretty sure the house will smell like burnt bacon forever.

Coughing draws my attention toward the doorway. Jake is standing there in jeans that hang perfectly on his hips, a bemused grin on his face and not a scrap of anything else. His hair is sticking up at weird angles and I'm positive I've never seen anything more mouth-watering.

"There are easier and much more pleasant ways to wake me up than trying to smoke me out of the bedroom."

"You said you're a fireman. I'm testing your skills. You passed," I say with a cough, my eyes watering so badly I can hardly see.

Jake walks around the island and props open the back door. Einstein, his giant, white-haired dog that I met last week, is sitting on the back porch, whining.

"Quick! Grab a Milk-Bone from the jar on the counter. You've deeply offended Einie's delicate sense of smell," Jake says. "You must make amends."

I can't help but grin as I grab the treat and head for the door. I step outside, give the dog his bone, and drag in a gulp of fresh air. Jake follows. Puffs of thick gray smoke are wafting out the door.

"Sorry about your bacon."

"Is that what that is?"

"Part of it. It began as an omelet, toast, and bacon, but it quickly deteriorated when I realized that I had no idea where anything was in your house."

"Like what? The off switch on the stove?"

"Ha. Ha. No, I mean like spatulas."

"Spatulas? Likely story."

"No, really. Everything was coming along just fine until I realized I had no way to flip the omelet."

"And then . . . chaos!"

"Exactly. Once the eggs started burning as I scrambled around looking for the spatula, they got all my attention for a few minutes. At that point, there was nothing I could do. I couldn't save the bacon."

"Okay, first of all, burnt eggs, scrambling around, saving bacon— I can't be expected to ignore any more clichés, so consider yourself warned. Secondly, why the big, elaborate breakfast?"

I shrug. "I thought it was the least I could do since you weren't mad that I hijacked your bed for a couple of nights."

"How could any man in his right mind be mad about that?"

"Because it's so rude! It's not like I asked or anything, which I should have. I was just so mad! And then, once I left my parents' house, I realized I had nowhere else to go. If I'd gone to the Sleep Inn, they'd have found me for sure. I mean, it *is* the only hotel in town."

"Well, now you have a place to stay, so you don't need to worry about it."

"Oh, no. I couldn't impose on you like that."

"It's not an imposition. It's an opportunity."

His grin is devilish.

"Dare I ask what kind of opportunity?"

"I don't know. Do you dare? Are you up for it? Are you *really* ready to take a walk on the wild side?"

"I . . . I . . . I guess that depends on what all is involved."

As if sensing my hesitation with where the conversation is going, Jake shifts into a lighter form of attack. Lighter, but no less effective. I can feel him wearing down my defenses with every passing second.

"Well, considering we just survived a nearly fatal breakfast," he begins.

"I'd hardly call that 'nearly fatal.'"

He ignores my interruption. "I should probably perform a thorough physical examination," he continues without missing a beat, stepping closer as he talks. Jake winds his arms around my waist. "Just to make sure there are no burns on your body. Or even red places. You know heat can make the skin feel very . . . sensitive. I'd be sure to treat any . . . sensitive areas right away. Massage them until they feel better. Much, much better."

My head is swimming—whether from oxygen deprivation or from Jake, I can't be sure—and a sublime feeling of contentment is threatening to overcome me. I should be leery, but it's hard to concentrate on much of anything when Jake is gently swaying against me, his lower body rubbing mine.

"As professional and . . . thorough as that sounds, I'm afraid there's a big mess to clean up now." Even as I decline his clever offer, a fire is still burning, this one in the lowest part of my stomach. It's a fire I know will soon need attention. And Jake will be the only one who can do anything about it.

"I'll let it go for now. But I won't rest until I've at least checked your lips. You know, in case you burned them tasting something."

I roll my eyes and sigh dramatically. "If you must. I mean, you *are* a fireman." He waggles his eyebrows comically as his head descends toward mine.

I'm loving this playful side of him. He really is charming. Which makes him even more dangerous. I didn't realize just how extensive his allure is.

Or maybe I did.

Maybe that's why I've been trying to keep a safe distance.

His kiss is light and teasing at first, but it quickly turns to more. Within seconds, I find my fingers delving into his hair and my body straining against his, craving closer contact. Craving . . . more.

When he leans back, his smile is gone and we're both breathless. His pupils dominate the golden irises of his eyes. "Are you sure you won't let me examine the rest of you? I can make you gasp in ways that have nothing to do with smoke inhalation."

I laugh nervously. It seems with every word and every kiss, I'm getting closer and closer to saying yes. To jumping.

"Believe it or not, I have no doubt that's absolutely true."

"I guarantee you the reality of what I'll do to you is far better than anything you can imagine."

My heart is pounding and I'm finding it harder to remember why I shouldn't be playing with fire this way. "Jake, I—"

"No excuses. No explanations. I know all your reasons and all your hesitations. And you don't owe me any of them. The only thing I want to hear from those luscious lips of yours is one word. 'Yes.' And until you say it, this is what you'll get," he says, crushing his lips to mine in a kiss that sears me all the way to my soul. When my insides are like melted butter, he releases me and backs away. "But try not to burn the house down in the meantime." He grins, turning to walk back into the house.

The smoke has dissipated considerably, but it still smells terrible. "So this is what hell is like," I murmur as I curl up my nose and look around.

"Does that make me the devil?" Jake asks, looking back at me with one brow raised in challenge.

"The jury's still out on that one."

He laughs. "So, since ruining breakfast, you now have two choices for the start of your day. Option number one—which just so happens to be the one I most highly recommend—you let me carry you to the shower where I can give intense attention to making sure every inch of your skin is free of smoky residue. Option number two, we go for a run and *then* we come back and take a shower, after which *I'll* be fixing *you* breakfast. One that's not toxic."

"You cook?" I ask, changing the subject before I impulsively choose option number one, which I'm becoming increasingly interested in.

"I'm a fireman. My chili-making skills are the stuff of legend."

"Chili for breakfast?"

"Oh, no. I'll tantalize your taste buds with my culinary delights. You'll be so smitten with me, we'll spend the following two hours in bed, where you'll be worshipping my body as payment for such epi-curean awesomeness."

"Epicurean awesomeness?"

"Yep."

I narrow my eyes and wrinkle my nose. "Tough choices, but I think I'll go with option number two point five."

"I don't remember offering any such option."

"Then I'll just have to surprise you," I say, prancing away from him as I make my way to the stairs. I have to get some distance from him before I make a big, big mistake. "You're not the only one with skills."

That one raven brow arches and a slow smile spreads across Jake's face. "Decided to take up the gauntlet, did we?"

"Maybe."

"Not gonna be the good girl after all?"

"Maybe not always."

"Oh, this is gonna be fun."

"I think you might be right."

With that, I mount the steps, feeling a little bit scared, a little bit uncertain, and a little bit giddy. But most of all, I feel free.

As it turns out, I lack imagination. And courage, evidently. At least I lack the courage to really step out and be the bad girl. To take the risk.

A dozen different ways to end a run with Jake went through my mind, some sexy and some not so much. I ended up chickening out and opting to bring him out for breakfast. Sweat and all.

So, here we are. Sitting at the bar of the one diner in town that serves breakfast all day (and looks like a single-wide trailer).

"So this is point five," Jake muses, shaking his head and looking around Rita's.

"Point five?"

"According to you, option 'two point five' would be daring. I didn't think you meant daring in the way of salmonella."

I give him a dubious look. "You know good and well the food here is great."

"Yet that's not the point, is it?"

I look into his discerning amber eyes and I say nothing. He's right. And he knows it.

"Are you really that afraid of taking a little risk? Or is it just that you're afraid of taking a little risk *with me*?"

Before I can answer, a familiar voice sounds behind me, making the hairs on the back of my neck prickle.

"So, this is what it's come to? My daughter comes back home for a visit and I have to casually run into her at the diner just to see her?"

I turn on my stool to see my father standing a few feet behind me, his hands stuffed casually in his pockets, his expression bland. Well, bland to those who didn't grow up under his roof. For those of us who did, there is a storm brewing just beneath the surface, a storm that comes with an hour-long sermon-slash-lecture attached to it. I've only been the recipient of a couple. I was always a good girl and avoided trouble of this kind. But still, I got one every once in a while. Not fun. And even now, several years into being an adult, I still feel the urge to shrink under his disapproval. But, mindful of Jake at my side, I hold my ground.

"Not at all, Daddy. We were just out for some breakfast. You remember Jake Theopolis, right?"

My nerves are jangling. I know how my father feels about Jake. Jake does, too, after last night. I just hope he doesn't embarrass us all by showing it *in front of* Jake.

"Sir," Jake says with a nod, coming to his feet to face Daddy. He extends his hand politely toward him.

At first my father just looks down at Jake's hand like it's dirty, but then he smiles and gives it a quick shake.

"So, you're the one that's lured my daughter into a life of sin," he says, as amicably as if he were talking about the weather.

"Daddy!" I exclaim, mortified.

"Not that I know of," Jake says with an unaffected smile as he resumes his seat next to me. I get the feeling he isn't nearly as relaxed as he appears, however, when he leans back against the bar facing my father, crossing his arms over his chest. That's clearly a defensive posture.

"Are you saying that she hasn't been staying at your house? Because I can't think for the life of me where else she might've gone."

"I didn't say that. But I've been working at the fire station, so she's had the place to herself."

My father nods, but I can tell he's still not satisfied. He wants blood. Jake's blood.

"Well, regardless, you can imagine how something like that looks. How it reflects on her fine character."

"I imagine that those inclined to judge others will find something undesirable in the purest of people."

"And yet we must keep up good Godly appearances, isn't that right, Laney?"

He turns his intimidating stare on me, but somehow, in the face of how manipulative he's been about Shane and how he's so openly antagonizing Jake, I don't wither as much as I usually do.

"That's probably the *right* thing to do, Daddy, but that doesn't mean it's the thing I'm *going* to do."

"Laney, I didn't raise you to—"

"This is not about how you raised me, Daddy. This is about you not being happy with my choices. But, lucky for both of us, you don't *have to be*. I'm an adult and I can live my life how I see fit. I can make my own decisions and make my own mistakes. I can decide for myself who's worthy of being part of my life and who's not. That's not your business. And it's certainly not your role to mend a relationship that I've ended. In fact, I'd appreciate it if you'd just stay out of my life right now. I've got enough to worry about without staying awake at night wondering if I've disappointed you."

Without meaning to, I've come to my feet, like I'm braced and ready for battle, and as much as I hate to cause a scene, I've done just that. I can feel every eye in the place focused on me. Evidently my voice rose as *I* did.

I turn to Jake.

"I've lost my appetite. You ready?"

Jake's expression is curiously blank. "Sure."

With that, he slides off his stool and holds out his arm for me to precede him. My father's disdain is palpable. Jake's apathy is, too.

I start to walk off with Jake, but Daddy grabs my arm before I can leave him and this humiliating conversation behind. "He'll be through with you once he gets what he wants, Laney. Don't waste your love on someone like that."

Before I can respond, Jake does. "She won't waste her love on me, sir. I'm unlovable. But you should trust her more because I'm sure *she's* not."

With a palm to my lower back, Jake urges me on. I keep my eyes straight ahead as we walk, avoiding all the accusing stares of the town folk. In their eyes, my father can do no wrong. But now I can.

My hands are shaking by the time we get to my car. "Here," Jake says, taking the keys from my fingers. "I'll drive." He opens the passenger-side door for me then walks around and slides in behind the wheel. "I knew we should've brought the Jeep. What are you, an elf?" He has to scoot the seat back as far as it will go just to accommodate his long legs.

I don't respond. I'm still too shaken by that run-in with my dad. I've never stood up to him that way, and I'm not sure I'm entirely comfortable with it. I don't want him to think badly of me, but I also don't want him meddling in my life so much. He's got to let me go eventually.

I'm also embarrassed by the things he said to and about Jake. I know I should apologize or something, but I don't even know where to start.

When Jake has started the car and pulled onto the main road, I give it a shot. "Jake, I—"

"Don't worry about it," he says abruptly.

"But I *am* worrying about it. I never wanted—"

"I know you didn't. I get it. You think your dad is the first father to disapprove of me? Hell, my own father hated me. Why should yours be any different?"

His voice drips with bitterness, but something tells me that there's more than that just below the surface, that somewhere deep down, he's hurting because of it. But what am I supposed to do? Or say? I hardly know him. How can I comfort someone I don't know? Over a situation I know nothing about?

"I'm sure that's not true," I assert weakly.

Jake's only response is a single harsh bark of laughter.

TWELVE: *Jake*

Laney's worked quietly all day. And I've let her. She's got some shit to sort out on her own. She doesn't need my help. And I wouldn't know how to help her anyway. I suck at family issues. Actually, I suck at family *period*. Whatever part of me that might've been good at being in a relationship of any kind died with my mother a long, long time ago. I've learned since then that "stick and move" doesn't just keep you from getting punched in boxing; it's a philosophy that can help you survive real life, too.

Besides, I wouldn't want to give Laney the wrong idea. That's not what this is about it. It's not what *we* are about. I don't want her getting attached to me. Have some fun, yeah. Have some sex, hell yeah. But get attached? Not a good idea. I'm not the kind of guy she needs.

It's getting close to dinnertime now, though, and I've got a mission to tend to—get Laney back in my bed tonight. And under me.

I figure it's just a matter of time before she says it wouldn't be right for us to share a room. What do I say? Bullshit! That's a cop-out. If she wants to stop being a good girl, she can start with me. I'm about as good at bringing out the bad in a girl as a man can be.

And bringing it out in a woman like Laney will be the sweetest of all.

My phone rings as I cross the yard to the back door of the house. I glance at the Caller ID and see the department's main number on the screen. I stop and hit the green button. After a few short sentences exchanged, I hang up and slide the phone into my pocket.

Just like that, in a single act as simple as answering the phone, my plans to seduce Laney tonight are shot all to hell. With a sigh, I continue on to the house, detouring toward the dining room where Laney works.

Her head is bent over the table, her eyes focused on some papers. When I lean against the doorjamb, it creaks, giving me away. Her head snaps up. When she sees me, her lips curve into a welcoming smile.

"I didn't hear you. How long have you been standing there?"

"Just a few seconds. Didn't mean to scare you." I push away from the doorway and move to bend casually over Laney's shoulder, as if to see what she's working on. Her light scent teases my nose, and I heard her catch her breath when my chest brushes her arm. "What are you working on now?"

"Um, just the contents of the safe. There's a lot of paperwork in there to go over."

I can practically hear her pulse jumping around. I know she wants me. And I know it makes her uncomfortable. She doesn't quite know what to do with it. But that makes only one of us, because I know *exactly* what to do with it! Just not tonight.

With a sigh, I straighten away from her. No sense getting both of us all excited when I have to leave.

Dammit!

"One of the other firemen called in sick. Seems like all the shit work is gonna go to the new guy. You know how that goes."

Laney turns toward me. "Oh," she says, disappointment clearly written across her face. Perversely, I'm satisfied to see it. "Okay. I'll feed the dog until you get back."

"No need. There are food and water dispensers for him out in the barn. He knows how to work them."

"I wondered why he wasn't very interested in the food I was giving him."

"You fed the dog?"

"Of course! I bought some cans of food at the store. I thought you'd just left him here to starve."

"You're kidding, right?"

"Sort of. At first, I really did think that. But then, when he wouldn't eat the food I put out, I thought maybe you'd made arrangements for someone to feed him elsewhere, like at a neighboring farm or something. I mean, he disappears for hours during the day. I figured he had to be eating *somewhere*."

"I appreciate your confidence in me, but—"

"I only thought it for a second . . ."

"Uh-huh. Sure."

"Really. I don't think you're that kind of person. Not really."

"Good to know," I reply tersely. I'm a little irritated that she could think so little of me, even for a second.

When the silence stretches on, she speaks. "Well, when will you be home?"

For the space of a few accelerated heartbeats, I feel a wave of panic suffocate me. Hearing her say it that way—"When will you be home?"—makes it sound like I'm answerable to her. Like I'm in a relationship. Responsible for not breaking her heart. Or hurting her. Like I'm something to her that I could never be.

But then it's gone. It ebbs once I remind myself that we aren't playing house, and she's not mine to care for. I remind myself that there's no obligation. She's staying in my home for a reason, one that has nothing to do with me.

"I'm not sure. I guess you'll know when I show up," I say nonchalantly, hoping to subtly drive my point home. To her as much as to myself.

She doesn't react.

"I guess so," she agrees quietly. "I hope it, uh, goes well then. And safe. Luckily there aren't a lot of fires in Greenfield."

"Yeah, but that makes for an incredibly boring shift."

"Probably still better than hanging around here, though. I'm sure I'm terrible company." Her tone is full of melancholy.

This is undoubtedly a bad time for me to be leaving. I mean, she did just have a big-ass fight with her dad. In public, no less. And partly over me. If it were me, I'd want to be alone. But with Laney, I bet she'd rather *not* be. She wouldn't want too much time to think, I bet.

"You could always come and visit. Break up the monotony. I could show you around the station. You know, they're pretty impressive places. Second only to the International Space Station."

She grins. "Oh, I'm sure. All that mind-boggling technology, like . . . water hoses and big red trucks."

"Don't underestimate. Getting things wet is one of my favorite pastimes."

Her cheeks pinken and she looks away, although I can see her lips twitch. She seems to be getting a little less defensive with every comment I make. And I like that she's loosening up. It just further assures me that I'll have her right where I want her in no time.

"Well, the offer stands if you get cabin fever being stuck out here. When I get back, I'll take you out into the orchard. Didn't you say you needed to tour the property?"

"Yes. It'll be formally surveyed and appraised, but I need to get a lay of the land to put in my final report."

"Oh, I can give you a lay of the land."

Her cheeks flame a little brighter, making me feel very proud of myself for some reason. It's fascinating to see how she reacts to me. Although I could see where it could be habit-forming—teasing her— I'm not worried. I'm not the kind of guy to get wrapped up in a chick that way. I've lived without love for too long to go back now. I like things just the way they are.

But still, I can see how it could happen . . .

To someone else . . .

Someone better suited to loving and being loved.

But not me.

Definitely not me.

"I'll plan for it then."

"For me to give you the lay of the land?" I ask, quirking one brow suggestively. She's so much fun to taunt.

"Well, not *that kind* of lay," she replies, making me raise my other brow.

"Very nice! Well done. Maybe you've got some potential after all."

At my words, her expression slowly falls into one that's sullen and pensive. Her sigh is deep and long. "I don't know. Sometimes I think whoever loves me will just have to love me the way I am. Whatever way that is."

In an uncharacteristic moment of empathy, I feel bad for Laney. I know what it's like to worry about being loved. I did it for years. Until I learned to stop. Until I learned to stop caring and stop trying. But for Laney, I don't think she ever will. It's obviously part of who she is.

As gently as I can, I tweak her chin and reply. "And someone will, Laney. Someone will."

Her smile is small and a little sad.

"I'll have my cell with me. Call if you need anything. Not that I can really do anything about it, but if you're burning the house down, I'll know which truck to bring."

She laughs. It's a good note to leave things on.

THIRTEEN: *Laney*

My phone rings. It's Tori. Again. For a few seconds, I hover over the green button to answer the call. But after a crystal clear image of her in bed with Shane flashes through my mind, I go straight toward the red decline button.

I get up and move away from the dining room table. With Jake gone, it's lonely around the house. Not that I'm used to him being there or anything. But I'm liking his company more and more as time goes on. Besides, with Tori and I on the outs, and my parents and I on the outs, it's a pretty lonely world right now. I could use the companionship I've found in Jake.

You can tell yourself that's all it is all day long, but you know there's more to it.

I push aside that voice. More than ever, I don't want to think too much, to overanalyze things. I just want to have some fun. To forget about life and pain and trouble and responsibility as much as I can. I'm here to do a job, but there's nothing that says I can't have a little fun on the side.

If I'm even capable of doing something like having a little fun.

Frustrated, I walk to the fridge. My eyes move over the peach preserves and the butter, and the milk and the pack of ham, but nothing strikes my interest.

Until I see the peach wine.

It's Saturday night. There would be nothing wrong with me having a glass of peach wine. Nothing at all. But thoughts of having one alone make it much less appealing.

I glance out the kitchen window, the sun now barely visible on the horizon. It'll be dark soon. Another night alone. Another night without Jake.

Everything in me pauses on a gasp, it seems.

Unless I pay him a visit.

As soon as the thought enters my head, I instantly think of at least ten reasons why I should *not* go visit him. But, still wrestling with getting rid of the girl I've always been, I stand in front of the open fridge until the bottle of peach wine and my desire to test the flames of attraction overwhelm my reservations and mute them into silence.

Impulsively, before I can change my mind, I take the stairs two at a time. When I walk into Jake's room, I think absently about how I probably should've moved into another room already. But rather than exploring the reasons why I haven't, I focus on picking out a change of clothes instead. That's much more fun and much less stressful.

I'm glad I hadn't unpacked at my parents' house yet. My exit the night they dropped Shane on me would've been much less dramatic if I'd had to spend half an hour packing up in my room. But as it was, I just tossed a few things in my smaller bag, zipped all my belongings into my bigger one, and took off. At least I have everything I need and no reason that I *have to* go back if I don't want to. Because I don't. At least not yet.

Speeding through a quick shower, I slather on some scented lotion and slip into a little white, summery skirt and a peach-colored top with spaghetti straps. After I slide my feet into white platforms that make me look taller and my legs look longer, I step back to appraise myself.

"Oh, well in that case . . ." I say, feeling like a complete idiot. "I guess I'll see you there."

I start to turn away, but he grabs my upper arm. "Hold on, what's this?" he asks.

It takes me a minute to figure out what he's referring to. "Oh, it's, uh, it's peach wine. From your house."

"You brought wine? To a fire station?"

His grin isn't meant to make me feel small. No, I'm managing that quite well on my own.

I dig out the strong woman, the person in control, from way down deep. I'm not sure how much she's ever in control, but at least she puts on a good front. "I guess that was pretty silly. It was an impulsive thing. I was bored. And I thought it would be nice to share a little of your hard work."

Jake takes the bottle from my hand then wraps his fingers around mine and pulls me inside. "See, it would be a crying shame for such a gesture to be wasted. Let me show you around, and then we'll get into this wine the right way."

I don't ask what that means. I simply go along, silently. I've already made enough of a fool of myself for one night. Best to just keep the mouth shut and hope I don't make matters worse.

We ascend a set of grated steps painted an austere yet spotless pale gray. At the top are two doors, also painted a drab gray. Jake takes me through the first one. It opens onto a long hall with doors on either side. "This is where the living quarters are, as well as the office."

I nod, looking around. "Everything is very clean. And . . . gray."

We pass a couple of doors, both shut, both clearly marked who they belong to. The third door has a window in it. A blast of mouth-watering air hits me in the face when Jake opens it.

I peek around his shoulder to see three guys sitting at a round table pushed off to one side of the combo room. Opposite the table is a small kitchen, in front of that is a pool table, and in front of that is a couch and two chairs, all facing a television.

My hair is still in a messy updo from the shower, something
actually goes quite well with this particular outfit. My makeup c[
use some freshening, so after a quick swipe here and there, I'm re
to go.

Downstairs, I grab the peach wine from the fridge along with
couple of leftover chocolate cupcakes, toss a bone on the back porc
for when Einstein shows up, and hit the door running.

I'm still trying to outdistance my better judgment. My cautious
self. I've had enough of her for a while and would rather she just
shush and let me get on with some semblance of a life.

It's not until I turn into the lot of the fire station several minutes
later that I begin to get nervous.

What the hell were you thinking?

With the engine still running, I sit in the parking lot, staring at
the closed bay door, debating the wisdom of what I'm about do. The
wine bottle in the seat beside me draws my attention. Reaching for
it, I unscrew the cap and take a sip as I think. I take several sips actually. Enough to calm my jangling nerves and give me the courage to
turn off the engine and get out of the car.

I straighten my clothes and make my way to the main door. It's
locked, of course, but there's a lighted red buzzer to the left that says
PUSH HERE FOR ASSISTANCE. So I do.

Within a few seconds, I see a shadow through the frosted glass. It
appears at the top of some steps. After a few seconds, I see it move
lower, coming down the stairs.

My stomach twists into a sick knot.

Just before I can bolt, the door opens. And Jake is standing there.
Smiling.

"Damn if you're not a sight for sore eyes! Did you know I was
leaving?"

I stare at him, gape-mouthed, for a few seconds. "You're leaving?"

"Yeah. Ronnie just came in to relieve me. He wanted the overtime. I was heading home."

"Hey, I'm gonna take a friend of mine for a quick tour before I go. See you dicks in a few days."

Three heads turn toward the door, eyeing me curiously. "You sure you don't wanna hang around?" This from a thirties-looking short guy.

"With you apes? Nah, I think I'm good."

"I meant her, dumbass. 'Course, if you're afraid I'd steal her from you, I'd understand."

"She's not a lesbian, Johnson," Jake says acerbically. "Oh wait, you're supposed to be a dude, right?"

The other two start laughing, and Johnson just shakes his head. "That's just wrong, man," he says woefully. The others laugh that much harder.

Without another word, Jake, grinning, backs me out the door, and we continue down the hall.

"Seems like you're all getting along well."

"Yeah, they're pretty good guys."

We pass two open doors, one on either side of the hall. Jake pauses, and I scan the insides. Both rooms are identical.

"These are the sleeping quarters."

There are two twin beds in each room. All four are made up with plain white sheets and depressing brown blankets. Very utilitarian.

"Not very homey," I murmur.

"I'll tell the guys to pick something flowery next time," Jake teases.

"It's not that. I just think they could've made the beds a little more appealing."

"I know exactly what you could do to make *my* bed more appealing."

I slide my eyes over to Jake, where he's looming at my side. He's standing perfectly still, his chest brushing my shoulder. His honey gaze is fixed on me, and it's scorching. There's nothing lighthearted about him now. He's all intensity and heat. Predatory.

Suddenly the hall seems narrow. The air has disappeared along with my ability to breathe it. I feel stalked. Ensnared, like helpless prey that can't get away. Only, I'm not sure that I want to. And I think Jake knows that.

"What's that?" I ask softly.

"Do you want me to describe it to you in graphic detail?" he asks.

I say nothing, only nod.

He steps forward.

Instinctively, I step back.

Again and again we do this—he steps forward, I step back—until I feel the press of the wall, firm against my spine. I have nowhere else to go. Nowhere else to run.

"You could let me watch you strip this little thing from your body," he says, his breath fanning my cheek as he runs his finger back and forth under the thin strap of my top. "You could cup those perfect breasts of yours, pretending that it's me, until your nipples are hard and your panties are wet." He eases up closer to me, flattening me against the cool concrete blocks. He bends his knee, sliding it between mine. The denim of his jeans is rough against the bare skin of my thighs. "You could wiggle out of this tiny skirt and that damp cotton underneath, then go stand on the bed. With your high heels on. And nothing else." He leans in closer, his lips grazing the shell of my ear as he speaks. "Then you could whisper that you want to feel me inside you. My fingers. My tongue. My cock. That's what you could do to make my bed more appealing."

My heart is beating so loudly I can barely hear him. But I can hear enough.

He's so close I can feel heat radiating from his body, warming my entire front. It pulls me to him, drawing me in. Drawing me closer.

After a few seconds, he pulls away. "Come on. Let me show you my pole."

With a wicked gleam in his eye, Jake takes my hand and leads me on. Not into one of the rooms, but farther down the hall to another door.

He opens it and steps through. Blindly, anxiously, I follow.

It's a small room with a thin shelf of catwalk around an open center, dominated by a shiny pole that disappears into the darkness below.

"Since you're wearing a skirt and heels, I'll go down with you so you don't hurt yourself. I'd hate for you to tear the skin on those pretty thighs of yours," he says, his eyes dropping to my legs. Instantly, they feel warm, as if he'd actually touched them.

And oh, how I wish he would. This heat, this anticipation is quickly becoming unbearable.

"Here, you hold this," he says, tucking the wine bottle into the curve of my arm. I gasp when he grabs me around the waist and pulls me toward him, my legs slipping over one of his. With his eyes on mine, he gives me one quick squeeze, forcing me up on his thigh a little more. The friction is delicious. And wicked. "Can't have you sliding down a metal pole in a skirt."

Turning his body slightly, angling me toward his hip, Jake leans forward and grips the pole then swings carefully forward, holding me against his side. I clamp him with my legs as he lets us slide slowly down the pole.

When we reach the bottom, Jake whirls me around and presses my back to the pole. His lips are on mine. His tongue is in my mouth, teasing me, making me promises of unspoken delight.

The wine bottle vanishes and then my hands are free to grip his wide shoulders, delve into his thick, spiky hair. Hold him close. Pull him closer.

"Do you know how crazy you make me?" Jake whispers. I crack my lids to look at him. His eyes sparkle in the shadows. The only light is the dim cone that pours down on us from above. Everything else is pitch-black. "Coming in here with your shy smile and your sexy skirt. I bet you're sweeter than that wine you brought. And damn you, tonight I'm gonna find out. Tonight, I'm gonna taste you."

With a growl he takes my lips again, his hands roaming my sides, searing me through my clothes.

And then there's nothing between his warm palms and my skin. I feel them gliding up the backs of my legs, slipping under the hem of my skirt, sinking into the flesh of my butt. He squeezes, pulling me tight against him, rubbing his hard length against me.

"Tell me I can taste you. Tell me you want me to. Right here. Right now."

I can't think. I can't breathe. I can only feel. And I know I want more. I want all Jake can give me.

"Yes. I want you to taste me." My voice is husky and breathless, even to my own ears. "Right now."

Like taking a tiger off the leash, Jake becomes fierce. He drags his hands into my hair and tugs until it tumbles free around my shoulders. Then he's kissing a hot trail down my throat. His hands are cupping my breasts, pinching my nipples through the thin material of my shirt, driving me crazy with want.

I feel his lips against my stomach. Then his tongue in my navel. His hands are under my skirt, then they're on my thighs, nudging them apart.

Willingly, I spread them, leaning back against the pole for support, closing my eyes as I gasp for breath, aware of nothing more than Jake and what he makes me feel.

He presses his lips against me through my panties. All I can think is that I want more. I want it all.

I feel him push them to the side. And then his fingers are inside me, moving deep and slow.

I moan aloud.

"Shhh," he whispers against me, causing my knees to nearly buckle. "Be quiet or they'll hear you."

Warmth gushes through me, knowing what Jake is doing to me while those men are upstairs. That all they'd have to do is look down the pole to see me being ravaged by his lips and tongue.

And then his hot mouth moves down to replace his fingers. His lips move against me, like he's kissing me as his tongue swirls around over my most sensitive part, pushing me higher and higher. "Oh my God, you taste so good," he moans against me, the vibrations sending chills down my legs. Faster and faster, he penetrates me with his fingers until I can't contain it anymore. I reach up to clamp one hand over my mouth as my body bursts into wet flames, pouring over Jake where he kneels between my legs.

As spasms wrack my body, I feel his tongue thrusting rhythmically into me, hot and deep, prolonging the pleasure that's coursing through me.

I pant behind my hand, my eyes squeezed shut against the burst of light that shines behind them. And then Jake is pulling at my wrist, moving my fingers away from my lips, driving his tongue between them. He licks the inside of my mouth, sharing with me what he found.

"See how sweet you taste," he groans. It's such a wicked thing to do, feels so naughty and forbidden, I feel another gush of warmth pool between my legs. I know that whatever Jake asked me to do right now, I would do. Wherever he wanted me to go, I'd go.

"I need more," I say, mindless in my passion. "I need you."

I don't know what it is about those words that stop him, but they do. I feel him tense and cool, as though a puff of cold air whipped through the room.

"What?" I ask, confused. "What's wrong?"

In the low light, his eyes search mine. For several long seconds, he says nothing. Then he reaches for my neck, pushing my hair away from my throat and kissing my pulse. "Nothing," he replies. But I don't believe him. "We'd better go. I doubt people would look kindly on me corrupting the preacher's daughter this way." His smile is wry, but I think he's hiding something else behind it. I just don't know what.

I know my smile is tremulous at best. I feel it melt almost as quickly as I could conjure it. "Okay."

With that, Jake grabs the wine bottle from the floor (I was barely aware of him taking it from me), takes my hand, and leads me through the dark room to the door.

FOURTEEN: *Jake*

I'm more grateful than ever that Laney's not the talkative type. Any other woman would've probably asked me a thousand questions about what happened back at the fire station. But not Laney. If anything, she's just quieter.

We've only been back at the house for a few minutes, and now she's making her excuses to get the hell out of Dodge.

"I think I'm going to move my stuff to another room and hit the sack. I'm pretty tired."

I know what she's doing, but I choose not to acknowledge it. She's better off thinking the worst of me. That way, she'll never get attached. Or have any expectations. Or, even worse, fall in love with me. She deserves better than that. I wouldn't wish me on my worst enemy. I'm a black hole for love. It's the way I was born.

"There's no reason to do that. I'm not gonna take advantage of you in your sleep," I assure her. "Unless you want me to." I grin.

She frowns in confusion. I'm sure she doesn't understand the swift shifts. And that's fine. She doesn't need to know all about the things that have made me who and what I am.

"If you're sure . . ."

"Of course I'm sure."

"All right then."

Cautiously, as though she's been singed if not actually burned by my earlier actions (actions, I'm sure, she sees as rejection), Laney makes her way up the stairs. And I let her go.

It's almost three hours later before I follow. I stand in the doorway, looking at her where she's spread out in the center of the bed. Her hair is like a platinum waterfall, spilling over the pillow. Her face is relaxed in sleep. Gone are the mistrust and the cool shell she sometimes hides behind. Gone is the hurt from earlier. It makes me uncomfortable how much I hate that I put it there. I remind myself it's for the best.

For the best.

For the best.

I walk to the bed and gently touch her side. Her brow wrinkles and she mumbles something, but she scoots over and I slide in beside her. It isn't long before she rolls back toward me and curls up with her head on my chest.

Damn, she feels good there.

My mind blinks back to the way she responded to me tonight, pressed up against a cold metal pole and not seeming to care. Sugar and spice.

For my own good, I try to put her out of my mind.

But it's her face and her body that fill my dreams.

It's hot and I'm sticky, and I could use a break. With Laney. I'm feeling a little restless and I think she sounds like the perfect distraction.

Heading into the house, I find her holed up in the dining room, as usual. This time she has a book and a bunch of pictures of different items in the house spread out in front of her.

"Wow," I say as I take my customary place leaning against the jamb, watching her. "That looks boring as hell."

"Does it?" she asks, looking up at me. She's wearing glasses today. I've never seen her in them before, and I'm not normally fond of that look (or that type of woman, for that matter), but these are a turn-on. At least they are on Laney. She looks like a hot librarian or something. Uptight and all. And boy is she uptight today, especially since last night! It makes me that much more anxious to get her loosened up.

"It does. But lucky for you, I have the perfect antidote. Come with me."

"I really need to get this done."

"This is work, too. Just a variation. Something with a little more fun worked in."

"And just how do you plan to make work fun?"

"Well, for starters, I'll be with you. How can you go wrong?"

She grins and rolls her eyes, but it's a playful expression.

We're off to a good start.

"What does this 'fun work' that you speak of entail, exactly?"

"It's a surprise. But I can tell you that it will involve some walking, so you'll need to change." I let my eyes drift over her prim form, sitting so straight and tall in her chair. "Not that I don't love the thought of loosening every one of those buttons . . ." I say, looking pointedly at where her breasts are straining against little pearl closures down the front of her shirt.

Although still casual, she's wearing some slacks and a little blouse, something far too dressy for this house. But, more importantly, it's far too dressy for this excursion. I wasn't lying, though. Seeing her in her standoffish clothes really does make me want to get her out of them even more. To leave her with nothing for cover, nothing to hide behind.

She eyes me wryly, but it doesn't hide the pretty blush that stains her cheeks. Although I have no desire to pursue any kind of relationship with her, I don't want to leave her in any doubt that I *want* her.

Badly.

"Come on. Chop, chop!" I prompt.

Laney lays her glasses aside and gets up. When she's even with me in the doorway, I lean down and whisper, "If you need help with those buttons, holler."

I wink when she looks up at me.

"I think I can manage," comes her sassy reply, but I can tell by the way her eyes dart away that I'm making her nervous. And, for my purposes, that's a very good thing.

"Suit yourself. Just hurry. We need to be back by dark."

With that, she moves off a little more quickly.

Less than five minutes later, I'm standing at the bottom of the steps when she hits the top one. She's twisting her hair up and securing it with a clip. The action makes the thin material of her yellow tank top stretch across her chest. I can see the outline of her nipples perfectly. My mouth waters with thoughts of having one of them against my tongue again.

I look away from her chest to take in legs that look a mile long in her khaki shorts, feet covered in cute little hiking boots. I'd much rather throw her over my shoulder and carry her to my bed, but that's not an option.

Yet.

"You brought a little bit of everything when you left your dad's, huh?"

Laney stops mid-descent and looks down at herself. "What do you mean?"

"Hiking boots?"

"I always bring them when I come home. I hadn't unpacked yet, so I just grabbed my bags and took off. Pretty much everything I own is on your bedroom floor."

"That's exactly where I picture your clothes every time I look at you."

"You could do this all day long, couldn't you?"

"Do what?" I ask, assuming my most innocuous expression.

"Tease me."

I wait to answer until she's on the next to last step, nearly tall enough to look me in the eye. "Baby, I haven't even begun to tease you."

"Well, maybe it's best if you don't."

As I suspected, she's still stinging from last night.

"No, I can guarantee you that it's best for *both of us* if I do."

"How would you know what's best for me?"

It's not a sarcastic question, but more a genuine one. I wonder if she asks herself that same thing often.

I step up on the last step, my chest close enough to brush hers. "You need to let your hair down a little. And I can help you with that. Neither of us wants anything serious. It's perfect. You're perfect. And I'm perfect *for you.*"

"You're perfect for me *right now* maybe, but normally . . ."

"I know, I know. Normally you're a good girl. And I'm the kind that corrupts them. Normally, you'd stay far away from me. And I'd probably stay away from you. But this isn't normal. I'm willing to go with it. And I think you are, too, if you'll get the hell out of your own head." I reach out to take a thin wisp of hair that's lying by her ear. I wind it around my finger. "Leave 'normally' behind, Laney. Leave all this shit with your dad and your friend and your shithole-of-an-ex behind. Give me a try. I promise I'll make you glad you did."

I see her swallow. Hard. "What if I can't do it? What if I'm not this girl?"

I stroke her trembling bottom lip with my thumb. "We already talked about this. Trust me. You're this girl."

To show her what I mean, to show her how good we are together and how much her body knows that her mind denies, I bend my head and press my lips to hers. I take it slow and easy at first, brushing her mouth with mine, tracing the outline of her lips with the tip of my tongue. When she parts them for me—not because I ask her to or because I'm pushing her, but only because she wants to taste me as much as I want to taste her—I slide my tongue between them and lick it like I licked her last night. Like I'm tasting the world's finest ice cream. Like I'm savoring every last bit of it. Of her. And I am. Something about her is sweet. The sweetest I've ever tasted. And it's got me hard and ready for her, even now.

As much as I want to take her back upstairs, I pull away instead. That'll come soon enough . . .

And then so will she.

"Believe me now?"

She looks down at my chin and pulls her bottom lip between her teeth. It's a shy gesture, but she nods in agreement.

"Good. Let's go." I take her hand in mine and lead her from the house and across the yard toward the orchard gate. "You wanted to see the property, right? Well, there's a lot to see, but today I think a good place to start would be the east grove. It butts up against the river, which will be a cool and refreshing place to visit on a day like today."

She stops dead. "I'm not wearing a suit. And I'm not going skinny-dipping."

"Damn, you really *are* going to be difficult. But who said anything about skinny-dipping?"

I tug her hand, and she reluctantly resumes her walk at my side. I tell her what I know about the orchard—number of acres, average yield each year, labor and upkeep, the average season length. She takes it all in.

She listens and looks around as we walk, never saying a word or asking a question. Then we fall silent. It's when she speaks after a few minutes that I realize why she's been so quiet. She hasn't been thinking about the orchard or work at all.

"What did you mean when you told my father that you were unlovable?"

I sigh.

Aw hell! Don't start this, Laney, I think in exasperation.

"Nothing. I was just making a point."

She looks up from the piece of grass she'd been twirling in the fingers of her other hand and watching intently. Now she's watching me intently.

"No, you weren't *only* making a point. That was sincere. And I want to know why you think that."

I think long and hard before I respond. "I don't do this, Laney."

"Do what?" she asks, puzzled.

"Do the whole spill-your-guts thing. We aren't dating. I don't date really. What I'm offering you is pretty much all I'm capable of."

"But why? That has to be a choice. You're smart and charming, you're driven and competent. You're funny on occasion."

I laugh at her qualification. "On occasion, huh? You're so generous."

"Don't change the subject."

"I don't feel the need to know people very well. And I don't think they'd want to know me very well, either. So I just avoid that kind of thing."

"But why? What makes you think you're so unworthy?"

"A lifetime of living with me, that's what."

"Maybe so, but there's something else, Jake. I'm not stupid. And if you simply don't want to talk about it, fine. Just know that I don't know if *I'm* capable of having this kind of . . . thing with someone I know nothing about."

It's my turn to stop. "But you do know me. You're getting to know me every day. You just said I'm brilliant and witty and charming and drop-dead gorgeous. Not to mention sexy as all hell. What more do you need to know about me? Maybe I'm just not that deep. Maybe there's only a puddle where you think there's an ocean."

She narrows her eyes on me. I can't imagine what she's thinking. This part of a woman's mind is a mystery to me. And I have no problem letting it stay that way. Having feelings about something every two seconds and then obsessing about them for days—that shit's for the birds.

Finally, she shrugs. "Maybe . . ."

But she's not fooling me. Not only does she not believe that for a second, but she's nowhere near letting it go. I can tell by the way she still watches me, like she's trying to see what's going on behind my eyes.

"Come on," I say veering off the path to the left. "I've got something to show you."

She makes no comment, asks no questions. But she follows. That's how I know she's still in this. There's something inside her that wants to pursue this. I just have to give her good reasons not to change her mind.

I hear the roar of it long before it's within sight. The air smells a little bit different here. Fresher. Cleaner. This is one of my favorite places. Always has been. And it's the only waterfall in the county.

We step through the trees. The cascade of white water gushing over the rocks and hitting the pool below creates a spray that makes rainbows in the sun. I glance down at Laney. Her eyes are wide and her lips are slightly parted.

Yeah, this was definitely the right place to bring her.

Although it wasn't my original plan, I can see it was the right choice, all things considered. I don't normally bring people here and risk spoiling it for me, but in this case . . .

I don't even know what "this case" really is. It's not just to get Laney in my bed. I could do that other ways. Maybe it's to put her mind at ease about me. Maybe it's to share something of mine, some part of me with her when she so obviously needs it. Anything beyond that, I'd rather not consider. I just want to sleep with her. That's it. End of story. And that's the way it has to stay.

It has to.

I could never risk loving someone, much less someone like Laney. She's actually a nice person. She deserves much better.

"Wow! It's . . . it's just . . . . wow! Breathtaking."

"Funny," I say softly, reaching out to touch her smooth cheek, "that's just what I was thinking."

When she looks at me, I know she knows I'm not referring to the waterfall.

"Come on. Let me show you the other view."

I take off upriver, along the bank. I know there's a path that cuts through the trees that leads to the top of the fall. There are a couple of tricky spots, especially where it gets rocky and the moss is thick. I turn and offer my hand to Laney, pulling her along safely behind me.

When we reach the top, I carefully walk the exposed rocks over to the center of the river. I stop to look down. I revel in the rush of adrenaline from the height and from seeing the water crashing into the pool below.

I hear Laney gasp beside me. "Oh Lord! That's a long way down. It doesn't look that far from the bottom."

"Nah, it's not *too* high."

She throws me a sidelong glance. "Too high for what?"

I give her my most persuasive grin. "To jump."

"Have you lost your mind? There's no way in the world I'm jumping off this thing."

"Oh, come on. I'll be down there to catch you."

"Catch me? Don't you mean to drag my dead, lifeless body from the water after I drown?"

"Of course that's not what I mean. If it were dangerous, I'd never suggest you jump. I just think this would be good for you."

"How, exactly, would risking my life be good for me?"

"You need to let go a little, Laney. I know you want to. You need to take some risks. Be spontaneous. Stop thinking so much. Do some things you wouldn't normally do. Trust me, when you surface down there, your adrenaline will be all jacked up, and there's no feeling like it in the world."

"That's not the kind of thing I was hoping to achieve."

"You want to forget. To escape. This will consume you. And sometimes we all need to dive into something else and be lost. Even if it's just for a little while. It's worth it, Laney. I promise."

She leans over and looks down again, nervously worrying her bottom lip. "I don't know, Jake. That's a long way down."

"You'll be in the water, all safe and sound, in a matter of seconds."

"My clothes will be ruined," she says, trying to find reasons not to do it.

"Take them off."

"I told you I'm not skinny-dipping."

"This isn't skinny-dipping. This is more like cliff diving. In the buff. And it's safer if you aren't wearing clothes that you could get tangled up in. And certainly not shoes that could weigh you down."

"So you want me to jump off this thing, naked, and then climb back up here to get my clothes? I think not."

"Fine," I say, sighing. "I'll climb back up here afterward and get them for you. You can watch my bare ass from down there. Maybe you'll even want to reward me for my heroics." I waggle my eyebrows at her, trying to lighten the mood, to make her feel less afraid. I don't want her fear completely gone, though. That's part of the experience. It'll heighten what she feels. And that rush . . .

Damn! That rush and the way everything else vanishes is worth almost anything.

She doesn't say no right away, which tells me that she'll agree to it. Eventually.

I grab the hem of my T-shirt, pull it over my head, and throw it toward the base of a tree on the bank. I step to a rock nearer the edge of the fall as I take off first one shoe and sock, then the other, tossing it all over to where my shirt landed. When I'm standing at the edge, with the hiss of gushing water at my back, facing Laney, I meet her eyes and grin.

Her gaze is glued to mine, as if she's trying her best to look at my face rather than what I'm doing with my hands. I open the snap of my shorts. Then I unzip them. I'm not wearing any underwear, so there's nothing to obstruct her view of me when I step out of my shorts and throw them to the bank.

"See you down there," I say quietly, smiling when her eyes flicker low and then back up to my face. I see her cheeks burn bright red and I laugh just before I turn around and jump straight over the waterfall.

And everything else disappears.

Except for the feeling that I'm flying.

And free.

And alive.

And that nothing else matters.

FIFTEEN: *Laney*

Oh sweet Jesus! He did it!
My heart is like a runaway train. His whoop of delight is still echoing in my head as I step onto the rock closest to the edge and look over, holding my breath until I see Jake's head break the surface away from the white spray.

Ohmigod, ohmigod, ohmigod, I can't do this!

Blood is rushing behind my ears even louder than the water. My pulse is racing and I feel short of breath.

I look left and right. The mossy bank looks a thousand miles away. Then I look down at Jake's handsome, laughing face, and so does he.

"Your turn," he calls up to me as he shakes his head one more time, making his hair stand up in spikes.

"No way," I reply, feeling a little panicky that I'm up here by myself.

"Come on, Laney. You can do this. Trust me."

"Trust you? You're obviously insane. Why should I trust you?"

It seems an inordinately long amount of time passes before he replies. And, even then, I have to strain to hear his low voice.

"Because trusting everyone else has gotten you nowhere. Take a chance for once in your life. Take a chance on me."

Common sense and self-preservation are locking horns with the lure of Jake and all that he represents as he stares up at me from the churning pool below.

I feel frantic. On edge. Literally and figuratively. But, again, something rises up and takes a dominant position. I don't take the time to examine it. Or reason with it. Like I've wanted to do, I just surrender to it. To freedom. To escape.

To Jake.

Closing my eyes, I bend and pull off my boots and socks. I hear Jake's holler of delight. "That's my girl!"

I can't help but smile.

He really is the devil.

I chuck them as hard as I can toward the shore. They land not far from Jake's clothes. Swallowing every bit of shy, responsible, fairly chaste Laney, I pull my tank top over my head and throw it at the tree. Then my shorts.

When I'm standing at the top of a huge waterfall, wearing nothing but my underwear, staring down at a guy who takes my breath away, I shred the last little bit of reservation that I have.

Along with my bra and panties.

And then, without another second's thought or hesitation, I leap.

The chains of who I've always been, of who my family is and what's expected of me, break away as I fly through the air. Dropping, dropping, dropping, everything fades away but for the sound of the water, the feel of the wind, the thrill of the moment, and the man at the bottom.

He's waiting for me there. All sorts of new and unexplored things are waiting for me there. This is an existential leap, as much as a physical one. There's no turning back now. I might as well embrace it.

The cool water swallows me up, slowing my descent and stealing the air from my lungs. The muffled sound of churning water swooshes by my ears as the undertow pulls at my legs.

I swim for the surface and don't stop until I feel the sun on my face.

And I open my eyes to see Jake. He swam to get me, just in case I didn't come up. Just like he promised.

He's smiling. And I am, too. All over. Every cell. I can feel it.

I've never felt lighter. Happier. More optimistic. And I don't even know what I'm optimistic *about*.

He's laughing when his arms reach around me and drag my body to his. All I can think of is how I want this moment—here, with Jake, feeling like this—to last forever. And there's only one thing that could make it better, that could cement it in my head and in my heart.

Digging my hands into his hair, I pull Jake's mouth to mine. His lips are cool and soft, and they taste of the water and the fresh air.

Brazenly, I slip my tongue into his mouth, asking him for things I don't have the courage to say, offering him things I don't have the strength to hold on to.

Then he's kissing me back, his hands roving my back, tugging at my hair. His smooth chest is teasing my nipples, his firm thighs are tangling with mine.

And then I'm weightless again. I don't even open my eyes to see where Jake is taking me. All I know is that my body is still pressed to his and the world cares only for what's happening between us right this minute. Nothing else matters.

The grass is soft and cool against my back. Jake's body is hot and hard as it covers mine. I groan into his mouth and arch against him, a silent plea for more. Just . . . more.

Spreading my legs, I reach around and dig my fingers into Jake's smooth, hard butt and I pull him toward me, craving him in places that ache with want of him. With a growl, he drags his lips away from mine and kisses a fiery trail down my throat to my breast.

When his mouth closes around my cool nipple, I gasp. The sensation is stronger, deeper. Heightened. The sky swirls behind my eyes. The river rushes behind my ears.

Jake licks and sucks his way from my nipples to my navel, and the earth collapses into a pinpoint of pleasure when I feel him move farther down to settle between my thighs. The first touch of his tongue to my throbbing flesh brings my hips up off the ground. Relentless, he lays his arm across my stomach to hold me still as he mouth plunders my every slick crevice and hidden desire.

Over and over, his tongue sweeps across my most sensitive part, bringing me higher and higher, further and further away from reality. Until, like the waterfall, my climax crashes down over me.

His lips sucking at me, his fingers penetrating me, Jake perpetuates my orgasm until I can barely breathe. My head is spinning with it. My body is drenched with it. The world is alive with it.

"Are you on the pill?" he asks, his voice nothing more than a muffled groan.

I nod in answer, unable to find words in the midst of what he's doing to my body.

"Do you trust me? I promise you I'm clean."

Again, I nod. And, truthfully, I do. Or I wouldn't have jumped off a waterfall and into his arms.

His fingers disappear as Jake shifts his weight. I want to cry at the loss, but then, reality splinters again when he enters me.

He's so big, stretches me so tight, I cry out. Not in pain, but in the most exquisite pleasure I've ever known.

When he starts to move within me, I feel the tension return, stronger than ever and threatening to overwhelm me completely.

"Oh fuuu—" he moans into my ear as he withdraws and plunges into me again. "Oh my God, I never thought it would feel like this," he says, his voice sounding nearly pained in his passion. "You're so tight. And so wet." More excited than I've ever been, I'm panting, almost delirious with what is happening between us.

"Jake, don't stop."

"I won't, baby. I'm gonna make you come all over me again and again. I wanna feel you squeeze me. I want you to feel it running down your ass. And then I'm gonna lick you until you come again." His words are an aphrodisiac, his body the sweetest torture device. Fiercely, he pumps into me, as if he knows I'm close. So, so close . . . "And then, I'm gonna put my cock back in and you'll come with me. I'll fill you up, baby. I'll fill you up with *me*."

With one hard, deep thrust, just as his mouth covers mine, it happens again. Wave after wave of it, sweeping me further away from all the things that never really mattered. Right now, *this* matters. *Only* this matters.

True to his word, Jake withdraws from me and moves down my body, using his lips and his tongue and his fingers to send me tumbling from one orgasm to the next. My legs feel limp when he spreads them even wider, placing his hand behind one knee and pushing it against my chest. I'm convinced I don't have anything left to give him.

But he persists. And I let him. I'm putty in his hands.

When Jake enters me this time, I feel it all the way in my stomach, like his body is merging with mine. I can feel every long, thick inch as he pulls out. And I can feel every long, thick inch as he plunges back into me. The friction is delicious, the pleasure undeniable.

Much to my surprise, as Jake manipulates my body, the tension builds once again. I'm convinced it will lead nowhere. Until I feel Jake's hot, pulsing release. With a growl, he grinds his body into mine, triggering spasms deep inside me.

True to his word, he's making me come with him. I can feel my muscles clutch at him, pulling him farther into me, milking him until I feel his shoulders shudder beneath my hands.

"That's right, baby. Take it all. Uhhh," he groans through gritted teeth as he strains against me. And then he collapses on top of me, spent.

We lie, joined together, for what seems like an eternity. My body feels numb, but it also feels like there's a hum of tingling nerve activity right below the surface of my skin.

When Jake finally raises his head to look down at me, I feel him twitch inside me. He's still hard.

"How is that possible?" I ask before he can speak.

His brow wrinkles. "How is what possible?"

I'm not even sure I know what I was asking. How can he make me feel this way, how can he make my body do what it just did, how can he still be hard after all that—I don't know how to be more specific.

"This?"

He smiles, his eyes twinkling down into mine, and he kisses the tip of my nose. My heart melts, bringing with it a prickle of unease that I push to the side for later examination. "Hell if I know, but I can tell you I'm dedicated to finding out and doing my best to duplicate it."

He runs his lips along my jawline as he flexes his hips. I feel the pang of something waking in the lowest part of my belly.

"You can't be serious," I whisper, using all my strength just to keep my eyes open.

"Oh, but I am," he says, pulling out and thrusting back into me. A wave of awareness steals my breath. Again. "But you need to rest a little first."

As sweetly as anything I could ever imagine a good man being capable of, Jake withdraws from me and rolls to the side, bringing me into the curve of his body.

"Jake, I—"

"Shhh," he interrupts, pressing his lips to the top of my head. "Relax. Enjoy the sun. I'll be here when you wake up."

He doesn't have to tell me twice.

SIXTEEN: *Jake*

I'm tired, yes. And I could probably use a little rest, yes. But not right now, I'm more interested in the girl curled up at my side, sleeping naked in the grass. The one who just rolled enthusiastically from one orgasm to the next. The one who let me devour her in the bright light of day, out in the open. The one who let me come inside her, and seemed to enjoy the shit out of it.

Can this be the same girl I kissed at the fair all those years ago? The same girl who blushes if I stare at her too long? The same girl who never curses? The same girl who probably never even had more than that one sip of wine until I put a purple people eater in her hand? What a very perplexing, yet very welcome walking contradiction.

I knew she had a little fire to her. Probably buried deep down, something she was raised to squash or ignore. And I knew she was itching to take a little stroll on the wild side. Or maybe just at the *edge* of the wild side. But I didn't expect this. I mean, damn! I want her again already. Right this second. My cock acts like it's seven a.m. on a Saturday morning after a two-month dry spell.

I hope to all hell that she doesn't get attached and ruin this for both of us, because I could stand to have a little more of this coming my way over the next few weeks.

I glance down at her body—at the arch of her neck, at the curve of her hip, at the perfect pink nipple that I can barely see, peeking out from under her arm where she's lying on her side—and my mouth waters. And my dick gets harder.

I'm debating waking her up the right way when she sighs and tilts her head up to pin me with her soft blue eyes. Judging by her expression, I know she still feels that lazy, bone-deep relaxed feeling that only comes after having some really good sex. And this sex? Sweet hell! It was that and then some!

But then they freeze, as if she suddenly remembers what happened. I watch her eyes round into Os nearly as large as the one her mouth makes. I hold my breath, not knowing whether to expect her to get up and walk out of my life forever or give me the coldest shoulder this side of Alaska.

True to what I've seen of her this far, though, instead, she surprises me.

"Can we do that again?" Air rushes from my lungs and my chest relaxes as a wide smile settles across her lips.

"Which part?" I ask, unable to help myself.

The blue of her eyes sparkle like stars in a midnight sky. "All of it."

I find my own lips curving. "Hell yeah!"

"But maybe backward this time," she says, sinking her teeth into her bottom lip in that shy way that I love. "Kissing . . . and . . . stuff first; jumping off the rock second?"

"Oh, *hell* yeah!" I murmur again as I roll my body onto hers and suck one delicious nipple into my mouth.

And then we do it all again.

Only backward.

* * *

It's long past dark by the time Laney and I drag our tired asses up the stairs to my bedroom. "How 'bout a nice long, hot bath to ease any . . . sore places you might have?" I ask this with a mischievous wink because I know there's no way on God's green earth she's ever had an afternoon like the one we just spent. As many "encounters" as I've had in the course of my life, *I've* never even had a day like today. To say it was spectacular would be a disgrace to the word *spectacular*. Makes me think it's been far too long since I've had really good sex.

Surely that's what it is.

"I can barely wiggle. I'll come along if you'll do all the heavy lifting," she says, winding her arms around my neck and smiling charmingly up into my face.

"Don't you start thinking you can use that beautiful face and this amazing body of yours to manipulate me," I warn.

"Please," she says coyly, rubbing up against me like a cat.

"Done," I say, grinning at her. She laughs when I sweep her off her feet and carry her to the bathroom.

I set her on the counter while I run the bath full of extremely warm water. When it's over half full, I strip, set her on her feet and do the same for her before we climb in.

"Aaah!" she squeals when the hot water hits her skin. She starts to hop back out, but I grab her arm to still her.

"Just give it a second. It only stings at first, then it'll do great things for your muscles. And . . . other things."

I sit down and spread my legs, holding my arms out wide for her to join me. When she does, she hisses.

"I didn't need to be on the pill, did I?"

"Huh?"

"There's no way a single sperm could possibly survive this. And obviously you've done it before."

"Once or twice."

After a few seconds, her voice sounds less pained. "So, is this a fetish?"

"Is what a fetish?"

"Luring unsuspecting women to your home and then boiling them."

"Oh, come on. It's not that bad, drama queen. Besides, isn't it worth it to share a hot bath with all this?" I say, curling my fingers in toward myself and giving her my cheesiest, most arrogant smile.

Boldly, she peruses me, which is kind of a turn-on when she lingers on my cock, which is nestled against her hip. "We'll see. What about you? What's a hot bath with *me* worth to a guy like you?"

I reach forward and pull her around and into my arms, her back to my chest, leaving her entire front open to my roaming hands.

"After today? Quite a bit, actually."

I nuzzle the side of her neck, the scratch of my stubble sending chills down her chest and tightening her nipple. I feel my body jump against her ass where she's sitting between my legs.

"Re-ally?" she purrs, tilting her head to one side to give me better access to her neck.

"Mmm."

"Then maybe we can talk a little."

I feel the sigh swell in my chest, but I hold it in.

Not this again.

"What do you want to know?" I ask after a long pause.

Laney says nothing for several seconds. Instead, she grabs a bar of soap and rolls it between her palms, creating a nice thick lather. She lays the soap aside and starts to wash one arm. I watch her begin at her wrist and make slow circles all the way up her arm to her shoulder. The closer she gets to her chest, to the curve of her breast, the tighter my entire body gets, like a clock winding up.

She's too innocent to know what she's doing will drive me crazy. My guess is that it's the easiest spot to wash first, as nearly everything else is submerged.

That or I'm not giving her nearly enough credit.

"What was it like, growing up on the orchard? What was your family like?"

It's an innocuous enough question, one that doesn't overtly stimulate any touchy areas. I don't mind answering if it keeps her doing what she's doing.

"Not much different than most childhoods, I'd say. At least not around here. I played outside most of the day, climbed trees in the orchard, sometimes helped pick peaches, skipped rocks at the wide place in the river down by the northern border."

"What were your parents like?"

"Just like regular parents. We ate meals together. Played games together. Watched television together."

I'm mesmerized as I watch her soap her chest, her hands inching her way toward her breasts. "And then Jenna came along," she says, letting her fingers play over the smooth, round globes.

"Yep," I say almost absently, my eyes glued to her hands.

When she uses her index finger to ring her nipples, my breath hitches in my throat. My balls throb with the sudden need to lift her up and plunge her down on my cock, to watch that perfect ass of hers move up and down as she rides me.

And then she kills off my hard-on with one question, with the one question she's been sneaking up to.

"Why do you think your father didn't love you? It sure sounds like he did."

"Laney, I told you—"

She cuts me off by whirling around in the tub to face me, her hands splayed across my chest and her eyes pleading with me.

"Please, Jake. Please talk to me. I want so much to be okay with this, but it's . . . it's just . . . it's hard. I *need* to know you. At least a little bit. Just tell me something about your life here. Tell me something. Just a little bit."

I want to kiss her. And shake her. And walk away. And hold her close. I've never been with someone like her, someone who actually *tries* to be . . . less. Most of the girls I've known *just are*. But not Laney. She's trying to be casual and easy, jumping into a sexual relationship with someone she barely knows. But it doesn't come naturally for her. Oddly, as bass-ackwards as it sounds, that makes me respect her all the more.

This time, I do sigh.

"My mother was already sick when she got pregnant with Jenna. She wouldn't even consider terminating the pregnancy to save her own life. She knew the risks, but she valued Jenna's life more than her own." I swallow hard. It's never easy to think about all this shit, much less talk about it. Which is why I don't.

Ever.

"Jake, I'm so sor—"

I hold up my hand to cut her off. I can see her sincerity in the big, glistening pools of her eyes. But she wanted it. Now she's gonna get it. At least part of it. There's still a part I'll never share with another living soul.

Ever.

"So when Jenna was born, Dad was busy taking care of her and Mom just kept getting sicker. There was a point where there was nothing else the doctors or medicine could do for her. Other than to just let nature take its course."

"How old were you when she . . ."

"Eight. I was eight years old when my mother died."

I lean my head back against the cool ceramic of the tub, closing my eyes against that time in my life. I feel Laney's lips, light as twin feathers, brush first my mouth then my cheek, my jaw then my chin, before she settles down on top of me. She rests her head on my chest and her right hand over my heart.

I can feel the sympathy and the regret rolling off her in nearly tangible waves. But I don't want her sympathy. I don't want anybody's sympathy. I just want the past to be left alone. It's already brought me enough pain in life without having to dig it all up again.

My tiny smile is bitter when I think to myself that Laney probably won't be asking any more questions any time soon.

SEVENTEEN: *Laney*

I can't help but smile as I smear cream cheese on a bagel half for Jake. It's such a domestic thing to do—fix breakfast for the man with whom I share a house and a bed—that it makes me feel happy all the way to the bone. I could see this being my life for a long, long time.

Over the last four weeks, I've been bungee jumping with Jake, white water rafting with Jake, cliff diving with Jake, done all sorts of things I never thought I'd ever do, and as much fun as it's been, some part of me still craves this—a home and a family. Mundane activities like making breakfast for the people I love.

As always when I think about my feelings for Jake, I feel the frown pucker my brow. I know he cares about me, and I care about him. Do I love him? I don't know. Whatever it is I feel for him, it's fierce. And passionate. And deep. It's different than the way I felt about Shane. A *lot* different. The thing is, I don't *want* to be in love with Jake. He's made it perfectly clear that he's not in it for love. He just wants to have some fun.

And we do. We have a lot of fun.

He loves my body. I know that for sure. We have some of the most amazing sex I've ever had. Better than anything I even *thought* could be experienced. So there's that. But it's not enough.

Sometimes, when I catch him staring at me or when I fall asleep on his chest while watching television on the couch and I wake to find him watching me or rubbing my cheek, I'll think to myself that he *must* love me. But I'm not crazy enough to believe that actually means it's so.

But do I want it to be?

Yes, I think I do. Despite it all—the unsavory reputation, the bad-boy ways, the thrill-seeking streak, the aversion to relationships—I still want him to be all mine.

But I don't know if a guy like Jake will ever be all anybody's.

And time is running out for me to try to win him over. I've already put in for two extensions with work. Another couple of weeks are all I'll be able to get before I have to turn in my reports and leave the account with my boss.

The back door bangs and I jump, startled. I turn to see Jake walk into the kitchen, sweat beading on his forehead and a satisfied smile on his face. "Mmm, are you what's for breakfast? Because I'm starved." He bypasses the fridge and heads straight for me. He takes the bagel and the knife and sets them aside and then threads his fingers into my hair and kisses me long and deep, enough to set my skin on fire. When he lifts his head, I'm breathless and wanting something much more . . . personal than breakfast.

"I think I could probably arrange something."

"No arranging necessary," he says, his fingers already at the zipper of my shorts. "I have everything I need right here."

The instant I realize he's serious, heat floods my core. I run my hands over the slick skin of his chest and then down around his waist, tugging at the elastic of his shorts. He pushes at mine until they pass my hips then he sets to work on my panties as I pull his shorts down enough to free his long, strong length.

Chills spread down my back when I wind my fingers around it, the tips barely meeting around his thick base. It never ceases to amaze me that something so large will fit inside me. Yet I'm not at all surprised that it brings me so much pleasure. Jake knows his way around my body like he's been loving it for years.

With a growl, he grabs my hips and turns me toward the cabinet. He reaches around and slides his palm down my stomach to the fire that's raging between my legs. I spread my thighs for him, stepping out of the tangle of my shorts and panties as I do.

When he thrusts a finger inside me, my knees get weak and I take hold of the counter for support. Jake pushes me forward until I'm bent at the waist. With his thumb grazing my clitoris and his fingers thrusting into me, I'm quickly approaching the edge.

I pant breathlessly as he brings his other hand between my legs from behind. His fingers are making circles and diving in and out of me, all at the same time. He leans over me to lick and then bite my shoulder. "Is this enough or do you want more?"

I'm breathless and my head is swimming. "More," I breathe. "I want more."

"Tell me. Tell me what you want."

I feel his hardness pressing against my hip. "I want you. Inside me."

"Tell me you want my cock. Tell me you want to come all over my cock," he snarls as his fingers move over me, winding me up like a pocket watch. His words are like gasoline poured on an already raging fire. My muscles clench as the tension in my body reaches fever pitch.

"I want your cock. I want to come all over your cock. Please, Jake. Please."

I'm so close, but I want him inside me. And he knows it. He's holding back just long enough . . .

And then he's sliding wetly into me from behind. One deep, sharp thrust. I cry out, unable to hold it in one second longer. His fingers bite into my hips as he pumps into me.

"That's right, baby. I wanna hear you. Let me hear you," Jake demands from behind me, thrusting into me harder.

I can't hold in my gasps of breath or my moans of pleasure. This was so sudden and so raw, I feel like I could growl.

I curl my fingers around the edge of the counter, holding on to the world, to my sanity, as Jake stiffens behind me. I feel his fingers tangle in my hair and tug as he shoots liquid heat deep inside me. Then, with his name on my lips in a voice that I barely recognize as my own, I shatter like a stained glass window.

Shards of multicolored crystal explode behind my eyes. Jake's thrusts are vicious. And all my body can say is *Give me more!*

When the spasms subside and I'm collapsed on the counter with Jake draped over me, both of us drinking in huge gulps of air, I marvel at the intensity of what we just shared. Rather than things losing their luster or becoming too comfortable or ordinary, it seems they're going the opposite direction. It's as though every minute of every day, every time we make love, it gets better and better. Hotter and hotter. More and more earth-shattering.

And more and more meaningful.

After the tingling wore off from my waist down, I finished smearing sweet spread on our bagels. Now, I'm sitting across from Jake as we munch on a late breakfast.

A very late breakfast.

"How's work coming?" he asks, out of the blue.

"Fine," I say, noncommittally. I swallow a piece of bagel, feeling it stick in my suddenly dry throat. "I don't have much left to do. Soon, I'll be out of your hair."

I keep my attention on my food, carefully tearing off another bite of bagel, but not putting it in my mouth. My appetite seems to have disappeared.

When finally I look up, Jake is watching me. His expression is fathomless. His golden eyes search mine for several long seconds before he starts to nod slowly. "How would you feel about a camping trip this weekend?"

I grin. It's like a stay of execution, this invitation. I love the thought of spending more time with him, especially out away from the world. Something secluded like a camping trip sounds wonderful.

"Sounds like fun." I try for a mild answer, which I'm sure is belied by my bright smile.

"That way we can be gone on Sunday, too. I know how much it bothers you not to be going to church."

My heart melts a little at his thoughtfulness. I had told him that very first Sunday that I stayed here that I felt guilty, that any time I was in town, I attended my father's church on Sunday. At the time, Jake made no comment, but now I know he heard. And it means the world, not only that he listened, but that he cares enough about me to be mindful of my comfort.

Don't read too much into it, Luney, I caution myself, but I know it's too late. It's just another little thing that I'll dwell on, wondering if it means he has deeper feelings for me.

I shrug. "It's not that big a deal."

Jake is quiet for a few seconds before he speaks again. He clears his throat. "You know, if you want to go, you can. And if you need me to go with you, I would do that."

I would give anything to be able to control the gush of tears that floods my eyes. But I can't. Before I know it, my eyes are burning and Jake is blurry. Quickly, I look down at my plate, but I know I wasn't fast enough.

I hear the scrape of wood against wood as Jake pushes his bar stool away from the island. I don't bother to look up. I don't want him to see the pain in them now, behind the tears. I knew this would be too much for him. Too emotional. Too . . . real.

But, much to my surprise, Jake rounds the island and comes to my side to turn me around on my stool. I keep my head down, but, with a finger under my chin, he lifts my face until I'm looking into his eyes.

"It's all right that it bothers you. It should. Your father is a good man. Misguided at times, but I think his intentions are good. He loves you. That much is obvious." I blink and tears spill down my cheeks, unchecked. Jake's eyes follow one all the way down to my jaw where he brushes it away with the backs of his fingers. "You're lucky to have him. I'd have given anything for my father to feel that way about me."

For just a few seconds, the real Jake, the one behind the tough guy, peers back at me from somewhere inside those guarded amber eyes. I want so much to talk to him, but I know better than to try. I know better than to ask any questions. No matter how much I want to know, I'm well aware that there are some things Jake won't tell me until he's good and ready. Which he may never be. But I know enough. Somehow, his father hurt him. Badly. And Jake has never gotten over it. That much is clear.

"Anyone would be a fool not to love you," I blurt, caught up in the moment, in the haunted look that's in his eyes. When I realize what I said, I feel a moment of sheer panic. But then Jake smiles, and I mentally exhale.

His expression is wry when he says, simply, "Thank you, but you don't know me as well as he did. He had his reasons."

As I watch, the curtain falls back into place and, just like that, tender, broken Jake is gone, replaced once more by the person who pretends to feel nothing. Who *wants* to feel nothing.

"But I want to know you, Jake," I confess candidly, and not for the first time.

"I know you do. But I also know what I'm saving you from. Trust me, it's for the best."

With that, he kisses my forehead and backs away. "How about we divide and conquer? I know you've got some work to do, but do you think you'd have time for a quick trip to the store? If you can get that, I'll have everything else ready and we can leave after lunch tomorrow."

Back to business as usual.

I hide my sigh behind a sniff.

"Sure. Just tell me what to get."

"I'll text you a list. First, though, I need a shower." He gives me a casual smile, a peck on the lips and then he turns to walk away. Jake has an enviable way of just moving on, not dwelling on things he can't control. He can't fix the past so he doesn't want to talk about it, doesn't want to think about it. He just . . . moves on. Some might call that hiding, but Jake's no coward. I think this is just his way of conquering it. By not letting it conquer him.

While I admire his determination, it still makes me feel so sad. "Okay. I'm heading to the office," I say with a smile. We now refer to the dining room as my office.

Jake tosses me a wink and takes the stairs two at a time. I don't move on nearly so quickly.

True to his word, my phone chirps about an hour later. It's a text from Jake. A list of things to get from the grocery store. As I'm scrolling through it, my phone rings and startles the crap out of me. When I finish fumbling to keep from dropping it, I see that it's Tori.

Again.

She's called me at least a dozen times in the last week. It's not that I don't want to hear what she has to say. Well, I don't, but now I feel a little more willing to. She's been my best friend for a lot of years. The least I can do is listen to her.

No, one of the biggest reasons I don't want to talk to her is that I feel like Jake and I are living in a bubble, one that could pop at any moment. And I want to enjoy every second of it while I can. I don't want anyone intruding on our time together. Tori included.

I hit the red button to decline the call and set my phone back on the table.

Maybe later. Right now, I'm going to the store. I don't really have time to talk to her.

At least that's what I tell myself.

After running a brush through my hair and putting on some lightly tinted lip gloss, I text Jake that I'm leaving and head for my car. He's out in the orchard. Somewhere.

It only takes me about fifteen minutes to get to the one and only grocery store in Greenfield. I look at the clock when I pull into a parking spot in the lot. Two forty on a Thursday afternoon. I shouldn't be running into anyone I know at such an odd time.

I grab a buggy and pull up Jake's list on my phone. I start in the produce section. For having such a hellion reputation around town for most of his life, he sure does practice mostly clean living. He drinks a beer or two on occasion, but mostly drinks water and eats healthy foods. He runs almost every day and he stays active. He doesn't smoke or do drugs. He's in outstanding physical condition, something I can personally attest to, and I can't think of one thing I'd change about him.

Unless it was that he'd fall in love with me . . .

I mutter to myself all the way through the fruit, chastising my stupid, stupid emotional self for going there. I'm not even sure that's what I'd want.

The hell you're not!

I have to smile when the thought pops up. It sounds in my head like Jake would say it in real life. Same tone, same kind of expression. Same . . . Jake.

I sigh. I think it's safe to say that, no matter my intentions or how hard I tried *not* to let it happen, Jake got under my skin.

"Just how the hell long are you gonna ignore me?"

I jump when Tori's furious voice barks from behind me. I was so lost in thought, I didn't even hear her approach me.

I sigh again.

"Tori, I just didn't want to get into it yet. Can't you give me some space?"

"Space?" my oldest friend says, her bright blue eyes flashing and her very ample bosom heaving. With her long blond hair thrown over one shoulder and her chin lifted in defiance, she looks like the cover of a magazine. "I've seen you once all summer. The only bigger space than that is death!"

"Don't be so dramatic."

Tori's lip pooches out in a pout. "You're making me dramatic. What do I have to do to get through to you? All I want is for you to hear me out."

I knew it was coming. I had just hoped to avoid it a little while longer. "Fine. You talk, I'll shop."

"Really? I've been your best friend since the womb and I get half your attention while you shop?"

I grit my teeth. This is really unhandy.

"All right, then let's go to the café and have a cup of coffee."

"The coffee here sucks," Tori says with a curl of her lip.

"Tori! Not the point."

"Right, right, right," she says, shaking her head like she's clearing it. "Okay, that's fine."

I turn the buggy around and head back toward the front of the store and the little lunch-area-slash-café that dominates one side of the building, just past the pharmacy. "How'd you find me, anyway?"

"I saw you pull in. In a town this small, it's a miracle you've been able to avoid me this long."

"I'm guessing you haven't talked to Mom or Dad then?"

She looks at me like I've completely lost my mind. "Hell no! Are you nuts? And get the lecture of a lifetime on what a devil-worshippin' skank I am? I think not."

"What-ever! You know my parents would never say any such

thing. And to be honest, they don't even know what happened. I haven't, uh, I haven't told them yet."

"Really? So they have no clue why you dumped Shane?"

I shake my head.

"Well, I'm gonna be honest. That doesn't bother me one bit. I'd rather they not hate me until you've heard the whole story."

I make no comment. I just keep steering the cart toward the café until I find an empty booth to park it beside. I throw my purse in first and slide into one side of the booth. After I'm situated, I take a deep breath and fold my arms on the table in front of me, lacing my fingers together.

"Stop that!" Tori blurts.

"Stop what?"

"Stop doing that. You look like you're just biding your time until you hand down my death sentence."

"I'm not your judge, Tori. God is."

"Thank goodness for that. At least *He* knows what I was trying to do."

Even though the wound from the whole episode has gone practically numb (no doubt thanks to the attentions of one Jake Theopolis), it still irks me to remember finding her in bed with Shane. And that she's now going to sit here and try to explain it away.

Whatever, I think with an internal roll of my eyes. It'll all be over soon enough.

"So, say what you need to. I've got some shopping to do."

Tori gives me a withering look, but says nothing. After a few seconds, she sits up straighter in her seat and clears her throat.

"Okay, let me just remind you that it's *me* who's been telling you for over two years now that something's not right with Shane. I told you, he's a hound dog in sheep's clothing."

My laugh is bitter. "Thank you for so kindly showing me that you were right."

Tori slumps forward and reaches out to cover my hands with hers. "You needed to see it, Laney. You needed to see it to believe it. Before you married that jackhole. No matter what I told you, you always believed in him. And that's great. Until the person you have so much faith in isn't worth it anymore." She pauses, as if to let her words sink in before she continues. "Laney, I love you. I would never, never, never do that to you. If you'll remember, I *knew* you were going to Shane's early. You texted me that morning to say that your pedicure had been cancelled and that you were going to surprise Shane."

"Yeah, but even *you* wouldn't have expected me *that* early. I didn't tell *anyone* that I cancelled my dentist appointment, too."

"Do you really think I'd be stupid enough to risk it, though? Really, Laney?"

Tori looks so sincere. So desperate for me to believe her. And for the first time since it happened, I begin to feel a little niggle of doubt. Could she be telling the truth?

"Okay then, just for the sake of argument, tell me what happened. Exactly."

Tori takes a deep breath. "Okay, here goes. So, for a while now, I'd been getting the feeling that Shane was coming on to me. Just a little comment here and there, a little flirting when you weren't in the room, casual 'bumps,' things like that. But one day about a month ago, I had gone to his place, thinking you'd be there, but you weren't. He said you'd be back shortly and that I could wait. So I did. Well, he asked if I wanted a beer and, you know me, I said yes. So he brought us both a beer and he sat down on the couch beside me.

"We chatted about random things. He asked me about school, I asked him about work. You know, all that boring shit. Things didn't used to be that strained between us. You knew I always liked Shane. Well, at first I did. Anyway, I finished my beer and asked if I could have another. He said, 'Sure. Help yourself.' So I did. It was when I was in the kitchen at the fridge that he came up behind me. I turned around so fast I just about fell into the butter, he scared me so bad. And then he kissed me. Just like that. Like he thought that was okay."

When she pauses, I wait for her to continue, but she doesn't. "So what did you do?"

"Nothing. When he leaned back, I told him I had to go. So I grabbed my shit and I left."

"And that's it?"

"I was freaked out, Laney! Wouldn't you have been? I mean, imagine what kind of position that put me in. Yes, I'd been warning you about him, but to say he tried to kiss me would only make you think badly of *me*, which is really sad but true."

"So you're saying that because I had faith in my fiancé, you felt you had no choice but to sleep with him to prove a point?"

"God!" Tori exclaims, throwing her head back. "Laney, no. I'm just saying that I knew you'd have to see it for yourself to believe it. That's all. Cheese and crackers, woman!"

I'm too angry to be softened by the expression—cheese and crackers—that Tori has used all our lives, one that I always loved. At the moment, I have no tender feelings toward her at all. I just feel manipulated. And foolish.

"And now I'm supposed to thank you for sleeping with my fiancé to open my eyes? Well, forgive me if I just can't muster up any sincerity for something like that."

I can't help the bitter edge to my voice. She's lucky that's all she's getting. I jerk my hands out from under hers and sit back in my seat, needing a physical distance from Tori.

"Laney, that's what I've been trying to tell you. I. Didn't. Sleep. With. Him."

"And you expect me to believe that?"

"Why wouldn't you? When have I ever shown the tiniest bit of interest in Shane? I think he's a total girl. I like my men *manly*, you know that."

I narrow my eyes on her. "But we both know you've mistakenly fallen into bed with the wrong guy before."

Her cheeks turn a little pink. "I won't argue that, but never with *your* guy, Laney. Never. I would never do that. I knew you'd be home. I knew if he was the kind of man I thought he was that he'd do it in a heartbeat. I'm just sorry that I was right." Tori closes her eyes and whispers, "I'd give anything for him to have proved me wrong."

Suddenly, I feel . . . too much. I feel trapped. Suffocated. I feel tears threaten. I feel stupid and alone and confused. And I feel the need to get out of here.

"Tori, can we, um, can we finish this later? I really need to get going." I don't look up as I grab my purse and slide from the booth. Tori doesn't move to follow me. Or try to stop me. But before I can wheel my cart far from her, she reaches out and touches my arm as I pass.

"I love you, Laney Holt. I always have. You're like my family."

I wait until she moves her hand before I walk away. I push my buggy back to the produce aisle, where I left off. Tears are streaming down my face the whole way.

EIGHTEEN: *Jake*

I give the last strap a tug, tightening it around the bundle of supplies tied to the small bed at the back of the Jeep. I check the other tethers to make sure they're secure. When I'm pretty confident all our shit won't fall out in the middle of a mudhole, I turn to Laney.

"Ready?" I ask.

She smiles widely and nods her head. It's the first time she's seemed really . . . herself since she got back from the grocery store yesterday. I don't know what happened, and I'm not about to ask. I'm not sure she'd tell me, anyway. That thing where Laney's not like most women—the ones who feel the need to spill their guts on a regular basis—works against me in some cases. Like now. I wonder what's wrong, but I don't want to give Laney the wrong impression by seeming concerned.

You don't want her to think you care, you asshole?

I hide my frown as I open the passenger door for Laney. I don't know why I don't want her to know that I care. I just know that I don't. Maybe it's because caring comes with responsibility, and Laney doesn't know that I destroy the things I care about. She doesn't know that I *can't* be responsible for her. It's not just that it's more comfortable for me. It's that it's best for *her.*

We're both quiet on the drive up into what we locals call the "mountains." To those people who grew up around real mountains, these are more like really big hills covered in trees. But for people who live in a state that has a lot of flat land, these are mountains.

When we get to the tricky parts, the areas that travel over stretches of the river and go up and down really sharp inclines, I notice Laney grab the handle above the door and brace her feet against the floorboard.

"Now you know why they call them 'oh shit' handles," I tell her with a grin.

She smiles, but her eyes are wide, which makes my grin that much bigger.

A couple of times I hit a deep spot in the river and it jars us both pretty good. Laney gasps, but doesn't say a word. She's just flushed-faced and beaming when I look at her. She's learning to enjoy the shocks and surprises in any given moment. The thrill of a rush. The pleasure in not watching life from the sidelines. I know she was kind of looking for it when we met, but I can't help but watch her with a little bit of pride, to look at her when she's enjoying herself and think to myself that *I* did that. It makes me happy in some way, in some place I'd rather not explore too deeply. I just know I'm not ready to give it up quite yet. I'm not ready to give *her* up quite yet. So I'm gonna make the most out of this weekend.

"How much farther?" she asks at one point.

"Maybe four miles. Something like that."

She once admitted to me that she'd never been camping. I couldn't believe it. But it seems to be true, if I'm only judging by her level of excitement. And that's fine with me. I'm excited, too. Just for a different reason. I plan to have as much sex with this woman as I can possibly cram into three days and two nights. I need to start working her out of my system. I need to get this thirst for her under control. We don't have much time left, and I have to be ready to let her go.

As always, thinking about her leaving is like having a storm cloud settle over my life for a few seconds, which is exactly why I don't spend too much time dwelling on it. She needs to move on with her life and so do I. Once this is all said and done, we'll go our separate ways and that's that.

But still, I don't really *enjoy* thinking about it.

Up ahead, I see the clearing come into sight. When we top the knoll, I pull to a stop on one side of the camp and cut the engine. The instant the Jeep's throaty purr can't be heard, the sounds of nature seem ten times louder. Birds chirping, water rushing over rocks, the wind rustling the leaves—it's the most peaceful loud in the world.

I get out and start unpacking our supplies. Laney comes to stand behind me, holding out her arms. "Okay, gimme something."

I quirk one brow at her. "I'll give you something," I say suggestively.

She grins broadly. "I mean give me something useful."

I say nothing for about three seconds before I lunge for her. She's ready for me, though, and she takes off across the clearing, screaming at the top of her lungs. It only takes me a few long strides to catch her, and when I do, I wrap my arms around her waist, pull her back up against my chest and swing her like I'm going to throw her. "What was that you said?"

"Nothing, nothing, nothing," she half laughs-half squeals.

"I could've sworn there was an insult to my manhood in there somewhere."

I swing her around again, her legs flying out in front of us. "No, there wasn't! I just said that I wish I was useful."

"That's not how I remember it," I say, setting her on her feet.

"It's not my fault you're old," she mutters playfully.

"Oh, you really *are* asking for it." I turn her around in my arms and bend her back over them, teasingly biting at her throat. She giggles and arches her neck, grabbing at my shoulders with her hands.

"A girl's gotta do what a girl's gotta do to get your attention," she replies hoarsely.

I lift my head and look down into her face. "All you have to do is look my way and you've got my attention. My *full* attention."

Laney's blue eyes are light and sparkly and . . . happy. "And I can't ask for more than that," she says softly, staring up at me. She reaches up and touches my cheek with her fingertips, her smile fading into seriousness. "Jake, I . . ."

Like hitting the panic button, her words trigger a marked response in me. "Come on," I begin, hauling her upright. "We need to get this camp set up before it gets much later. We should be at the river, fishing for supper, in a couple of hours."

Laney nods, her smile bright once again. Almost too bright, in fact. And I can tell by the way she tucks her hair behind her ear that she's a little off-kilter.

Back at the Jeep, I hand Laney small things as I unpack them, telling her where they go.

"The way the fire pit is positioned, we'll put the tent over there," I say, pointing to the edge of the clearing that backs up to the ravine. I hand her the bound tent and poles. "Just set it over there. We'll put the cooler and kitchen-related stuff to the right and the two chairs in front of that ring of rocks. Inside that is where the fire will be."

"Sir, yes, sir!" she says, giving me a sassy salute as she prisses off with the tent.

"That's a little more like it. I love a woman that knows her place." Laney looks back over her shoulder and sticks out her tongue at me. "Do that again and see what happens," I tease. Rather than give me some pithy reply, she just keeps moving.

I watch her as she walks to the place I indicated and lays the tent down then turns to make her way back. She stops to dust something off her shorts, drawing my attention to her amazing legs. I immediately picture them wrapped around my waist, Laney's head thrown back, her nipples pointing at the sky, her tight body settled around me, and I wonder what she was going to say. Would she have told me she loves me? Or was it nothing like that at all? Although it would be a disaster for both of us if she had, I must admit that I like the thought of her being mine. All mine. Body, heart, and soul.

But that would be a disaster.

Especially for her.

After the Jeep is unloaded, I get the rubber mallet. We spread out the tent and I start pounding in stakes. Laney helps me when I need it and, otherwise, busies herself setting up the little table we brought to keep food stuff off the ground. Although I can't hear her, I can tell by the set of her mouth that she's humming. She does that often when she's doing something domestic, I've noticed. Obviously, it makes her happy. Yet another reason she doesn't need me in her life. I'm far from domestic.

When the tent is set up, I unzip it and hold open the flap for Laney to crawl inside. I try not to look too long at her perfect ass or think about the fact that she's down on all fours, the perfect position for me to sweep in and take her from behind.

My dick twitches inside my shorts, so I make a point to think of something else. *Anything* else.

"Hand me the sleeping bags," she says before I can duck inside.

I get the two rolls and toss them in to her before I join her inside the little dome. I watch as she rolls them out straight, side by side. Looking at them, I realize that I object. And not for sexual reasons. Chances are, we'll have sex in dozens of places and not one of them might be inside those sleeping bags. But that's not the point. The point is, I don't like the thought of not being able to feel her curled up at my side, like she's been every night for a couple of months now.

"If you unzip one and lay it out flat, we can zip the other one on top of it and make it a double," I propose.

"Oh, that's smart," she says, moving to do what I suggested. "That way we can share body heat."

"Yeah, if you say so," I murmur.

She looks at me over her shoulder and grins. "Among other things."

"That's more like it," I say.

With the bags set up properly, she turns toward me. "Now what?"

I don't think she's trying to be provocative. With Laney, I don't think she ever really *tries*. She just *is*. Everything she does is sexy as hell and makes my dick as hard as a chunk of granite. My . . . appetites have always been pretty voracious, but with Laney, they're even worse. I just can't seem to get enough of her.

"I can think of so many ways to answer that question, but I guess we'd better get down to the river."

"Whatever you say, Davey Crockett," she responds pluckily as she bends forward to crawl past me. This time, I have to grit my teeth as she passes me.

It's dark. Laney and I are sitting in front of the fire. She's between my legs, leaning back against my chest. We just finished our hot dogs. "Those were for an emergency, you know. *Just in case* we didn't get much out of the river."

Laney shrugs. "How was I supposed to know it would bother me so badly? I told you I'd never been fishing. It's not like Daddy is exactly outdoorsy."

"But Laney, God put fish here for us to eat. People would've starved to death in the old days if the women were like you."

She tilts her head to one side and looks back at me. Her eyes are big, soulful drops of sky blue that glisten in the firelight.

"Maybe they didn't go. Maybe their men just brought them back fish filets to throw in a skillet and cook." She nods as if that explains it all.

I shake my head and sigh. "Maybe. All I can say is thank God for hot dogs."

She grins and rests her head back against my shoulder. "Thank you for throwing the fish back."

"I think it's weird that you'd rather eat Porky Pig than a damn cold fish, but . . ."

"I didn't have to *catch and kill* Porky Pig. *That's* the difference."

"You're such a girl," I say mildly.

"And you're such a guy."

"Damn straight."

"But that's the way it's supposed to be. The men are the ones who are supposed to be okay with doing these heartless things. The women are the ones that stay back at camp to patch up skinned knees and dry tears."

"I can see you doing that."

"Can you really?" she asks, looking back at me again.

"Definitely. Sometimes I get the feeling you're trying to do that to *me.*"

"Do what to you?"

"Patch me up."

"Is that such a bad thing?"

"No. I just don't want you wasting your time on a project like me. Some things can't be fixed, Laney, no matter how much you wish they could."

"Maybe you just need to let someone try."

"You think?" I respond casually, looking away from her eyes.

"I do."

"Well, if you wanna know what *I* think, it's that we need some marshmallows. What say you?"

Her lips curve into a smile, but it's a sad one.

"Marshmallows sound good."

The mood is a little somber as we peel down the tips of the green sticks we used to roast our hot dogs to make way for marshmallows. Several times, I find myself glancing over at Laney, watching her fingers work, admiring how satiny her skin looks in the flickering light.

If I'm being honest, I know she's developing feelings for me. I should've put a stop to this a couple weeks ago when I started suspecting. But the truth is, I didn't want to. Still don't. Why? Because I'm a selfish bastard.

It's been so long since I've let anybody get close to me. And now that I have, I find myself wanting to enjoy it for a while, whether it hurts her or not.

But that's not fair to her. It's not her fault I'm this way. And, ultimately, she shouldn't have to pay the price for it.

As Laney eases her stick into the fire, letting the marshmallows hover just above the flame, the metaphor is not lost on me—her getting too close to the flame, her in danger of getting burned. Badly. I know what she's doing. And I know I should stop her. And I will.

Just not yet.

I reason that she's not past the point of no return yet. I've still got a little time to enjoy what we have before I have to make my move.

And enjoy it I will.

One of Laney's marshmallows catches fire and she jerks back her stick, blowing the flaming blob until the fire is doused. Gingerly, she picks off gooey globs of sticky sugar and plops them in her mouth.

"To never have been camping before, you sure have this part down pat," I observe, smiling as she licks white cream from her fingers.

"Any kid who's ever been near a fire of any kind has roasted marshmallows."

"Ahhh, so you're an old hand at it." She nods and smiles. "Obviously you enjoy it."

"They're made of sugar. And they're melty. What's not to love?"

I stare at her beautiful face, the one that matches what seems to be a beautiful soul.

What's not to love, indeed.

A big blob drops off Laney's stick and hits the front of her shirt. "Awww," she whines, picking at it to salvage what she can. "I hate to waste even one bite."

Before I can even suggest it, as if reading my mind, Laney lays her empty stick to the side and slips her shirt over her head. Her bra is the color of the setting sun and, in the soft light, makes her skin look like it glows.

Within a fraction of a second, my body is as hot as the fire I'm sitting in front of.

A month ago, she would never have done something like that. Hell, a couple of *weeks* ago she wouldn't have done something like that. She's come a long way.

Where has the time gone? And how can I get some of it back?

When she's finished picking marshmallow from her shirt, I catch her before she can put her shirt back on. "I'll make you a deal," I tell her. "I'll share some of my marshmallows with you." She's paused with her arms half raised above her head and she's peeking at me over her hands. "On one condition."

One of Laney's eyebrows rises, something she's just started doing. Something that drives me wild. "What's that?"

"I get to feed them to you. But I'm messy, so you'd better take the rest of your clothes off."

Even in the low light, I see her pupils dilate. She doesn't answer me. She just lowers her arms. Slowly.

At first it seems she isn't going to answer me at all. But then, with her eyes locked on mine, she stands to her feet and reaches for the button on her shorts. She unbuttons then unzips them.

Very deliberately, very carefully, she wiggles her hips back and forth as she slides the khaki material down her long legs. When she straightens, I see that she's not wearing any panties. She must not have put any back on after she changed out of her wet clothes earlier.

I get hard immediately.

"Where do you want me?" she asks, her expression the picture of innocence.

I pat the ground beside me. "Right here. You'll stay warm near the flames." Gracefully, Laney steps toward me then sinks down to the ground. "Lie back," I tell her.

And she does.

I hold the stick of marshmallows over the flames for a few seconds to make sure they're nice and hot before I dip my finger into one. The crispy outer shell gives way to a hot, sticky center that coats my finger. I trace it over Laney's bottom lip. "Lick." I watch the pink tip of her tongue sneak out to snatch the sugar from her lip. My mouth waters. "My turn," I tell her.

I get some more marshmallow on my finger and I drag it from her chin down to the valley between her breasts. I bend my head and use my lips and tongue to lick her skin clean.

"Mmm, delicious," I say when I raise my head and meet her eyes. Laney says nothing, but I can hear her short, heavy breathing. She's excited. And when she's excited, I'm *even more* excited.

I scoop some more marshmallow onto my finger and hold it to Laney's mouth. "Open," I tell her. Wordlessly, she parts her lips. I slip my fingertip inside. It's all I can do not to strip and dive right into her when I feel her suck on it and swirl her tongue around the tip.

With my eyes locked on Laney's, I reheat the remaining marshmallows. After a few seconds, one catches fire. I hold the stick up to Laney's lips. "Blow."

Obediently, she puckers her lips and puffs out the flame.

"My turn again," I state, leaning forward to hook my finger under the edge of her bra strap and tug it down. When one button-like nipple is exposed, I pierce the browned marshmallow and dip my finger inside, transferring the warm gooeyness onto Laney's nipple. I hear her gasp at the heat of it. I look up at her face and see her eyes drift shut in ecstasy. "So sweet," I whisper as I bend over her to suck away the sticky sugar.

When I straighten, Laney opens her eyes and looks at me. Her lips are parted, and I'd be willing to bet if she were wearing panties, they'd be soaked.

"Where else can I put some?" I ask.

I see her pearly teeth sink into her bottom lip and I suppress a growl. I tighten the hold on my libido. I want to draw this out a little longer. No matter how much it hurts me.

I smear a shiny, white streak down Laney's stomach to her navel, where I deposit a blob of cream. Leaning forward, I lick the trail and then lap up every last bit of marshmallow from her belly button.

Her stomach trembles as I lick a little lower. My cock jumps in response. She knows where I'm headed next. She knows what I'm going to do. And she's practically vibrating with anticipation.

Straightening, I put the stick in the fire once more. I heat the remaining marshmallow. When the outside starts to darken, I remove it. I blow on it until it cools enough that I can handle it. And then I stick my tongue right into the hot center. It burns, but not enough that I can't tolerate it.

Bending over Laney, I nudge her legs farther apart with my elbow and run my sugar-coated tongue between her folds, leaving a hot, sticky sweet trail all the way down the crease to her opening. The noise she makes is somewhere between a gasp and a moan. To me, it just sounds like a plea for me to continue.

"That's it, baby," I say, moving my lips against her, "you know I wanna hear you."

I lave her slick flesh with my tongue, enjoying the sweet taste of marshmallow mixed with the sweet taste of Laney. I suck her clit into my mouth. She digs her fingers into my hair and holds me to her, her hips moving against my face. I push one sticky finger inside her. She's warm and tight and so, so wet. I move it slowly in and out of her, in a rhythm that matches my tongue. I hear her start to pant, so I slide another in beside it. More aggressively, I penetrate her with my fingers as I lick her into a frenzy.

Her hips move in time with me, and when I feel her muscles tense, I thrust another finger in alongside the first two and slam them into her until I hear her cry out.

Laney's voice echoes through the ravine below, my name bouncing back around us. But I'm not done. And neither is she.

Sliding my tongue down, I thrust it inside her, licking her higher and higher into her orgasm. My need for her is building.

I smell her delicious body, more mouthwatering than the marshmallows. I taste her natural sweetness, pouring onto my tongue and mingling with the sugar. I feel her everywhere—her hands in my hair, her legs brushing my face, her body writhing against my chest.

"Jake, please," she whimpers softly. "Please. I need to feel you inside me."

I lift my head and look at her. Her eyes are heavy. Her cheeks are flushed. Her nipples are puckered. Her lips are trembling.

I strip off my shorts as fast as I can and position myself between her legs. For a second, I feel frantic, too, but I make myself slow down.

I lean back on my heels, poised between her spread thighs. I look down as I rub the glistening head of my cock over her swollen lips. I tease the entrance and I feel her slippery cave clutching at me. I bite back a groan.

I glance up at her. Her chest is heaving with every breath she takes. She's right on the edge of another one. And if I wait just another second . . .

I put my palms on the insides of her thighs and I push them farther apart, easing an inch into her. "Lean up," I tell her. "I want you to watch."

Laney levers her body up onto her elbows. I withdraw fully so she can see the light flicker off the wetness covering me. "See that? That tastes like sugar. *You* taste like sugar," I say, slowly slipping the head back into her and rocking it in and out. She's sucking at me, begging me to fill her up. "You're all over my tongue," I say, thrusting a little farther in. "I can still taste you."

I look up at Laney. She's watching me tease her, her mouth a silent O of pleasure, her eyes little more than slits as she struggles to keep them open. I pull out and circle my fingertip over the head of my cock then reach up and drag it over Laney's bottom lip. I feel like I might explode when her tongue sneaks out and licks it off.

"So good," I whisper. "I want you to see how good we are together." I moan, straining to keep my strokes short and shallow. "I want you to watch me come inside you. I want you to feel it. Filling you up." My control is slipping. "Filling you up and running back out." My heart is racing and I can't hold off much longer. "I want you to see the mixture of us dripping from my cock. Us. Together."

Her face looks pained, but I know what she's feeling—desperation. She wants this every bit as badly as I do.

Pulling her hips in closer to mine, I angle my body and drive as hard and as deep into her as I can. She takes every inch of me and her cry tells me what I can already feel.

She's coming again. That's all it took for her. She came undone. And with every spasm of her body around mine, I know I'm not far behind.

I watch Laney watching us, watching my thick cock crash into her over and over again. And then I feel it. It steals over me like darkness. It robs me of sight and sound for a few seconds, and all I can sense is the tension in every muscle of my body.

And then I'm coming. I spew into her, knowing she's watching, and I love it.

I've never come so hard before. For a few seconds, I lose touch with reality. Like an animal, I arch my back and throw back my head and growl. I growl as I spill everything I have deep inside Laney.

As she watches.

I can feel it oozing out of her, all around me. And when I pull out, I can see it dripping off me. And so can she.

NINETEEN: *Laney*

I hear Jake get up, but I don't feel like moving yet. Every inch of skin, every fiber of muscle, and every last nerve is supremely satisfied. My stretch is languorous, making me feel like a cat.

I lean up on one elbow to watch Jake climb out of the tent. Even if I weren't attracted to him—which I am, and which I fear is becoming very dangerous for me—I could appreciate his beauty. His legs are long and muscular. His butt is hard and round. His waist is narrow and trim. His back is V-shaped and his shoulders are wide. And everything is covered in flawless, golden skin.

When he turns to look back at me from just outside the entrance, I see him from the front. I feel my cheeks flush when I look at him. I still can't believe it's that big. And that it fits in me.

But it does. Oh, how it does!

Chills spread down my arms and chest, and I feel a gush of warmth. I look quickly back to Jake's face. He's grinning.

"You're very much awake now, aren't you?"

I nod slowly, grinning broadly.

"Hold that thought. I'll be right back."

I lie back and snuggle down in the sleeping bag, smiling happily as I listen to the sounds of the forest waking up. In the distance, I can hear the babble of the river, which reminds me that I actually have to pee.

Dang it!

Throwing on Jake's big T-shirt, I slip out of the tent and find a place in the nearby woods that has a marked lack of poison oak. I see a fallen tree and head for it. It's always good to have something like that close at hand. That way, if I lose my balance, I can reach out and grab it rather than falling onto the ground while I'm trying to pee.

I turn my back to the log and lift Jake's shirt. Before I can squat, a sharp pain tears through the back of my left knee. I yelp, partly out of surprise and partly due to the discomfort.

I whirl around toward the fallen tree, looking for what assaulted me. I feel the blood drain from my face when I spy the beautifully patterned, rust-colored snake coiled inconspicuously on the back side of the log. Its head is still lifted and it's facing me as though ready to strike again. Pain is radiating down the back of my calf already and all I can think, in total Jake style, is *oh shit, oh shit, oh shit.*

I know virtually nothing about snakes, so I don't know whether I should move or not, or how much trouble I'm in. I do the only thing I can. I yell for Jake.

"Jake! Help!"

My pulse is pounding in my ears and my leg is on fire as I stand perfectly still and watch the snake. I'm relieved when I hear the crashing of Jake coming through the woods toward me.

As if sensing that danger is on the way, the snake slithers off its perch and sneaks into the bracken surrounding the fallen tree. Overwhelmed with relief and feeling a bit lightheaded from the pain in my leg, I sink to my knees just as Jake finds me.

"Laney, what's wrong?" he asks. There's panic in his voice, which actually makes me feel like smiling. But I don't. The pain in my leg seems to be increasing by the second.

"A snake bit me," I breathe.

"Where? And where is the snake?"

I roll slightly to the side and point to the back of my leg. Jake examines it and then looks back to my face. He gently takes my chin between his fingers and looks closely at me.

"Which way did it go, Laney?" he asks quietly.

"Off the back of the log, into the woods."

"I need to find the snake. I need to know what bit you. Stay here. I'll be right back," Jake promises. He brushes my lips with his, so tender and sweet it makes me want to cry, before he stands up and turns a complete circle. Before I can ask what he's doing, he takes a good-sized rock from the ground and hefts it a time or two, as if to check its weight. With it tucked against his palm, Jake walks to the log, steps cautiously over it, and moves farther into the forest.

I pray hazily for God not to let him get bitten, too, as I lie back against the cool ground. I would be devastated if something happened to him because he was trying to help me.

I don't know how much time has passed when Jake comes back. Gone is the rock, replaced by a length of wiggling snake body.

I gasp in shock. "Jake, it might—"

He holds the snake up just long enough for me to get a good look at it. And see that it's missing its head. "Is this what bit you?"

I look closely at the snake. The color and markings are unmistakable. "Yes, that's it."

"It's a copperhead," he says, tossing it back into the woods. Jake's face is solemn, which worries me. He bends and gently sweeps me into his arms, careful not to jostle my leg or put too much pressure on the bend of my left knee. "We need to get you out of here."

I'm not panicking. Mainly, I'd say, because my leg hurts so badly it's hard to think of much else. I just want the pain to stop.

"Copperheads are poisonous, right?"

"Yes."

"Aren't you supposed to cut it and suck the poison out or something like that?"

Jake grins, but it doesn't completely erase the look of concern on his face. "Do you *want* me to cut you and suck the poison out?"

"Well, if that's what you're supposed to do . . ."

"With some venomous snakebites, that might be the case, but with a copperhead, fortunately their strike is their warning, so they don't often inject very much venom. I'm going to get the first aid kit and clean it then we'll head down the mountain."

I consider this new information, feeling somewhat relieved. But still, my leg is hurting so bad!

"What about all your stuff? The camp?"

"I don't care about all that shit. My main concern is getting you to the hospital so they can give you some antivenom and something for the pain."

Jake sets me in one of the chairs in front of what used to be the fire. I watch him dig through a metal box in the back of his Jeep and produce a small white square. As he walks back, I notice the fresh blood on his arm and one thigh. When I twist my leg and look down at it, I see the blood running from the wound at my knee.

"Bleeding is a good thing, right? To clean out the bite or something?"

"Copperhead bites bleed quite a bit. It has something to do with the way the venom affects your blood cells." Jake kneels in front of me, opens the white box and sets it on the ground at my feet. "This is gonna sting, but I need to clean it before I put some gauze on it, okay?"

I nod.

Whatever Jake pours onto a cotton ball is liquid hell. I'm sure of it when he presses it to my already hurting leg and it makes it hurt even more.

"Almost done," he says, dabbing gingerly.

I glance down and see the blood trickling even as he swipes at it. Nausea creeps over me like a swell of unbearable heat. Sweat beads on my forehead. "Jake, I feel sick."

"Slow deep breaths. We'll be on the road in a minute."

With quick-yet-competent movements, Jake folds a few squares of gauze into a thick pad and presses it lightly to the snakebite. He then winds a roll of gauze loosely around my knee and fastens it with tape. It's just enough pressure to keep the gauze in place.

"Not the best job, but it'll do," he says, closing the white box and then standing to his feet. "Let's blow this joint."

Before he can scoop me up into his arms, I have a moment of clarity. "Aren't you going to get dressed?"

He's still naked. And I'm still mostly naked.

Jake looks down at this body then back up at me. "Well, you're wearing my shirt. How 'bout we settle on a pair of shorts for both of us?"

I nod. "Sounds good."

Jake ducks into the tent and, after a few seconds, emerges wearing shorts and tennis shoes, carrying my shorts from last night. "Here," he says, holding the shorts open at my feet, "step into these and then I'll carry you to the Jeep."

He pulls me slowly to my feet and I put my hand on his shoulder to steady myself as I step into my shorts. It's so sweet that, before I can do it for myself, Jake pulls the shorts up and fastens them at my waist.

When he meets my eyes, he winks. "Strange. I never seem to fantasize about getting you *into* your shorts."

His calm charm makes me feel more at ease. Careful to mind my leg, Jake reaches for me, swinging me up into his arms and heading for the Jeep. I lay my head on his chest. I know I should be afraid. Up here in the mountains, hurt. All alone with a bad boy, someone the whole town looks down on. But I'm not afraid. I'm in good hands. I have no doubt.

The drive back down the mountain seems twice as long, although, according to the dashboard clock, it's actually shorter. Of course, I wasn't in pain on the way up, either.

When we pass over the river at a spot I remember as being fairly close to the bottom, Jake takes out his phone and powers it up.

"I should have signal by now," he says by way of explanation. He punches in a short couple of numbers and then holds the phone to his ear. "Yes, ma'am, I'm on my way down the mountain behind the Theopolis peach orchard. I have a friend with me who's been bitten by a copperhead. Could you send the paramedics?"

Jake answers a few of her questions and then gives the woman his address. After a few seconds of listening, he thanks her and hangs up.

"Why did you do that? I can make it to the hospital." I'm not sure how to take his actions, but I'm not feeling good about them. Should I be more worried? Is this bite more serious than I think? Or is Jake just trying to get rid of me?

"You need the antivenom as quickly as possible. The sooner you get it, the more effective it is. By calling it in now, the ambulance can be at the house by the time we get to the bottom of the mountain, giving you at least twenty minutes. And by calling it in *as a snakebite*, the hospital can make sure the ambulance has it on board when they come out."

"Oh," I say with a nod. That makes sense. False alarm.

We ride in silence the rest of the way down.

The paramedics are just coming down Jake's driveway as we drive up from the field. They pull to a stop, we pull to a stop, and then Jake hops out and comes around to the passenger side to get me. He carries me to the back of the ambulance just as the EMTs are extending the legs on the stretcher. He sets me gently on the thin mattress and backs away.

The emergency techs are both older guys, which makes me feel at ease somehow. Maybe it just seems that the older they are, the more experience they should have. Or at least that's my way of thinking.

"Where were you bitten?" This comes from paramedic number one, on my left.

"The back of my left knee."

He nods to paramedic number two, who begins placing a cuff around my arm as paramedic number one lifts my leg to examine the bite.

"What's your name, ma'am?" the one on my right asks as he starts placing stickers on my chest.

"Laney."

"Is this your husband, Laney?" he asks, nodding to Jake.

"No, he's, um, he's a friend."

I use Jake's term. It feels just as cold and hopeless as it did when I heard him use it on the phone.

"Do you have family in the area, Laney?"

I feel a moment of dread. I gulp, feeling tears threaten. This is not the end I had thought our wonderful camping trip would have. Not at all. And now my parents will be involved.

"Yes, I do."

"What are their names?"

"Graham Holt is my father and—"

"Graham Holt, the preacher?"

"Yes, sir."

"Well, all right then, Laney, we'll get a hold of your father and have him meet us at the hospital."

"I'd prefer you not, actually. Can't Jake just come with me?"

The men look at one another across me, and then the one on my left clears his throat and answers. "Sure he can, but we'll need some family member present in case something should happen."

My stomach sinks and I nod. "Okay."

I look to Jake. His smile is tight and his hands are shoved down into his shorts pockets. "I'll meet you at the hospital, Laney."

I nod and smile, knowing that it's a pathetic one, what with my chin trembling.

"Laney, are you allergic to any medications?" EMT number one asks.

"No, sir."

"Good. When we get you in the back here, I'm going to start an

IV and give you some pain medication. Then I'll be giving you some medicine to help neutralize the snake venom, okay?"

"Yes, sir."

"It's important that you tell me how you're feeling, all right?"

"Yes, sir."

With a jolt, the two men collapse the legs of the stretcher and stuff me in the back of the ambulance. I lift my head and my eyes meet Jake's as one of the guys closes the doors. He looks pale. And upset. And it's all because of me. I've ruined what was supposed to be a fun weekend. What could quite possibly be our *last* weekend.

When I can no longer see him, I don't hold back the tears. I let them flow.

"I'll have that pain controlled in just a few minutes. You hang in there, Laney," he says as he unwraps tubing and punctures a bag of fluid.

I give him a watery smile. I don't think he can numb the pain I'm feeling right now. It has nothing to do with a snakebite.

I know I've looked at the doorway a dozen times. Where is Jake?

In my stomach, there's a sinking feeling that he just won't come, that this will be the end of us. This isn't the fun he was looking for. This isn't the kind of rush he enjoys. And I'm probably not the kind of girl that he'd ever give more than a few weekends to.

The doctor finishes examining my leg. He's tall and gaunt with a head full of wild salt-and-pepper hair, but he has a warm smile. "Well, Ms. Holt, you're one very lucky young woman. You're not out of the woods yet, but based on the reaction of the tissue surrounding the site, I'd say you were only very lightly envenomated. What that means for you is minimal tissue destruction, no systemic effects like nausea, vomiting—"

"Sorry to interrupt, but she said she was nauseous right after she was bitten."

My heart swells inside my chest. He came.

"Jake," I say, unable to keep the silly smile off my face. He winks at me quickly then turns his attention back to the doctor.

"Sorry I'm late, sir. I'm Jake Theopolis. I was with Laney when she was bitten."

The doctor nods, taking in this new information then turning back to me. "Are you feeling nauseous now, Laney?"

"No, sir."

"It was only something you experienced directly following the bite?"

"Yes, sir. I, um, I . . ." I feel my cheeks sting. I already feel stupid for what I'm about to say. "I get that way sometimes at the sight of blood. Especially my own."

He smiles kindly. "That's nothing to be embarrassed about. And it was a traumatic experience, which only heightens your senses. But it's a good sign that you're not feeling poorly anymore. If you'd been more heavily envenomated, you'd be experiencing nausea and vomiting now, along with a variety of other side effects of a copperhead bite. What I believe is that you'll have some local reaction like pain and swelling, possibly some bruising, but for the most part few lasting effects or disability in your leg. I think this young man's quick thinking probably saved you quite a bit of suffering."

Jake looks unaffected by the doctor's praise, but he doesn't look as miserable as he did at the house, either, so I'm sure it's welcome, whether he'd admit it or not.

"So when can I go home then?"

"Not for a couple of days." The doctor flips through my chart and glances back down at me. "But I'll do my best to have you out of here before your birthday." With a wink and a fatherly pat to my hand, he nods to Jake and then turns to walk out of the room.

"You've got a birthday coming up?" Jake asks.

"Yeah. Thursday."

"Why didn't you—"

"What on earth is going on here, Laney?"

I feel the blood drain from my face when I hear the booming voice and then see my father appear behind Jake.

"Nothing, Daddy. I'm fine."

"You're lying in a hospital bed. You are most certainly not fine." He comes around and sits on the edge of the bed, taking my hand in his. "What happened, baby girl?"

I see the worry in his eyes, etched on his face. "I went camping and got bitten by a snake."

He closes his eyes and brings our joined hands to his forehead. He's silent for the longest time. I know he's praying. "Thank the Lord you're okay," he says finally, opening his eyes to look at me.

"If it hadn't been for Jake, things might've turned out much differently," I say, hoping Jake's heroics will help my father to look more favorably upon him.

"Well, who were you camping with?" Daddy asks.

"Jake. That's what I mean. The doctor says his quick thinking probably saved me a lot of suffering."

"But isn't he the reason you're in this predicament *at all*?"

"Of course not! My getting bitten has nothing to do with him." I tug my hand free of my father's and sit up straighter in the bed. I don't like feeling as though he has such an advantage over me. He's lorded over me my whole life, and with him sitting and me half lying, it makes me feel intimidated. And I don't want to feel intimidated. I want to have the guts to make my father see what I see in Jake. Not what he thinks he knows about him.

"Well, if he hadn't taken you up in the mountains unsupervised you wouldn't have been bitten by a snake."

"Unsupervised? Daddy, I'm an adult. In a few days I'll be twenty-three years old. I'm long past needing supervision."

"That may be the case, but if you weren't up there doing things you weren't supposed to be doing, maybe this wouldn't have happened."

"And how do you know *what* we were up there doing?"

My temper flares. I can only imagine how Jake must feel, being the object of such harsh judgment and criticism most of his life.

"I'm not stupid, Laney. You think I don't know what happens when a man and a woman shack up together?"

"It's not like that, Daddy. Jake let me stay there when I didn't want to stay with you. If anything, that's on *you* for not respecting my decision about Shane."

"You can't blame me for loving you and wanting what's best for you."

"No, I can't. And I don't. But I do blame you for using such underhanded tactics. And for being so domineering. Daddy, you have to butt out of my life and let me make my own decisions. I don't need you to run my life."

"It appears that you do. Look what a mess you've already made of things."

"I haven't made a mess of anything. Things are going along just fine, just the way I want them to."

"Is this what you want? Is *he* what you want?"

His question isn't overtly insulting, but the emphasis he put on the word *he* makes his opinion of Jake crystal clear. And what's worse is that, with Jake looking on, I don't know how to answer that without incriminating myself. But I have to say something.

"What if I said yes? Would you stop?"

"Laney, you can't expect me to just step aside and watch you ruin your life."

Jake clears his throat and steps forward. The look on his face is unfathomable. But something in it breaks my heart. And makes me feel panicky. "Mr. Holt, it was nice to see you again, but I'll be leaving now. I don't want to upset Laney. She's been through enough today."

And with that, he turns and walks away.

The bigger man. And, in this case, the better man.

Tears sting my eyes. "How could you be so cold and mean, Daddy? What happened to the loving man I used to know?"

"I'm still that man, Laney. Can't you see that I do all this *because* I love you? *Because* I want what's best for you?"

"Don't you get it, Daddy? *He* is what's best for me. I'm in love with him."

The words slip out before I can stop them. They pour from my heart in anger and frustration, but also in truth. Truth I hadn't even consciously admitted to myself.

My father leans away as if I slapped him. "Don't be ridiculous. You are destined to be with Shane. Everyone can see it but you."

"No, I'm not. And everyone can see *that* except *you*."

TWENTY: *Jake*

There's a lot to do around the orchard. Between that and working a few shifts at the fire station, I'm keeping busy. The problem is, none of it is enough to make me stop thinking about this mess with Laney.

I wasn't ready for it to be over just yet. But it *has to be* now. As if it weren't enough to hear how terribly I fit into her perfect life and perfect future (at least in her father's eyes), fate stepped in and let her get bitten by a snake. Her hospitalization and subsequent inability to continue immediate work on my family's estate meant that the law office sent someone else to tie it up. Turns out that Laney was finished but for a few minor things that the new guy wrapped up in two days' time.

I don't know if she was dragging it out because of me, but if she was, that just means it's even better that it's over. At least for her. I'm no good for her. I knew that going in. I thought she did, too.

As for me, I'll just have to scratch this itch somewhere else. No, I've never had a woman get under my skin like this, but as I've heard numerous times throughout my life, I'm better off alone. And that means fleeting interludes with women, not real relationships. Nothing lasting. Certainly nothing permanent. And that's what Laney needs—forever. What she's ultimately after in life. And I just can't be that for her. So the best thing I can do is step aside and let someone who can give her that have a chance to do it.

But knowing all this, knowing that it makes the most sense from every perspective, doesn't make it bother me any less. The fact is, I don't *want* to scratch this itch with someone else. I wanted to get it out of my system with Laney. Sort of overdose it. Overdose with her. Flood my body with her until I didn't crave her anymore.

Damn that woman! What the hell has she done to me?

TWENTY-ONE: *Laney*

It's been nearly a week and no Jake. Deep down, I knew—*I just knew*—that he had feelings for me. I would've bet money on it. We had settled into what was very close to a marriage for a while. And he was thriving and happy. Or at least he seemed to be. But evidently I was wrong.

He hasn't been by to see me in the hospital since that first day, when my father acted so horribly. He hasn't called. Hasn't returned any of *my* calls. He just disappeared. Like he never was.

Only I can't seem to forget him. I can't pretend that he never was, because to my heart, he still *is*.

I lay my cell phone to the side. There's no point in leaving him any more messages. It's obvious that he's done with me. I just need to let it go.

I roll onto my side, willing myself not to cry, not to shed one more tear over him. I hear a throat clear behind me and my heart stutters. But when I turn over, I see Tori standing in the doorway.

"Hey," I say, unenthused.

My lack of zeal has nothing to do with her. I'm very ready to forgive her and move on. It has everything to do with the fact that she's not Jake. But she can't help that. Only Jake can fix that.

"I was going to stay away, but . . ."

She eases into the room, and I scoot into a sitting position in the bed, patting the space beside my legs. She gives me a small smile and comes to sit with me.

"So, how are things with you?" I ask.

Tori tilts her head to the side and gives me a disdainful look. "I'm not here to talk about my boring life. I'm here to visit my best friend who got bitten by a snake in the woods with *Jake Theopolis*." Tori's mouth drops open and her eyes sparkle. "Oh my God, Laney! You always said when you went wild, you'd do it your way. You weren't kidding."

I can't help but laugh. "Where'd you hear about that?"

"Well, your parents could only keep things hush-hush for a while. With you in such a public place as a hospital, there was nothing they could do to keep word from spreading. And spread it did!"

I lay my head back against the pillows and close my eyes. "Great," I sigh.

"Nah, it's not that bad. Pretty much everyone sees you as the victim. You know, big bad Jake lures sweet, innocent Laney into a trap."

"This town . . . Why am I not surprised?"

Tori shrugs and pushes her long hair back over her shoulder. "This is the kind of place that needs a villain. And Jake has always given them one. You know, taking advantage of girls." She snorts and adds, "As if he'd even have to ask twice."

I smile but say nothing.

A slow, mischievous grin creeps over Tori's face. "So, you wouldn't be willing to throw a girl a bone, would you? Tell me all about it?"

I give her a sad smile. "It's nothing you'd want to hear about."

Her eyes get big as saucers. "Are you kidding me? Laney, I've wanted to be on that guy's radar since kindergarten!"

I grin. "You have not."

She gives me a dubious look. "Laney. Come on. You know I developed early . . ."

She makes a good point. "For you and your hormones, kindergarten is probably right."

Tori gets a wistful look on her face and stares out into space. "Ahhh, the third grader that woke my sleeping body . . ."

That makes me giggle. "I don't think even *you* were quite that bad."

Tori palms her generous chest and gives them a shake. "I had boobs by the time I was nine. Trust me, everything else was just as early." Smiling, I just shake my head at her. "So come on. Spill."

I feel my smile die. What happened between me and Jake wasn't just a sexy sidetrack in my life. Sharing it with Tori would just make it feel dirty and . . . well . . . just less. "Nah, there's nothing really to spill." I fiddle with the edge of the sheet, avoiding her eyes.

I hear her gasp as she grabs my hand and stills it. "You didn't fall in love with him, did you?"

My eyes sting. Even *Tori* thinks I made a mistake. Is it so impossible that Jake could ever love someone like me?

It must be.

Tori says nothing for a couple of long minutes, minutes that give me time to collect myself.

"You know, Laney, I was thinking about the stuff with Shane. I hate to even bring it up again, but maybe you should just forget everything I said, forget everything that happened and give the guy another chance. I don't want for you to miss out on your happy ending because of what I did or what I think. That's a decision you need to make on your own, without my help and input."

I growl in frustration. "Not you, too!"

"I'm not saying you should marry the guy or take him back with open arms. I'm just saying that maybe you ought to at least give it one more chance. See how you feel. See how things go. I couldn't live with myself if I thought I cost you the dream you've had since childhood."

I meet Tori's bright, sincere blue eyes. People have always said we look a lot alike, only Tori's more vibrant. I know most meant it with regard to coloring, but I've always felt like I pale in comparison to her in *every* way. Shane choosing a free spirit like her only underscored it.

But now, just because I don't want to be the sweet goody-goody anymore doesn't mean I'm cut out to be vibrant like her. Someone who could ever hold the interest of Jake. Maybe I was overreaching by thinking someone like him could settle down with someone like me. Or settle down at all.

"Maybe my dream changed, Tor."

She gives my hand a squeeze. "Just make sure, Laney. Make sure you're doing things for the right reasons. Don't let me sway you. Or your dad. Or anyone else. Do what makes *you* happy."

Already, a plan is forming in my mind. I lean forward, giving my friend a smile. "You know what would make me happy?"

"What's that?"

"A birthday party."

"You're in the hospital, Laney. I hardly think—"

"I mean when I get out. A belated birthday party."

Tori's face lights up. "Now that's what I'm talkin' about."

TWENTY-TWO: *Jake*

I t's been well over a week since I've seen or talked to Laney. There's a guy at the market who knows her dad, and he says she's recovering very well so I know she's fine. And I know I'm doing the right thing by keeping my distance, but she's not making it easy.

I listen to her message. She left several earlier on, each of which was light and fun, even though I know she was bothered by my sudden disappearance. But this one is the only one I've listened to more than once. This is the one that's tempting me. It came in after I hadn't heard from her for a day or two. And the tone is just . . . different.

Hey, Jake. It's Laney. Since my leg is doing so much better, I got out of the hospital yesterday. One of my friends is throwing me a little belated birthday party at Lucky's Thursday night. I hope you can come. I'd like to buy you a drink before I leave.

Before she leaves. She's going back home. Back to her real life. The life she had before she met me. She's ready to move on. Surely it would be all right for me to go and have one drink with her, wish her a happy birthday.

Surely.

I don't call her back, but I already know where I'll be Thursday night.

Saying my good-byes.

TWENTY-THREE: *Laney*

My leg looks almost totally back to normal. The swelling around my knee is almost gone. Gone enough for me to wear a cute little skirt.

I know I shouldn't be setting myself up this way—wearing a skirt just because Jake always said he loved my legs, hoping to spur him into a confession of love if I make one first—but I can't help it. I've never really taken any huge risks in life until I met Jake. And this is the most important one of all. I *have to* tell him how I feel. Even though I cringe at the thought of making a fool of myself, I have to do it. I might not get another chance. When things are settled up with the orchard, Jake might leave, and I'll never be able to track him down. It's now or never.

And I choose now.

Because I can't stand the thought of living with the never.

Putting a few more curls in my hair and then piling it all up on top of my head, I spray some perfume at my throat, give my lips a coat of gloss, and then make my way to the door.

I guess this is as ready as I'll ever be.

TWENTY-FOUR: *Jake*

When I walk through the door at Lucky's, I search the crowd for Laney's familiar blond head. She's at a table in the corner, laughing with some friends. There are eight or ten people there with her. Some look like faces I remember seeing in high school. Maybe in one of the classes behind me. Probably Laney's age.

I make my way to the bar. I see *several* familiar faces here. This was my element before I left, starting with my first fake ID that everyone knew was fake, but didn't care. I always ran with the older, wilder crowd.

"Well, if it isn't Jake Theopolis," the girl behind the bar purrs. Her name is Lila something. She's a good ten years older than me. We had a thing when I was still in high school. I'm sure she had "things" with a lot of guys around town. "Where you been, sugah?"

I slide onto a bar stool. "Around. Working mostly. Gimme a beer. Whatever you've got on tap is fine."

Her heavily made-up green eyes flicker back to me several times as she pours my beer. "This one's on the house," she says, placing it on a napkin in front of me. "Call it a welcome home present. The first of a few." She winks at me, which tells me that one of my presents will be her. Naked. Riding me like a wild stallion. I remember that about her. She likes it on top.

Unbidden, a vision of Laney on top of me interrupts. I frown.

Damn the woman!

I glance over at her table. She's preoccupied with her company. I'll wait and talk to her when she's alone. Or at least *a little more* alone.

"Did I hear her say you're Jake Theopolis?" a voice asks from my right. I turn to see a guy lean on the stool next to me. "Single malt scotch, neat," he says to Lila, tossing a bill on the bar.

"Yep, that's me," I tell him, taking a sip of my beer. There's something about him that I don't like right off the bat. I'm not sure if it's the perfectly combed hair that's undoubtedly loaded with all kinds of styling shit, or if it's the dress shirt with unloosened tie that makes me think he's a pretentious asshole. But something about him makes my lip want to curl. "Do I know you?" I ask, knowing full well that I don't.

"No, but I think you know my fiancée."

I arch my brow at him, doubting very much that I do. "Oh yeah? And who's that?" I sip my beer, wishing the guy would just take the hell off before he makes me get rude.

"Laney Holt."

It's all I can do not to spit a mouthful of beer all over the bar in front of me.

"Laney Holt is your fiancée?"

"Yep. We got engaged a few months back. Had a little bit of a misunderstanding before she came back here to sort out on your family's case, but we got things worked out while she was in the hospital. Now I'm hoping we can set the date and get this thing done."

Get this thing done?

He makes it sound more like a formality than the day when he'll pledge his undying devotion to the love of his life.

"Is that right?"

"Yeah, that's right," he says, sipping the scotch that Lila just set in front of him. He leans in toward me, his eyes suddenly flat. "Look, I don't know what happened between you two while we were . . . having problems, but you need to know that it's over. Laney Holt will be my wife. And there's nothing you can do to stop it. There's no need for you to make a fool of yourself by trying. Just let it go and I won't have any reason to pay you a visit."

I turn on my seat to fully face this guy. "Surely you didn't just make the mistake of threatening me."

"It's only a threat if you choose to pursue Laney. If you walk away, I'm man enough to say no harm, no foul. I've forgiven her. End of story. Now *you* just need to walk away."

For a dozen different reasons, everything in me wants to break this jackass's jaw like it's made of glass. But even though I don't quite believe this guy, something is making me pause. Why would he say these things if they weren't true, knowing that Laney is close and all I'd have to do is go ask her?

As much as it pains me to engage in civilized conversation with him, I grit my teeth and do it. I need to know if he's telling the truth. I need to know if Laney really has moved on.

"You'll understand if I need a little more than just your word to go on," I tell him tightly.

His smile is as hard as his cold gray eyes. "Of course." He glances at the table where Laney's sitting. One of the girls sitting near her looks in our direction. I see this guy, Shane I think his name was, motion for her. The girl grabs her empty glass, says something to one of the others, and then heads our way.

"Harmony, you go to church with Laney, right? You two have been friends for years, right?"

Harmony, a small girl with springy black hair, looks around nervously. "Hush with the name calling, Shane. You know my mother would kill me if she found out I was here."

"We're not telling anybody anything. I just wanted you to clear up something for my friend here. He doesn't believe that Laney and I got engaged. He thinks I'm still the same guy from college. You know, the confirmed bachelor." The guy winks at her conspiratorially, making me think that what happened with him and Laney's friend, Tori, was probably legitimate on his part. I'd say this son of a bitch is a creeper. I'd be willing to bet on it.

"You two went to college together?" she asks me. "Aren't you from around here?"

"Yeah, originally, but I moved away a while back."

"Ohhh," she says, eyeing me appreciatively. "Well, sorry. You're gonna lose the bet. Shane and Laney have been engaged for months. No one knew what to think when she showed up at church without him those few times. We couldn't believe she'd let a guy like Shane go."

She gives him a smile and Shane winks at her. I want to puke.

"You're sweet, Harmony," Shane oozes, "but it all worked out in the end. Thanks for clearing that up, honey."

"Sure," Harmony chirps, sliding onto a stool to get a refill of her drink.

"It's on me," Shane tells Lila, who nods her understanding. "So, any more questions, *brother*?"

"Just in what orifice you'll be wanting my foot if you call me *brother* one more time."

Shane throws his hands up in surrender, but there's a smug expression on his face that clearly says he thinks he won.

And I guess, truth be told, he did. I didn't realize I was even in the game until just now. But this was a much-needed reality check. While Laney is far too good for a dirty bastard like this guy, she's far too good for me, too. And there's only one of those two things I can help her with.

Not that she needs any help. Laney is perfectly capable of making her own choices. And if she chooses a douche bag like this, then he's the luckiest douche bag in the world.

I wash that bitter thought down with a long pull of my beer before I toss a couple bills on the bar and get up. "Good seeing you again, Lila," I say to her, never taking my eyes off Shane. "As for *you*, all I can tell you is that if you hurt her, you'd better hope to God that you've got a damn good hiding place. You don't want to be seeing me again." Just to prove my point to both of us, I half lunge at this pompous prick. I grin when he flinches. "That's what I thought."

I aim for the door, but as I glance to my right, I see Laney's platinum head, calling to me like a beacon in the dead of night. Detouring, I make my way over to her, leaning around the person closest to her so I can whisper in her ear. "Happy birthday, Laney. Be happy."

With a kiss to her cheek, I turn to leave.

"Wait, Jake!" she calls, struggling to get around chairs and bodies. "There's something I wanted to tell you."

I put my hand up to stop her. This doesn't need to go on any longer. I hurt the things I love. That's why I don't love. And Laney deserves better. "Don't bother. I already know." I give her a wink. "I'll be heading out soon. Stay and enjoy your party. I'll see you around."

And, with that, I turn and walk away, leaving Laney and whatever she might've felt for me behind.

TWENTY-FIVE: *Laney*

A thousand things are running through my head as I watch Jake walk out of the bar. And out of my life.

He said, "See you around," but we both know that will never happen. Once he goes back home, that'll be it. I'll probably never see him again.

And he obviously wants it that way. He knows that will happen, too.

Slowly, I sink back into my seat, debating the wisdom of chasing after him. But what purpose would that serve? Just to further embarrass myself? I knew what he was like. I knew what he wanted, what he was capable of giving in terms of a relationship. I was just stupid enough to think he might change. Or that I could change him. Or that what we had might make him *want* to change.

Only it didn't. Nothing changed.

Except for me.

I barely feel like the same person that came back to Greenfield at the beginning of summer. Fall is approaching and, like nature that undoubtedly feels the death of winter coming on, I feel the death of

my heart coming on. I got what I wanted—an escape from my life
and who I was. But it came at great cost.

My happiness. My heart.

Where do I go from here?

"Laney," I hear from what seems like a thousand miles away. I
look up and find Shane standing on the other side of the table, watching me with a sad expression on his face. He tips his head to one side,
a silent invitation for me to come around to him. On numb legs, with
my mind elsewhere, I get up and maneuver my way out from behind
the table and cross to him.

"What is it, Shane?" I can't keep the irritation from my voice. A
conversation with my ex, no matter how short, is the last thing I need
right now. I want to strangle whoever it was that told him about my
party to begin with.

"I wanted to tell you I'm sorry," he begins.

"Shane, not now. I know what—"

"Not about that, although I'm sorry about that and I still wish
you'd let me explain my side of the story. But that's not what I meant.
I just wanted you to know I'm sorry about what happened with that
Jake guy. Nobody deserves to be treated the way he treated you."

I frown. Shane has my full attention now.

"What do you mean?"

"I just talked to him at the bar. He was dreading coming in here
to tell you good-bye. He was afraid you'd make a big scene. Try to
follow him or something."

I narrow my eyes on him. "What? That's ridiculous! He would
never say that."

Or would he?

"If you don't believe me, ask Harmony. She got a refill on her
drink when we were talking."

I turn to Harmony, who is sitting on the other side of the table,
talking with a couple of our friends. "Harmony!" I call. She looks up

and smiles. "Did you see Shane talking to Jake Theopolis a few minutes ago?"

"Is that who that hot guy was?" She laughs. "Yeah, I did, but I got your back, Laney. Don't you worry." She winks at me and raises her glass. My stomach squeezes into a tight knot, as if it's shrinking away from the explosion that's happening inside my chest.

I glance back at Shane. He looks genuinely sympathetic.

"I feel like this is all my fault, Laney. I should never have believed Tori when she said it was just a prank we were pulling. I—"

"What? Tori did *not* tell you that!"

"She did! Hand to God," he says, holding up his hand as if he's swearing.

I shake my head. It's all just too much right now. "It doesn't matter now, Shane. It's done. Over. No hard feelings, okay?"

He looks down as he takes my left hand in his and begins fiddling with my ring finger. "Is there any chance my ring will ever find its way back here again?"

I pull my hand away. "Shane," I say, backing away. From him. From the crowd. From the pain. From this place. "I just can't do this right now."

And with that, I run. I just run.

TWENTY-SIX: *Jake*

I can feel sweat running down my chest as I sit, perched on the edge of the big boulder, gulping down a bottle of water.

"You're gonna puke if you don't slow down," a familiar voice says from behind me. I turn to see Jenna walking casually up the path toward me. "And, dude! There's no puking on my rock."

"This isn't your rock," I argue good-naturedly. "This is family rock."

"Which, in this family, means it's mine."

I shrug. "Yeah, pretty much. Spoiled brat."

"Arrogant dickweed."

She climbs up the back of the rock and scoots down to sit beside me facing the river. We used to sit like this when we were little. When we'd help in the orchard on hot summer days, we'd come here to swim in the river and cool off, then we'd get up on the rock to dry. We weren't allowed in the water without Dad around, but we did it anyway. I was the only one who ever got in trouble for it, though. Of course. Dad would always catch me in my room later to give me the big lecture on how my carelessness had already cost him one family member, that he wouldn't allow it to happen again.

"What're you doing here? Finally get up enough balls to come home?" I ask, pushing against her shoulder with my own.

"Something like that," she answers vaguely. "How're things going with the estate?"

"The inventory is complete. I guess now we just wait on the hearing."

Jenna nods. "God, I hope she doesn't get this place. It would kill Daddy."

"She won't get it, Jenna. I told you I'd take care of it. Stop worrying."

I've already decided that I'd use every dime of my savings to pay off our aunt if need be. She's a money whore. I think that would be like speaking her language. But if *that* didn't work, my next step would be to threaten her, which I'm not above doing if it means saving this place from her. But Jenna doesn't need to know the details. She just needs to know it's taken care of. And it will be. One way or the other.

She's quiet for a few minutes before she changes the subject. "So what are you still doing here? I figured you'd get Einie and be gone the instant the lawyer's people left."

I shrug. I don't know how to answer that. "I'm not sure what my next move is just yet."

"What do you mean? You go back to your life. You live it just like you planned. What's not to know?"

I shrug again. "Maybe it's time for something different."

"Such as . . ."

I shrug yet again. "I don't know. Where I *was* just doesn't hold a lot of appeal for me right now."

"So move. Find another job in another town. Some place where there's skydiving. And lots of girls. That's all you seem to need." I look at Jenna. She's grinning.

I smile back. "Yeah, I'm pretty easy to figure out, huh?"

"Hell yeah! As long as there's a fire to fight, a few skirts to chase, and something to jump off of, you're a happy camper." I say nothing, so she nudges my shoulder. "Right?" I shrug. Yet again. "I swear to God, I'm gonna slap the shit out of you if you shrug one more time. What is *wrong* with you?"

"Did you drive all the way down here just to harass me?" I snap.

"No. I drove all the way down here to see my brother. I'm afraid that after you leave here, I won't ever see you again."

Surprised, I frown down into her face. "Why would you think that?"

I see her chin tremble. This isn't like Jenna at all.

"You've never been really . . . *into* family. And now with both Mom *and* Dad gone, and this place up in the air, I'm just afraid you'll travel off to parts unknown and I'll never see you again." Jenna turns her dark eyes up to mine. They're so much like I remember Mom's being, especially now, glistening with tears. And a lot of love. "Jake, you're all I have left. Absentee grandparents don't count."

I wrap my arm around Jenna's shoulders and pull her in for a hug. "You're all I've got, too. And I promise you'll see me again. Hell, who knows. I might even end up here. Stranger things have happened."

Jenna leans back to look at me. "What? Why the hell would you wanna do that?"

I shrug, and she slaps my arm. "I don't know. Maybe I'm just getting older, thinking about all the stuff I've missed out on all these years. Maybe it's time to finally settle down. At least a little bit. I mean, it's not like I can't travel wherever I want to. You know, to jump off things." I grin at her, and she grins back.

"As much as I'd never want to live here, it would make me really happy if you did. I won't lie."

"I'm not saying that's gonna happen. I'm just telling you that, right now, I'm not sure where I'll end up. But I promise to keep you in the loop, 'kay?"

"'Kay."

Over the last couple of weeks, since that night at Lucky's, I haven't looked too deeply into my reasons for suddenly wanting to stick around Greenfield. I know one thing's for sure: It can't have anything to do with Laney. I mean, she's got a life in another town, and for all I know could be marrying someone else. There would be no reason for me to stay here for *her*. But still, there's something in me that's just not ready to move on yet. A gut instinct. And, for a guy, I'm fairly intuitive, so I listen to my gut. And my gut's telling me to stay. At least for a while.

TWENTY-SEVEN: *Laney*

S ummerton. It was always the perfect place for me. It was far enough away from my parents, but not too far. It was bigger than Greenfield, but not too big. It had stuff to do, but was still a good place to raise a family. It had more job opportunities for me *and* for Shane, yet it wasn't so big we could never move up in the world.

What a difference a few short months makes!

I unlock the door to the apartment I've barely stayed in. I rented it shortly after getting my first job. I signed the lease for one year thinking that I would only need it for a short time. I figured Shane and I would be getting married within that year and then moving into our first home together.

Now, I look around the cute space—the bright eggshell walls, the cheerful yellow curtains, the comfy ecru couch with its yellow and white throw pillows—and I feel nothing but disappointment. With . . . everything. Nothing turned out like I thought it would. Not that I'd really want that version of my life now.

It didn't take me long to realize I didn't love Shane. Not really. He *seemed* like everything I wanted. He fit the description to a T. The problem was that, until recently, I didn't know who *I* was, much less how to go about finding what would make me happy. I'd still love a husband and a family and a home to take care of, but all that has shifted to encompass so much more. Laughter, excitement, passion. True love.

But it's looking like I'll never have any of that. At least not the vivacious version that I felt for a few short weeks. I might be able to find some watered-down version of it with a man that will . . . do. But what girl ever dreams about going through an entire lifetime with a person she settled for?

Not me.

For the thousandth time, I hold back tears. I've mourned Jake enough for three or four lifetimes. I need to move on.

The problem is, I don't know how.

There was no real ending. No closure. We just . . . stopped.

Would I rather have spilled my guts and had to watch Jake awkwardly try not to further crush me? No. But in a way, that would've been preferable. At least it would feel over. Final. Not like it does now. Every day, I wake up like I'm in limbo. I go through the motions of living, but I'm not alive at all. Not really. It's like I'm stuck back in those weeks with Jake, the weeks when life held so much promise.

Now it just seems bleak.

Hopeless.

Empty.

TWENTY-EIGHT: *Jake*

When the lawyer's office called to tell me they were sending someone out, I should've asked who it was. But I didn't. Maybe I didn't want to expect Laney. Or maybe I didn't want to *not* expect her. I'm not sure which is worse.

But now, waiting on the porch, I wish I'd asked. The anticipation is killing me.

I've thought of what I'll say. I'll congratulate her on her engagement and ask if they've set a date. That will tell me if it's legit. Then I'll ask if he makes her happy. If she says yes, I'll move on. There'll be no reason to ever think of Laney Holt again.

If only I can manage to get her out of my head. Out of my blood.

But what has me on pins and needles is wondering what I'll say if she says no. What if he doesn't make her happy? What if she's reconsidered and realizes that she can't live without me? Then what will I say? What will I do? Nothing has changed for me. Not really. I'm still bad for her. I'm still bad for anyone to get close to.

But damn, how I want to!

Never has my past haunted me like this. Like a demon. Like something I can't shake no matter how hard I try.

Probably because I've never tried before. I've never wanted to be anything other than who I am. Who I was.

Until now.

Until Laney.

But that doesn't seem to change anything, either.

Disappointment sets in when I see a shiny black sedan making its way along the driveway toward me. Even if Laney had gotten a new car, she'd never get something like this. This is an old, stuck-up, rich-guy car. And Laney is none of those things.

When it pulls to a stop in front of me, I'm already out of patience for the visit.

I guess I really should've asked if Laney would be coming.

Now, I'm just cranky.

The driver's side opens and a tall, heavyset, white-haired man gets out, tugging on his vest then buttoning his jacket.

Pretentious.

He leans into his car and brings out his briefcase then closes the door and walks toward the porch. "You must be Jake. Robert Wilkins, but you can call me Bob."

His handshake is firm, but his smile is pleasant. He's much less of an asshole than I expected. Nice surprise.

"Come on in," I say, turning for the front door.

"We can stay out here if it's all the same to you. There's something about a big porch and fresh country air . . ." He inhales deeply and unbuttons his jacket as he lowers himself into one of the four straight-backed rockers. "So, young man, you've had a lot on your plate lately. How you holding up?"

I shrug, which aggravates the shit out of me. I never used to do that. I never used to feel like I didn't know exactly what I was doing, where I was going, and what I wanted. Until now.

And now, all those things seemed to be wrapped up in one person that I can't have and shouldn't want.

"I'm okay. Just ready to get this over with. Obviously, I'm willing to do whatever is necessary to keep the orchard with me and Jenna."

"Well, it's looking like the gods are in your favor."

"And why is that?"

"Your aunt's attorney contacted me this morning, shortly after I filed the inventory. It seems her husband has come into quite a bit of money and they'll be leaving the county, which means she'd have to hire someone to run the operation here if she were to gain a controlling interest. Evidently, that just wasn't very appealing to her, so she has submitted that she'd like to revert to an arrangement similar to what she enjoyed with your parents. Just a monthly sum that'll be deposited into her account. No real say in the day-to-day operations."

While that's definitely good news, I hate to have her involved in this place in *any* way. Who's to say she won't pull this same stunt again if Turkey (her husband) loses his ass out there?

Nobody. So it's up to me to do what I can to prevent it.

"I'm glad she's found some other means of making money in life, but you'll understand if I'm not comforted by her rash decision. She could just as easily come back at a future date and try this again."

Bob nods. "Which is why I would suggest that you make an offer to buy her out with one lump sum. You've got some valuable assets that you could probably part with and not feel the sting of it quite so much, if you get what I mean."

"Yes, I do. What did you have in mind?"

Bob proceeds to explain to me that there is a small tract of land, deeded to the orchard but not actively used, which has quite a bit of value simply because of its situation in regards to the river and the national forest. "If you had that appraised and then offered her the proceeds from the sale of that tract as an incentive to let you and this place alone, why, I think she'd likely take that deal and run. We could have her sign away all past, present, and future rights for the amount of the sale."

This is a sly old man. I can see it in the twinkle of his sharp brown eyes. Meeting him and spending a little time with him leaves me in no doubt as to why my parents felt safe leaving their possessions and their legacy in his hands.

Just over an hour after his arrival, Bob is shaking my hand and heading back to his car. Strangely, I'm glad he came. As much as I'd have liked to see Laney, it's better this way. And now, there's a plan for handling my aunt, Ellie, and possibly being completely free of her in the future.

Now if only my own future was so clear-cut . . .

TWENTY-NINE: *Laney*

My cell phone rings. I sigh when I look down to see Shane's number pop up. Never would I have thought I'd be friends with him again, but when there's no one else, sometimes a familiar face is a welcome face.

"Hello?"

"Hey, beautiful. How about some lunch?"

I sigh again. He hasn't given up giving me the full-court press. He swears he's going to win me back. I keep telling him I'm just not ready and that I might never be, but still he persists.

But then there's the loneliness that plagues me . . .

"Sure. Where can I meet you?"

"I'll pick you up at one."

I glance at my watch. That's about six minutes from now. "Okay, see you then," I say before hanging up.

I sit staring at the blank screen. The office is quiet around me. Bob is hard at work trying to free Jake and his family from his greedy aunt.

He didn't tell me until after the fact that he'd gone to Greenfield to meet with him. That was almost two weeks ago. Two weeks since my last chance to see Jake flew right on by without me even knowing about it.

Now there's just a constant ache and an ever-present sense of melancholy that I can't shake. It's like nothing that used to matter is very important anymore, and nothing that used to make me happy even gets me out of bed.

My parents have called dozens of times. I always answer and chat with them, but they're astute enough to know that something is terribly wrong. But they're also astute enough not to make a single comment about Jake.

Other than that, it's me and Shane and my job here. Tori is back in Greenfield. She's my only real friend, as I hadn't lived here long enough before my breakup with Shane to make any more. Not that they would be much help now, anyway. There's only one person who could possibly make me feel better.

And he's long gone.

My phone rings again, stopping me from giving in to the threat of another round of tears. It's Tori this time.

"Thank God," I say by way of greeting.

"I know I'm the answer to prayer, woman, but damn!" she teases.

"Today, you really are." This time my sigh is one of relief. "You're not in town, are you?"

I'm hoping she'll say yes, but I've learned to live with disappointment.

"No, but in just a few seconds, I'm gonna be begging you to come to me instead. Why don't you save me the groveling and just tell me you'll come home, okay? Okay!"

I can't help but smile. I miss my friend. "You know, simply in the interest of helping you to preserve your dignity, I think I can manage that. But just this once. I'm not a fan of missing out on begging. Next time, it may cost you twice as much."

"Duly noted," she says easily. "I'll bring my kneepads next time."

"Wise choice," I say with a giggle. "So, what is it that is so important that you'd beg me to come home?"

"Umm, if I told you, I'd have to kill you. And I love you too much to harm one lovely golden hair, so . . . there you go."

"Lucky for you, I don't need much of a reason to visit you. Mind if I borrow your couch?"

"Still avoiding the parents?"

"No, not really. I just think space is a good thing. I didn't cut the apron strings too well the first time around. This time, I'm not making the same mistake."

"Finally! Ohmigod! Boy, this summer sure was good for you, Laney." As much as I love Tori, and even though I've forgiven her for the stuff with Shane, I still haven't really felt comfortable talking to her about Jake. At least not about how my life is like a barren wasteland without him. I haven't told anybody that. It feels almost like, if I keep it a secret, it'll just go away and not be this way anymore. Eventually.

If only . . .

"Yeah, I did a lot of growing this year, didn't I?"

"You sure did. And all for the better, I might add."

I'm glad when I hear the front door open. I'm sure that's Shane. Just in time to rescue me from a torturous conversation about how wonderful this summer was.

It seems that, no matter how hard I try, I can't *forget* how wonderful it was.

But sometimes I wish I could.

"I've gotta go, Tori, but I'll see you home tomorrow night, okay?"

"Sounds good. Meet you here around seven. The key's under the mat if you get here before I get home."

"Okay, see you soon."

"Be safe."

"Yes, ma'am."

"You know that's right," Tori says before making a kissing noise and then hanging up.

"Who was that?" Shane asks as he saunters through my office door.

"Just Tori."

"Mmm," he murmurs neutrally. "Ready?"

"As ready as I'll ever be," I say, wondering how I ever thought this man was enough to make me happy.

You didn't really know yourself at all back then, did you?

No, I sure didn't.

THIRTY: *Jake*

You still wanting overtime?

A text from the fire chief.

Hell yeah!

Keeping busy is tantamount to staying sane, but I can only stand being at the house by myself for so long. It's not really that I'm lonely per se; it's more that I see Laney everywhere and it's getting harder and harder to stay there without her. To cook in the kitchen, to watch television on the couch, to shower in my bathroom. To sleep in my bed. She's everywhere. I can't escape her. Even when I sometimes want to.

Come on in at 6 then. 48-hour shift. May end up being longer.

I make a mental note to myself to fill up Einstein's dispensers in the barn. Just thinking about them reminds me of Laney's surprise that he used them.

She had been under the very mistaken impression that I just left my dog to fend for himself. She tried to cover by saying she then concluded maybe one of the neighbors was feeding him. When I told her about the system I'd rigged up, she didn't believe me so I took her out into the barn and showed her.

The contraptions are really nothing more than levers that release a premeasured amount of food and water down into bowls, respectively.

"See," I'd told her. "Einstein just walks up and high-fives the lever, and he gets fed and watered. There's enough in here to last him at least a week if he's not a total pig."

"You're telling me that your dog is smart enough to come in here when he's hungry, press these levers, and get his own food and water?"

"That's exactly what I'm telling you."

"And you expect me to believe that?"

I grinned at her. She was so uptight back then. But over the summer, it's like she opened up. Just for me. Like a flower to the rain. She needed me in order to see who she really was, to see how beautiful and perfect she was deep down, past all the outward appearances and polite ways. What she never knew was that I saw it all along. She was always perfect to me, inside and out.

I whistled and called for the dog. "Einstein! Come!" It was still early so I figured he'd be around somewhere close, probably staying cool in the shade under the house or in one of the barns.

After a few minutes, Einstein showed up, tongue lolling to one side. "Good boy," I praised him, wooling his fuzzy, white head. "Get a drink, Einie. Drink!"

After watching me for a few seconds with his sharp brown eyes, Einstein walked casually over to his water bowl, lifted his paw and smacked at the lever, and then waited until the bowl was full to get himself a nice cold drink of water.

Laney watched the whole thing with her mouth hanging open. "That's the smartest dog in the world," she finally surmised.

"Why the hell do you think we named him Einstein?"

Even now, I smile when I think about her. But it's bittersweet. It's like having the most precious thing in the world, but yet not really having it at all.

And then losing what you didn't have.

How's that for a conundrum?

Back in the present, I text my boss before I get lost in the past and forget about the present entirely.

Will do. See you soon.

THIRTY-ONE: *Laney*

It's Friday. And for the first time in a while it *feels* like Friday. That relief that the workweek is over and the fun is about to begin, that's how it feels. Well, my version of that, anyway. For me, it means that I get to spend some time away, out of my own head and away from things and people and places that make me sad. And even though going back to Greenfield should qualify as something that *makes* me sad, for some reason, I'm still looking forward to it. It almost seems like just being in town again will make me feel closer to Jake.

Even to me that sounds crazy, but it's true, nonetheless.

I let myself into Tori's apartment. She hasn't had it very long, but she'd been unpacking and settling in as quickly as possible, and it's come a long way since the last time I visited.

It's decorated in vibrant colors, much like Tori's vibrant personality. The living room is huge compared to mine and it's done in rich jewel tones—ruby, sapphire, and emerald. It's anything but soothing, but I don't think Tori really wants or needs soothing, so it fits.

I set my stuff off to one side of the kitchen and make myself a drink. When I sit down on the couch, I have no intention of taking a nap, but that's exactly what happens.

More than two hours later, Tori coming through the door wakes me up. "What the hell are you doing, lazy ass? You're supposed to be ready!"

"Ready for what?" I ask, trying to shake the fog from my brain.

"The party."

"What party?"

"The party I told you about."

"You didn't tell me about a party. You just said it was a surprise."

Tori stops with her hands in midair as she was taking the clips out of her hair. "Oh. Well . . . surprise!"

I roll my eyes and flop back onto the couch. "You can go without me. I'm tired."

"Oh, no! You did *not* come all the way home just to crash on my couch, young lady. You will have fun this weekend if it freakin' kills me. Do you hear me?"

"I'm pretty sure *everyone* hears you," I tease, sliding off the sofa.

"Shower for you, my friend. You've got exactly forty minutes to wash, shave, and pamper that pretty ass or I'm taking you as is."

I mumble all sorts of things about what she can do with a razor and a bottle of shampoo as I make my way to the bathroom.

Before I can close the door all the way, Tori shows up to press her face into the crack. "Were you giving me attitude? And did I hear a 'up your *tight* ass' thrown in there?"

Tori's expression is comical. She's probably never heard me say the first curse word. I grin at her. "Maaaybe."

She squeals and pushes the door open to give me a bone-crushing hug. "Eeee, I love this new you!"

I can't help but laugh as she darts out the door and slams it shut behind her. I don't tell her that she's got Jake to thank for *this* Laney.

"Um, why are we at the church?"

I look suspiciously through the windshield at the bright lights pouring out of the detached fellowship hall windows. Suddenly, I have a bad feeling.

"I'll explain in a minute. Just come on," Tori says, hopping out of the car and running around the hood to jerk open my door. "Move it, slowpoke."

Earlier, I was curious why Tori didn't want me wearing jeans and a T-shirt tonight. She insisted that I wear her little black cocktail dress, the one she reserves for special occasions. That right there should've been a huge red flag.

"What are you up to, Tori?"

I'm not sure at all that I want to go inside.

Tori takes my hands and pulls me to my feet. Even though we're both wearing heels, she looks down into my face. "Lancy, you know I love you. Please. Just trust me."

Something in her eyes tells me that this is important to her, important to her proving herself to me like she's tried to do for months now. That's the only reason I go with her when she tugs me along behind her all the way up the walk to the front doors.

When we step inside, every head (of which there are literally dozens) turns toward me and everyone starts clapping. I smile uncertainly as I look around.

It looks like the cheesiest high school prom in the world is getting ready to take place. There are white streamers dangling from the ceiling, there are white silk roses gushing from vases on every surface and there is glitter sprinkled on the tables and floor.

All my church family is here, as well as my parents, who are standing at the front of the room in front of the lit gas fireplace that's flanked by two long tables. Each is draped with a white paper cloth. My mother looks like she's about to cry, and my father looks impressively smug.

The crowd seems to part as I make my way to them. A few of them move just enough that I can see who is standing at my father's side.

Shane.

He's wearing the worst car salesman smile I've ever seen. And he's standing beneath a printed banner that reads, CONGRATULA-TIONS, SHANE AND LANEY!

I stop. Dead in my tracks, right in front of everyone, I stop. And I turn toward Tori.

"What the hell is this, Tori?"

She takes my hands in hers again and holds them up to her chest.

"Laney, you are my best friend. I've only ever tried to do what I think is right and what's best for you. I would never, ever hurt you. If I ruined what was between you and Shane, please accept this night as my most heartfelt apology. I'm giving you back everything that I cost you. All you have to do is accept it. If, for some reason, a life with him isn't what you want, then I still offer this as a gift to you. Tonight's the night, Laney. You've come so far, and I know you have this in you. You can either walk down there and take Shane back, set a date to marry him, and live your life with him, just like you planned. Or you can tell him to go to hell, tell the rest of these people to kiss your ass, and you can take my car to Jake's house and tell him how you feel about him. You go forward with him. Or back to this," she says, sweeping her arm toward the front of the room, toward my parents and Shane. "It's up to you. This time, you'll get no interference from me. I'll love you no matter what you decide. I just want you to be happy."

I don't even know what to say. My mind is quite effectively boggled. "Did you rehearse that?" I ask quietly.

"About four hundred times. In front of the mirror. How'd I do?"

"Nailed it."

She grins. I grin. And then she steps out of my way and gives me the very physical choice of which direction to go—forward or back.

My foot twitches, but I still it. There's one more thing to consider. Well, not really. My mind is already made up, but there's one thing I need to know.

"You said drive to Jake's house. I thought he was gone."

Eyes sparkling, Tori shakes her head.

I lean up and kiss her on both cheeks, then I take a deep breath.

And I turn to walk up the aisle. Toward my parents. And toward Shane.

THIRTY-TWO: *Jake*

Some people don't believe in premonitions and shit like that. I'm one of them. I do, however, believe in instinct. Especially when it comes to working fires.

And something tells me tonight is gonna be a busy night.

While everyone else is in the kitchen, shooting the shit and scarfing down potato chowder, I'm making sure everything is stocked and in order on the truck.

Call it a hunch. Call it whatever. It doesn't matter. They are what they are.

But I never ignore them.

And they're never, ever wrong.

THIRTY-THREE: *Laney*

As I walk toward them, I can't decide whose grin is bigger, Shane's or Daddy's. Not that it matters. Neither will be wearing it very much longer.

I smile and nod to first my mother then my father. "Thank you both for coming. I'm sure you know this is a surprise to me, but I'm glad you could be here for it. I think that's important." My mother covers her mouth with her hand and my father squeezes her narrow shoulders.

"We love you, pumpkin."

We shall see . . .

I turn to Shane. "I take it you had a hand in this, Shane?"

"Of course," he answers proudly. "Nothing's too good or too big for my girl. And that's why," he says, taking a black velvet box out of his jacket pocket, "I have this for you instead."

And here come the first round of fireworks . . .

Everyone in the hall quiets when Shane, still grinning like a peacock, drops to one knee in front of me. He takes the ring out of the box then reaches for my left hand before he clears his throat.

I'm sure he wants everyone to hear his proposal. As well as my answer.

Or maybe he doesn't . . .

"Laney Holt, love of my life, future mother of my children, will you do me the honor of once again agreeing to marry me?"

He looks so proud of himself, I think absently, *like he has no reason in the world to think I might turn him down. To him, all is forgiven and it's as good as water under the bridge.*

But little does Shane know, my heart belongs to someone else.

"Oh, Shane. If only you'd asked me before you went to all this trouble." For just a few seconds, I hold my tongue as I revel in the sight of his face going from shit-eatin'-grin to what-the-hell-is-happening. "I don't love you, Shane. What you did to me was the best thing to ever come my way. It helped me to see who I really am, what I'm capable of, and what I want out of life. And I'm sorry, but you aren't it."

I could be cruel and say more, but there's no call for that.

Little gasps and titters begin all around me. The buzz is already starting. I'll be the talk of the town. And not in a good way. And for the first time in my life, I really, genuinely don't care. I've lived my life under the microscope of these people for far too long. It's time to show them who Laney is. The real Laney.

Shane tries to recover as I reclaim my hand. "Is this some kind of a joke?" he hisses.

"What kind of a sick joke would this be, Shane? Something sick like trying to play off you cheating on me as part of a 'prank'? Is that what you mean?"

I hear my parents gasp and I smother my satisfied smile. Now they know.

Shane stands to his feet, all evidence of the suave, composed gentleman gone. He leans in close to me. "You're nothing but a filthy little whore," he spits into my ear. I simply roll my eyes. I hope my parents are close enough to hear this part, too. Maybe they'll get to see what

Shane is *really* like. Maybe they can have someone new to hate, someone other than Jake Theopolis.

"I guess that's just your opinion, Shane. Now, if you'll excuse me."

I spin on my heel, ready to make my grand exit, when Shane reaches out and grabs my upper arm, jerking me to a rough stop. "You know what, whore? I would've given Tori the ride of her life if she hadn't stopped me. You were never enough woman for me."

I half laugh, half sigh. "Nice, Shane. Real nice."

Shaking my head, I wrench my arm free and turn to walk away, not giving anyone an explanation. They can make up whatever story suits them. I've got a life and a future to tend to.

It's as I'm nearing the door that I hear the explosion. And I feel the gush of heat.

THIRTY-FOUR: *Jake*

I'm not at all surprised when the siren goes off. I knew something would happen tonight. I just knew it.

When the call comes in, I think little of the address. The church's fellowship hall. If I'm not mistaken, it's equipped with a full, commercial-style kitchen. Grease fires happen all the time in places like that. Makes a shitload of smoke, but generally they aren't too out of control, staying confined mostly to the kitchen.

But then, just as four of us are piling into the truck, we get word that it was a propane tank explosion. And that the hall was full of people. For an engagement party.

My never-wrong gut twists and I feel a cold sweat break out on my brow. I have one thought. Of one face.

Laney.

It's her. I know it's her. Laney's in town. She's there and there's been an explosion.

I don't even try to imagine what kind of function she might be in town for that's held at the church. The dull ache in my chest seems to think it's to celebrate her reunion with her fiancé. But right now, it really doesn't matter *what* she's in town for. I don't give a big ugly shit about her fiancé. All I care about is that she's not in danger. That she's not lying on the ground somewhere, burning alive.

A burst of nausea tears through my gut at the mental image of Laney covered in third degree burns. I've seen it too many times, been to too many fires that were raging before we could make it to the scene.

I squeeze my eyes shut against the image, reminding myself that this is a small town. It will only take us a few minutes to be onsite. Helping. Saving lives. Controlling the fire.

Saving Laney.

When the truck makes the turn onto the street, I look out the window. The first thing I see is a sign at the front of the street that says, CONGRATULATIONS, SHANE AND LANEY. My heart sinks at that.

And it sinks even lower when we pull into the lot and I see the wreckage.

"Looks like the tank wasn't full or it would've blown that place to bits," Ronnie says.

I'm not comforted. One wall was blown out completely. Fire is eating away at the rest. And the roof is hanging precariously over it all.

"Respirators on, guys," Chip yells. I look around. They're already in place. We all know what to expect.

My heart is racing by the time we pull to a stop and everyone jumps out to do what we do best.

Behind the shield of my helmet, I process the scene as I approach. I scan the tear-streaked and smoke-smudged faces. I search the bewildered and terrified eyes. I see it all. I take it all in. But the one thing I want most to see, the one *person* I want most to see, is nowhere to be found.

Turning my body 360 degrees, I scan the crowd once more for Laney. There are a lot of people out here. Surely this is the majority of those who were in attendance. The building isn't *that* big. But in all these faces I don't see the only one I care about. The only one that matters. And I know, deep down, that nothing will matter again if I don't find her. Dead or alive.

I ask one of the more coherent people I pass, "Is anyone left inside?"

She nods, sobbing all the while.

"Is Laney in there?"

Again she nods. "She went back in a few minutes ago. She was helping people out, but there were some still inside . . ."

Before the woman can finish, I turn to Chip and motion that I'm going inside. I run up the short flight of stairs and step through the doorway, careful not to touch anything.

The room is ablaze. The curtains are on fire. The flower arrangements on the tables are on fire. There are flaming pieces of paper floating through the air. There are blazing bits of banner scattered across the floor. Some of the exposed beams from the ceiling have let go on one end to form what looks like a flame-soaked obstacle course.

Across the room, I see the gaping hole where the one wall was blown to bits. I also see where the remaining three are struggling to support the weight of the sagging roof.

This place is gonna go any minute now.

I *have to find* Laney.

I look through the bright orange haze, searching the billows of smoke for her pale head, but I see nothing. I see no upright bodies. No movement. No life.

I feel the beginnings of desperation set in. I look ahead and see a path that could possibly lead me safely into the center of the room, where I'll have a better vantage point. Cautiously, I walk in that direction.

I turn the valve on my mask, something I know I shouldn't do. "Laney!" I call, knowing full well that with the roar of the fire and the crackle of the structure giving way there's no way she can hear me. But I yell again anyway. "Laney!"

As I duck beneath a huge wooden beam, I see the most glorious sight in the world—a shiny, blond head. I see Laney. She has something wrapped around her face, but I'd recognize her anywhere, wearing anything.

She's making her way into the flames, going farther into the room. Lurching forward, I reach out for her, stopping her before she can go in any deeper. I spin her toward me and look into the face I've missed so much. I see recognition light her eyes, and she throws her arms around me.

So tight I could probably hurt her, I wrap my arms around her and lift her off the ground. Holding her against my chest, I turn and hurry back the way I came. My heart is racing, but this time with gratitude. And relief. And something else.

When I reach the door, I'm hesitant to release Laney, but I feel her struggling, so I let her down. There are tears in her eyes when she looks up at me. Tears and sheer panic.

"Jake, there are still people in there!" she says frantically.

I push her hair back from her face to get a good look at her. She looks all right, just freaked out. "Shhh, Laney, it's okay. We'll get them out. Don't worry."

"No, Jake, you don't understand. I have to go back in there. Please."

"Laney, let us take care of it. It's—"

Chip taps my shoulder and cuts me off. I turn to him, and he's shaking his head. "The roof is collapsing, Jake. No one goes back in until we can get past the tank in the back and through that blown-out wall. Stay put."

I look to Laney. Her eyes are wide and terrified.

"Wh-what does that mean? They're not going to just leave them in there, are they? Jake, I have to go back in there. I—"

"Just give us a few minutes to get in through the back. He's saying it's no longer safe to cross the room. We have to get in through the back."

"No!" Laney starts to run past me, but I grab her around the waist. She struggles like a wild thing. "There's no time!"

"Laney, stop! You have to—"

"You don't understand. It's my father. He's in there. He and Shane were at the very front when it happened. Jake, my father is in there!" she cries, her agony tearing through my chest like it's my own. "Please let me go back in there. Please!"

For a tenth of a second, my mind scrambles for the best way forward. None of the firemen will go back in until Chip gives the go-ahead. I'm sure as hell not letting Laney go back in there. But I couldn't live with myself if this heartbreak, this utter devastation was the last thing I saw on her beautiful face.

That means there's only one thing I can do. One thing I can do for Laney. For once in my life, I can *help* and not hurt someone that I love. For once in my life, I'll prove my father wrong. Even if it kills me. Even if it means giving up my life for the two people in hers that I dislike the most.

It's for Laney. And that's all that matters.

Before anyone can stop me, and without another word, I turn and run back into the flames in search of Laney's loved ones.

THIRTY-FIVE: *Laney*

"N**ooo!**"

The word is ringing so loudly in my ears, I hear nothing else. Pain is resonating in my chest so deeply, I feel nothing else.

I know that there are arms wrapped around me. I know that someone is preventing me from going after Jake, from stopping him. From saving him.

I didn't want for him to risk his life for theirs. I simply wanted him to let me go, let me make the choice, make the sacrifice if it had to be made.

But not Jake.

Never Jake.

A burn more devastating than ten fiery buildings is consuming my heart as I watch the very spot where I saw him disappear into the flames. My entire being, my entire world is focused on that one sliver like my life depends on what comes back out.

Because it does.

I won't be able to live with myself if Jake doesn't come back out. I won't be able to survive the rest of my days without him. And knowing that he died to save the people I love . . .

I crumble inside the arms that restrain me, my legs no longer strong enough to support me. I hear someone screaming Jake's name in the distance. The voice sounds like mine, but it can't be. It can't be me. I can't move. I can't speak. I can't even think past the mind-numbing panic that's coursing through my body, through my soul. All I can do is stare, stare at the place where I saw him last and wait . . .

It seems an eternity has passed when I see movement. My lungs cease to expand, my heart ceases to beat until I see the clear form of Jake cutting through the haze. My relief is more profound than any emotion I've ever experienced.

Until he lays down his human cargo and turns to go back inside.

The arms that held me suddenly disappear, and I see people rush to the man lying prone on the ground. After a few seconds, I see my mother come into my view, falling to her knees beside the person just sitting up. It's my father. I squeeze my eyes shut over my tears when I see him wrap one arm around her shoulders and lean into her.

But then an even more painful realization slices through me. Jake went back in.

To get Shane.

He's risking his life for a man like Shane. Because he thinks it matters to me.

The tears come freely now, and without end. I sit on the ground, surrounded by hurt people and emergency workers and stretches of hose, and my heart melts right inside my chest.

"Please God, please God, please God!" is all I can make out. Over and over and over again. Every nerve, every cell, every bit of light that I am as a person cries out to Him for mercy. And I watch the doorway . . .

When Jake appears this time, he sets down the body he's carrying. As he turns, stripping off his helmet as he goes, his eyes search for me. I struggle to my feet, to stand until he can see me.

And he does.
And he waits.
He waits for me.
Maybe like he's always waited for me.
Like I've always waited for him.

THIRTY-SIX: *Jake*

I watch Laney take shaky step after shaky step toward me. Toward *us*. Shane, her fiancé, is lying in the grass just behind me. If ever there was a choice for her to make, now's the time. Her actions will speak volumes. And I'll do nothing to influence them.

Closer and closer she gets. Harder and harder my heart beats. What will she do? What will she do?

When she's five or six steps from me, she glances down at Shane and my chest gets tight. But then, as if she was only paying him the simplest of courtesies, she launches herself into my arms and smashes her lips to mine.

I've always heard Jenna and her friends go on and on about all the different things a kiss can mean. Now I think I understand what they were talking about.

In this kiss is declaration. In it is acceptance. In it is passion and perseverance, hope and happiness. In it is everything I've ever needed and everything I never thought I'd want. *It's* everything because *she's* everything.

All the voices, all the sounds, all the activity around us is muted when she leans back and looks deep into my eyes. "You saved me, Jake."

I smile. "You saved me first."

For a few seconds, I think of spilling my guts, right here in the middle of a disaster area. But I think better of it when I hear a voice to my left.

"All right, hero, was there anyone else inside?" Chip asks. "If not, we need to get these flames put out and wrap this up."

Leave it to a guy to interrupt such a great moment. I feel like snarling at him, *Can't you see I'm in the middle of something here?*

But I guess my personal affairs are actually doing the interrupting. I'm here to do a job. To save lives and put out fires.

One down.

One to go.

I set Laney on her feet and wipe away a smudge from her pale cheek with my gloved finger. "Are you all right? Really?"

Her smile is wide and bright, and she nods enthusiastically. "I know it sounds weird, but I've never been better."

I grin down at her. I know just what she means.

"I've gotta finish up here. I'll find you later, 'kay?"

She nods again, her smile still intact. "Okay, I'm gonna go check on Daddy."

She walks backward for a few steps, as reluctant to leave me as I am for her to go.

"Stay away from this building," I say as I move toward the side of the hall, getting ready to replace my helmet. "You hear?"

She nods again and turns to walk to her father. I round the smoking structure to make my way to the back, to put this baby to bed.

Almost six hours later, I'm on my way home. The chief called in the backup shift to help with cleanup, which is something the bigger fire departments don't get involved in. But Greenfield is small, and it's more a neighborly gesture than anything else. With the reinforcements onsite, it allows those of us who were first-responders to come home for a break before resuming our shift.

My first thought was to go to Laney, but that might not be the best thing. If she's still at the hospital being medically cleared with the other people from the church (which I heard had the ER backed up for hours) then there's no reason for me to bother her there. If she's at home sleeping, I definitely don't want to bother her there. So I figure the best thing I can do is wait until morning. What I have to say can wait until then. It's waited this long . . .

Coming down my driveway, my headlights hit a patch of blue just barely visible through the trees. That's when I know I won't have to wait. Laney's at my house.

I pull up and park beside her car. The house is dark. I'm assuming she's asleep since it's late and she had a big night.

I cut the engine and get out, reaching into the back to get my gear. I jump when I hear a soft voice from the opposite side of the Jeep.

"Took you long enough."

"Holy hot damn! You scared the shit out of me!"

Laney giggles. She must've been on the front porch, waiting.

I can hardly make her out on such a cloudy night with only a sliver of moon to see by. It looks like she's changed clothes. She's wearing something pale and, when she puts her foot on the tire and swings up into the Jeep, I can see that it's short. Even in the low light, I can see lots and lots of long, tan leg.

My pulse picks up, and it has nothing to do with her sneaking up on me.

"What are you doing up? I figured you'd be asleep. You need rest."

Laney moves to stand on the backseat, her bare feet on the cushion and her back braced against the roll bar.

"Who can sleep after a night like tonight?" She pauses before she adds, "And I don't mean the fire."

Here we go!

I take a deep breath. I knew this was coming. By giving in to what's between us, that means I have to be open with her. She'll expect that. But hell, she couldn't even wait until morning?

For a few seconds, I have a burst of doubt. How will she react? Will it change anything?

Setting my bag on the ground, I hop into the backseat of the Jeep, repositioning her feet to the space on the seat between my legs. She might as well get comfortable. If we're gonna talk, there's no time and place like the present.

THIRTY-SEVEN: *Laney*

Jake settles my feet back between his legs and leans his head back. Looking down on him, all I can see is his shadowed face and the occasional sparkle of the low light in his eyes.

I didn't come here to pressure him. I came here to . . . to . . . I don't know what. To be with him. To see if what happened was real. To see where we go from here.

I came because I couldn't stay away.

And because, once again, I feel hope. And, this time, I need to know if it's shared.

But I don't want to move too fast. Jake has ghosts. Demons. Things he hasn't wanted to share. Since I don't know what they are, I can't possibly know if I'm about to step on a landmine. It makes proceeding tricky. But not impossible. I just have to be patient.

That's what I'm telling myself when I hear him sigh and feel his fingers touch the top of my bare feet and start absently making slow circles.

I'm thinking of how to start, of *where* to start when Jake speaks.

His voice is low. And distant. He's somewhere else in time. And, this time, he's taking me along with him.

"When I was little, before Jenna was born, Mom and Dad used to take me out into the orchard with them almost every day. Sometimes we'd pick peaches. Sometimes we'd play hide-and-go-seek in the rows of trees. Sometimes we'd walk in the shallow parts of the river. We had breakfast and lunch and dinner together more often than not. Even after Mom got sick, we did a lot together. It was after she got pregnant with Jenna that things got so much worse."

Surprisingly, there's no bitterness in his voice. Obviously, he doesn't resent Jenna for what happened to his mother.

"Her cancer fed on the estrogen. It spread like wildfire while she was carrying Jenna. After she delivered, Mom started chemo and radiation. She took treatment for a couple of years, but the disease was always a step ahead of the cure. The last few months, all the doctors could do was keep her comfortable. Even as young as I was, I knew what was going on. I guess I just didn't know how much it would change things. And what my new role would be.

"Dad was busy taking care of the orchard and Jenna. Mom was in bed all the time, so I was kind of lost. I spent a lot of time in there with her. I'd color on the floor in her room or play with my cars. Sometimes we'd watch TV together or she'd read me a story. If I ever went out to play, it was always by myself, which was never fun, so I didn't stay long. I always ended up back in Mom's room. With her. I got an up close and personal view of what she went through and how miserable she was."

I listen with rapt attention. My heart bleeds for Jake the child, as well as Jake the man. I can't imagine what it must've been like for a little Jake to have to watch his mother go through so much, and to have to do it all by himself for the most part. In the midst of it all, everyone got busy with life and Jake got pushed to the side. Forgotten.

"It was nothing unusual for her to ask me to bring her something—ginger ale, ice chips, a washcloth—so the day she asked me to hand her one of her pill bottles, I didn't think anything of it. I guess some part of me wondered why Dad had started keeping them up in the cabinet rather than letting her take them by herself like she'd always done. But at eight years old, you just don't really think about stuff like that. So I didn't hesitate to get them for her."

Pulse pounding and lip trembling, I have an idea where this is going. It's all I can do not to cry bitter, heartbroken tears for this man that I love.

"She had me hand her the glass of water that always sat on her nightstand. Then she had me get up on the bed so she could hug me. She told me she loved me and that I would always be her big, strong boy and then she told me to go play outside until dinnertime. So I did." His pause is deep. And dark. And haunted. "That was the last time I saw her alive."

I can barely swallow past the lump in my throat. The ache in my chest explodes into an unimaginable spray of sympathy at his next words.

"My mother overdosed. She killed herself. But she didn't kill herself out of weakness or selfishness. She didn't do it to end *her* suffering. She did it to end ours. I once heard her tell Dad that she could live with what she had to go through, but that it was breaking her heart to see what it was doing to us. Dad told her we were fine, that we would *always* be better off with her around. No matter what. But she didn't believe it. I could see it in her eyes more and more every day. She thought her life was hurting us. So she took it."

I'm doing everything I can to let my tears fall in silence, to let Jake have this time, without interruption.

"When Dad found her, he yelled for me to come upstairs. He was sitting on the floor crying, holding Mom in his arms. The pill bottle was still in her hand. All I remember is him screaming at me, 'You did this! You did this!' I tried to explain, but he wouldn't even listen to me. He told me to get out, that he didn't even want to look at me. So I left. I went back outside for a while.

"For hours, I watched the door. I kept waiting for him to come back downstairs, but he never did. I remember that it got dark and I was so hungry, so I went into the kitchen and opened a can of SpaghettiOs for me and Jenna and we ate 'em cold. Nothing was ever the same after that night.

"She turned four two days later.

"Dad got her a cake and presents, and celebrated like nothing was wrong, but every time he looked at me, I could see how much he hated me. How much he blamed me. It went on like that for a couple of years. Until I finally got up the nerve to ask him about it. He told me he could never forgive me for taking her from him. He said there was something wrong with me. He said I didn't know how to love the right way, that I only hurt the people I was supposed to care about. He never let me forget it, either. After that day, he only hid his feelings from Jenna. Never from me. He blamed me for everything after that. If Jenna fell off her bike and scraped her knee, it was my fault for not watching her closely enough. If she got in a fight at school, it was my fault for being a terrible big brother. He never said anything in front of her, though. He wanted her to have a good life, one without all the pain we'd known. And so did I. I didn't want her to have to feel like I did all the time. I even tried not to love her. I was afraid if I loved her like I did Mom, something would happen to her. Like Dad said. So I never did. And nothing bad ever happened to her. I learned early on that the best thing I could do for people I cared about was to stay away from them. To care as little about them as possible. And it's worked. I haven't lost another person I loved since the day Mom died. And neither had Dad."

A sob is torn from my throat. I clamp my hand over my mouth to hold it in, but like pressure building up behind a kinked water hose, the dam eventually breaks. And when it does, nothing can control the flood. I bury my face in my hands and let go.

Even behind my hands, behind my closed eyes, I see the picture of Jake's tortured face. He's learned not to let his pain show, but for these few seconds, in the quiet night and pale, silvery moonlight, he let me see. And it's almost too much to bear.

I feel him lean over me and wrap his arms around my shoulders, smoothing my hair with his wide palm. "Shhh," he whispers. "I didn't mean to upset you."

I wind my arms around his waist, lay my face against his chest and I cry. I cry for Jake. From the deepest, darkest part of my soul, I cry for him. For all he's been through. For all he's lost. For a lifetime of feeling he's to blame. And for a lifetime of missing out on something so simple yet so profound as love.

"Oh God, Jake, I'm so sorry! I'm so sorry you've been through so much. No one deserves that."

"It's over now. I just wanted you to know who I am. Who I was. But that's in the past now. There's no need for you to cry."

I lean back and look into his handsome face. "*You're* comforting *me?*" I reach up to cup his cheeks. "If there was some way I could help, some way I could take away the pain, I would do it, Jake. I would do that for you. I'd give anything to go back and make things different for you. You've missed out on so much. So much love and happiness."

Jake grabs my wrist and turns his lips into my palm then smiles a small smile. "But it's made me who I am today. And today, I'm a different man. Because of you." Reaching up to brush his thumb over my cheekbone, Jake's eyes pour bits and pieces of his heart into mine. "Today, I realized that I'm not the person he thought I was. Today, I realized that I don't always hurt the people I love. Today, I realized that I'd rather walk into a fire and carry out your father, who hates me, and your fiancé, who's marrying the woman I love, than to see you hurting for one more second. Today, for the first time in my life, I felt like I could love somebody like they deserved to be loved. Like I could love *you* the way you deserve to be loved."

Taking my face in both his hands, he tilts it up to his. "Laney, I don't deserve you. I could never deserve you. But I can promise you that there's not another man on the planet that will love you like I do. That would lay down his life for your happiness. That would give up his whole world if it made you smile. And I'm not letting you go without a fight. I watched you walk away once and it nearly killed me. I won't let it happen again."

I'm crying again. But this time, tears of pure joy. My heart is near bursting from the most intense, overwhelming happiness I could ever imagine feeling. Nothing else in my entire life has ever come close to this. And I have a feeling that nothing else ever will.

"I love you, Jake Theopolis," I whisper, scattering kisses all over his face. "I love you more than anyone has a right to love another human being. Do you hear me? Promise me you'll never leave me. Promise me."

In my fervor, my lips cross his. And, like always, there's a spark. Only this time, there's more. There's love. And there's salt. And there's tenderness. And there's hope.

And, right in the middle of it all, there's heat.

"Never," he murmurs against them, his tongue licking over the crease.

Like the fire at the church—sudden, explosive, raging—everything I feel for Jake and everything he feels for me bubbles to the surface. We are hands and lips. We are mouths and tongues. We are passion and desperation. And it is beautiful.

When Jake slips his hands beneath my skirt and tears my panties off, I reach behind me for the roll bar, winding my arms around it. I hear him fumble with his zipper and then he's lifting me off my feet, slamming me down on him, rocking me against the cushioned bar.

My legs around his waist and his long, thick hardness buried inside me, Jake moves me against him. Over him. Through him, it seems. And when I come apart, in a shower of bright white stars and crackling heat, I hear his hoarse, velvety voice breaking the silence. With every stroke, he whispers, "I love you. I love you. I love you."

Those three simple words have never meant so much.

THIRTY-EIGHT: *Jake*

Two months later

"What the hell is wrong with you?" Jenna asks, stabbing me in the ribs with her pointy elbow.

"There's not enough room in this kitchen for both of us, dammit!" I snap.

I'm glad that Jenna has finally overcome her grief enough that she can come into the house, but we are tripping all over each other trying to get shit ready for this cookout.

"God! You're so grouchy! When was the last time Laney stayed over?"

"I haven't seen her all week. Does that answer your question?"

"Yes. It. Does. We are Theopolises. We need our . . . attention."

"Ewww, could you please refrain from making me nauseous right before supper."

"That's not me making you nauseous. That's nerves. You think I don't know what's going on, but I do-oo," she gloats in her singsong voice.

"And just what do you *think* is going on?"

"I think you invited the big bad preacher over here because you're gonna ask for his daughter's hand. And I think that's why you're so grouchy. And I think that's why you're so nervous. And I also think it's the sweetest thing ever!" With a squeal, Jenna throws her arms around my neck and kisses my cheek loudly. "I hope he tells you no just to yank your chain. And then, when I jump in to restrain you from kicking his ass, he'll tell you to please take his daughter to the bedroom and ravage her immediately, and you'll live happily ever after."

When she finally leans back, I frown down at her. "What the hell have you been smoking?"

"Oh, come on!" she says, slapping my arm. "You need to ask that girl to marry you before someone else does. I've never seen you this happy. And you're just enough of an idiot to do something stupid, like wait too long and screw it up. I can't stand the—"

"Damn, Jenna, take a breath. And hush that loud mouth of yours," I say in a quieter voice. "They'll be here any minute."

"What does it matter if they hear me? If you weren't planning on asking—"

I clamp my hand over her mouth and growl into her ear. "Fine, you're right. Now would you shut the hell up?"

Squealing even louder, Jenna bounces up and down, clapping her hands excitedly. "Yaaay! I'm gonna have a sisterrr!"

"Jenna, shhh," I hiss. But I can't really get mad at her. I feel a lot like that on the inside. Just more nervous. And, truth be told, I'm not nearly as nervous about Mr. Holt saying no as I am about Laney saying no. Although she's opened up and loosened up a ton since we met, her still waters run very deep. She's never *said* she has any reservations about me or us, but that doesn't mean she isn't harboring any. And there's no time like a proposal to make you start considering all things, weighing all things. Seeing things from all angles. Seeing all the rough edges.

For me, the thought of spending the rest of my life with Laney makes me happy. Happier than I've ever been. She's what I want out of life. And I'm more certain of it with every passing day. With time, rather than finding things I don't like or things that drive me crazy, I think I love her more. And the more I find out about her, the more I find to love.

I hear Einstein barking and my pulse speeds up. Jenna looks at me with wide eyes and whispers, "He's here."

I'm sure it *is* Mr. Holt. I purposely told him and his wife a slightly earlier time than anyone else. I knew I'd want to get it over with rather than worrying about it the whole time.

I take a deep breath and look at my beaming sister. "Wish me luck."

Her eyes start to water when she responds. "You won't need it. I've always believed you deserved all the happiness in the world, even when you didn't."

I pause on my way to the door, looking back at my sister. "Jenna, I . . ." I don't even know what to say to her, how to explain what I'm feeling. "I love you."

In all our years together, I've never told her that. I hope that she realizes the significance, even if she doesn't fully understand it. I want her to know that she means a lot to me, whether I've ever shown it or not.

"I know," she breathes, shakily. "I'm just glad you let go of whatever it was that's been holding you back all these years. I won't pretend to get it, but I'm glad you're not hiding from it anymore. You deserve better than that."

Impulsively, I walk back to her and kiss her cheek. "Now don't say anything to embarrass me, and for the love of all that's holy, watch your trashy mouth."

Jenna sniffs loudly and tosses her hair over her shoulder. "I stop cussing for no one." I give her my sternest look. She sighs and smiles sweetly. "Except for you. Just this once."

"Better. Now, go make yourself scarce. I've got some charming to do."

She probably doesn't think I hear her whisper as I leave the room, but I do.

"Go get 'em, Jake."

So I do.

THIRTY-NINE: *Laney*

My pocket feels heavy. I feel lopsided, like everything in me is leaning. Leaning and holding its breath.

I've never been more nervous. Yet I've never been more certain.

Over the last couple of months, Jake and I have talked about all sorts of things—our hopes and dreams, our fears and trials, our plans and timetables. Hearing him say that he wants the same things I want, one by one, has been the most amazing unfolding of my life. It's like the dreams I've had since I was little were right on target, they were just missing one vital ingredient—the perfect man to tweak them just a tad.

Yes, I still want to get married. Yes, I still want to have a family. Yes, I still want a place to put down roots and call home. Yes, I still want a love that will grow better as we grow older. I still want all those things. But now, they have a face. All of them. They all revolve around Jake.

He took them and made them *ours*, not just mine. And he brought his own special brand of wild to them. Never have I wanted to travel and experience new things in life, but now I do. I want to take off to parts unknown and go cliff diving with Jake at my side. I want to parasail in warm Mediterranean waters and hang glide over rain forest treetops. I want to do it all. And then I want to come back home to the life we've built and sit in front of the fireplace on cold winter nights, and skinny-dip in the river on warm summer ones.

All my life was ever missing was Jake.

It all starts and ends with him.

I just hope that he feels the same way about me.

I'm always hoping . . .

FORTY: *Jake*

I usher the Holts into my backyard. Jenna appears within seconds, wearing a huge smile. Mentally, I roll my eyes. She's a shitty secret-keeper!

"Can I get you two some lemonade?"

"That would be lovely," Mrs. Holt says. Mr. Holt nods.

"This is my sister, Jenna. Jenna, Mr. and Mrs. Holt, Laney's parents."

"It's a pleasure," she says brightly, then disappears back inside to get the lemonade.

"Beautiful place you've got here. You've done a good job keeping it up after Cris passed," Mr. Holt says. I'm sure, for someone like me, that's his highest compliment.

"Thank you, sir. Would you like to walk the front of the orchard? It's just right along the fence that circles the house."

I can almost feel his sigh. "Sure."

So enthused.

I tell him things he probably already knows as we walk from the backyard to the split-rail fence that borders the east portion of the orchard. When we stop there, I start to roll right into talk about the orchard operation, just to have something to say, but I stop myself. My patience was thin to begin with. This isn't helping. So I just go for it.

"Mr. Holt, there's something I'd like to talk to you about."

His pause is a long one. "What's that?"

He turns and leans back against the fence, crossing his arms over his chest and narrowing his eyes on me. Anxiously, I chew the cinnamon toothpick between my teeth. Then, thinking he might see it as a sign of weakness—my nervousness—I take it out and throw it into the orchard.

"Look," I say, running my fingers through my hair. "We both know I've never had the best of reputations in this town. And, in all fairness, I've earned most of what I've gotten. But I didn't bring you here to try and explain away my past. I brought you here to talk to you about your daughter, Mr. Holt. And our future," I say, letting my thoughts drift to Laney and all that she means to me. "The best way I can describe what Laney is to me is to say that she's been like *life*. For reasons I won't go into, I was never quite alive until I met her. I had no idea what I was missing until she came along. She loved me before I did one single thing to deserve it. And, although I don't ever see myself being good enough for her, I can promise you one thing. I will love her and care for her better than anyone else on this earth. And that includes you. She's everything good in me. She's everything I could ever want. She's everything I could ever hope to achieve in life. And I'll spend my very last breath making sure she's happy. There is no one else for me, sir.

"Laney gave me a chance when no one else would. She saw something in me that I didn't even see in myself. I hope you can do the same. And, with your permission, I'd like to ask her to marry me."

Now I'm just spent. If I weren't waiting for an answer, and it wasn't rude as all hell, I'd turn around and walk right back to the house and crack open a beer. But, as it is, my entire future is hanging in the balance, so I guess I'd better not.

"You know, a parent always wants certain things for their children. Safety, security, love. The best of everything. But sometimes, we can't see what's close to us as clearly as we think we can. I'm man enough to admit I woefully misjudged you. That was wrong, and there's no excuse. You proved yourself to be the better man when you pulled me out of that fire just to see my daughter smile again.

"It seems I stopped teaching Laney how to be a good person, how to succeed in life, a long time ago. In fact, here lately, *she's* been teaching *me*. With you, she reminded me to look upon a person's heart and nothing else. Jake, regardless of your past, I know you make my daughter happy. And I believe you love her. I can't understand how anyone *couldn't*. But I'm through trying to push her into doing what I think is right. I'm learning that she's smart enough to figure out what's best for her. And I'll stand by her, *what*ever and *who*ever she chooses in life." Mr. Holt pushes away from the fence and starts to walk by me. He stops when his shoulder is even with mine—him facing the house, me facing the orchard—and he turns to clap me on the back. "It just so happens that this time, I agree with her." With a nod and a smile, he walks a few steps beyond me and then looks back, as if he's waiting. I exhale and move forward until I reach his side, and we walk back to the house. Together. In silence. Perfect silence.

FORTY-ONE: *Laney*

The cookout went off without a hitch. My parents seemed happy and forgiving, which is enormously important to me where Jake is concerned. In my opinion, he should have every member of this town's respect for what he did on the night of the fire. But I'm not worried about the whole town. I'm just worried about Daddy. I'd hate for him to make me choose between him and Jake.

He'd be disappointed by my choice.

But it seems that might not happen, if tonight is any indication. Now, the dishes are done, my parents are gone, and Jenna is waiting on the front porch for Rusty, her fiancé, to arrive.

And, for a few minutes, I have Jake all to myself.

I feel my nerves come back full force.

We're lying in the hammock out back. Jake's drinking a beer and chewing his toothpick at the same time. It sounds disgusting, but it's something that I find kind of endearing now. Jake just does what he wants. He marches to whatever beat he happens to hear and like at the moment. And I love that about him.

I lean up on him, looking down into his face. His eyes are closed and his lips are curved in a little half smile.

"Jake?"

"Laney?"

I grin. "Were you serious when you said you could see yourself living out your days here?"

He cracks one eyelid open. "Why do you ask?"

Oh Lord, oh Lord, oh Lord! Here I go!

I push myself into a sitting position, causing the hammock to rock precariously. "Haven't you ever heard that expression 'don't rock the boat'?" he asks, hanging on to the edge so it doesn't tip him out.

"Of course. And I'm so glad we're not in a boat right now," I say with a grin. Jake grins back. "But I digress. So were you? Serious, I mean?"

"Yes. Why do you ask?"

Clearing my throat, I reach down to subconsciously pat my pocket. I don't even realize what I'm doing until I see Jake's eyes follow the movement. He frowns, but says nothing. "Did you mean here, as in this town? Or here, as in this place? The orchard?"

Jake shrugs. "Either one, I guess. But I think it would be kinda nice to hang on to the orchard, to stay here. There are still some things to work out with Ellie before I'll ever know that this place is mine forever, though. Why?" he asks again.

"What if I told you I could make that happen? Would you be mad?"

"Mad? Of course not! I just told you I'd love nothing more. Why, Laney? What are you getting at?"

Jake is getting impatient, and I don't want that ruining this moment, so I scoot out of the hammock and stand up, wiping my damp palms nervously on my jeans.

Jake sits up in the hammock and looks up at me, curious. For a few seconds, I get lost in his warm honey eyes. But then I remember why I'm nervous, what I'm supposed to be doing.

"Your aunt came into the office a few days ago. I may have talked to her. And I may have convinced her to sign over the orchard to you. All of it. Forever. She has no financial or legal interest in it whatsoever."

He laughs. That kind of laugh that says he's pleased, but speechless. "Wow! Are you serious?"

I nod, chewing my lip.

"That's great! How did you do it?"

I resist the urge to kick my toe in the dirt or fiddle with my fingers. "I may or may not have slightly exaggerated the work that you'll have to do at the orchard to keep it going. I may or may not have slightly exaggerated the expense of running and maintaining it now that it's grown to its current size. I may or may not have slightly exaggerated the number of employees she could expect to have to hire for next year's harvest. And I also may or may not have slightly exaggerated the amount of money she'd have to invest out of pocket just to get her through the first harvest before she *might* see a profit."

Jake is smiling a proud, pleased smile.

"And you did this just for me?" *And there's the catch.*

I say nothing for several seconds. I don't move, either. I'm totally frozen, wondering if I've overstepped my bounds.

But I have to take the risk. Jake is worth it. Worth all this and more. He's worth everything.

I drop to my knees in front of him, digging the metal out of my pocket. I let my hair swing down to hide my face as I spread the rings out on my palm.

"One day a couple weeks ago, I was helping Daddy clean up at the fellowship hall ruins and I saw something glistening in the sunshine. It was embedded in a chunk of concrete that had been busted up by the blast. When I bent down to look at it, I saw that it was a ring. Stuck in the concrete. I got a rock and I chipped away until I could get it loose. But buried there, right beside it, was another one. Two plain gold rings." I pause and take a deep breath, taking a quick peek up at Jake's face to gauge his reaction before I continue. I have his full attention. And he hasn't run off yet. I think that's a good sign. "Daddy saw me looking at them. I told him where I'd found them. He smiled, but he didn't say anything for the longest time. But when he did, he told me that when he and Mom had gotten married, there was an old church where the fellowship hall is now. It burned down, too, and Daddy bought the empty lot right after he got the call to preach. He wanted to build a church back there. He said he and Mom used to go up there and sit on the ground where the old church was and where part of the new church would one day be, and they'd talk about the future and their plans, about the church and their life, and their family. Years later, when the foundation was poured, Daddy bought him and Mom new wedding bands and they went up to the new church site and they put their old rings in the concrete. Pushed 'em way down deep while it was still wet. He said he was planting a seed on holy ground for the health and happiness and prosperity of his family and his church."

I tuck my hair behind one ear and look up at Jake, meeting his eyes as bravely as I can.

"I know the night that church burned down you thought I was gonna marry someone else. But since then, you've learned different. In a way, I feel like that fire burned away all the stuff that was coming between us, like it cleared the air and paved the way for us to just love each other. The way we couldn't in the beginning. The way two people should love each other. Forever." I feel the tears come and I can't stop them. My voice is trembling when I ask, "Jake, would you marry me? I know it's crazy for the girl to do the asking, but I'm afraid to go for one more day without you knowing that I'd pledge my life to you right here in this spot, right here in this very minute if I could. You're the only thing in this world that makes me happy. Without you there's . . . there's . . . there's just nothing. You're my everything. And I want to spend the rest of my life showing you how much I love you."

That's all I can say before I start sobbing like a two-year-old who lost her cat.

I hear the creak of the hammock and then I feel strong, warm arms come around me. Jake pulls me in close to him and whispers against my hair, "You stole all my best lines."

I lean back to look at him. He's smiling a beautiful, perfect, happy smile down at me. "Is that a yes?"

"No. That's a hell yes!"

The tears are still streaming down my cheeks, coming in a great flood of happiness and relief. "I don't know if they'll fit. Or if you'd even want to wear them, but—"

"If they don't, we'll put them on chains and wear them around our necks. This will be a reminder of one of the happiest days of my life and I'll never let it go. Just like I'll never let you go."

My heart feels like it has melted and run all over my body, making me warm and more content than I can ever remember being. "Please don't. Don't ever let me go," I say, breathing in his skin as I tuck my mouth against his neck.

"You don't have to worry about that. I couldn't survive without you. And I don't even want to try. You make me the kind of man that I've always wanted to be. You make me a better me. And without you, I'm nothing."

"But to me, you're everything."

"That's just proof."

"Proof of what?"

"That love really *is* blind."

"Not this love! I see very clearly. And I love what I see."

"Well, if you've got a few minutes, I can give you a lot more to look at," Jake says, his grin suddenly playful. He stands to his feet, pulling me with him and into his arms, where the heat rises by several million degrees.

"A few minutes? Is that all it'll take?"

"Oh, no! You did *not* just ask me a question like that! Challenge accepted."

Tossing me over his shoulder, Jake takes off at a run for the back door.

"Jake, stop!"

"You'd better enjoy that word, baby, because that's the last time you'll be saying it for a very, very long time."

I squeal as he flings open the door, races through the kitchen, and takes the stairs two at a time.

He needn't worry about me ever asking him to stop. I'll never want him to stop loving me.

To preorder the next Wild Ones novel,
There's Wild, Then There's You
visit mleightonbooks.blogspot.com.

Wild Child

Dear Reader,

I'm here today to prepare you for the arrival of Rusty and Jenna. They're finally getting their own story. Yay! It's called "Wild Child," and it is sandwiched right here between Jake and Laney's happy ending and the teaser of book three, There's Wild, Then There's You. *This is a bonus story for you amazing readers, a show of my deep and humble appreciation for all the love you've shown me and all these wonderful characters. I can't even begin to explain how excited I am! Can you tell by my complete and utter abuse of exclamation points?*

For those who haven't read The Wild Ones *(I hope you will remedy that posthaste *big smile*), Rusty and Jenna are the two spirited best friends of Trick and Cami, the main characters of book one. The attraction between them is breathtaking and immediate. They meet and sparks fly, but you never really get to see where those sparks lead. Do they hit dry grass and spread into a raging wildfire? Or do they get carried away by the wind until they fizzle? Well, you're about to find out.*

It was a fascinating story for me to write. Jenna is so lively and full of spunk, it's impossible not to love her. But in this *Wild Ones installment, I got to see the depths of her personality, and how hard it can be for someone like her to* really *let go and love. Especially with a guy like Rusty.*

Rusty is wild and fun and passionate, everything Jenna likes, but he's got a past that keeps him from being able to give her what she really needs. *Rusty is bold and gorgeous, funny and brave, but he's also broken—broken in ways he doesn't realize until he is faced with losing the one thing he holds most dear.*

It was the struggle that they faced in finding each other that left me reeling from this story. Sometimes life throws you punch after punch after punch to see if you'll keep getting up. And sometimes you don't want to. But it can be that last time, the last time that you struggle to your feet to fight for what you love that can be the most worth it.

Life and death, love and loss, ups and downs—you'll find it all in this story. I hope you enjoy the journey as much as I did.

Happy reading!
Michelle

ONE: *Jenna*

May

"**N**o sex before the wedding. For me and Trick. *Or* for you and Rusty," Cami says.

With my mouth hanging open, I watch her unpack her suitcase. She's staying with me during this ridiculous celibacy thing she's insisting she and Trick observe the last couple of days before the wedding. She said nothing about dragging my libido into it.

"What?" I exclaim as she crams some shorts in a drawer beside the few belongings I brought home for the month. Having just graduated college, I didn't pack much. I didn't think there was a need. Now, seeing all the crap Cami travels with, I'm glad I didn't. There's not enough room for both of us in here. "No sex for me, either? What the hell kind of twisted joke is this?"

She laughs. "I knew you'd love it."

"Um, excuse me. Have you *met* me?"

"I knew you'd love it . . . when I told you how good it would be for the boys. I read an article about the benefits of anticipation.

Sexually speaking. But then I started thinking about how much it would make the guys miss us if we weren't so . . . accessible. How much more they'd appreciate us, and how they'd realize how lucky they are to have us." Cami nods her head slowly, meaningfully until I see what she's getting at.

"Ohhh, I think I see where this is going."

Cami grins. "That doesn't mean we can't tease them. And make them *wish* we were more . . . available. We just won't be. Until after the wedding."

"Riiight," I say, nodding along now.

"But you have to stick with it, Jenna. No caving."

I'm already recognizing the merit of her plan and how it could lead to very good things for me and Rusty. "No caving," I agree. "Unless Rusty finally drops the L bomb. If that happens, I'll be on him like stink on shit." Cami wrinkles her nose as she eyes me. "Okay, bad analogy. I'll be on him like a cheap suit. Better?"

Her brow smoothes. "Much." She reaches into her suitcase and takes out more clothes, these on hangers. She walks to the closet and begins hanging them on the empty half of the rod. "So, still no progress on that front?"

I sigh. "No. I know he loves me. Well, at least I *think* he does, but it's like he's blocked when it comes to this stuff. He just won't break down and tell me."

"Well, as long as you know . . ."

I feel a pout come to my lips and I can't seem to stop it. "But it's not enough. I *need* to hear it. I *need* to know for sure, beyond the shadow of a doubt."

"Some guys just aren't the type to spill their guts like that, Jenna."

I plop down on the bed, shoulders slumping forward as I pick at the bedspread. "I know. But I hope Rusty's not one of them. You know how I am, Cami. I tell it like it is. I don't think I could live my life always wondering if maybe I was wrong, if maybe I'd imagined it and he really *doesn't* love me. Not the way he should, anyway. I don't want to make plans for my future, plans that include him, and—"

Cami's gasp interrupts me. "Does that mean you got the interviews?"

I can't help but smile. "Yep. Both of 'em."

"Jenna, that's awesome! Ohmigod, this is just what you wanted."

"I know, but you see why this is stressing me out? I don't want to make plans for my future until I know where Rusty stands. I mean, he already thinks I'm the leaving kind, and this will just make it seem like he's right."

"The leaving kind?"

"Yeah. He's always teasing me about being too restless for this town, about having plans that are too big for it. I've never tried to hide how much I hate it here or how I want to live in a bigger city. Maybe Atlanta. But sometimes, I think he sees us as . . . temporary because of it. He thinks I'm some sort of wild child that will never settle down."

"You *are* a wild child, Jenna. But that's not a bad thing. It's who you are. It's what makes us all love you so much."

"But that doesn't mean that I'm gonna bail on someone I love."

"No, it doesn't. And I'm sure Rusty knows that. Deep down."

"That's the problem. I'm not sure that he does. His dad abandoned him and his mom when he was little and I think it effed up his head."

Cami shrugs. "Maybe, but he can overcome that. You can show him that you're here to stay. With him, I mean."

I sigh again. "That's what I'm trying to do. But sometimes I'm just not sure it will ever be enough. Maybe it's *Rusty* who's the leaving kind. Maybe his fear will always keep him from committing, from loving someone like he should. Like he *could*. But that's the thing—I need to know so I can move forward, one way or the other. But I'm scared shitless to tell him about the interviews. What if it makes up his mind for him? What if he thinks it's me saying I'm leaving *him* and not just this town? What if—"

"He'll come around for you, Jenna," Cami interrupts as she finishes hanging her clothes. When they're all neatly arranged in my closet, she comes to sit on the bed with me, bumping me with her shoulder until I look over at her. "For *you*. Trust me. That boy loves you, no matter how much he might try to deny it. Just give him time."

"I'm trying. I'm trying."

"See? My plan is a good one. Maybe he'll realize that he can't live without you. That he doesn't even want to try."

"I was hoping he would see that during one of the many, many weeks we were apart while I was at school, but it's not looking like he did."

Cami pats my knee. "But now you're back home. And school is over. Maybe he'll see how much he likes having you around. And how awful it would be if you got a job in Atlanta and didn't get to come back here as much as you did during school."

"I hope so. I can't wait forever."

"You won't have to. I promise."

I just hope she's right.

Shaking off the depressing thoughts that are threatening to infringe on my bestie's good mood, I hop off the bed and pull Cami up with me.

"Come on, old wise one, I'd say Fab Dad has something delectable waiting for us in the kitchen."

We've both referred to my father as "Fab Dad" for as long as I can remember.

"God, I wish my dad cooked like yours. And was as sweet as yours."

"But then he wouldn't be Jack Hines, now would he?"

Cami sighs. "No. And God forbid I have even *one* family relationship that doesn't give me indigestion for the rest of my life."

"You and Trick are too perfect. God gave you drama everywhere else to even the playing field. No one's life is perfect. Yours was just getting too damn close," I offer as we walk into the kitchen.

"Language, young lady," my dad, Cris Theopolis, scolds from the other side of the island.

"Sorry, father," I respond formally in jest.

"So," he begins conversationally as he piles a heap of French toast and bacon onto two plates, "what are my two favorite girls up to today?"

I watch as he drizzles his homemade peach syrup over the toast. My mouth waters accordingly. "Oh, just girl stuff. Wedding stuff. You know, *fun* stuff."

"This'll be good for Jenna, Cami," Dad says as he slides a plate in front of her. "Maybe it'll make her want to settle down and give her old man some grandkids."

"You're not old enough for grandchildren, Daddy."

"Of course I am."

"You don't look it."

"If you're sucking up, you're off to a particularly good start."

"I know. I got your stunningly youthful genes *and* a winning personality."

"Let's not forget a double dose of humility," my father says wryly.

"How could I forget that?"

"How indeed," he says with a roll of his eyes. "Well, this ought to give you girls enough energy to tackle any amount of wedding hoopla, so eat up."

I glance over at Cami. She's already put away a piece and a half of toast. "You don't have to ask us twice."

Dad winks at me and leans across the island to scrub my head, like he's done for as long as I can remember. He's one of the best things about coming home. This town isn't exactly my favorite place, but there are a few positives. And two of them are in the room with me right now. If it weren't for them, and Rusty, of course, I'd probably never come back.

Rusty, I think with an internal sigh as I take a bite of toast. *The wild card in my future.*

TWO: *Rusty*

"Who the hell came up with this piss-poor idea?" I ask.

Trick pops his head up from under the hood of a '67 Chevy truck. "It's hard to say. My money would be on Jenna. This sounds like some wicked plan of hers, don't you think?"

Giving it a few seconds' thought, I have to agree. "You're probably right. She probably read in some magazine or something that it would make sex better or some such bullshit."

"That sounds like Jenna. And, while I'm all about great sex, I can tell you right now that this is needless on my part. I don't think it's possible for our sex life to get any better."

"Same here. Jenna's a damn hellcat in bed."

Trick laughs. "I'm not surprised. I kinda get that impression."

"Right. So what the hell?"

"Who knows? They're women. I don't think God Himself understands what they do sometimes."

"Duuude," I say, holding out my fist for Trick to bump. And he does. "Couldn't agree more."

"Of course, maybe Jenna wants to show you what you're missing. You know, since you're a pansy about telling her how you feel."

"I'm not a pansy, you prick! Jenna and I are on the same page. We both know she's not the kind to stay around here."

"No, she's not, but you always wanted to open up a garage somewhere near a bigger city so you could do high-end classic restorations. So what's the problem?"

I shrug. "There's no problem. Jenna's restless. It is what it is. Sometimes people leave, no matter how much you want them to stay. Trust me, Jenna knows the score."

"Man, I think you don't know that girl half as well as you think you do. That or you're just *trying* to lose her."

"Now, why would I want to do that?"

"Hell if I know. You're the one with the issues."

"Issues? Kiss my ass. I don't have issues."

"Of course not. It's perfectly normal for a guy to be so much of a pussy about telling a woman how he feels that he dicks around until he loses her."

"Actually, that probably *is* perfectly normal. That shit comes with having balls."

"Or *not* having balls."

"God, you're ornery this morning. What's your deal?"

"You think *I'm* looking forward to sleeping alone just because *your* girlfriend thought it would be a cool experiment?"

"Hey, we still don't know whose brainchild this was. Don't blame *my* girlfriend. It was probably *your* fiancée. You *are* getting married in a couple of days after all. Maybe there's some kind of ancient superstition that Cami read about."

Trick raises his head again. "Why are we still talking about this?"

"Because I've got blue balls already, that's why."

Trick quirks one eyebrow. "Well, then we'll just have to make them suffer until they come begging for this stupid thing to be over."

My grin is slow, and I can see it reflected on my best friend's face. "Oh, hell yeah we will."

I like the sound of this already.

THREE: *Jenna*

I can't wait for Rusty to see what I'm wearing. I dressed specifically with torturing him in mind.

Cami and I made all kinds of salads and desserts this morning to bring to her house for the cookout-slash-bridal shower. It's an unconventional event, but she wanted Trick to participate in everything *with* her. Therefore, the bridal shower now includes the groom, and tomorrow night's bachelorette party will include the bachelors. Crazy as hell if you ask me. But she didn't. She wants Trick around for all of it, and who am I to try to talk her out of it? Besides, she *did* let me plan the bachelorette party. That alone was worth a thousand other compromises.

There are already a dozen cars parked along the side of the road leading to Cami's house, but someone put a sawhorse on the side of the driveway where she usually parks. My guess is it was Trick, saving a spot for his fiancée. I won't deny that it makes me a little green, what they have. I want it for myself. With Rusty. If he ever gets to that point.

And that's a big if.

I get out and move the sawhorse so Cami can pull in. We waste no time in loading up our arms and taking all the foil-wrapped dishes straight down into the backyard.

I look around as we walk, but Rusty is nowhere to be found. He and Trick must be doing some manly stuff inside. Whatever that may be. If I had to guess, I'd say it involves them pounding beer somewhere in the house.

Cami and I are setting dishes on one long, cloth-covered table when I see the patio door open and Trick emerge. I know Rusty won't be far behind. And he's not. He comes out next, holding a beer just like Trick. They're both laughing at something. I turn to face him and wait for his eyes to find me.

When they do, I feel the warmth of those bright blue orbs, and I smile when he stops dead in his tracks. Even from this distance, I can tell exactly where they are on my body. He starts at my feet, taking in my strappy, sexy platforms. Then he works his way slowly up my legs, making them tingle. I can tell the instant he gets to the ragged hem of my cut-off blue jean shorts. I can almost *feel* his fingers tracing the edge of them, teasing the elastic of my panties underneath. I squeeze my thighs together to stop the ache that started the instant I saw him. No sense in getting all worked up when I can't do anything about it.

His eyes finally continue to rise, traveling over the slice of exposed skin on my stomach to the edge of my T-shirt and then stopping on my boobs. I see his chest rise and fall with his deep breath and my nipples pucker into points. Rusty's mouth drops open a little bit and I wonder if he can see them through my shirt. I'm sure he knows they're begging for his mouth.

When his gaze meets mine, I know I'm right. His eyes are shooting blue flames at me. And my body reacts accordingly.

Very slowly, he walks toward me. I can't help but get excited as I watch him. His loose gait is like that of a lion, stalking his prey. And

I'd love to be Rusty's prey. For him to stalk me until he catches me, to grab me with his hands and hold me down so he can devour me.

Shit a monkey, woman! You've got to stop thinking like this!

Rusty's body is almost as familiar to me as my own. As I take in his dark auburn hair, sticking up at all different angles, his wide shoulders, encased in snug navy cotton, and the ripped jeans that hug his thighs so perfectly, I consider throwing Cami's plan right into the toilet and asking Rusty to take me upstairs and let me give him a few more tears in his clothes.

But when I meet his eyes, I don't. I see lust there, but I also see something else. Something I know is worth waiting for. At least until I can't stand to wait any longer. That alone is why I just smile when he stops in front of me.

"Damn you, woman," he breathes, inhaling so deeply I feel his chest brush mine.

I give him my most innocent expression and blink wide eyes at him. "What?"

"You wore this just for me, didn't you?"

I trail my fingers from my collarbone, down between my breasts to my stomach. "What, this old outfit?"

"Yeah, 'this old outfit,'" Rusty says, glancing left and right then taking another small step closer to me. I can feel his thighs against mine. And I can feel the growing bulge between them. "This shirt that makes my palms itch to feel your nipples," he says, tugging at the hem of my shirt, the back of his hand tickling my stomach. "And these shorts that are so short I could slide my fingers right up under them," he says, reaching one hand down between us to barely stroke my inner thigh. "And feel those damp panties of yours."

I'm breathless. Already. And I know from experience that it will only get worse. Rusty does to me what no one else in the world can.

"What makes you think they're damp?"

"Because I know you, baby. I know you put them on with thoughts of me taking them off. I know, even now, you're wishing that I'd take you upstairs and pull them slowly down your legs so that I could . . . do things to you."

"Maybe you're right," I whisper. "But we both know that won't happen, so it doesn't matter."

"This is going to make you just as miserable as it will me."

"Maybe."

Rusty grins. "Oh, no. It will. I'll see to it."

I lift one brow. "Is that right? Well, then bring it! Touché, pussycat."

"Touché, indeed."

With a wink that turns my insides to mush, Rusty reaches around and slaps my butt before he moves past me, his shoulder brushing my aching nipples. I close my eyes for a second, wondering if this might actually hurt me *worse* than it does him.

I flop down in one of the deep cushions of the patio chair. "Phew! I'm glad that's over."

I hear Cami's sigh. She's sitting on the outdoor sofa with her legs curled under her, leaning into Trick's side. "Me, too. That was exhausting!"

"But at least it wasn't embarrassing. I was just sure Rusty's present would be a sex swing and you'd have to explain it to your mom."

"Rusty what?" Rusty asks as he appears at the door, stepping out onto the patio.

"I was just telling them I figured you'd get them something like a sex swing."

He grins and comes to sit in the chair beside mine. "That's why I wanted to shop for it without you. I wanted to show you I could be *un*guy-like sometimes."

"So you're saying the wine fridge-keg cooler combo unit was your *only* consideration?"

"I didn't say *that*."

"Aha! I knew it!"

"Look, I'm a guy. Of course I thought first of a sex swing. But I figured some prudish old blue-haired woman might have a heart attack when it was unwrapped. Or that Cami's dad might whip my ass."

"I'd gladly let Jack whip your ass for a present like that."

"Of course you would, dickhead! But even *I* don't love you that much."

"Well, I think you did a great job, baby," I croon to him.

"Great enough to get some kind of reward?" he asks, waggling his eyebrows at me.

I pause for a few seconds. "Sure. What did you have in mind?" I know exactly what he has in mind, but I want to hear it. Even if we can't do it, I still like hearing what goes on in his head.

"How 'bout a lil skinny-dippin'?"

I perk up instantly. Not only does that sound cool and refreshing, but it sounds like fun. Hot, playful fun.

"You're on," I say, coming to my feet. "You two coming?" I ask Cami.

She looks at Trick and grins. "Yeah, I think we will."

"We will?" he asks.

"If you want to see me in anything less than what I'm wearing right now, then yes, we will."

"I'm in," Trick replies enthusiastically. We all laugh.

The four of us strike out across the yard, bathed in warm breezes and pale moonlight. It already looks like the perfect night for a naughty tryst, which will make it that much harder *not* to . . . indulge. But I think Cami's right. I think maybe this will be a good way to make Rusty see what he's missing out on. Maybe he'll realize he doesn't want to be without me. It's worth a try, anyway. Rusty's worth a lot of tries.

We drop into single file formation as we trek through the woods. I've heard Cami talk about the pond on their property and how much she and Trick *love* to visit it, but I've never been. When the trees part to reveal an oval clearing dominated by a sparkling freshwater pond and absolute silence, I can see why it's a favorite of theirs. It would be a favorite of mine, too.

Trick and Cami drift off to one side. I can barely make out their whispers and Cami's giggles from where I'm standing. It's just enough privacy for everyone without there being . . . trouble.

When I feel a palm brush my butt and Rusty appears at my side, I quit thinking of anyone except him.

"Need some help with these?" Rusty asks, trailing his hand over my hip as he walks around in front of me.

"I think I just might. This zipper can be awfully hateful," I say with mock seriousness.

"Mmm, I figured as much," he says, stepping in close to me again. I can feel warmth radiating from his body as though there's nothing between us at all—no clothes, no air, no emotional separation. Just . . . heat. "But we'd better start with your shirt. I don't want to get tangled up in it as I'm working on that faulty zipper." His eyes appear black in the low light, his dilated pupils overwhelming the azure of his irises.

"I'll trust your judgment," I reply, my heart already racing.

"Lift your arms," he commands quietly, his eyes never leaving mine.

Obediently, I lift my arms over my head and wait. Rusty watches me for several seconds before he presses his palms to my waist and slides them slowly upward, caressing my rib cage, thumbs teasing my nipples as he drags up the material of my shirt. I close my eyes for a heartbeat as he runs his palms up my arms, bringing my tee with them. When Rusty gently removes the shirt from my head, I open my eyes again, falling headlong into the desire I see in his.

"Thank you," I breathe.

"Now for this pesky thing," he muses as he slides a finger under the strap of my bra. "I'm sure it could get in the way."

"I'm sure," I agree, trying hard to remember my objective so that I don't get lost in the moment.

Rusty reaches around me and pops open the hook of my bra with one flick of his fingers. He runs his hands up over my shoulders and down my arms, removing my bra straps as he goes.

I see his eyes flicker down. My nipples tighten when I hear him suck in a breath through his clenched teeth. I know he wants to touch them. He loves my body. He's told me a thousand times he worships every inch of it. But this time, he'll have to love it from a distance. Even if it's a short distance.

"My shorts," I prompt, knowing I'm dangerously close to giving in to my need of him.

Rusty's gaze comes back to mine. He doesn't move. Or speak. He just watches me. I know he's fighting touching me. And I let him.

Finally, he drops to one knee and reaches for my waistband. Carefully, he unbuttons my shorts and then slowly unzips them. He doesn't touch me in any way except when he leans forward just enough to press his lips to the top edge of my panties.

Heat pours into my core and my body throbs for him to kiss me lower. Then lower still. But he doesn't. With his face so close I can feel his breath, Rusty pulls my shorts down my legs then follows them with my panties.

When I'm standing before him, wearing nothing but my shoes and a passion for him that never seems to die, he looks up at me. For a few seconds, I think it's over. The game is over. He's going to kiss me and I'm going to let him. But he doesn't. Instead, Rusty stands slowly to his feet and says, "Your turn."

I kick off my shoes, take a deep breath, and curl my fingers in the hem of Rusty's shirt. I pull it up, letting my hands touch his hard, smooth skin as I go. I can feel every ripple of his abdomen, every hard bulge of his pecs, but I don't give in to my urge to press my lips to them.

I stretch up on my tiptoes to tug his shirt over his head. He's taller than me, so I have to sway slightly toward him to reach high enough.

My breasts graze his chest and I gasp. I can't help it. The sensation of his skin touching my nipples flashes through me like a bolt of lightning, hot and electric.

"Jen-na," he warns gruffly.

"Sorry," I pant. I throw his shirt to the side and drop to my knees in front of him. I reach for the button of his jeans. I pause with my fingers tucked just inside his waistband, and I look up at him. His face is set in stone and his jaw is clenched. I know this is hard for him. And when I let my eyes travel down, I can see the enormous bulge that assures me just *how* hard it is for him. Impulsively, I lean forward and press my lips to it. I hear him moan and his fingers wind into my hair, holding me to him for a few seconds before he tugs my head away.

"You'd better hurry it up or this is all over with," he says hoarsely.

I grin up at him. "Can't handle it?"

He opens his mouth to say something, but stops, clamping his teeth shut with a click. He watches me for a bit before his lips curve into a smile. "We'll see who can handle what," he responds, crossing his arms over his chest. "Continue."

He's steeling himself against wanting me, which makes me want to tease him that much more. I *want* to break him. I *want* him to give in because he just can't stand it. I *want* him to forsake all else for me, for the want of me, for the love of me. That's all I've ever wanted from Rusty—his devotion. The same kind of devotion I have for him.

With determination, I smile up at him and unbutton his jeans. I reach for the zipper and ease it down over his erection. I ignore the pulsing between my legs. *This* is about Rusty.

I run my hands around his waist and slide them down over his butt, pushing down his jeans as I stroke the backs of his thighs, letting my chin graze his belly as I look back up at him.

With glittering eyes, Rusty watches me. I feel him shift as he kicks off his shoes and steps out of the jeans now pooled at his feet. And then he waits. Waits for me to finish.

I trail my fingers up the outsides of his legs and tease the bottom of his boxer briefs, running my fingers up high enough that I can feel the crease where his thighs meet his hips. I see him twitch behind the white cotton.

Bringing out my hands, I reach up to grasp the elastic band of his underwear and I tug, carefully freeing his shaft before I drag them down his legs. When he steps out of them, I hold onto his thighs as I rise. As my mouth passes his erection, I stick out my tongue and drag it along the thick vein that runs from base to tip.

I hear him growl, and I smile as I straighten in front of him. "Ready?"

"To skinny-dip with the devil? Sure," he replies, a slow grin coming to his face.

With speed a striking snake would envy, Rusty bends and throws me over his shoulder. I squeal in surprised delight as he takes off running toward the water and jumps off the bank, plunging us both into the cool, black pond.

FOUR: *Rusty*

It's been hours, and I still can't sleep. Cami and Jenna had asked that I stay with Trick during this forced period of celibacy. I think each of us is supposed to watch the other, making sure no one cheats by paying any late-night visits. And it's probably a good idea, because if there was ever a night I'd be likely to climb a tree to try and get to Jenna through Cami's window, tonight would undoubtedly be it.

Just the thought of hearing Jenna laugh as we played in the water, just the memory of her playfully wrapping her arms and legs around me and pressing her cool lips to mine, just the knowledge that her tight, hot body was within centimeters of my granite-hard cock— well, it's enough to keep a man up at night.

With a growl, I throw back the covers and stomp through the living room and into the kitchen. I have to laugh when I find Trick sitting at the island, in the dark, nursing a beer.

"What the hell, man?" he says when I turn on the light.

"If we ain't sleeping, we're drinking. Now go get your stash of beer from downstairs. We're gonna need a lot more than what's in the fridge. We've got some hot blood to cool."

"This is gonna be a long week, isn't it?"

"Hell yeah, it is!"

We both sigh, and Trick gets up to go downstairs. I walk to the fridge and take out the rest of the cold beer in there to make room for more. I figure we'll have these downed in less than an hour.

I shake my head as I think again of Jenna. I don't know what that girl's trying to do to me, but if it includes death from overexcitement, she's well on her way.

FIVE: *Jenna*

It's after lunch, and Rusty is on my mind even more than usual, which is always a lot. This whole look-but-don't-touch (or at least don't touch anything too much) is eating me up. But in a really good way. For whatever reason, I almost feel closer to Rusty, like we're sharing a private joke. I guess we are, actually. A private joke that's like the ultimate foreplay. And neither of us knows how much we can take before we give in.

But wading through every sweetly torturous moment is half the fun.

"So they *are* meeting us there, right?" I ask Cami, who's sitting in the passenger seat of my car, fiddling with her phone.

"Yes. For the millionth time yes! They're supposed to be there by 1:30."

"Okay," I say with a smile. Cami turns her attention right back to her phone and types something out furiously. "Just what the hell are you doing?"

Cami's head jerks up and she glances guiltily at me, shielding her cell phone against her chest. "Nothing. Why?"

I gasp. "You're sexting!"

"Am not."

"Are, too! You are a dirty little sexter! Don't even bother to hide it. Your cheeks are blood-red and your pupils are *huge*!"

Cami grins. "Are they really?"

"Ohmigod, you two are horrible!"

"You say that like *you* don't do it."

"I haven't texted Rusty one naughty thing since you told me what we were doing with this no sex thing."

"Really? I'm impressed."

"You should be, you cock-blocking guttersnipe!"

"Cock-blocking guttersnipe?" She laughs.

I giggle. "I don't know where in blue blazes that came from. See what a lack of sex does to me?"

"I figured you'd have caved already. You're not the celibate type."

"Neither are you. At least not where Trick's concerned."

She smiles wider. "He *does* make it awfully hard to do without."

My sigh is wistful, as thoughts of Rusty's talented . . . parts come to mind. "Gotta love a man with magic in his pants."

At 1:22, Cami and I are pulling into the parking lot outside the Crazy Clown Costume Shoppe in Summerton. It's the nearest more-than-one-horse city to our hometown of Greenfield, South Carolina. We get out and walk to the door, both of us stopping to stare at the cardboard cut-out standing on the sidewalk like a proud, bipolar sentry at the shop entrance.

The guy is wearing a fuzzy red wig and a squishy red nose and his face is painted white with a big, black smile around his mouth. From neck up, he's a clown. But from waist down, it's a different story. He's wearing a Chippendale bow tie, forearm cuffs like Conan the Barbarian, underwear with an elephant trunk at just the right place, and chaps to finish him off. He's sort of a costume clusterfu—

"Please God, tell me you didn't pick any of this for Trick," Cami pleads as we approach the door, interrupting my thoughts.

I giggle. "Well, not all of it."

She looks at me from the corner of her narrowed eyes, and I smile as angelically as someone like me can smile.

A chime sounds as we walk through the door. A short, olive-skinned, small-framed guy dressed in full drag—and I mean *full drag*—greets us from near the cash register.

"Welcome, ladies," he says with something similar to a lisp.

His clothes are girly enough—pink sequined mini dress, black feather boa, black fishnets, pink polka dot platforms—and the silky, straight pink wig even matches. But it's the flat masculine nipples visible above the plunging neckline of the dress that gives the clerk's gender away. That and the bulge about six inches below his navel.

"I'm Loretta. Can I help you find something?"

Loretta?

What I'd thought was a female smoker's voice over the phone was apparently . . . not. Loretta is a man.

"I'm Jenna. I called a few days ago about some coordinating costumes."

Loretta throws his hands in the air and his mouth forms an O of excitement. "Oh, girl! I've been waiting for you. I can't wait for you to see what I got in for the guys."

Platforms and all, Loretta races toward me and takes me by the hand to start towing me toward the back of the shop. Quickly, I reach out and grab Cami's wrist. If I go, she goes.

The back wall of the store is lined with rows and rows of rolling metal racks. Loretta doesn't stop until we are in the far right, rear corner facing a rack parked under a sign that reads THEOPOLIS.

"I already pulled aside two or three different sizes in all the costumes you asked for. I brought 'em back here with the ladies', just to keep 'em straight. It's the only thing I like straight," he says with a wink and an elbow to my ribs. "They start at large and go through two X. I know how big these corn-fed country boys can be." He waggles his eyebrows comically and delicately slaps my shoulder. I laugh outright.

"Well, you know your men," I say, stating the obvious. "Most of the ones coming in are pretty husky."

"Mmm, I love me some husky," Loretta says with a wicked grin. "Now which one of you gets what outfit? Wait! Don't tell me. Let me guess."

Like the expert that he obviously is, Loretta describes exactly what I had envisioned us wearing.

"Damn, Loretta, you're good!" I say in awe.

"Girl, I own a costume shop. I've got an eye for the inner beast," he says confidently.

"Well, two of the guys should be here in a few minutes. They're the two that are giving us the most trouble about the costumes. You know how pigheaded men can be . . ."

Loretta rolls his eyes. "Mmm-hmmm, don't I know it."

"So we've decided to put on a little show for them so that maybe they'll be a little more . . . agreeable."

Loretta's eyes light up. "Oh, a costume montage? Sign me up!"

"I was thinking something a little more . . . private."

Loretta smiles. "Not that I don't appreciate what you're thinking, but this *is* a public business."

"Oh, not *that* private. I was just thinking maybe put on a little show for the boys. You know, get them a little more excited about dressing up. And seeing *us* all dressed up."

"Ohhh, I see where you're going. Start the engines up. Get the appetite going. Girl, I like where you're head's at. And I think the dressing rooms in back will work just fine."

I hear the chime of the front door and my pulse skips. That has to be them.

Loretta yips in excitement. "That must be them. You girls go on back," he says, pointing to a curtained door. "There are two separate rooms you can use for fitting. Ms. Theopolis, you go left. Honey, you go right," he says, speaking to Cami. "I'll roll the whole cart back there when I show your guests to you." His eyes are bright and sparkling. It's easy to see that he really loves his job. And men. Hot, corn-fed men.

"Sounds good," I say, grabbing Cami's hand. "Come on, woman. We've got some torture to inflict."

Before we disappear, I loud-whisper to Loretta before he's out of earshot. "Loretta! I get the redhead."

He nods and gives me a wink. Cami and I are both smiling on our way through the curtain.

SIX: *Rusty*

I doubt many things would've surprised me more than the man in drag who greeted me and Trick at the door of the costume shop. I think my mouth was still hanging open when he pushed us to the rear of the store and through a curtain to where Jenna and Cami were waiting. Somewhere.

"I'm Loretta," the guy says by way of introduction. "I'll be your host for this afternoon's display. Can I get you boys something to drink?"

Trick and I look at each other then back at him and shake our heads. "No, thanks."

"All right then. You have a seat right here," Loretta says, leading me to a comfortable-looking, bright red chair positioned in front of a private little cubby with a black velvet curtain covering the door. "And you come with me," he says to Trick, disappearing around the corner. "Let's get this show on the road," I hear him say as they're walking away.

I'm sitting in my chair, feeling like a dumbass, when I hear the crackle of speakers coming on line a couple of minutes later. Music pours out around me just before the ambient lights dim and a spot-light pops on to illuminate the thick curtain.

I recognize the music. And the song. It's called "You Can Leave Your Hat On," and it has an old, burlesque feel to it. It sets a mood; I'm just not sure what for.

Until I see the curtain wiggle.

It parts just enough that I see a knee poke out. In time with the music, the leg straightens. It's curvy and covered in fishnet stocking, with a garter halfway up the thigh. On the foot is an obscenely high, shiny black heel. The curtain parts farther, and Jenna steps slowly out of the dressing room.

"Oh damn," I breathe, suddenly warming to the idea of costumes. Jenna smiles and then, pausing, coyly bites her fingertip, looking up at me from beneath her lashes. "I seem to be having some trouble finding juuust the right costume. I'm looking for . . . sexy. What do you think of this one?" she asks, her lips curved the slightest bit, just enough to be suggestive. I let my eyes slide over her outfit. She's in a pink and black bustier that her tits are practically spilling out of and some frilly little panty-type things. And the fishnets. And that's it.

"Does it fit okay?" she asks softly, letting her palms glide over the swell of her breasts. "It feels a little . . . tight." Before I can answer, she slinks over to my chair and turns, peeking back over her shoulder at me. She wiggles her ass just enough to draw my eye. "How does it look from behind?"

I glance up at Jenna's face. I see the playfulness in her eyes. And the heat. She's toying with me, but she's enjoying it, too. I've always loved that about her.

"The fit is good, but what about the material?" I ask, reaching out to touch her. Before my fingers meet her body, though, she straightens and starts to walk away.

She stops in the doorway of the dressing room, smiling back at me. "Let me try another one. Maybe something else will tickle your . . . fancy a little more."

When the curtain closes, I lean my head back and close my eyes. It's been a while since I've embarrassed myself in public. If this is the way the afternoon's gonna go, maybe I should start thinking about baseball. Or Margaret Thatcher. Naked. On a cold day.

Before I can conjure one distracting thought, however, I hear the rings on the curtain jingle. Then, all I hear is the music. And the thud of my heartbeat in my ears.

I open my eyes to Jenna masked and dressed in a black leather catsuit with one sparkling silver zipper that goes from throat to crotch. She struts over to me this time, cracking a black leather riding crop over her palm.

She stops in front of the chair and raises one leg to set her stiletto-shod foot on the arm. With her legs spread, I watch as she drags the tail of the riding crop up one long thigh, stopping only when it grazes the V that makes my mouth water.

"How do you like this one?"

I look up at her face. I can see the glimmer in her eyes as she watches me from behind her black domino mask. She flicks the riding crop between her thighs. I see her lips part like she gasped, only I didn't hear it. She might be doing this to torture me, but she's enjoying the hell out of it, too.

I'm just about to take that crop from her hands and show her how *I* could use it on her when she turns on her heel and walks back the way she came. My eyes are glued to her ass. Blood pumps through my body with each exaggerated swing of her hips.

As I wait, try as I might, I can't think of baseball or naked, old British women. I can only think of Jenna. And what she might be wearing next. And how much I wish I was in there while she changes.

When the curtain parts a third time, Jenna appears wearing a teeny tiny white dress with a red cross over the left breast. The top is split to the navel and, if she moved just right, I could probably see nipple. On her feet are red shoes. Around her neck is a red stethoscope.

She starts toward me again, but before she reaches me, she stops, dragging the stethoscope from around her neck. She lets it dangle from her fingertips for a few seconds before she drops it onto the floor behind her.

With wide, round eyes, she purses her lips and says, "Oops!" covering her mouth with her fingertips in a gesture Betty Boop would be proud of. Then, in slow motion, she pivots on her high red heel and bends at the waist to pick up her stethoscope.

As the short dress rises over her hips, I see the curve of her ass and the dark shadow between her legs. Damn her, she's not wearing any panties!

I give absolutely no thought to where we are, or the fact that I'm supposed to be keeping my hands off her. I simply get up and go to her. Jenna affects me like that. She consumes me. Completely sometimes.

She yelps in surprise when I jerk her upright and whirl her around. I pull her up against my chest and raise my finger to her lips.

"Shhh," I mutter, backing her up into the dressing room she just vacated.

Once inside, I pull the curtain shut behind us. With that song still playing, I reach around Jenna to feel for the zipper on her skimpy costume. Her breathing is heavy as it hits my lips. She's panting.

I ease down the zipper and then pull the white material from her shoulders, peeling it down to her waist. She's not wearing a bra underneath, either; the outfit is cut too low for one. Gently, I palm one plump breast, rubbing my calloused hand over the nipple. Jenna's mouth drops open, and I remind her again, "Shhh."

I tweak the pebble and smile when she sinks her teeth into her bottom lip. I bend my head and suck one nipple into my mouth as I push her costume down over her hips. I let it fall down her legs to pool on the floor.

Jenna's breathing is ragged as I kiss my way down her stomach. Cupping the back of her knee, I push back so that she leans into the corner for balance as I bring her foot up off the ground and prop it on my shoulder, opening her up for me.

I place one kiss on the inside of her thigh before I slide my mouth over to nuzzle the silky, wet flesh between her legs. I flick my tongue over her, just once, and I inhale. "God, I miss this." I feel her shudder when I exhale warm, moist air on her. Slowly lowering her leg, I straighten to stand before her. "I miss *you*."

Jenna's eyes are heavy and her lips are trembling.

"But I'm right here. I've always been right here."

"Still, I can't have you, though, can I?" She watches me with her hazelnut eyes, but says nothing. I wonder if she's thinking the same thing I am. "Let's go home. Before I commit a felony in here."

"Don't let me stop you," she replies softly.

"Oh, no. When the time finally comes, I want you screaming my name. More than once." With a grin I know will drive her nuts, I back out of the curtain, telling her just before I close it, "Just remember this when I see you tonight."

I smile all the way out the door. The funny thing is, Trick's already outside waiting on me.

SEVEN: *Jenna*

When we walk into Lucky's, the only place Cami would agree to have this joint bachelor-slash-bachelorette venture, my eyes immediately scan the crowd for Rusty. I'm not sure what the female equivalent of blue balls is, or if there even *is* one, but if there is, I've got it!

Since walking out of the shop with the three of them and getting a chaste kiss on the cheek as Rusty opened the car door for me, I've been unable to think about anything other than his lips on me. And how much I want them on me. Now.

I don't see him at first, so Cami and I make our way to the cluster of tables that Daryl, the manager of Lucky's, let us push together under the giant banner that reads CONGRATULATIONS, TRICK AND CAMI! Behind that, in front of the stage, is a curtain I borrowed from the local funeral home. They use it as a partition when the need arises. It's super-sized, solid black, and thick as hell, perfect for what I needed. It conceals the night's two main attractions.

I grin when I take in the costumes of the members of the wedding party who have already arrived. I picked them out specifically so they'd match.

One of Cami's bridesmaids is wearing a Playboy bunny getup. Her husband is wearing a Hugh Hefner–style smoking jacket, a cravat, and a gray wig. Another girl is wearing a nurse's costume, one that gives me chills when I look at it because it reminds me of this afternoon. Her counterpart is wearing a surgeon's outfit. There's also a Pocahontas and brave couple, a Marilyn and JFK couple, and a Pamela and Tommy Lee already here.

As Cami gives hugs all around, I turn again to look for Rusty. This time I spot him.

And he takes my breath away.

Rusty is gorgeous anyway, but his costume highlights his stellar body. He's shirtless, with only a bandana wrapped around his throat and a cowboy hat on his head. From the waist down, he's all long, muscular legs, tight jeans, and dusty boots. I'm sure those are his, because I didn't pick out boots to go with his costume.

He hasn't noticed me yet, so I can look my fill. His broad shoulders are tan and muscular. His chest is wide and well-developed. And his stomach . . . God help me, I love that stomach! It's trim and ripped, and there's a thin trail of hair that leads from his navel to the most incredible . . . appendage.

I smile as I think about it. Rusty would probably have a stroke if he knew I was calling it an "appendage."

Suddenly, he turns and his eyes meet mine. It's almost as though he could feel my attention on him. He raises one dark brow, no doubt wondering what I'm grinning about. I smile even wider, knowing it will eat at him until he finds out.

I'm not surprised when he grabs his beer and walks toward me. He's halfway across the bar when he starts to slow down. It seems that he's just now noticing what I'm wearing.

And I'd say he likes it very much.

I suck in my stomach and hold out my arms before settling my hands on my hips to let him look. His eyes roam me from my own black cowboy hat, down to my fringed, suede bra, to my bare stomach and on to my chaps, completely open all the way to my boots, but for the frilly little panties I'm wearing underneath.

His mouth drops open the tiniest bit and I feel my heart speed up. I have no doubt if we were alone, or even in a different venue, Rusty would take me by the hand, lead me to the first semiprivate place he could find, and bury his body in mine until we both lost the ability to think straight.

It's what we do. It's how we affect each other.

And it's wonderful.

He resumes his walk to me. Cami passes in front of him and he watches her go, shaking his head at her outfit. She's wearing a black leather dominatrix ensemble, and Trick is wearing the matching submissive one. I watch her cross to Trick, and I laugh out loud when he turns and sees her. His jaw goes slack and I'd be willing to bet he got a hard-on instantly. I wouldn't be the least bit surprised if they use these costumes again. In private.

"So, the next surprise in Jenna's World of Wedding Wonders?"

"You mean the costumes weren't enough?" I ask. "Don't you like mine?" I look up at him from beneath my lashes, purposely coy as I tease the fringe that hangs from my bra.

"I'd be happy to show you what I think of your costume. Later."

"You would?"

"Mmm," he purrs, leaning in to kiss my neck. Chills spread down my arms.

"Well, since I'm off limits, maybe the other things I've got lined up will take your mind off me. And all the things I'd like for you to do to me in this outfit." I lean in to Rusty, my lips less than an inch from his, and I whisper, "And out of it."

"You're evil. Did you know that? You'll probably go to hell for doing this to me."

I run my fingers up his bare chest to his chin, then I trace his bottom lip with my bright red fingernail. "Come burn with me."

"You lead the way," he growls hoarsely, like the heat between us has singed his vocal cords.

I plant my hand on his chest and push. I give him my sauciest grin. "Maybe later," I say, taking a step back. "Or maybe not."

Rusty's breath hisses through his gritted teeth and I laugh outright. Who ever thought this would be so much fun? Torture, for sure. But fun, anyway.

EIGHT: *Rusty*

never thought it could be so hard to keep my hands off someone. Of course, I've never really tried. All I can say is that, when I finally get between those long legs of Jenna's, there's gonna be an explosion of epic proportions.

And it won't just be *me* doing the exploding.

As I watch Jenna, I can see invitation in the way she moves. She might as well be shifting against me, close enough for me to touch her. The things she does with her hips and her hands, the way she bends over with that delicious ass of hers tipped perfectly in my direction—all of it is for me, like she can feel my eyes on her. Like she *wants* to feel my hands on her.

I know this because she keeps looking back, making sure I'm watching. Teasing me. I'd be willing to bet those ruffled little panties she's wearing now include a wet spot. We're engaged in the ultimate game of cat and mouse, and it's keeping us both turned on.

I watch her as she backs toward the curtain that's stretched across the back half of the room. I know there's a stage back there, but there has to be something else. It's a big space she's got concealed!

"Seems like we're missing something in here, doesn't it?" Jenna asks, raising her voice so the rest of the party can hear her.

Shouts go up all around and she smiles, taking a handful of curtain and dragging it along the makeshift line that's stretched across the room. Bit by bit, the edge of a thick black and red mattress is revealed. That's all I can see because it's so dark behind the curtain.

With a flourish, Jenna flings back the curtain. A single spotlight flips on, shining down on a dull, black mechanical bull. The crowd goes nuts.

All I can think about is watching Jenna ride that thing.

"Holy shit, it's gonna be a long night," I mutter to myself.

Jenna is grinning from ear to ear. "All right, now that I've got your attention, who's gonna be the first to ride the bull? We gotta get some use out of this thing before the operator gets bored and goes home," she says, gesturing toward the clearly unenthusiastic plaid-clad old man who's sitting on a stool in the corner, leaning over a small console. He probably came with the mechanical bull. I think he might be asleep under the wide brim of his enormous hat. I can't be sure. "Come on, ya bunch of pansies! Who's gonna pony up and ride it first?"

There's lots of shouting and whistling and general loud-mouthing, but no one steps forward. I can see several people trying to get Trick to go first, but he's resisting, content to sit by his hot fiancée.

I hear Jenna's name above the fray, called once, twice, then multiple times. In a few seconds, everyone is chanting for her to give that bull a ride.

With an exasperated shake of her head, she turns toward the bull. "Fine. I'll show you how it's done. I just hate to make the rest of you look bad," she teases with a cocky grin.

The old man, awake and alert after all, slides off his stool and hobbles over to Jenna to lend her a hand as she climbs up onto the bull. When she's seated on its wide, leather back, I see her frown. "Something else is missing," she muses loudly, pausing for a second before she shouts, "Music!"

The lights over the stage come on in a burst of color. Standing with their instruments, and one member sitting behind his drums, are the members of Saltwater Creek, the band I used to play in. I glance over at Trick. He's howling happily, his arms raised into the air. He used to play with us, too. He looks at me and smiles. I know this probably makes his night that much better. I return his smile then look back to the stage.

"Something's still missing," Jenna yells. "Oh, I know what it is. We're gonna need more bass."

Heads start turning toward me, and I finally look up at Jenna where she's sitting atop the bull. She's looking right at me, grinning. She tips her head toward the stage and I look back in that direction. Everyone in the band is watching me, smiling, and Sam, the bass guitar player, is taking the strap of his guitar off his shoulder. He walks to the front of the stage and holds it out to me.

Quitting the band was a tough decision, but it was the right one. Business at the garage started picking up and it was a matter of growing up and facing my responsibilities, laying the groundwork for my future, or playing with the boys.

Adulthood won out.

But getting a chance to get back up on stage still holds a special lure. And Jenna knows that.

I can't hide my smile as I hop up on the platform and take the guitar. Sam nods at me and I nod back, slipping the leather strap over my shoulder and taking the pick from his outstretched hand. I lay my palm against the body of the guitar and curl my fingers around the neck, settling in to the feel of the cool metal against my skin.

I look out at Jenna, and her eyes tell me she knows I'm on top of the world right now. It reminds me of all the things that I love about her that have nothing to do with her body, but with her heart and her soul. She winks and calls out a question that doubles as a song request.

"Who feels like makin' love?"

A rowdy bunch, pretty much everyone in the bar yells out in agreement, so I close my eyes and reach back in my memory for the chords to the song. For a few seconds, everyone quiets and the world fades away as they all wait for me to start picking out the notes. With the first one, I remember how much I love the feel of the strings under my fingertips.

After eight beats, the rest of the band jumps in. I open my eyes and look back out at Jenna. She takes her hat off and gives her head a shake, her dark hair shimmering down her slender back. When she puts it back on her head, her eyes find mine and she winks at me from under the brim. I could easily drop my guitar, jump off the stage, and spread her out on that bull and eat her like dessert. But before I can really finish the thought, she reaches down for the leather strap and nods for the bull operator to wind it up.

The rotation starts out slow, like the operator is trying to match the beat of the song. Jenna's body moves in perfect time with it. It's like everything between us and around us is in sync.

It's almost painful to watch her ride that damn bull. Her back arches with each buck of the machine and her hips swivel fluidly, like she's connected to it. Her cheeks are flushed, her lips are parted just a little, and I can see the tip of her tongue grazing her teeth. I hope she's thinking what I'm thinking—that the only thing better than this would be if it was *me* between her legs.

The operator increases the speed and Jenna's body shifts and sways in time with it. All too clearly, I can imagine us in front of a mirror with her moving just like that on top of me. Up and down on my cock, her thighs clamped around my sides, her creamy body squeezing me.

My jeans get tight. Real tight. As the song winds down and the operator slows the bull again, Jenna glances up at me. The look she gives me says she knows what I'm thinking. And I mutter again, "Holy shit, it's gonna be a long night!"

NINE: *Jenna*

After getting so turned-on by Rusty watching me ride the bull, it's all I can do to keep my composure for the rest of the night. I want him so bad I ache with it.

But stay composed I do. Somehow, I manage to keep it together while cranking up the heat. It's my mission to make the want as painful for Rusty as it is for me. And every time I look at him, I know it's working a little more. The crotch of his jeans is probably extended to the tensile limit of denim. I can't stop the satisfied smirk that comes to my lips as I think of it.

I glance over at Rusty as he watches another girl ride the bull. As if sensing my eyes and my thoughts on him, he turns those bright-blues on me. I wink sassily at him and he raises one eyebrow.

I make myself turn away after that. I'm tempted to go order another shot when I hear the bartender ring the bell that signals last call. I resist the urge, because part of my deal with Daryl in him letting us "borrow" Lucky's tonight was that I'd lock up after closing and then come back bright and early in the morning to meet the truck when it comes to collect the mechanical bull. The last thing I need is to be shitfaced while trying to secure a bar that isn't mine.

Less than an hour later, the house lights flash three times in a row and the lights over the stage shut off, my signal to start shooing people out the door. Luckily, the band stopped playing about an hour ago, so no one cares about the stage anymore.

When the bar is empty, but for the little old man who operates the mechanical bull, I give him a fifty dollar tip and push him out into the lot, too, flipping the lock behind him so I can make my way around, cutting off lights before I go home.

I find off switches for every light in the place except the one over the dance floor, the dance floor that, for tonight, was occupied by a mechanical bull. I walk behind the bar, searching for a hidden switch. I look through the small storage and break room in back. Still no luck. The only thing I find back there is the radio, which is clearly labeled LEAVE ON, but no other light switches. I decide to check the other side of the building, somewhere near the stage, hoping I can find the controls there.

As I round the corner back out into the bar, I come to a sudden stop, a gasp bubbling up in my chest. There's someone sitting on top of the bull.

I'm only startled for a few seconds, though. My pulse speeds up for an entirely different reason when I recognize the figure straddling the machine.

It's Rusty. And he's watching me.

My feet move me slowly across the room toward him. My heart thumps wildly against my ribs. My mouth goes completely dry as I take him in.

The wide brim of his cowboy hat casts a shadow over his face. But even so, I can feel Rusty's glittering blue eyes fixed on me. The light pouring down on his shoulders accentuates every ripple of muscle in his arms and bathes his perfectly defined abs in a soft, golden glow. His big hands are resting on his thighs, motionless. Chills spread down my arms when I look at those long fingers, remembering all too clearly the pleasure they can bring.

I take a deep breath. "Bar's closed, mister," I say casually as I approach him.

He doesn't respond immediately. When he does, I feel a hot flush move through my core.

"Thought I'd grab a slow ride before you locked up. I missed my chance earlier."

My stomach twitches at his insinuation. He's asking me. Outright. And he's perfectly still as he waits for my reply.

Adjusting my trajectory, I veer to the right and walk to the podium that houses the bull controls. I look down at the console I watched the little old man working earlier. I glance back at Rusty, knowing that if I turn it on, I'm giving him my answer.

My pause is barely that of a heartbeat before I reach up and flip the red switch up to the on position. To hell with resisting him! I'm not the one getting married.

"How slow do you want it?" I ask provocatively, the sultry music from the radio only adding to the intensity of the moment.

"As slow as you can make it," he replies, a wicked grin twisting his lips.

I ease the lever up the tiniest bit, just enough that I can barely hear the whir of the machine's motor turning. With a groan, the bull moves slightly forward and down, making a leisurely turn on its post. Rusty doesn't move but for the motion of his hips as he rides fluidly on the swiveling bull. When it revolves completely, leaving him facing me again, I see the almost imperceptible tip of his head. "You coming?"

I don't answer him. I don't need to. I step out from behind the console and walk toward Rusty, an answer in and of itself. Anticipation pours through me when I step up onto the thick, black mat and stop at the base of the slow-moving machine.

Without a word, Rusty holds out his hands. Without a word, I take them.

Effortlessly, he pulls me up onto the bull with him, my back pressed to his chest, his hard body folding in around me. "Put your hands here," he whispers in my ear as he leans forward to show me.

I do as he asks, excitement curling in my stomach. I feel Rusty drag my hair away from my neck just before his lips touch my skin. My nipples pucker reflexively.

"Do you know how much I wanted to be up here with you tonight?" He pushes his hips against my butt. I can feel how hard he is, just as hard as I knew he would be. "Watching you arch your back," he says, trailing his fingers down my spine, causing me to bow outward. His hand rises back up to the band of my bra, his fingers easily unsnapping it. Slowly, he runs his palms up to my neck and then down over my shoulders, not stopping until he brushes my fingertips, pushing off my top. "I kept imagining how hard your nipples would be if I were touching them while you rode this bull."

He cups both breasts in his hands and squeezes. My breath hitches in my throat and heat puddles between my legs.

"I know you were wishing I was up here with you, too. I could see it in every sway of your hips," he murmurs against my neck, the fingers of one hand tracing circles around my nipple as his other travels down the center of my stomach. "And I know that if I could've touched you right then, I'd have found these wet," he whispers, dipping his hand down into my panties and cupping my burning flesh. "Mmm, just like this."

The lights swirl around me, framed by the pitch-black of the empty bar. I close my eyes, abandoning myself to the moment, to the feel of what Rusty's doing to me as he slips one finger inside me.

I moan and let my head fall back against his shoulder. He rolls my nipple between finger and thumb as he thrusts the fingers of his other hand in and out of me. Long, deep movements, like the rhythm of the bull.

"I knew you'd be dripping. Watching me watch you. Wishing you were riding my cock up here on this bull. Fantasizing about coming for me. In front of all those people. I know you'd like that, wouldn't you?"

Lazily, he drags his fingers out of me to tease my clit with leisurely swirls. I move my hips against him, breathless as the familiar tension builds inside me.

I feel Rusty lean away from me before he puts his hands around my waist and lifts, turning me around on the bull to sit facing him, but not straddling him.

The look on his face is ravenous as he takes off my hat and flings it into the darkness. "Do you think there's anyone outside right now, Jenna? Out there in the dark? Watching us through the windows?"

His lips crash down on mine before I have time to answer. His tongue licks along mine as his hands roam over my breasts and my stomach, my back, my hips. He's touching me everywhere except the place I need him to touch me most.

When he tears his lips away from mine, he puts his palm between my breasts and pushes gently, urging me to lie back. I relax over the head of the bull, letting the slow, easy movements of the machine set the pace for what's to come.

Rusty drags his hand down my stomach, not stopping until he reaches the juncture of my widely spread thighs. I feel him move my panties to one side. There's a pause that lasts a lifetime. It's filled with heat and electricity and wild anticipation. And then I feel the hot lick of his tongue. I buck at first, like the imitation bull beneath me might. But then I relax under his mouth, easing my legs back down over the sides of the machine, opening them wider and giving Rusty full access to my body. The blood is rushing to my head, making it swim lightly, and I feel the tightening of my muscles as Rusty pushes two fingers inside me. In and out, he moves them as his tongue flickers over my sensitive flesh.

"I wonder if someone's watching me lick you, watching my tongue when I do this," he says, removing his fingers and replacing them with his tongue. He works it into me, penetrating me as deeply as he can, his lips pressing against my most sensitive part as he does. When he moves back up to flick the tiny muscle, sucking it briefly into his mouth, I lose my breath completely.

"Rusty," I manage to say above the twirling lights and dizzying pleasure.

"I bet every man in this bar was wishing he could have a taste of you tonight, to taste that sweet come pour out of you onto his tongue. But I'm the only one who gets to taste you. I'm the one who gets to make you come tonight," he says, the vibration of his words traveling through his lips and stimulating my pulsing flesh.

"Rusty, please."

"Please what?" he asks. "Please eat you in front of whoever might be watching? Or please sit you up so you can ride me until your come runs down my cock and onto this bull?"

I can't *think* with him *saying* these things to me. I can't *breathe* with him *doing* these things to me. All I can do is *feel*. And I feel need—need for Rusty's body. Filling me up. Stretching me tight. Pushing me to the edge.

And I need it now.

"Please," I repeat breathlessly.

Rusty's hands leave me for a few seconds. But then he's winding my legs around his waist, pulling me upright, and slamming me down onto his hard, thick length.

I cry out. I can't help it. Nothing has ever felt more perfect. Or more right.

Our loud moans of pleasure mingle. I can't tell the sounds apart. I just know that there's no better feeling in the world than Rusty, inside me. All around me. With me.

His hands are in my hair as he eases me up and down on him,

deeper and deeper with each slow buck of the bull. I shudder against him when he takes my nipple into his mouth and sucks it hard against his tongue.

I knock his hat off and thread my fingers into his hair, holding him to me as he moves my body on his. "I hope someone's watching when you come on me, Jenna," he says hoarsely as he tugs my head back and sinks his blunt teeth into the flesh of my breast. "I want someone to see my mouth on these nipples. I want someone to see your beautiful body riding my cock. I want someone to see my fingers biting into this delicious ass."

Just then, he leans back and flexes his hips, his fingers digging into my backside. I fall more fully onto him, taking in every long, strong inch. With that one stroke, I explode into a shower of muted sounds and blurring lights. My body spasms around his, squeezing it tight, drawing it in. Rusty grinds his hips into mine before he picks me up and drops me back down onto him, one, two, three times.

Rusty's body goes rigid beneath me, and I open my eyes a crack, just in time to see him throw his head back. He lets out a growl that tingles along my nerves. Then I feel the hot pulse of his climax, pouring into me. I feel it inside me, all around me, as the shudder of his body vibrates through my core.

Still awash with sensation, I collapse against Rusty and we sway gently to the rhythm of the bull. After several long minutes, with only the sound of our heavy breathing and the music in the background, Rusty lowers his head to meet my eyes. "Don't ever take this away from me again," he says softly.

"Don't ever ask me to," I reply. As we watch each other, the light shining down on the angles of Rusty's face and the tenderness pouring out from the depths of his eyes, a swell of emotion overcomes me. "I love you," I murmur.

Rusty says nothing. His eyes search mine as he reaches forward to stroke my cheek with his fingertips. Finally sliding his hand around to cup the nape of my neck, he pulls me toward him and captures my lips with his own. The kiss is sweet. Profound. Enigmatic. It says *something*. I'm just not sure *what*.

TEN: *Rusty*

I ease open the unlocked front door of Trick's house. I'm hoping he's already in bed, sleeping off his zillion shots of Patrón and his undoubtedly painful set of blue balls before his wedding in the morning. I close the door quietly behind me.

"You are the shittiest best friend ever!" he mumbles from the darkness.

"Holy mother of hell! You scared the piss out of me!"

With no lights on, I can barely make out Trick's silhouette where he's sitting at the island. I see his arm move as he tips back a bottle. He's drinking. Again.

No sex'll do that to a man!

"Don't you think you ought to knock that off and get some sleep? I'm pretty sure you're supposed to be presentable when Cami meets you at the altar."

"Kiss my ass, man! I'm trying to drown my libido so I can honor my fiancée's wishes. Unlike *some* people."

"Hey, I'm not the one getting married, dude. I have no clue how Jenna and I ended up involved in this."

"Because you're our best friends. You're supposed to do it for moral support."

"I *was* doing it for moral support."

"Then where have you been for the last two hours?"

I chuckle. "Damn, has it been that long?"

"You dawg," Trick shouts, jumping to his feet. "You *have* been with Jenna!"

"I thought that's what we were talking about."

Trick flicks the kitchen light on and I can see that he's grinning. "I was just yanking your chain, man. I didn't think you'd really cave *that* fast. You really *can't* stay away from that girl, can you?"

I hadn't really thought of it that way. "I don't have the same motivation as you. *I'm* not the one getting married. Besides, you've got the rest of your life to bang your wife. My time with Jenna is much more limited."

"That's your choice, dumbass."

"It's not a choice. It's just the way it is."

"Just because she has interviews doesn't mean she's gonna take either job. Besides, there's nothing holding you here. Nothing saying you couldn't be with her somewhere else."

I feel like I've been kicked in the teeth. Or in the chest. Jenna has interviews. And she hasn't said a single word to me about them. I don't really know what to say. I can tell by Trick's expression that he knows he's stepped in it. If he weren't shitfaced, he'd never have told me and I'd never have known. Until she was already gone.

Why would she hide it, though? Was she just planning on bailing and never saying a word? Because that doesn't sound like Jenna. Even though I expected her to go—eventually—I can't imagine her doing it like that.

But still, she didn't tell me. For a reason.

"Jenna's in love with you, idiot."

"Sometimes love isn't enough."

Trick shakes his head. "Whatever. You want a beer?"

"Nah," I say, suddenly feeling tired. "I think I'm going to bed."

Trick drains his beer. "Yeah. Me, too. Tomorrow, my suffering will come to an . . . explosive end."

"Too much information, dude!" I mumble as I walk away. "Too much information."

ELEVEN: *Jenna*

Spending the entire morning being lavishly pampered, scrubbed, buffed, massaged, made up, curled, and dressed with my best friend on her wedding day is a ridiculous amount of fun. And memories of Rusty last night, his hard body between me and a mechanical bull, only make my mood that much lighter.

Once we are as perfect as professional hands can make us, we move into one huge room full of mirrors to get dressed. I pull on my dress, zip it up, and spin in front of the mirror.

"You really are the best friend ever," I tell Cami.

"I know, but what did I do to make you say that this time?" she asks with a mischievous grin.

"Only the bestestest friend in the whole world would take such pains to pick a bridal color that suits both her *and* her best friend's complexion, especially when they're basically polar opposites." Cami has dark red hair, blue eyes, and fair skin, while I have black hair, dark eyes, and olive skin. There are, like, ten colors out of a zillion that would look good on both of us. Yet Cami picked one of them to use on arguably the most important day of her life.

Cami shrugs. "I can't very well have you looking all washed out, standing up there behind me, now can I?"

She winks, but I know that had nothing to do with her choice. She's just that kind of a person—caring, considerate, selfless. Even on her wedding day.

The royal blue dress complements my coloring surprisingly well. My skin glows like bronze, my eyes sparkle like drops of onyx, and my lips needed very little red stain. And the cut of the garment is superb. The pencil-slim design makes my waist look narrow, my ass look round, and my boobs look like they're tucked up under my chin. On top of that is my sexy hairdo—black curls pulled up on the sides with tendrils dripping down to kiss my shoulders. All in all, I can't wait for Rusty to see me.

After my confession last night, I feel the need to knock his socks off. For my self-esteem's sake as much as anything else.

As we are being herded out of the salon toward the curb, I see the familiar face of Trick's mom, Leena, hovering at the edge of a crowd of giggling girls. I look to my left to find Cami, only she's not beside me anymore. I turn to find her stopped dead in her tracks, staring at Leena.

"Come on," I say, reaching back to take her hand. "It's your wedding day. You can do this." Her wide eyes dart to mine, and I can see in them that she's not convinced. "You won. Just remember that. You. Won."

I tug on her hand, pulling her behind me as we make our way to the waiting limo. All the other girls pile in and, before we can duck inside, Leena makes her way to Cami. I start to let go of Cami's hand and get into the limo to give them some privacy, but she tightens her grip, urging me to stay. So I do.

Leena jumps right in, not giving Cami the chance to say anything. "Cami, I'm not trying to ruin your wedding day and I'm not trying to make your life harder by showing up like this. I just . . . I just wanted to talk to you beforehand. Without Trick." She pauses, and I see her take a deep breath, like she's gathering courage to do something she doesn't want to do. "I love my son more than you can imagine, but I'm not ready to be around your family just yet. I don't know if that will ever change. I'm working on seeing you for *you*, not for the mistakes of your family. And that's why I wanted to come today. I'm sorry I didn't come to any of the other events. I just didn't think I could be around . . . everyone that much just yet. I want to be part of your life, part of my son's life and the lives of my grandchildren, but I can't promise much more than that right now. Just know that I'm trying. And that I'm here for Trick." She pauses, looking away again. "And for you."

Cami cups her hands over her mouth and squeezes her eyes shut. I see her fingers tremble. I can't imagine what she must be feeling. But, to her credit, she recovers quickly, dropping her hands and taking Leena's in both of hers.

"Thank you, Leena. I'll take whatever you can give."

Leena glances up, obviously uncomfortable, gives Cami a small smile, and then steps away, gesturing toward the limo.

"You'd better get going."

"Won't you come with us?"

Leena's smile is more genuine this time. "That's no place for an old lady, much less the groom's mother. You go. Enjoy yourself. Enjoy this day."

Cami smiles sweetly and nods her head before she turns her glistening eyes on me. "Ready?"

Tears are streaming down her cheeks and she's not even trying to stop them. But she's smiling. She doesn't have to say it, but her wedding will be perfect now. This was all she needed to be the happiest bride on the planet. And I'm glad she got it. I'm glad Trick got it, too. I know it's been weighing on him more than he'd ever admit. I nod, swallowing the lump of emotion in my throat as we climb into the back of the waiting car.

The ride to the church is pretty . . . enthusiastic. We ladies chatter and giggle and tease Cami about the pervy gift set we hid in the trunk with her luggage. Since there was no dedicated "bridal shower," a couple of the girls took it upon themselves to make Cami a bridal . . . survival kit instead. It's a lovely cloth-covered keepsake box full of lotions and candles. It just also happens to contain edible body paint, crotchless panties, and a few more creative things, some of which involve batteries. In short, it's a box full of shit that will make Cami's face turn eight shades of red when she unpacks it in front of Trick.

"Maybe he'll spank you for being such a naughty girl, Cam," I taunt playfully.

"Ohmigod, Jenna!" She's already turning the shade that's one step up from "beet."

Such fun being a girl and having a delicate best friend!

When we arrive at the church, all the guests are inside. The neighborhood is quiet and the lawn is empty, as are the steps leading up to the front doors.

Within seconds of our arrival, Xenia the Wedding Planner, much like Xena Warrior Princess only with less leather and more taffeta, comes to the door and peeks out. It's like she has a Spidey sense that can detect the location of the bride and groom at all times. It's kind of creepy actually.

She sticks one perfectly manicured hand out the door and folds her fingers in toward the church twice. I can almost hear her saying in her schoolmarm voice, "Come come!" And then she disappears back inside, no doubt off to swat some poor noisy child's knuckles with a ruler.

While she might seem like the devil, holy hot damn can she plan a wedding! I bet even the flowers don't have the nerve to drop a single petal until the festivities are over and she's gone.

Yeah, it's like that.

We all shuffle out of the limo, up the steps, and into the vestibule. When I take my place at the front of the line and the noise on the other side of the doors quiets, the energy and excitement and significance of the day finally seeps in to take over everything else. Just like it should.

This is my best friend's wedding day. She's marrying the man of her dreams and getting the life she's always hoped for, the life every little girl prays she'll one day be blessed with.

I should wanna slap the lucky bitch.

But I feel nothing but love and happiness and elation for her. And I know it shines from the smile I turn on her when I look back between all the other perfectly coiffed bridesmaids' heads and meet her eyes. She nods. I nod. And, between us, an entire conversation happens in the blink of an eye.

I could cry.

But I won't.

I'm not sure the salon used waterproof mascara, although they'd be complete imbeciles if they didn't.

A door to the left opens. Rusty walks through and pauses. My heart stops beating right inside my chest. If I thought I looked hot . . . holy effin' cow!

His tux is black, his shirt is white, and his cummerbund is the same beautiful blue as my dress. His hair is dark and looks freshly washed. His shoulders are impossibly wide and strong as ever. His waist is narrow and flows smoothly into his long legs.

But it's his eyes that capture me. Just like always. They are fastened on mine when I meet them, after I finish appraising him. They're brilliant blue. And very intense. It makes me wonder what's going on behind them. Because something definitely is.

Letting the door fall shut behind him, he moves slowly toward me, not stopping until he is standing so close that my boobs almost brush his lapels.

I get short of breath when I see his eyes travel down to my cleavage and back up again. They run all over my face, taking in every detail, even flickering up to my hair and back again.

Finally, they settle on mine, making my nerves flare up. "Hello, handsome," I say playfully, hoping I seem natural rather than insecure.

"You look . . . amazing," he says softly. Sincerely.

The blood that stains my cheeks is genuine. I don't blush easily, but something about his comment seems so heartfelt that my body reacts in a very physical way.

Just as I begin to search for something else to say, it registers that there's music playing on the other side of the door. I take a deep breath, thankful for the notes that saved me from further embarrassment, and I tip my head toward the interior of the church. "Shall we?" Rusty nods and I smile, turning toward the sanctuary just as the ushers open the door.

Everything flows perfectly, just like we'd practiced at rehearsal. I do my best to enjoy my best friend's perfect day without letting doubts and insecurities about Rusty tarnish it. It's hard, but I keep my focus on the bride and groom, and that makes it easier.

When it comes times for the vows, Trick clears his throat and asks if he can say a few words. The minister nods and smiles. He doesn't look the least bit surprised, which leads me to believe that he knew Trick would do this.

The church is absolutely silent around us, every person, no doubt, waiting with bated breath to hear what he has say. I can imagine all too easily how Cami must feel right now. If I were in her shoes and Rusty were getting ready to say something special to me, I'd be a mess behind my veil.

"Since I was a kid, I've always known what I wanted to do with my life," Trick begins. "I wanted to work with horses. I didn't much care about the how, the what, or the where, as long as I got to be around them. I thought that's all it would take to make me happy. Until I met you. Without you, those dreams were just . . . empty. It didn't take me long to see that without you, I could never be happy.

"Whether you knew it or not, I was yours from the second you looked up at me with the most beautiful eyes I've ever seen. I knew you'd mean more to me than all the riches, all the horses, all the *things* the world has to offer. And I was right. Cami, I love you with everything I am, and everything I ever hope to be. From this moment on, I'll spend the rest of my days making sure you never regret picking me."

His words float through the church like they're on angels' wings. I'm pretty sure every heart has stopped, just like mine has. To know a love like that is everyone's dream, whether they admit it or not. And to have someone look at me the way Trick's looking at Cami is *my* dream.

If he hadn't said a single word, the look in his eyes says it all. All he sees is Cami. And that's all he needs to see. It's right there on his face, for all to behold. Just like he said, she's everything to him. Everything.

My eyes flicker to Rusty. He's watching me with a strangely puzzled expression. I look away. My heart can't stand the pain of it.

TWELVE: *Rusty*

I grab Trick's arm after the photographer finishes taking a blue million pictures. I want to catch him before he heads toward the reception hall with Cami.

"Hey, man, can I talk to you for a sec?"

"Sure," he says, kissing Cami's cheek and telling her he'll be right back. We walk a few feet away. "What's up?"

"Would I be on your shit list forever if I bailed?" He says nothing, just eyes me suspiciously. I rush to explain. "I've got some major work to do on that car I just got in and—"

Trick starts shaking his head. "Stop right there, man. You don't have to make excuses for me. I know you're full of shit. There's nothing that's *that* important, that you have to do today." I have nothing to say to that. Because he's right. That has nothing to do with me wanting to get the hell out of here. "*But*, you're my best friend and I love ya. I'm grateful you did this much for me."

I feel like a steaming pile of shit. "If it really means that much to you, I can—"

"Go, dude. Get out of here," Trick says with a smile as he claps me on the shoulder. "Go do what you need to do."

I know by his expression and the look in his eye what he means by me doing what I need to do. He may not understand it completely (hell, *I* don't even understand it completely), but he knows me well enough to know I need to get out of here. And he doesn't ask questions, which I'm grateful for.

This whole day has me feeling flustered. Jenna's confession last night caught me off guard, although I guess I suspected that she loves me. The fact is, however, that it doesn't change anything. I know the *type* of person Jenna is. I've seen it before. With my father. Already, she's trying to hide her plans to leave. She couldn't even really meet my eyes in the church. You can love somebody and still end up leaving them. Some people are just made that way—to always want greener pastures. I've seen it before. And I'm not getting attached to a person like that again. I guess today just reminded me of that. And it feels pretty shitty.

I pull Trick in for a quick hug and a manly slap on the back. "Be happy, man. And enjoy the hell out of that honeymoon."

Trick laughs. "Oh, I will, but I'm not waiting for Tahiti to get this damn dry spell behind me. I plan to get Cami out of that dress *myself* here in about an hour."

I laugh, too, leaning back to pound my fist against Trick's. "Get it done, my friend!"

Trick nods and turns toward the reception hall, so I slip off, over the hill, through the trees and down to the parking lot behind the church to get my car. I need some speed and the freedom of the road to clear my head.

I feel antsy as I slide in behind the wheel. I loosen my bow tie as I crank the engine. Within seconds, I hit the gas and steer the car back toward town, and then on toward the interstate. I want a long, straight stretch of road that I can open it up on.

When I clear the entrance ramp and see that there are no cars in front of me, or even really off in the distance, I punch it, milking every last one of the four hundred-plus horsepower that I can get with the modifications I made to my GTO.

I exhale as the landscape speeds by and the engine roars around me, quieting all the shit from my past that's mixing with the shit from my present to cloud my head. I don't want to think about then. I don't want to think about now. And I sure as hell don't want to think about the future. I just want to feel the road. And the speed. And the fine-tuned handling of the car I practically built from the ground up.

I'm so lost in the moment, I don't see the fine spray of gravel on the road up ahead. Until it's too late.

And I'm spinning out of control.

I wake to the sound of a stranger's voice. "Can you hear me, sir? Sir? Can you hear me?" he repeats.

I feel like I'm hanging upside down, and when I try to open my eyes, they won't cooperate. I try to move, to right myself, but someone or something is holding my arm. I try to jerk free, but pain shoots through my whole right side. I hear a deep scream.

And then there's nothing.

Something's covering my face. I try to raise my hand to knock it off, but my limbs feel too heavy to move. I feel pressure on my right arm, like something is squeezing it tight.

My head feels like lead. Thick, numb lead. Again, I try to open my eyes. This time they obey, and I crack them just enough that I can see bright lights overhead, but none that look familiar. It seems like I'm moving, too.

"Sir, can you hear me? Can you tell me your name?" The voice sounds the same, like the same guy I heard before. I want to tell that bastard that if he doesn't stop asking me the same questions, I'm gonna kick his ass, but no words come out. I hear only someone moaning.

And then there's nothing again.

There's a weird beeping sound. And I smell some kind of harsh chemical, like antiseptic or something. When I try to turn my face away, pain sears my brain like a branding iron.

What the hell?

The beeping speeds up, and I try to open my eyes to see what's making that god-awful noise. I see a flash of hospital green, then bright lights again.

I hear a woman's voice. "Take deep breaths, Mr. Catron. Slow, deep breaths. You're gonna be just fine." She sounds reasonable enough. "Count to ten for me," she says.

I don't hear my voice, but in my head I count.

One. Two. Three.

And then there's nothing.

Again.

"Mr. Catron? You're all done. Can you open your eyes?" I recognize her voice, even though it sounds like it's coming to me through a tunnel a mile long. My head feels a little fuzzy, but it doesn't hurt as bad as it did.

"Yes," I manage to answer. My tongue feels like it's covered in cotton and my throat has never been rawer. "Drink," I croak.

"Can you open your eyes and look at me?"

I'm a little annoyed at her request, but I comply. With what seems like an inordinate amount of effort, I crank my lids up and try to focus on the face hovering above me. I blink twice and things seem to work a little better.

"Very good. Now I'm going to slip a piece of ice into your mouth, okay? Don't swallow. Just let it melt on your tongue."

God, ice sounds wonderful! I open my mouth a little and feel like sighing when the tiny, cold sliver hits my tongue.

I close my eyes for a second, enjoying the liquid before I open them again, focusing more easily on the woman.

She's young and very attractive. Her hair is dark red and pulled back into a ponytail. Her face is pretty and free of makeup. She's wearing nursing scrubs. I recognize them because I saw my mother in them nearly every day for the last fifteen years. After Dad left, she put herself through nursing school. She worked the night shift for years while she went on for her master's degree. She doesn't wear scrubs anymore, but she still works at the hospital.

"You're a nurse," I say, stating the obvious. I don't even know why I make the comment.

"Yes, I am. Do you know where you are?"

"I assume at the hospital."

"Yes. You're just coming out of surgery. Do you remember what happened?"

I try to think back, but it all seems pretty blurry. I remember feeling the car start to slide, and I remember seeing snatches of grass go tumbling by. I vaguely remember hearing some loud, metallic sounds, but none of it really makes sense. The best I can gather is that I was in a wreck, but the details just aren't there.

"I suppose I wrecked, but I don't remember much else."

"Yes, you were in a car accident. You suffered a severe concussion, numerous contusions, and your right arm was nearly torn off. You were taken to surgery within an hour of arriving in the ambulance. You'll be spending some time in ICU until we can make sure you don't suffer further complications. Are you in pain?"

Her words jumble around in my head. "Uhhh . . ." She's telling me too much too fast. I can't think.

"On a scale of one to ten, one being *no pain* and ten being *the worst pain* you've ever experienced, where would you rate your pain?"

I only feel pain in one spot. "My head. It hurts."

"You have a headache?"

Isn't that what I just said?

"Yes."

"That could be from the anesthesia or from the narcotics. Once we get you upstairs, I'll get you some Tylenol."

I nod, feeling grumbly and irritated all of a sudden.

I close my eyes against the sight of rectangles of light passing by overhead, and I relax against the mattress of the gurney. As we roll through the halls, I digest what I've just been told.

"Which arm was hurt?" I ask, unable to clearly recall everything the nurse said.

"Your right."

A mild feeling of alarm passes through me, but the world is too fuzzy for me to process it or dwell on it.

"Can I use it?"

"You'll need some physical therapy, but the doctor repaired everything as best he could."

"My car?"

"I don't know about that, but considering the shape you arrived in, I'm thinking it's going to need a lot of work."

Dammit!

After a brief trip in the elevator, the nurse wheels me down a short hall and through automatic doors. The world gets quiet all of a sudden. I barely hear the click of the doors closing behind us.

As the nurse rolls me farther into the new area, I hear muted whispers and faint beeping sounds. I open my eyes again just as I'm being backed into a room. To my left is a window that looks outside. The curtain is pulled shut against the setting sun. To my right is a wall of windows that look out into a semicircular configuration of countertops—a nurse's station. This must be the ICU.

Within a few seconds, there's a loud thump as the nurse sets my bed's brake, and then I hear my mother's voice.

"Was he able to fix it all?"

I lift my head to try and locate her, but it falls right back onto the pillow. It must weigh at least fifty pounds. "Mom?"

I feel her cool hand take my left one. "I'm here, Jeff," she says in her calm, practiced, nurse voice. I feel like smiling. She's the only person on the planet that calls me Jeff. Jeffrey when she's mad. "Give me just a few minutes to talk to the nurse. I'll be right back."

She kisses my forehead, and then I don't hear their voices anymore. I want to wait for her to come back and answer all my questions, but damn! I'm so tired all of a sudden. Maybe if I rest for just a few minutes . . .

When I wake, my eyes open immediately and effortlessly.

'Bout damn time! I think to myself.

I raise my head and, despite the dull throb that starts up instantly, look around. There are some people behind the tall counter of the nurse's station. All the lights are on, and, when I turn to look out the windows, I see that it's dark outside. But what puzzles me is that I have to look past some kind of contraption to see.

My right arm is immobilized by a series of cords. My upper arm is casted and there are straps coming out of it at my elbow. They attach to some fixed point that I can't see. My elbow is bent to ninety degrees and my lower arm is casted, too. There are straps coming out from beneath it at my fingertips, and they attach to some wires that go up into a pulley that is counterweighted somewhere down around the foot of the bed.

"What the hell?" I say to no one in particular.

A shadow falls across me and I look back toward the door. My mother is standing there. Although not one short, strawberry hair is out of place and her clothes and makeup look like she has just come to work, there's a frazzled look about her I'm not used to seeing.

My stomach sinks.

"What? Something's up. I can see it on your face."

She walks farther into the room and gives me a smile as she perches on the edge of the bed. "Can't I just be happy you're all right?"

"Sure you can. Was there ever a doubt that I *would be*?"

"Not really. You're here just as a precaution, so they can keep an eye on you for the first twenty-four hours. You took quite a beating, and your head took a big hit."

"Well, then, why the worry?"

"Well . . . It's just that . . . Jeff, your arm is in pretty bad shape. And I know how impatient you are. You need to understand how important it is for you to let this heal right and to realize that you're going to be very limited for a while. But if you push it, son, you could have permanent damage."

"Push it? What the hell am I gonna push? They've got me strung up like a damn puppet!"

"For good reason. You were thrown from the car, and your right arm must've gotten tangled up in your lap belt somehow. Nearly tore it off. Your rotator cuff is torn, you dislocated your shoulder, your humerus is broken in two places, your—"

"Speak English, woman," I interrupt gruffly, trying to add a teasing note to my voice, but failing miserably. The fact that *she's* acting like this has me worried.

"You dislocated your shoulder, you messed up that joint, you broke your upper arm in two places, you broke both bones in your lower arm, sustained significant ligament damage in your right hand, cracked three ribs, and badly bruised your right hip. You also had a concussion, and they picked a bunch of glass out of your face. Is that plain enough for you?"

"So what you're saying is my whole right side is banged up?"

"Yes, to put it mildly."

"Okay, so how long will I be in here?"

"Weeks. You don't—"

"*Weeks?* Are you kidding me? Why can't they just put me in a normal cast and send me home in a few days?"

"Because your injuries are severe, Jeffrey. That's what I'm trying to tell you. You can't rush this or you could have permanent damage."

"Like what *kind* of permanent damage?"

"Like the kind that means you could never regain full use of your right hand and arm."

Oh shit.

Now I see why she looks so upset. My job, my livelihood, all my dreams depend on me being able to use my hands and arms to work on cars. Hell, I'd have been better off to have broken my leg than my arm. Or even my *left* arm. But not my right one. God almighty, not my right one!

What the hell am I gonna do about my garage? About the vehicles I've already been contracted to restore? I was just getting that part of my dream under way. It's been slow going, but I could see it starting to take shape. But now . . . After this . . .

"Well, I guess I'll just have to heal fast and right then."

"I know you will. *If* you do what they tell you."

"I will, I will," I snap, already aggravated and ready to leave this conversation behind. "Who else is out there? Anybody?"

Mom shakes her head. "You've only been out of surgery for a couple of hours, Jeff. Give them some time."

"Well, Trick's on his honeymoon, I'm sure. And Jenna probably doesn't even know yet, does she?"

"I talked to Leena. She called when she heard. She said she'd tell Trick, but I asked her to wait until they had a couple of days to enjoy their trip, and to tell them you were doing fine. I knew you wouldn't want them to rush home to see you. You'll still be here when they get back."

"No, I wouldn't have wanted that." After a few seconds, I ask her again about Jenna. "So you didn't call Jenna then?"

I hear her sigh. "Yes, I called Jenna."

"Is she coming?"

"I don't know. She hung up."

She hung up? What the hell does that mean?

THIRTEEN: *Jenna*

I've never been so torn and conflicted in my whole life! Granted, I was just turning four when my mother died, but I still learned to hate the hospital. Luckily, she wanted to spend her last days at home, which she was able to do, but I remember the smell and the hopelessness, and riding home with my father while he cried quietly in the front seat. All in all, I hate hospitals. With a passion. I feel short of breath just *thinking* about going to visit Rusty. So much so that I just freaked and hung up on his mother, which I'll have to call and apologize for. And I will. Later.

After I conquer step one—Rusty.

Despite my fear of hospitals, despite the fact that I probably just deeply offended his mother, despite the fact that I made one of life's biggest confessions and he said nothing, despite the fact that he totally bailed at the wedding, I'm going to see Rusty. At the hospital. Because I love him.

I was more than a little hurt when I found out that he left before the reception. Not only did he *not* find me and tell me, but he almost seemed to be avoiding me altogether. I just don't understand it. The only thing I can figure is that my use of the L word freaked him out. I'm sure Rusty knows I love him, but I've never gone out on a limb and *told* him. Until last night.

Maybe this all adds up to the fact that he really *doesn't* have deeper feelings for me. Maybe it's just great sex and great companionship, nothing more.

It's as I'm pulling on a pair of jeans, getting ready to leave that I find something else to be nervous about. What if he doesn't want me there? What will I do then?

I push the thought out of my mind. I can't think about that right now. I have to go. Not only is it the right thing to do, but it's Rusty. And I love him. And he was almost taken from me. I *have to* see him again. I have to.

FOURTEEN: *Rusty*

Time feels different for some reason. Slower. Like every minute is an hour. Maybe because I've slept so much. Maybe because I can't sleep now. Maybe it's because I'm waiting. On Jenna.

I don't know what to think about her anymore. I can't figure her out. And I'm not sure I should even try.

I was hoping I was wrong about her, that she's really *not* like my dad. He always thought there was something better somewhere else, too. So he left. He abandoned me and Mom, and never looked back.

I've always been bound and determined that I won't make the same mistake she did. And, the more I think about it, the more I realize that leopards don't change their spots. The things I loved so much about Jenna are likely some of the very things that will take her away from me. I guess you really *can't* have your cake and eat it, too.

Maybe I should just let her go. If she hated Greenfield before, she'd hate it twice as much if she felt like she had to stay to take care of an invalid who may or may not have a future at all.

No, the days of me having anything to offer Jenna that could compete with the rest of the world are over. I guess it's time to cut her loose before *she* cuts and runs.

FIFTEEN: *Jenna*

As it turns out, my memory (and probably my imagination, to some degree) had vilified hospitals much more than necessary. *At least so far*, I think as I ride the elevator to the third floor.

I'm inclined to rethink my bravado when the doors open and a long sterile hallway stretches out before me. The heavy scent of sanitizer stings my nose and makes me think of unpleasant things, of sick people and dying people and people who are lost without each other. In a way, at least in the way my memory reacts, it's like the hospital took my mother from me. Visit by visit, month by month.

The doors start to close again, so I step out in a hurry. After two deep, shaky breaths, I start to turn back, only to find them closed and my means of escape gone. For a second, panic strikes. I spin in a wild circle, looking for the glowing red EXIT sign. I feel my forehead prickle with sweat as the walls draw closer and closer and the air gets thicker and thicker.

Oh shit, oh shit, oh shit!

Finally, I spot the exit. I take a step toward it, but a swell of heat gushes over my face, making the room swim right before my eyes. I reach for the wall, anything that's steady in a world that's grown disturbingly unstable.

Why did I come? Why did I come?

My palm hits the cool concrete of the wall and I lean toward it, pressing my cheek to the pale, painted surface. My pulse is racing, my heart is thumping, and my addled mind is struggling to answer my own simple question.

Why did I come? Why did I come?

But finally, like a cool breeze to parched skin, my head clears enough for me to *feel* the answer.

Rusty. I came for Rusty.

I close my eyes and take a deep, steadying breath. Just the thought of him, of the fact that he was so nearly taken from my life in a very permanent, irrevocable way, gives me the focus I need to get a grip on myself.

I don't move for several long minutes as I wait for my calm to be restored. Still leaning heavily against the hard wall, I give my shaky legs a test. They don't feel strong by any means, but they're strong enough to support me. That's the main thing. I push away from the concrete and smooth my hair before I turn my back to the wall and face, head-on, the two intimidating wooden doors in front of me.

As I approach, I read the large, red lettering emblazoned across both panels. AUTHORIZED PERSONNEL ONLY. I hardly fit that description.

I chew my lip as I think of what to do now. As I look casually from left to right, I see the little buzzer to one side of the door. There's a sign below it that has a schedule of ICU visiting hours and the procedure for getting inside.

Following the directions, I depress the buzzer and wait. After a few seconds, a pleasant enough–sounding voice comes on. "May I help you?"

"Um, I'm here to see Rust—er, I mean, I'm here to see Jeff Catron."

"Hold please."

The line goes dead, leaving me standing in front of the door, staring at the box like an idiot. I look all around to make sure no one is watching me. I'm still alone, thank God.

Finally, she comes back on. "Room three-oh-four. Come on back."

A click is followed by a loud buzzing sound just before the two doors swing open in opposite directions, allowing me to pass into the sick people inner sanctum.

The center of the large, bland room is dominated by an enormous nurse's station. Arranged in a semicircle around it is a ring of patient rooms, all with glass windows and doors that allow the nurses to see inside unless the curtain is drawn. I look to my left and see room three-twelve. I figure Rusty is all the way at the other end, so I start walking along the rounded edge of the nurse's station until I get to his room.

The curtain is drawn and I hear no sounds coming from behind it. Hesitantly, I knock on the metal frame that surrounds the open glass door.

"Come in," I hear Rusty say. My heart skips a beat and I wipe my damp palms on the butt of my jeans before I pull back the nondescript beige curtain.

When I peek inside, I see Rusty lying in bed, his arm attached to all sorts of wires or ropes or something. His cheeks already show the signs of dark stubble, as though the strain of the last hours has taken its toll in a very physical way. The frown he's wearing only adds to that impression.

"Hey," I say weakly.

He narrows his eyes on me before he speaks. "Hey," he responds in kind, not making me feel any better about things.

"Can I . . . can I come in?"

"I just said 'come in,' didn't I?" I'm sure the small curve of his lips is an attempt to soften his snappy reply, but it doesn't sting my heart any less.

Pulling up my big girl panties, I return his tight smile and step through the curtain, heading for the only chair in the room. I perch on the edge, clinging to my purse like a lifeline.

"So, how are you feeling?"

"How do I look like I'm feeling?" he asks with a short bark of a laugh.

"I'm sure you've been better."

"Yeah, I've been better."

"What happened? I mean, obviously you were in a wreck, but . . ."

Rusty takes a deep breath and shrugs. "I'm still fuzzy on some of the details, but from what I remember, I hit some gravel on the interstate and slid into the median. Must've caught it just right and flipped the goat a few times."

Although he casually refers to his GTO as a "goat," which he does often, and his tone is matter-of-fact, I don't get the impression that he's so blasé about the accident. "That sounds bad."

He shrugs again. "Could've been worse."

"Yeah, like if you'd been killed. But my God, look at you. How many injuries did you have?"

"Torn rotator cuff, dislocated shoulder, multiple breaks in my arm, three cracked ribs, and a variety of cuts, scrapes, and bruises."

I cringe at the ache around my heart. It hurts me to think about Rusty being hurt. And, as I look at him, lying in the bed all bandaged and tied up, it hurts me even more to know there's nothing I can do to help him.

"How-how long until you're able to . . . how long will you be in here?"

I see his frown before he looks out the window behind my head, and I realize it wasn't the right question to ask. Something about it bothered him. But honestly, I don't know what to say. He's acting like he could care less that I'm here, and it's making me want to go all the more.

"Probably quite a while. Too long for you to be hanging around here," he says, not even bothering to look at me as he speaks.

His words are like so many daggers to my heart. My worst fear has been confirmed. Rusty really *doesn't* want me around. I guess I was good enough for some fun, but not good enough to keep.

With my heart shriveling inside my chest, it's all I can do to fight back tears. I turn to look out the window as well, staring into the increasing darkness as I collect myself. And as I think about Rusty and his brutal dismissal, I do what I can to keep it together.

I get mad.

"Well, that's probably a good thing. I hate hospitals," I say, turning back to look at him, forcing a smile onto my face.

"Don't feel like you have to come back then. It won't hurt my feelings."

More daggers. I want to scream at him, to tell him I went through hell just to get here, just to get to him tonight. But I don't. I don't want his pity. Or a pat on the back. I don't want him to be kind to me because I've "earned" it.

So, instead, I give what I'm getting. Tit for tat. Casual for casual. Unaffected for unaffected.

I nod as I lean forward, getting ready to stand. "Okay. Maybe I'll stop by again before I leave, if I have time."

"Before you leave? Running already?"

Something in his tone is snide. "I'm not *running*," I reply defensively. "I just graduated college. I've got to go get a job eventually."

"That should be easy. I'm sure you've got a few things lined up already. An escape plan." His tone is so bitter my heart drops through the concrete floor. Now I *definitely* can't tell him I've got interviews. I won't give him the satisfaction of knowing he's right.

It's my turn to narrow my eyes on Rusty. "What the hell is your problem?"

"Problem? What makes you think I have a problem?"

"You make it sound like I'm running away from something, when all I'm doing is starting my life."

"Right. And that's exactly what you *should be* doing. The timing is perfect. This is for the best. You need to get on with your plans *away* from here."

I sit, looking at his handsome face, while my heart is spewing blood around the wound of his sharp words. He continues, driving the knife in a little deeper. "You need to find a place you can make new friends. Find a job that you love. Find some happiness."

His words say he wants me to go and find happiness, but something about his attitude belies his well-wishing. In a way, I feel like he's blaming me for wanting more.

"Why is it that when *you* say it, it sounds like a bad thing?"

"I have no idea. Must be your imagination."

"It's not my imagination, Rusty," I say, standing to my feet. "Do you *blame me* for wanting to get a job using the education I spent the last four years getting?"

"Not at all. I knew that's what you'd do."

"Again, you make it sound like a bad thing."

"I'm not making it sound like anything. I'm just saying what we both already knew, Jenna. You're getting ready to go. It was just a matter of time."

"Oh, so now I'm a terrible person for not wanting to hang around Greenfield for the rest of my life?"

"I didn't say that."

"But that's what you meant."

"Don't tell me what I meant," he bites. "You're not the kind to settle, Jenna. That's all I'm saying. You're the kind who has big plans for a better life. And that doesn't include this town or the people in it. We both knew that. And it was fun while it lasted. No reason to drag it out."

That hurts. I told him I love him less than twenty-four hours ago. Although it *does* seems like an eternity now, Rusty acts like it never happened, like I never had any feelings for him. He makes it sound as though we were a convenient way to pass my time in Greenfield, nothing more. Like we were destined for failure.

"Wow," I say, trying to keep the hurt from my voice. I dig deep for a little bit of pride to help me get out of this without making things worse than they already are. "You've got me all figured out then, don't you, Rusty?"

"It is what it is, Jenna."

"I guess I won't be bothering you anymore then." Head held high, I stride across the room toward the door. I make each step as long as I can, giving Rusty every chance to stop me. To tell me I'm wrong. To ask me to stay.

But he doesn't. When he speaks, it's just to tell me good-bye.

"I wish you well, Jenna," Rusty says softly as I pull the curtain back. I don't turn around when I answer.

"Thanks, Rusty. You, too."

When I let the curtain fall behind me, I *do* run this time. I run until I'm in an empty elevator, holding a handful of tears.

SIXTEEN: *Rusty*

There's absolutely no doubt I have qualms about the last words Jenna and I said to each other. Unfortunately, she did as I asked and she stayed away. Not only has it been lonely and boring, but I've got too much time on my hands to think about her.

I teeter between regret and bitterness. On the one hand, I feel like I pushed her away. Maybe she would've proved me right and gone anyway. But maybe, just maybe, she'd have proved me wrong and she'd have hung around. If I hadn't practically pushed her out the door, that is.

But after dwelling on that for a little while, bitterness rushes in. Even if Jenna had stayed longer, it wouldn't have been permanent. And I'm nobody's charity case. I don't want her hanging around here because she feels sorry for me. Oh, hell no!

Needless to say, I'm pretty much a bear by the time Trick and Cami get home from their honeymoon and come to see me.

"Got a regular room now, huh, hoss? I heard you spent some time in the ICU," Trick says as he strides in, Cami's hand tucked firmly in his. They're both tan and glowing. And not just the skin kind of glowing. It's the kind that radiates from somewhere deeper, the kind that comes from being happy all the way down to your soul.

"Good God, it's about time!" I say. "I'm surprised there's anything left of her. How long has it been?"

Trick laughs. Cami blushes. "Just two weeks, you dick. What the hell's the matter with you?"

"Other than the obvious?" I ask.

"Yes, smart-ass. Other than the obvious."

"I'm in here. Isn't that enough?"

"I figured you'd be milking this and getting three sponge baths a day from Jenna," he teases.

"Not hardly."

Trick gives me an exasperated sigh. "All right, what'd you say to her? This *has to be* your fault. Otherwise, Jenna would probably be here right now, soaping up her sponge."

"You mean you haven't talked to her since you got back?"

"*I* haven't."

We both look at Cami. Her eyes get wide and her expression turns to that of a cornered animal. "What? We literally just drove in from the airport. I haven't seen *anybody* yet."

"Haven't *seen*, but have you *talked* to anybody?" Trick asks.

Cami's mouth opens a couple of times like she wants to say something, but finally she closes it and sighs. "Yes."

"Jenna?"

"Yes."

"And?"

"And, she asked if we'd been by yet. I told her we hadn't."

"That's it?"

"Pretty much." Cami looks from me to Trick and back again. She rocks back on her heels and drops Trick's hand to smack her own together. "So, where's the vending machine? I need to get a bottle of water or something. I'm thirsty."

Likely story, I think. But I don't say that. "I walked by some yesterday when they let me out of bed to do PT. Down the hall and to the left."

"They already let you out of bed?" Trick asks after Cami leaves.

"Hell yeah, they did! I almost kissed the poor guy that was my nurse yesterday when he told me. Before that, my arm was in traction. I couldn't even take a piss without it being a big production."

"How'd you do when you finally got to get up?"

"They wanted me to take it slow. Evidently I strained some ligaments in my hip pretty bad. But I was bound and determined that, come hell or high water, I was getting out of this damn bed. I wanted 'em to know I was ready to be discharged."

I pause before I finish telling him what happened. It's during that time that Trick, my best friend who knows me better than anybody, figures it out.

"Busted your ass, didn't you?"

I can't help but grin. "Pretty much. I was a lot weaker than I thought I'd be. When the therapist got me up, I tried to walk ahead. Thought I'd show him how self-sufficient I am. Well, I showed him all right."

Trick throws back his head and laughs. I shake my head, letting him get it out of his system. "Did it get better after they scooped up your pathetic ass?"

"Yeah, a little. I'm still kinda weak, but I'm doing as much as I can from the bed. I'll be out of here as soon as is humanly possible."

Trick nods his head, still smiling. When the silence stretches on, he steps closer to the bed. "So, what happened with Jenna? You did something stupid, didn't you?"

"Man, why do you always take her side?"

"Because I know you. You're a guy. We do stupid shit."

"Well, it wasn't me this time. She was getting ready to leave soon, anyway. I spared her the trouble of having to come back up here and babysit."

"You really *are* an idiot, aren't you?"

"No, because I was right. She's not staying around here, Trick. That was never her plan. And it still isn't. She's getting a job somewhere else. Period. The end."

"Just because she doesn't want to live in this town forever doesn't mean she doesn't want to be with you. Hell, *you* even talk about getting away from here and opening up a classic restoration shop near a big city. How is that any different?"

"Because I'd never leave someone I loved. Not for a job, not for anything."

"Have you ever *asked* her to stay? For you?"

"No."

"Why not?"

"I know she doesn't want to. Why would I ask her to stay when I know she doesn't want to?"

"Then how the hell can you be mad at her for leaving?"

I'm getting irritated. "Look, I can't explain it to you. You obviously don't get it. She's not the kind to stick around. That's it. It was a fun thing while it lasted. Now it's over. Leave it the hell alone, will ya?"

Trick just shakes his head, but he doesn't say anything more about it. Even though, in a way, I wish he would.

SEVENTEEN: *Jenna*

I wander aimlessly through the house. I stroll through the den, with its comfy brown sofa and dark cream walls, then into the dining room. I let my fingers trail over the chair backs, making note of the worn edges. It's the suit my grandparents gave to my parents as a housewarming gift when they signed over the orchard then left for retirement in Florida. It was brand-new once upon a time. Now it looks old and worn. And loved. Every smooth spot, every faded spot is the result of being handled thousands of times by Mom and Dad, and by Jake and me.

Although my father sent us off to school shortly after my mother's death, this house still holds a million precious memories. They're just not enough to make me want to stay here. Few things are.

I move on into the kitchen, noticing, as I always do, the faint smell of peaches. It must be permanently embedded in the wood of the floors and the plaster of the walls. The kitchen always smells sweet, just like the orchard outside.

"How much longer you gonna be able to put these people off, Jenna?"

Startled, I whirl around toward the back door. I find Cristos

Theopolis, my father, standing there watching me. His eyes are the same warm honey color as my brother's, only right now, they hold concern. That's the only difference, because Jake's never do. Somehow, life made his heart hard and mostly inaccessible.

I sigh. "A little while longer. It's just an interview, Daddy."

"Just an interview. *Just* the rest of your life, you mean."

"Who's to say I'd even like working there? A degree in business with a focus in marketing is hardly a narrow field. I could work anywhere, in any number of settings."

"It's a great company, Jenna. You're the one who tried to sell *me* on them just a couple of months ago. Why the sudden hesitation?"

"I . . . I . . . I don't know," I say with a shrug, making my way to the kitchen window to look out.

"What's gotten into you, Jen? Lately, you're so distracted. You seem restless and . . . well, unhappy."

I sigh. "I guess I was just hoping Rusty would be out of the hospital before I left."

"Rusty? I thought you two broke up."

"We did. If we were ever really together, that is."

"What does that mean?"

I sigh again. "Oh, nothing. I guess I'm just . . . waiting."

"On what? What is it you think will happen if he gets out before you go?"

"I don't know, I—"

"Do you think he might propose? I mean, you're broken up. Wouldn't waiting around be silly? Maybe you ought to move on."

His words hit a tender spot. "God, Daddy, I'm not stupid. I know he's not gonna get out and come to beg me back. But I'd like to make sure his life gets back to normal, you know?"

"And if it doesn't? What then? What is it you think you'll be able to do for him?"

"*I* can't do anything for him. I know that. But if things don't work out for him around here . . ."

"Jenna, you've got to stop this. You can't put your life on hold for a boy."

"He's not a boy, Daddy. And he's not just 'a boy,' anyway. I love him. If there's even a small chance that we could be together, I'll wait for it."

Even to my own ears, I sound deluded and pathetic. And that breaks my heart into even smaller pieces. I seem to be the only one who can't let go, who can't move on.

"You'd want him to come to you just because he's got nothing else left? You'd want him to choose you because there's no better option?"

That's like a scalpel to my stomach. "Of course not."

"Then how long do you wait, honey? How long is *too* long? Have you ever thought of that? What is the cutoff for him choosing you first? Because you deserve to be *first*."

For the millionth time, I feel the burn of tears at the back of my eyes. "I don't know. But I can't leave yet. I can't do it, Daddy." I feel like I'm hanging on by the world's thinnest thread of hope. But it's not enough to hold *me* together. I crumble. "I just can't do it. I can't leave him like that."

I bury my face in my hands. Within a few seconds, I feel strong, familiar arms come around me. One hand strokes my hair as my father soothes me. "Shhh, baby girl. It'll all work out. I promise. Just let it happen like it's supposed to. Don't fight it."

The problem with that advice is that I'm afraid I already know how it's supposed to work out. I'm just not sure I can live with it.

EIGHTEEN: *Rusty*

I guess that's what happens when you're a total asshole to pretty much everyone—they stop coming to see you. I was blaming my grouchy mood on being confined in a twelve-by-twelve room with one window, a door, and a lot of machinery, but now I'm beginning to see what the problem really is. Every person that walks through the door who's *not* Jenna pisses me off. Instantly.

Trick was coming to see me a few times every day at first, and staying for a couple hours each time, but now he stops by once a day and never really settles in. I can tell he's anxious to leave five minutes after he arrives. It doesn't help that, two weeks ago, after his first visit back from his honeymoon, I told both him and Cami that I didn't want to talk about Jenna. So we don't. Ever. They never mention her. And, of course, I never ask. I guess she's gone and gotten a great job somewhere. And I guess I'll never know unless I swallow some damn pride and ask.

But, then again, do I really want to know? Do I really want to know how happy she is, living somewhere else, without me? No, not really. That feels an awful lot like twisting the knife.

With Trick's visit for the day already over and done with, the only thing I have to look forward to is PT. They tell me that I'm doing so well with my deep breathing, my range of motion exercises, and my ambulation (a fancy word for walking) that I'll soon be discharged until my arm cast comes off. Then I'll start PT all over again.

That's all fine and good. I just want out of *this* place. ASAP. I need to get on with my life, too. Whatever kind of life that may be.

NINETEEN: *Jenna*

"So, how is he? Is he getting stronger? Did he get a discharge date yet?" I pound Cami with questions the instant she answers the phone. I know Trick was supposed to go for his morning visit and should be back by now.

"Whoa, whoa, whoa! Give me ten seconds to answer each one. Sheesh," she moans. I give her absolute silence as I wait. "Trick's still calling him a 'grouchy bastard' if that tells you anything about how he is. Still not happy about being in the hospital. Yes, he is getting stronger. He's aced all his PT stuff and is up walking the halls at all hours of the day and night, evidently. And yes, he got a date. Well, sort of."

I feel a gasp stick in my chest. "What do you mean, he 'sort of' got a date?"

"They're saying within the next couple of days. I have no idea what the date is contingent upon."

"Well, why didn't Trick ask?"

"Jenna! He doesn't think like you do. He's a guy. Remember?" She sighs.

"I know. I'm sorry. I'm just so curious."

"I know," she says, her tone quiet. Somber.

I pause, debating the wisdom of asking my next question. I've asked it a couple of times before and the answer always upsets me. But still, I can't seem to help myself from holding on to hope.

At least for a little while longer.

"Did he ask about me?"

There's a pause.

"No."

Although, yes, there's a stabbing pain through my heart, I also get irritated. How the hell can he just move on like that?

"So he hasn't mentioned me, not one time, since y'all have been back?" Static crackles on the line between us. And my heart drops through the floorboards of my bedroom. "Tell me, Cami. I need to know. I'm driving myself crazy, and if something has happened, I need to know."

"Nothing has happened . . ." she says vaguely.

"Then what was said?"

"The second time I went to see him, he said he didn't want to talk about you, not to bring you up."

"But why?" I ask, my voice small even to my own ears.

"He said he was tired of hearing about it."

I can hear the pain in Cami's words. She hates to tell me something so hurtful, but I cornered her by asking *juuust* the right question. Otherwise, she'd never have told me, never have hurt me with this.

But I needed to know. As much as it hurts, I needed to know.

I look down at my hand, shaking where it rests on my thigh. The air around me feels thick and unbreathable. My head throbs with the need to scream. Or cry. Or come apart.

I clear my throat then take a deep breath, refusing to let my best friend see how deeply wounded I am. She's seen enough, heard enough. I won't continue to do this to her.

"Well, in that case, I guess I have some phone calls to make."

"Jenna, I'm so sorry. I don't know what . . . I really thought . . ."

"Don't be sorry. We both hoped. And we were both wrong. Turns out neither of us knows Rusty very well."

"Wh-what are you going to do?" she asks carefully.

"I'm calling human resources at those two places I've been putting off. If they've still got openings, I'm going to set up an interview again. Only this time, I'm going. There's nothing holding me here. Nothing and no one."

And, for the first time since I met Rusty, I feel that's absolutely, one hundred percent true.

"Why don't you come over tonight? I'll rent some movies and we can hang out. Or we could go to Lucky's. Whatever you want to do."

I smile. Even though I'm hiding it from her, Cami knows me well enough to know I'm dying on the inside. And, no doubt, she's worried about me.

"Nah. I'll leave you two newlyweds to your perverted sexcapades. I think I'll stay here with Daddy. I need to spend some quality time with him since I won't be here much longer."

"Yeah, that's probably a good idea."

She sounds a little hurt by my choice.

"Because you know as well as I do that he won't be visiting me when I move, like you will. The man refuses to leave home."

"Yeah, what's up with that? What's so fabulous about staying in Greenfield all the time?"

"Well, it's not really Greenfield, it's this house. It's where he spent time with Mom. I don't think he'll ever love another place as much as he loves this one."

Cami sighs. "That's so sweet."

"I know. Unless it ruins your life."

"Yeah, love can go either way. If you let it."

"I guess so. I suppose sometimes you just have to cut your losses."

"Sometimes you do," she agrees.

The question is: How?

TWENTY: *Rusty*

I glance up at the clock on the wall. It's after seven in the evening. "What are you still doing around here?" I ask Mom when she wanders in. Normally, she visits me several times throughout the day and then goes home around six or so to do stuff around the house.

She doesn't answer me right away. She just walks toward me, arms crossed over her chest, and sits on the edge of my bed. She looks like she's deep in thought.

"Did I ever tell you that your father came back after he left that last time?"

I feel like shaking my head to clear it. Talk about out of the blue!

"What? What are you talking about?"

She looks off into the distance, a wistful smile on her face. "Your father had big dreams. And he was a very determined man. Stubborn. A lot like you. He thought there was more to life than small-town living."

I grit my teeth. It aggravates me to think of him, to think of what he did to Mom, to *us*, much less talk about it. "I know. He was an asshole. You deserved better."

"You'd get so excited when he'd come home. You were on cloud nine, right up until he left again. Then you'd be depressed for days. Sometimes you wouldn't eat. I'd get letters from your teachers. It was a cycle. It was hard on you."

"But once he left for good, we did just fine without him."

"You're right. We did. But he came back once, once that you didn't know about."

I shrug. "So? What's one more time?"

"He asked me if we'd go with him. He'd gotten a job with a country singer, on the road crew. Unloading equipment from the trucks. He just *knew* it would be his big break. And he wanted us to come with him."

I'm not sure how I feel about this new information, but I'm confused as to why she's telling me this now. "Obviously you told him no, right?"

"Right. I told him no. I knew nothing would make you happier than to have both of us together, but he wasn't thinking about you like he should've. He wasn't thinking like a parent. What about school? What about stability? You can't raise a child on the road, as a hired hand for a country singer."

"So he left us for his big dream. I already knew that, Mom, even if I didn't know he came back that last time."

"Yes, the end result was the same. But you know, I could've asked him to stay. And he would've. And things would've gone on like they always had. But I still loved him, and I wanted him to be happy. I knew he could never be happy around here. And I knew you needed more than sporadic visits or life on the road. So I made the only choice I felt I could. I told him to stay away. I told him to go chase his dreams, to find what happiness he could out there, but I told him to forget about us. I knew you'd never have a chance to heal if he kept coming in and out of your life."

Even though I understand *why* she did what she did, I'm not certain I can see why she kept it from me all this time. She let me think he abandoned us because he loved his dreams more than he loved us. In a way, that was true. But he would've kept coming around if she hadn't told him not to. And I'm just not sure how I feel about it now, how I feel about him. And her.

"Mom, why are you telling me this now?" I ask, my tone rife with frustration.

"Because I could always see how it hurt you when he would come and then go, but I never saw how much it hurt you that he left and never came back. But I'm seeing it now. And I don't want you to live your life based on a single event when you don't have all the information."

I don't even know what to say to that. I want to ask her what the hell she's talking about or if she's been taking someone else's meds. But I don't. Because the more I think about it, the more I think I know what she's trying to say. And the more I think she's trying to help me not lose someone I'll regret losing for the rest of my life.

TWENTY-ONE: *Jenna*

A loud bark at my right ear provides me with a very rude awakening. After spending a nearly sleepless night tossing and turning, agonizing over the situation with Rusty, I'm not entirely surprised when I roll over to look at the clock and see that it's almost noon.

Einstein, my eerily intelligent, solid white Labradoodle, barks again, throwing his muddy paws up on the side of the bed and scratching at me with his blunt claws.

"Einstein, no!" I chastise.

He stares me down for several seconds, panting heavily. Finally, he slides his feet off the bed then turns and trots to my closet. He brings back one tennis shoe, drops it on the floor beside the bed, and barks again.

"It's too early to walk," I tell him, flopping back down on my pillow. I hear his toenails on the hardwoods and a few seconds later the *thonk* of another shoe hitting the floor. Another bark. "Einstein, I said no!"

Another scrape from a big paw has me up and out of the bed. Angrily, I grab his collar and tow him toward the door. That's when I hear the sound of a loud engine pulling up in front of the house.

I stop and listen. Einstein is absolutely still as he watches me. He's a very smart dog, and this behavior isn't like him. A little thread of alarm snakes its way down my spine.

I hear the engine shut off. Then a door slam. Then another. And then someone is shouting, "He's in the orchard. This way." The voice is heavily accented and unfamiliar, making me think it's one of the pickers.

But if someone is hurt out in the orchard, why is a picker at the house doing the talking rather than my father?

Apprehension brings me fully awake. I reason to myself that it's probably because Daddy is still in the orchard. He's not the type of person to leave someone who's hurt. He'd send someone else for help. He probably called 911 from his cell phone and then told one of the pickers to go wait for the paramedics to arrive.

Jumping out of bed and rushing to the window, I pull back the pale pink sheer curtain and peek through the slats of my blinds.

There's an ambulance in my driveway. I catch the departure of a dark-haired guy, dressed in jeans and a white T-shirt (obviously the picker), leading two uniform-clad emergency workers through the gate and into the orchard. Something is obviously very wrong; they're wasting no time as they disappear into the trees, carrying the supply-laden stretcher between them.

Again, Einstein barks at me, urging me toward the door. His persistence is making me more nervous than anything, so I hurry downstairs to the kitchen and grab the walkie-talkie from the counter. It stays in the same spot at all times. Everyone knows never to move it.

I press the button and speak into it. "Daddy? Is everything okay?"

I hear a crackle of static followed by silence. I wait several seconds for a response. When I get none, I call again. "Cris Theopolis, what's your twenty?"

Using truck driver speak always, always, always makes me laugh. It always has, since I was a little girl.

Always.

Except for today. Today it's not funny. And the reason is because my father always, always, always answers right away.

Always.

Except for today.

Like I've swallowed a lump of lead, the pit of my stomach feels heavy with dread. Something is terribly wrong. I can feel it like cold breath on the nape of my neck. The skin on my arms pebbles with chills.

"Daddy?" I call again. I know there's anxiety in my voice. And that I probably don't sound very much like myself. It's hard to speak past the fingers of fear that are squeezing my throat.

Finally another crackle of static is followed by a voice, but it's not my father's. "Who this?" the man asks, his English broken.

Fear erupts into terror. "This is Jenna Theopolis. My father owns this property. I need to speak with him please."

"The men just now get here. They take him to hospital. Can't talk right now."

The line goes dead again.

And panic sets in.

I'm alone. I have little information and a nearly unbearable weight on my chest. And my father is out in the orchard. Somewhere. Hurt.

My heart is hammering against my ribs, threatening to break them into tiny pieces if I don't find out what's going on. Taking the stairs two at a time, I race to my room and throw on some clothes. Less than five minutes later, I grab the walkie that never moves and I hit the front door, fully dressed and ready to scour every inch of the orchard for my father if need be.

Something tells me I should wait, that going out isn't the best thing to do, but I ignore that voice. I'm not a "wait" kind of person; I'm an "act" kind of person. For better or worse, to make a move or to move on, I act. And now, I'm acting. I'm going in search of my father.

Einstein and I stop at the fence. I squat and grab his face in my hands, looking directly into his somber, intelligent brown eyes. "Take me to Daddy, Einstein. Take me to him."

With a bark, Einie takes off running east. I'm hot on his heels, oblivious to the tears streaming down my face and the ache in my legs as I dodge trunks and branches to pursue the dog as he runs through the trees rather than up the lanes between them.

Another bark and Einstein abruptly cuts left down a row. I hurry to catch him. When I step out into the opening, I see a picker leading the two paramedics toward me, back in the direction of the house. Between the emergency workers is the stretcher. Atop it is my father.

"Daddy!" I yell, my voice cracking with emotion.

Three pairs of eyes are watching me as I race toward them. My father doesn't move.

When I reach them, they don't stop. They are walking briskly. They don't even slow down long enough to let me talk to my father.

I walk alongside the stretcher. My dad is lying prone, covered in a white sheet and strapped in so that he can't move or fall off. An oxygen mask is covering the lower part of his face, a face that's unusually ashen. His eyes are closed and, when I reach out to touch the top of the arm closest to me, the lids don't even flicker.

"Daddy?" He doesn't respond. His eyelashes don't flutter. He doesn't turn his head. He doesn't move a muscle.

Oh God! Oh God! Oh God!

"What happened?" I ask in general, speaking to anyone who will answer me.

One of the EMTs answers. I can tell by his kind expression that he's trying to be gentle, which upsets me all the more. What is he hiding?

"We can't be sure, ma'am, but considering what this man has said, it sounds like he fell off a ladder and hit his head. We won't know anything for sure until we get him to the hospital. He's been unresponsive up to this point."

The picker falls back to walk closer to me. "He fall off ladder. Doesn't wake up. We call emergency."

In my head, I can picture it. The first pick of the season is done by my father. It's something he and my mother apparently used to do together, every single year without fail. And they always used the same ladder, the ladder that had been used by my mother's family for generations. That damn rickety, old, wooden ladder.

That ladder, that *ritual* meant the world to them. And it might have cost me mine.

Einstein leads us back to the gate. I don't leave my father's side as they carry him to the ambulance. With a flick, the paramedics lower the legs on the stretcher to let it rest on the pavement while they open the doors to the back.

No one looks at me. No one says a word. I'm terrified.

In shock, I wait while the paramedics collapse the stretcher legs and push my father into the empty rear compartment of the squad. One EMT climbs in behind him.

"You're welcome to ride along, if you're comfortable going now. If you'd rather drive, that's fine, but we need to leave now. Right now," he says emphatically.

I process very little of what he's saying. "My keys," I say, dazedly. I know I need to go get them.

The EMT nods. "Just meet us there."

I turn on shaky legs to run into the house and get my purse. When I reemerge, the ambulance is just pulling out. I climb into my car to follow.

My legs feel numb where they dangle below me. My foot feels leaden where it presses on the gas pedal. My hands feel frozen where they grip the steering wheel. Nothing seems to be working right. My thoughts are jumbled and dark, foreboding. Ominous.

In the back of my mind, I keep thinking there must be some mistake. Or that I'm still dreaming, that this can't be happening. That my father can't be hurt badly, that he must not have heard me calling his name. Surely he didn't, or he would've opened his eyes.

But he was so still. So very, very still.

My mind churns, mixing and remixing my emotions into a thick paste that rational thought can't penetrate. But one feeling lurks behind all the rest, like a still, black backdrop. It's the horrific, bone-deep, gut-wrenching certainty that something is so wrong that my life will never be the same again.

Never.

At the hospital, the dreaded hospital again, I follow the signs that say EMERGENCY all the way up to two wide, wooden doors that read AUTHORIZED PERSONNEL ONLY. Still confused by what the morning has held for me, I stare blankly at the sign until constructive thought can get a foothold.

With a muted click, the doors swing open and two nurses emerge. They smile at me as though my father isn't in a room back there, possibly slipping away from this world, taking with him the only anchor I have left.

As they continue past me, I slip through the doors, unnoticed. I make my way slowly through the labyrinth of identical halls with identical smells and identical workers, my eyes constantly searching for the familiar face of my father.

Unremarkable door after unremarkable door goes by, and still no sign of my father. I reach the end of the hall and turn the corner. Up ahead, I see the nurse's station to my right. As I walk toward it, I pass a room with a flurry of activity inside. Nurses are shuffling quickly in and out, carrying different things. A harsh male voice is barking orders, *demanding* different things. I realize as I watch that I don't need to ask anyone to help me find my father anymore.

I've found him.

The excruciating ache in my chest tells me so.

I stop just outside the room, staring through the window, watching the scene like I might watch a train wreck. A train wreck where my whole world is lying on the tracks.

I hear the word *clear* followed by an odd tapping sound. I know what it is. I've never heard it before, but I can guess. It's the machine that shocks a dying heart back to life.

I stand, mute and motionless, listening, watching, crumbling inside as the commotion dies down and I hear the same male voice, not so harsh anymore, pronounce time of death.

Like a silent movie, somber faces file out of the room, one by one. Some look at me in question as they pass; others don't meet my eyes. It seems they know who I am. Maybe they can feel the agony coming off me in waves.

Finally, the doctor emerges. I open my mouth to speak, to tell him who I am. I hear someone say my name. But surely that's not my voice, that broken sound. Surely not.

But it must be. The sad look of sympathy on the doctor's face tells me so. It says that he's the bearer of bad news. And he knows he's delivering it to me.

His words come to me from a long distance, like he's speaking from the other side of a large, empty room. I see him reach out compassionately and lay a hand on my arm. I feel his touch like I'm wearing layer upon layer of thick wool.

He takes me by the shoulders and turns me around, leading me to a tiny private room tucked away in a quiet corner of one hall. The soft blue furniture and soothing taupe walls are clearly meant to calm, but I feel only desperation.

Devastation.

Heartbreak.

I watch his lips move as he explains to me what happened. A few words echo through my mind in a disjointed way, things like *basilar skull fracture*, *fatal*, and *instant*.

I think he asks me about other relatives to notify and someone I can stay with, but I can't be sure. Like a radio with bad reception, I'm fading in and out of the world around me.

I hear that voice again, the girl's voice, the broken one. It asks to see "him." It spills my thoughts into the air, but it's nearly unrecognizable to me.

I watch the doctor nod solemnly. Then he's touching me again, leading me back through the halls into a now-empty room. Well, not completely empty. It's only empty of the living.

Gentle hands position me at my father's side then push me down into a chair. And then I'm alone. With my father. One last time. To say things he'll never hear and to beg for things he can never give.

His hand seems small and pale when I slide my fingers over the cold palm. He's always seemed larger than life, even his hands. But that's no longer the case. They're tiny in the face of death. Everything is.

I lean forward in my seat and brush my fingertips down his cheek. It's firm and cool. Still. Lifeless. Never again will I see the smile that graced his face so often. Never again will I see the love that shined from his eyes. Never again will I hear the voice that soothed my worried soul.

Never.

That's a word I'll have to get used to.

All the things I took for granted, all the things I thought there was plenty of time for, all the things that carried a tag that read *someday*, now bear one that reads *never*. All the somedays and one days, all the maybes and ifs are now nevers. Never is the new constant. The only thing that will always be true now is that he's gone. He'll always be gone.

I let my head fall onto his shoulder one last time. The spreading wetness beneath my cheek makes no impression on me. Nothing does.

I don't know how long I've been like this when a nurse comes to help me to my feet. She explains something about having to get him ready for the funeral home and then tells me I need to get some rest.

Something in me says that's funny—rest. Rest? Who could rest at a time like this? And what kind of person would even suggest it?

My radio fades in and out again, taking the nurse and her silly words with it. Absently, I wonder if I'll be able to experience true rest ever again. Right now, I'm not even sure I'll be able to experience true *feeling* ever again, much less rest. Or peace. Or happiness. Only numbness. Blessed numbness.

She leads me to the door and I look back, back at my father one more time. And then, with the one step that takes me from the room, I'm as gone from him as he is from me.

TWENTY-TWO: *Rusty*

I'm surprised when I see Mom come back through the door. It's Saturday, so she stayed home most of the day, stopping in after lunch to see me before she went downstairs to catch up on some paperwork and then go back home. Only she didn't. She's here instead.

"I thought you were going home?" She doesn't answer me right away, which gives me time to notice her expression. She's got bad news. I can see it in the way her mouth pinches in at the corners. "Please don't tell me they've decided to keep me another week."

"Son, I've got some bad news."

"Well? What is it?"

There's a long pause and a sigh before she answers. "I was going over some reports with the unit manager down in the ER when they brought in Cris Theopolis."

Using my good arm, I push myself up in bed. "What? What happened?"

"Evidently he was in an accident at the orchard. He passed away, honey."

I throw back the covers and climb quickly out of bed. I don't hesitate. Not for one second, not for one heartbeat.

"Jeff, listen to me. I'll do whatever you need me to do, but you need to stay put until they let you go."

"To hell with that! I'm going."

I walk to the closet to get the clothes Mom brought me a few days ago.

"Jeffrey, this could set you back. It could—"

Angrily, I whirl toward her. "I don't give a shit, Mom. It's Jenna." When she does nothing but stare at me, I repeat, "It's Jenna."

I pull on the jeans I was going to wear when they let me go. Turns out I'm going to wear them today.

When I go find Jenna.

TWENTY-THREE: *Jenna*

I hear the honking again. I wonder vaguely why people keep honking at me. I'm driving straight. I'm within the lines.

Another car goes flying past as though I'm standing still. It's then I realize that I am. Again. For the fourth time, I've stopped in the middle of the road and not even realized it until a car honks its horn angrily and then speeds by like a bat out of hell.

The nurse in the ER asked if there was family she could call for me. I stared blankly at her as I went through a mental list and came up with no one. My mother is dead. My father is dead. My brother is . . . well, he's somewhere. But not here. My answer to her was no, I have no family for her to call.

I could've had her call Cami, but she feels far from me today. Her life is happy and perfect, not a place for all my troubles and woes, let alone a place for death and loss.

Without her, I really am alone. All alone. The only other person who means anything to me in this town couldn't care less that my world just exploded. He made his feelings about me very clear.

As I pull off the road onto the long drive that leads to my house,

I remember how, just a few weeks ago, I was enjoying the feelings of comfort this part of the drive was bringing me. Now, it feels empty. Hollow. Painful.

Once I park in my usual spot at the house, I get out of the car and, on stiff legs, make my way up the steps to the porch. The door is slightly ajar; I didn't even bother to close it before I left to follow the ambulance.

I push it open and stop just inside the foyer to listen, to smell, to experience home the way I always have. But I can't. This isn't the home that I've returned to every year for so many. This is just the place that my dad no longer inhabits. It's just a series of rooms alive with only the ghost of his memory. Nothing more.

I hear a slow, steady clicking and look up to see Einstein standing in the kitchen doorway. His eyes are sober as he watches me. He drops to the floor and lays his head on his paws, a soft whine screeching at the back of his throat. He knows something is wrong. So, so wrong.

I walk past him to the kitchen. I see my father reheating fried chicken for me and scrubbing me on top of the head in that loving way he used to do. I turn away, back toward the den. There, I see my father laughing and eating popcorn, and giving me philosophical advice. I turn back toward the stairs and know that at the top is his bedroom—now and forever empty and cold.

There is no longer any happiness here, any comfort. There is pain and loss and a future without my father. The floorboards don't ooze peach syrup anymore; they ooze the most hideous kind of heartbreak. The walls don't shake with laughter anymore; they shake with grief. The air doesn't smell of home anymore; it smells of my own personal hell.

So I run.

I run back through the house, back out the door, back out into the driveway. And I stand there. Looking at the house. Knowing I can't go back inside. Not now. Maybe not ever.

Little by little, this town has taken every bit of happiness I've ever had. It has swallowed it up and left me standing, broken and alone, staring at an empty house with an empty life.

I feel the first drop like a cool tear to my cheek. I look up at the sky, at the dull gray clouds that mirror the bleakness in my chest, and I see the rain begin. Slow at first, like the sky itself is suddenly feeling my pain. And then, like the break in my heart, it opens up and weeps for me, pouring rain over my upturned face.

Impervious to the downpour, I stand in the driveway, in the rain, looking at the house. I wish with all my heart the drops would just wash it away. Along with the pain.

I glance up at the windows, gaping black holes staring back at me, mocking me with what is no longer behind them, with *who* is no longer behind them. And never will be again.

One second the tenuous hold I have on my emotions is intact, the next it's gone. And the dam breaks.

A scream echoes through my head like a coyote's cry echoes through a canyon, is torn from my lungs, from my chest, from my lips in one long, agonizing wail. The rain steals the sound and carries it to the ground, where it's as dead as my father. And I'm once again all alone in the deafening silence.

Turning from the house, I take off at a run for the gate, for the orchard that took my father's life. If I had a knife, I would cut the bark of every tree I pass until they bleed their life in thick, sticky rivulets. Penance for the life they stole.

I can't see past the tears, past the rain. Past the pain. My foot finds a hole and my balance is lost. I see the ground coming toward my face with alarming speed. My knees hit first, the impact jarring my teeth. I close my eyes and throw out my arms to brace myself. But before I make contact with the ground, strong fingers are winding around my upper arms, stopping my descent.

One heartbeat brings confusion. The next, recognition. I don't have to look back to know who's got me. Who caught me. Who saved me.

Rusty turns me toward him. I stare up into his eyes. They're deeply pained at the moment, as though they're a reflection of my own.

"Jenna," he whispers softly.

"What are you doing here?"

His eyes search mine. "I came for you."

"But why?" I ask, unwilling to give in to the hope that has left me so devastated so many times before.

"In case you need me," he responds simply.

Bitterness rises to the surface to mix with the pain. It blurs the lines of my feelings. "You shouldn't have," I spit. "I don't need you."

I see hurt flash through his eyes. "What if *I* need *you*?"

"But you don't. You made that all too clear."

"I was an idiot, Jenna. I was a proud, arrogant idiot. But I'm here now. Doesn't that count for something?"

"No, it doesn't. It can't. It *can't*," I hiss, my voice getting louder and louder as my emotions churn. "I can't wait for you anymore, Rusty. I can't lose anyone else. My heart can't take it. You had your chance and you blew it. Now let me go and get the hell off my land."

I twist my body, trying to wrench free of his iron grip, all to no avail. Despite the fact that one arm is in a cast, Rusty is still stronger than me.

"I can't," he growls down into my face.

"What are you even doing here?" I scream, channeling my rage at the world, my rage at *life* into fury at Rusty. "Aren't you supposed to be in the hospital, forgetting about me?"

"I was, but I left."

"Then go back. I don't want you here."

"I can't," he says again.

"Why not?"

"Because I came here for you, Jenna."

"Why? I didn't ask you to come here. I never asked you for *one thing*. But now I am. I'm asking you to leave. Just leave. Leave me alone!"

"I can't!" he repeats angrily, his face the twisted mask of a tortured soul.

"Why?" I rail back.

"Because I can't let you go. I love you too much!"

My heart stops for just an instant, torn between elation and devastation. But I can't afford to hang on to the elation. The devastation to follow might well be the end of me.

"You can't tell me that today. You don't get to do this to me today. I've lost everything. *Everything.* You can't come back into my life and then leave me again, you bastard," I cry, thumping my fists against his chest. "You don't get to do this to me today. You don't get to . . . do . . . this . . ." My words are choked out by the sobs I can no longer contain. Suddenly devoid of the ability to stay upright, I crumble into the mud, held vertical only by the grip of Rusty's hands on my upper arms.

"Jenna, please," he whispers, trying once more to pull me to his chest with his good arm. This time I let him, the will to fight having drained right out of me with the first few sobs. "Let me help you. Just give me this one day and I'll go. Just this one. Please, Jenna." In his pause, I feel a sigh expand his lungs. "Please."

Finally, exhausted, I melt into Rusty. On our knees, in the rain, in the mud, I bury my face in his neck and I cry. From my soul, I cry. Every sob feels as though it's torn from me, ripped viciously from a place that should never be touched so cruelly. And I'm left, alive but only physically, with nothing but gaping wounds and gushing blood that no one else can see.

When I'm so hoarse my sobs are nothing more than croaks and I'm so spent my tears give way to the rain, somehow, with only one fully functional arm, Rusty gently cradles me against him, gets to his feet, and carries me away from the orchard.

TWENTY-FOUR: *Rusty*

I carry Jenna toward the front door of her house, thinking only of getting her out of the rain. I barely hear it when she speaks softly into my ear. "Anywhere but there. I can't go back in there."

"Okay," I tell her, detouring toward my mother's car. I manage to get her into the passenger seat and start the engine, but then I draw a blank. Where can I take her?

Only one place comes to mind. The one place she'd feel best, I think.

Cami's.

I drive cautiously. It's a little unnerving for my first time back behind the wheel of a car to be in the rain, in an unfamiliar car, with a grieving Jenna in the seat beside me. Oh, and with my right arm in a cast. Hell, I don't think conditions could be much worse.

We finally make it to Cami's. I park and walk around to the passenger-side door. I open it and lean down to scoop up Jenna, not giving her any choice other than to let me carry her again. I feel like I *need* to carry her. Maybe more than she needs for me to.

Once she's in my arms, I realize she wouldn't have argued, anyway. She's asleep. I'm not sure that's a good thing.

I hurry to the door and ring the bell. Trick answers within a few seconds. "What the—" He frowns in confusion as he looks from me to Jenna, to her legs folded over my casted arm and then back again.

"Can I borrow your bedroom downstairs?" I ask quietly.

"Sure," he says without hesitation, opening the door wider so we can pass.

He doesn't ask questions, which I appreciate. It's a guy thing.

I'm making my way through the kitchen when Cami appears in the doorway.

"Ohmigod, what happened?" she asks, rushing toward me, her eyes on Jenna.

"Shhh," I caution. "She's okay. Just let me take her downstairs and I'll come back up so I can explain."

"No! You can tell me now. Is she okay? What hap—"

"Cami!" I snap, interrupting her. When she snaps her mouth shut and looks at me, I add, "Please."

Cami's violet eyes bore holes into mine as she narrows them on me. She says nothing for a few seconds. I'm sure she's debating the wisdom of leaving her best friend in my care when I've been such an asshole. But she relents.

"Okay, but you come straight back up here," she hisses.

I nod and continue on to the stairs that lead to the basement. I hit the light switch with my elbow and descend the steps into the cool quiet of the lower level.

I stop on the landing at the bottom. The light from the stairwell only penetrates the dimness a few inches in every direction. When I step out into the darkness, it's somehow like stepping into blessed peace. The light has shown me too much trouble lately. I could use some darkness. Darkness where there's only me and Jenna. And maybe one more chance for me to *not* screw it up.

From memory, I carry her to the guest suite Trick and Cami set up down here. I can barely make out the bed in the dying daylight seeping through the tiny window at the top of one wall. I head for it and lay her gently on the soft, pillowy top. She stirs very little.

I bend and press my lips to her forehead. I don't know if she even has a clue she's in the world right now, but I speak to her anyway. Just in case.

"Rest, Jenna. I'll be right back. I promise," I whisper. She doesn't respond. A few seconds later, she rolls onto her side and I hear her breathing become deep and even. "I'll be here every time you open your eyes. I swear it," I say. This time, it's more for my benefit than hers.

I make my way back upstairs. Cami's waiting on the top step, arms crossed over her chest, hell in her eyes.

"Dammit, Rusty, what is *wrong* with her? What did you do?"

"Keep your voice down," I tell her. "I didn't *do* anything to her. Her father was killed in an accident at the orchard today."

Cami's gasp is followed by her hands covering her mouth and her eyes filling with tears. "Oh my God! Oh my God! Poor Jenna!" She closes her eyes and slides her hands up to cover her whole face. Trick comes around from behind me to pull her into his arms. I give them a few minutes, minutes for Trick to comfort Cami and for Cami to collect herself. She's known Jenna's dad for years. No doubt she feels some sense of pain and loss, too, not to mention sympathy for her best friend.

When she uncovers her face and wipes her eyes, I continue. "Mom was down in the ER, and she came and told me right away. Jenna had already left the hospital, so I went to her house. I found her out in the rain. She didn't want to go back inside, so I brought her here."

"I'm glad you did," Cami says, kindness back in her eyes. "I'll take care of her. I'm sure you need to rest. You're not even supposed to be out of the hospital yet, are you?"

"I'm fine. And I'll stay with her tonight, if you don't mind."

"You really don't need to do that. I'll make sure she knows—"

"No offense, Cami, but it's not a request. I'm staying. Or I'm taking her with me when I leave."

Cami eyes me suspiciously, but again, she relents. "Okay, okay. Can I at least go see her?"

"I'll come get you when she wakes up, but *I* want to be there when she does."

Cami nods, possibly in approval. I can't be sure. "Fair enough."

She looks from me to Trick, and then turns and walks slowly back toward the living room. I know she doesn't like it, but at least she recognizes that I'm not budging on this. She can take it or leave it. Her choice. She chose to take it.

Smart girl.

TWENTY-FIVE: *Jenna*

Life, or what feels like the reasonable facsimile of it, has slowed. At first, it was a series of lightbulb-flashes of time and sounds, of people and places.

There were the various rooms of my house. Then there were the empty windows of the rooms upstairs. There was Rusty's face in the rain. Then there was the dashboard of an unfamiliar car.

I woke sometime later, in a dark room, to the faint sight of Rusty hovering over me. We watched each other for an eternity. Or for a few seconds. I'm not sure which. I stayed perfectly still while the mattress beside me sank and he stretched out beside me, drawing me into his arms.

There was more time after that. Hours or days, I don't know, but I woke again in the same dark room. Beneath my ear was a beating heart and deep, even breathing. I lifted my head to confirm what I already knew. It was Rusty. Rusty had fallen asleep holding me.

Still, there was more time. Still, I don't know how much. I woke, startled by a girl's screams. It took Rusty stroking my hair, soothing me with his calming words to make me realize that the girl was me. And that her screams were mine.

I remember daylight after that. And Rusty. Still. Always, it seemed.

There was worry on his face and in his eyes. But there was something else, too. Something I refused to think about. So I slept.

There were vague impressions, too. Fingers on my cheek, lips against mine, words whispered in my ear. Something that made my heart sing and cry, all in the space of a heartbeat. So I dove back into sleep, into escape.

When I could hide no more, I woke to the sight of Cami sitting in the rocking chair in the corner. I watched her for a few seconds before I moved. She looked tired as she swayed gently back and forth, her head resting against the cushion, her eyes closed. I wondered briefly what was weighing so heavily on her.

Her head straightened and her eyes opened, locking on mine immediately. I knew then what was worrying her. It was me.

She came to the bed, curled up beside me, threaded her fingers through mine and we cried. Together. I don't know how long we did that before I fell asleep again. When I woke she was in different clothes, standing in the doorway.

"Where's Rusty?" I'd asked.

"He said he'd asked you for one day, and that you'd given it to him. And that he would come back if you wanted him to."

My heart broke a little more. I'm not sure why. Maybe because it was already in a million tiny pieces and happiness hurt just as much as sadness. Or maybe because I couldn't tell them apart. Maybe they are one and the same. Or maybe there can't be one without the other.

After that moment, time sped up into a blur, a rapid succession of images and places, of fuzzy emotions and decisions, all set against the backdrop of an unimaginable pain and sense of loss. They ran together, beyond my control, like watercolors in a cold, hard rain.

There were arrangements to make, morticians to speak to, songs to choose, and gravestones to select. There were thoughts of telephone calls, but none to make, except to my brother, Jake. Although he's always been as far away emotionally as he has been geographically, he promised he would come. That moment stood out among the rest.

And now, somehow, I'm here. In a cemetery. In the sunlight. In a dress I don't remember buying, in front of a casket I can't remember picking out.

My brother stands beside me, looking like a brooding, bitter version of my father, with his black hair, dark skin, and amber eyes, and we address the dozens of people who have come to pay their last respects to my father. He nods politely, and I say things I really don't mean to people I really don't know as they drift by in single file. I watch them come and I watch them go, and all I feel is . . . empty. And alone.

Even my mother's jealous, vindictive sister Ellie's presence doesn't shake me from my stupor. I recognize her trailer-trash hair and her trailer-trash dress when she steps up in line. I recognize the smell of vodka on her breath and the way she curls her lip in disgust. But still, I don't feel like I'm present. Not fully.

I listen as she speaks, but I don't really understand what it is she's trying to say. And some part of me thinks that I don't really want to. At least not today.

"I'm so sorry to hear about your daddy," I hear her slur. "Have you already read the will and taken care of all the arrangements?"

I don't answer. I simply watch her, wishing she'd disappear. Or that I would.

"Well," she continues, "just let me know when to be there. I'm sure he's made some provisions for you two, like a good father would, but that orchard should come to me. Rightfully. And since you kids don't have an interest in living there like me and Turkey do . . ."

Some part of me, a part that I see and feel as if I'm observing it from a great distance, is getting angry. It threatens to penetrate my numb cocoon. But I resist.

"What's this about, Ellie?" Jake asks, protectively stepping closer to me.

"Jake, honey, you know as well as I do that you two don't want the orchard. And it should've come to me next anyway, so why don't we just talk to the lawyers and have them sign it over to me and Turkey. You'll feel better without having to worry about the homeplace."

"The hell I will," Jake bites. "My mother would roll over in her grave if she thought I turned the place she loved so much over to *you*."

Even from deep inside my fuzzy reality, I see Ellie's saccharine-sweet demeanor dissolve into one of contempt. "We'll just see what the lawyers have to say about that then. I tried to do this the kind way, but you're making it awful hard to be nice, son."

"I'm not your son," Jake growls. "And we'll see just who ends up with what. Now, take your raggedy ass on home before you *really* make me mad."

I know I should feel angry. I can see it in the way Jake glances at me, as if waiting for me to speak up. Only I don't. Because I can't. I can't feel anything right now. I simply watch, like I'm watching a game from the sidelines, as Ellie glares at Jake and takes her husband, Turkey, by the arm and drags him away. "Come on. I knew this would be a waste of time."

The line begins to dwindle. As it does, one random thought chases itself through my head, over and over and over.

What do I do after this?

No answer comes to me. I shake hand after hand, and accept hug after hug until there's no one left in line, and it's just me and Jake standing in the cemetery, all alone.

It's as I'm glancing at the gravestones that surround me, all glistening in the sun like so many black diamonds, that I see him.

Rusty.

Standing in the shade of a tree, he's wearing a black suit, the jacket draped over one shoulder. His right arm is free, covered only in a white, unbuttoned shirt sleeve that fits over his cast.

I have no idea how long he's been there, but some part of me says he's been there all along.

Across the distance, we stare at each other. Then, little by little, like dawn breaking through the darkness of the night, feeling begins to penetrate—the breeze on my skin, the sun on my face, the pain in my soul, the certainty in my heart.

Everything in my vision, in my world, in my *life*, comes into crystal clear focus as I stand, holding my breath, staring at Rusty. Waiting. Finally, with clarity that only great tragedy can bring, I *see* Rusty. Really *see* him. I see the fear he's lived with, and I see the insecurity he grew up with. I see the guy I fell in love with, and I see the man he's become since fate stepped in and brought us together.

I take one step forward and I stop. And I wait. Unmoving, he watches me, so I take another. And another. And another still, walking until I'm close enough to smell the scent of his soap, swirling around me like a comforting fog.

"I know I shouldn't have come," he begins.

"Then why did you?"

"Because I couldn't stay away. I had to know you were okay."

"I'm okay," I assure him, even though we both know that's a lie. "Is that it? I mean, are you just gonna leave now?"

"I don't want to, but I will if that's what you want."

"I've never wanted you to go, Rusty."

"And I've never wanted *you* to go," he replies. "But I knew you would. I knew you had to."

"Then why did you say the things you did?"

Rusty takes a deep breath and looks off into the distance before he returns his gaze to me. "I was trying to do what was right. For both of us."

"And now? What are you trying to do now?"

"Survive," he says simply.

My addled mind isn't working well enough to make sense of riddles, so I wait. Wait for him to explain.

"Jenna, I can *survive* without you. I can exist," he begins, the words slicing through me like a knife through butter. "But it wouldn't be any kind of existence that I'd want. *You* are what makes my life worth living. You're the sunshine in it, you're the laughter and the smiles. You're the warm nights and the cool breezes. You're like every good memory and moment and dream I've ever had all wrapped up into one. And if you go, you take the only living part of me with you. Without you, I might as well be dead. So, yes, I can survive without you. But that's all I'd be doing.

"I don't know how to apologize for being an idiot and an asshole, and for letting something as stupid as fear come between me and the only chance I'll ever have at happiness. I don't know how to tell you that I love you for every single thing that you *are* and every single thing you'll *ever be*. I don't know how to tell you that when my mom told me about your dad, I felt an ache in my chest—literally— at the thought of you somewhere, alone and hurting, and me not being there to hold you while you cried. I don't know how to tell you that I'd follow you to the ends of the earth, just to hear you say you love me one more time. Help me, Jenna. Help me say the right things. Help me *do* the right things. Help me to be the kind of man you could spend the rest of your life loving. Because that's who I want to be."

As I stand, chest to chest, with Rusty, listening to his hoarse voice, letting the sincerity in it wash over me like a cleansing tide, I realize that it is entirely possible to experience the most agonizing pain and the most wondrous happiness at the exact same time in life. And that maybe it's the presence of one that so magnifies the other.

I glance back over my shoulder, at the mahogany casket that's gleaming brightly on the other side of the cemetery, and I know my father is looking on. Just like I'd always hoped, he's here with me on one of the most important days of my life. And he always will be. I might not be able to reach out and touch him or feel his arms wrap around me, but he's here just the same. I'll carry him with me. Always.

With my first smile in days blooming across my face like an old friend, I turn back to Rusty.

"I don't need any of those things, Rusty. I never have. All I've ever wanted, all I've ever *needed* is your love. As long as I have that, nothing else matters."

"But I—"

"Shhh," I say, placing my finger over his warm lips. "No. No more apologies. Life's too short to go back, to *look* back. As long as you love me, that's all that matters. That's all that will ever matter."

"I've loved you from the moment I met you, Jenna. And I'll love you long after I'm gone from this world."

I reach up and wind my arms around his neck, giving him a mischievous wink. "What took you so long?"

He grins down at me. "Traffic was hell."

I laugh as his lips cover mine. And, in the sunshine, I feel my father smiling down on me—the two men I've loved most in my life, here with me. Always in my heart.

EPILOGUE: *Jenna*

Three months later

"I wonder what this is all about," I muse out loud to Rusty as he flies through the curves and turns that lead to Cami and Trick's house.

This is the first time we've been back to Greenfield in over a month. Jake, like a dog with a bone, is staying at the house, taking care of Einstein and doing everything he can to thwart my aunt as she tries to take our heritage. I'm relieved that he wanted to do it. I still have trouble walking through the front door of that place. But that doesn't mean I want to let Ellie have it. I just need time. And Jake is giving it to me.

As for Rusty and me, we've been busy—me with my new job, Rusty with physical therapy and getting his new garage set up in Atlanta. And both of us with making our new apartment "home."

"I've got my suspicions. Since Rags won his last race—and I don't even know how many that makes now—Trick has started getting all sorts of offers for breaking horses. And for breeding, too. Everybody wants a piece of Rags. But last I heard he hadn't made any moves on anything. I'm wondering if he just has or is getting ready to. Either way, you know how he is. The guy's about as dramatic and mysterious as my left nut. All this suspense has to be Cami's idea."

"Of course it is, silly. What guy is ever the dramatic one in the relationship?"

"Exactly, which makes me think it's—"

"Wait!" I yell, holding out my hand to stop him. "I take it back. I don't want to know what you think. I wanna be surprised."

Rusty shrugs. "Whatever."

I'm looking out the window at the passing landscape, just thinking, when we pass a little road I've never noticed before.

"Wonder where that goes?"

When Rusty doesn't answer, I glance over at him. He's looking in the rearview mirror. "I don't know," he admits, turning his eyes to me. "But how about we turn around, see where it goes, and have some afternoon delight before we hear this big news?"

"No, we can't do that. They're waiting for us."

"We won't be long," he says with a grin.

"Oh, so you're not worried about me at all. Is that what you're saying?"

"Are you saying you don't think I can work my magic on that delectable body of yours in such a short amount of time?"

"No, I'm not saying that. I meant—"

"Challenge accepted," he says with a grin, bringing the car to a screeching halt then making a U-turn.

Fourteen minutes later, we're back on the road, both of us wearing very satisfied smiles.

"Doubt me again," Rusty says with a cocky half grin. "See what happens."

"Gladly."

He reaches over and takes my hand in his, bringing my wrist to his lips before he sets our entwined fingers on his thigh. A little smile stretches over his lips as he navigates the road to Cami's. I lean my temple against the headrest and watch him. I can't help thinking of how life is full of the most precious moments imaginable.

Less than fifteen minutes later, we're sitting on Cami's couch, holding glasses of champagne, watching Trick and her grin at each other.

"For the love of God, tell me or face the consequences," I say when I can't take another second of suspense.

"You're so impatient! Give us a minute."

"Why? Are you working up the courage to get naked and ask if we wanna swap? Because I can save you some embarrassment."

"Oh God, Jenna! Of course not."

"Then get to it, woman! Chop chop!"

"It's not that easy. We're waiting for a phone call."

"A phone call?"

My curiosity is officially piqued.

The silence stretches on and, just when I'm about to mouth off again, Trick's cell phone rings.

He smiles and says, "She is?" Pause. "That's great news! And thanks for calling me with the results."

When I hear that, I cover my gaping mouth with my hand and fight back the tears stinging my eyes. "Ohmigod," I mumble.

Before I can say anything else, Trick finally speaks. "That was the vet's office. They just got back the blood work results from the lab."

I drop my hands. "The vet? What?" Obviously I was about to jump to a very erroneous conclusion.

"Yeah. I used some of the winnings from Rags's last race to breed Patty with a stallion who's won the Kentucky Derby twice and the Preakness once." Trick looks down at Cami and grins before bringing his attention back to us. "Her blood work confirms that she's pregnant. Male or female, we're naming the foal Justy, after you two. The godparents."

"Say what? I'm confused."

I look at Rusty, and he appears to be just as confused as I am. We both turn back to Trick.

"Man, you're gonna have to spell things out. We just christened some woods near here and our brains aren't fully functional yet," Rusty blurts honestly. I smack his arm for his confession, but when he winks at me, I can't help but grin.

"We'll talk about the rules and regulations for, ahem, *acceptable uses* of my property later," Trick teases sternly. "Right now, we're basically asking you two to be the godparents of our children."

"Ohhh," Rusty and I say simultaneously. "Of course we'll be godparents to your children. Why would you ever think otherwise?" I ask.

"Well, we kinda figured you would," Cami says. Her smile says there's more. When she doesn't say anything right away, I gasp and throw my hands over my mouth again. "Ohmigod, ohmigod, ohmigod!"

Cami's smile gets wider, and Trick's grin stretches from ear to ear.

"Am I missing something?" Rusty asks.

Cami turns glistening eyes to him as Trick bends from behind to wind his arms around her neck and hug her to him.

"I'm pregnant, Rusty. Trick and I are gonna have a baby."

Tears are spilling down my cheeks and over my fingers when Rusty gets up and takes Cami's glass of champagne and downs it in one swallow. "I guess you won't be needing that then."

We all laugh.

This just keeps getting better and better.

EPILOGUE: *Rusty*

Jenna's skin is still damp from the thorough plundering I just gave her. My fingers slide smoothly across her flat stomach. I rub circles over it, around her belly button and up between her ribs. It's times like this that I'm even more glad I healed so well. I'd hate to miss touching Jenna like this.

"What are you thinking about when you do that?" she asks.

"Do what?"

"Touch my belly like that."

"Do I do this a lot or something?"

"You have been the last few days. Am I getting fat or something?"

I roll my eyes, and she grins. She's not getting fat and she knows it. Jenna's got a body ninety-nine percent of the female population of the world would kill for. I'd kill for it, too. Just in a different way.

I go back to exploring the subtle landscape of her stomach.

"Well?

"Well, what?"

"Are you gonna tell me what that's all about or not?"

I shrug, trying to be nonchalant. "I've just been wondering what it would look like a little rounder, what you'd look like pregnant."

There's a long pause.

"Does that worry you?"

"Worry me? Hell no. I can't imagine what it would feel like to touch you like this, knowing that my baby, *our* baby, was growing inside you."

I hear a soft gasp and look up into the dark pools of her eyes. "What's wrong?"

She shakes her head, but says nothing.

"What? Does that bother you?"

She shakes her head again. I can see that she's fighting back tears. Her eyes shine in a different way when she's trying not to cry.

"Then what?"

It takes her at least a full minute to answer me, and even then, her voice sounds a little thick.

"I just didn't know you ever thought of things like that."

"Do you? Ever think of things like that, I mean."

"Sometimes."

"And?"

"And what?"

"Does it make you happy? Thinking about having my baby? Having *our* baby?"

I can tell she's getting choked up again. She just nods.

"I could spend the rest of my life touching you like this, watching our babies grow inside you, raising them together, chasing our dreams down and making them our bitches."

She laughs, which is just what I wanted. One of the dreams I have yet to tell Jenna about is watching her walk down a beautifully decorated church aisle toward me, toward our future and our life together. I'll tell her all about that one someday soon. When I give her the ring that's hiding in the top drawer of the dresser, under some old hunting socks I have. When I ask her to spend the rest of her life as Mrs. Jeffrey Catron. But right now, I'm happy just to hold her. And tell her I love her. And call her mine.

It's about time.

Keep reading for an excerpt from
the next Wild Ones book

There's Wild,
Then There's You

Available in June 2014 from
Berkley Books

Available now for preorder at all major retailers.
Please visit mleightonbooks.blogspot.com.

ONE: *Violet*

Ohne by one, I watch the people in the rows in front of me stand up and introduce themselves.

Oh, sweet Jesus! How do I get myself into these messes?

I don't know why I even ask. I already know. I help people. It's not only what I do; it's who I am.

By day, I'm a social worker. By night, I'm a chauffeur, a counselor, a nurse, a guardian, a suicide hotline, and, tonight, an addict.

As the first person in my row stands, my stomach turns a flip, and I look around once more for my best friend, Tia. The only reason I'm here is for moral support. Her moral support. And she hasn't even shown up yet.

That's what I get for trying to help her when she obviously doesn't want it.

Tia's fiancé, Dennis, insisted that before they get married, Tia attend at least ten sessions at an addicts meeting. That might sound ridiculous to some people, but it's probably not that much to ask, considering that Tia has cheated on him not one, not two, not three, not even four times. But six. Six times in three years, Tia has gotten drunk and slept with someone else. She regrets it immediately. Cries over it, apologizes for it, always confesses it, but it never seems to stop her when she feels a wild hair come on and a hot guy happens to be near. It doesn't help that she's gorgeous. With long, blond hair and pale blue eyes, Tia looks just like a Barbie doll. She has insanely big boobs, an enviably tiny waist, and ridiculously long legs. It's a package that draws the eye of practically every male within a ten-mile radius. And that only worsens Tia's . . . weakness. She loves first kisses. And butterflies. And excitement. And vodka. That combination lands her in more trouble than I care to comment on. It also lands me in more trouble than I care to comment on.

Like finding myself next in a long line of people standing up to explain who they are and why they're here. My mind is whirling as I listen to the lady beside me explain that her name is Rhianne and that she's been an addict for eleven years. People clap (why, I'm not sure) and she smiles before taking her seat again. Then the room falls quiet and every eye turns to me. My stomach drops into my shoes.

My turn.

Slowly, I stand. I give the guy at the head of the room a shaky smile and he nods me on in encouragement. I clear my throat and wipe my damp palms on my jeans. I glance quickly around at all the attentive faces, wishing silently that this moment was already over.

Just a few more seconds and it will be . . .

It's when my eyes collide with breathtakingly pale blue ones that I nearly forget where I am and what I'm supposed to be saying. Lucky for me, my speech is short. And exactly fifty percent untrue.

"Hi. My name is Violet, and I'm a sex addict."

ABOUT THE AUTHOR

New York Times and *USA Today* bestselling author **M. Leighton** is a native of Ohio. She relocated to the warmer climates of the South, where she can be near the water all summer and miss the snow all winter. Possessed of an overactive imagination from early in her childhood, Michelle finally found an acceptable outlet for her fantastical visions: literary fiction. Having written more than a dozen novels, Michelle enjoys letting her mind wander to more romantic settings with sexy Southern guys, much like the one she married and the ones you'll find in her latest books. When her thoughts aren't roaming in that direction, she'll be riding wild horses, skiing the slopes of Aspen, or scuba diving with a hot rock star, all without leaving the cozy comfort of her office. Visit her on Facebook, Twitter, and Goodreads, and at mleightonbooks .blogspot.com.